*Sinclair entered the library,
sat on the sofa, and studied
his new secretary.*

Something was wrong.

The lad was absorbed in his work, kneeling on the floor, his back to Sinclair. As he stretched to reach another pile, the tails of his coat fell to either side.

Sinclair couldn't take his eyes off him.

Quincy sat back on his heels, studying a piece of paper. Then he leaned forward to drop it onto a pile of receipts, his trousers stretched taut across his backside.

And then, suddenly, the earl realized what was wrong. Sinclair was no monk. His last dalliance had been long before Waterloo, but he hadn't lost his appreciation for a fine female derrière . . . and that's exactly what he was staring at.

Mister Quincy was actually a Miss!

Other AVON ROMANCES

Coming Soon

And Don't Miss These
ROMANTIC TREASURES
from Avon Books

ATTENTION: ORGANIZATIONS AND CORPORATIONS
Most Avon Books paperbacks are available at special quantity discounts for bulk purchases for sales promotions, premiums, or fund-raising. For information, please call or write:

Special Markets Department, HarperCollins Publishers, Inc., 10 East 53rd Street, New York, N.Y. 10022–5299.
Telephone: (212) 207–7528.   Fax: (212) 207–7222.

SHIRLEY KARR

What An Earl Wants

AVON BOOKS

An Imprint of HarperCollinsPublishers

This is a work of fiction. Names, characters, places, and incidents are products of the author's imagination or are used fictitiously and are not to be construed as real. Any resemblance to actual events, locales, organizations, or persons, living or dead, is entirely coincidental.

AVON BOOKS
An Imprint of HarperCollins*Publishers*
10 East 53rd Street
New York, New York 10022-5299

Copyright © 2005 by Shirley Bro-Karr
ISBN: 0-06-074230-5
www.avonromance.com

All rights reserved. No part of this book may be used or reproduced in any manner whatsoever without written permission, except in the case of brief quotations embodied in critical articles and reviews. For information address Avon Books, an Imprint of HarperCollins Publishers.

First Avon Books paperback printing: January 2005

Avon Trademark Reg. U.S. Pat. Off. and in Other Countries, Marca Registrada, Hecho en U.S.A.
HarperCollins® is a registered trademark of HarperCollins Publishers Inc.

Printed in the U.S.A.

10 9 8 7 6 5 4 3 2 1

If you purchased this book without a cover, you should be aware that this book is stolen property. It was reported as "unsold and destroyed" to the publisher, and neither the author nor the publisher has received any payment for this "stripped book."

To Steve Wicker, high school teacher extraordinaire. Bet this wasn't exactly what you had in mind when you invited me to take your journalism class, was it?

In memory of Jack, beloved writing companion, who stayed beside me from the very first page, flipping his tail across the keyboard, purring his appreciation of my prose.

Acknowledgments

Special thanks to my friends and critique partners, Betty, Jessica, Joey, and Maggie, whose unflagging encouragement and affectionate harassment kept me going.

None of this would have been possible without the loving support of my husband. Without you, I wouldn't have been able to finish and sell the @#$% book.

Chapter 1

London
March 1816

"**I**t ain't my job," cried a feminine voice out in the hall.

"'T'ain't mine, neither," a male voice replied. More voices joined in the squabble, and the volume rose.

Benjamin, Earl of Sinclair, leaned forward in his leather chair and wondered what else would go wrong today. He stared at the young applicant seated across the desk from him, who stared calmly back, unfazed by the shouting match. Just as Sinclair was about to rise to quiet down the servants, the group moved on. Silence reigned at last.

"Why should I hire you, Mr. Quincy?" Sinclair sank back into the chair cushion.

Blast. Now he couldn't see over the ledgers and papers piled on his desk. He sat forward again, studying the young man seated opposite. "I've already interviewed five other secretaries this morning, each with more experience than you. I doubt you even shave yet."

Quincy adjusted one clean but frayed cuff, his gaze never leaving Sinclair's. "Is shaving a requirement for the position?"

Sinclair blinked in surprise. He propped his boot heels on one corner of the desk, sending a pile of folios sliding to the floor. They disappeared amongst other piles already littering the carpet. He stared at Quincy from around a remaining, quivering stack. "I haven't decided yet."

Another commotion in the hall made them both glance at the door. Voices rose and fell, then faded away altogether, and Sinclair returned to the task at hand. He picked up a sheet of foolscap from a pile still balanced on his desk. "Since you've only had one previous employer, and you say Baron—" he glanced at the signature at the bottom of the sheet "—Bradwell recently died, I can't even verify this reference. How do I know it's not a fake?"

"You don't." Quincy pushed his spectacles farther up on the bridge of his nose, concealing the expression in his gray eyes. Or were they green?

Sinclair studied the lad. Though wearing a threadbare coat, the set of his shoulders spoke of confidence, and the set of his chin suggested a stubborn streak. Quincy might desperately need this job, but he wasn't begging for it. Another, still louder commotion in the hall interrupted Sinclair's perusal.

It was beyond Sinclair how being short by just one maid could cause such chaos. Why weren't the upper servants handling this? Sinclair slid his heels off the desk, stalked to the door, and yanked it open. Half his household staff stood clustered in the hall, abruptly silent at his appearance. "Do you mind?"

The servants scattered amid a chorus of "Beg pardon, milord" and "Won't 'appen again, milord."

By Juno, he'd had more peace and quiet when they camped a mile from Boney's forces. Sinclair returned to his chair with a sigh and propped his feet once more on the desk. "Give me one good reason why I should hire you, Quincy. Just one."

Quincy gestured toward the door. "I could get your business affairs in order, so you would be free to get your household affairs in order."

Sinclair shook his head. "Any of the men I interviewed

this morning could do that. Why should I hire *you*?"

Quincy pushed his spectacles up again. "I can forge your signature."

Sinclair's feet slammed to the floor, all annoyance gone. "The devil you say."

The young man continued as though discussing the weather. "As my employer, you could supervise my activities. Make certain they were in your best interest."

Sinclair raised one eyebrow. "I could have you thrown in Newgate."

"You could, but that would be a waste, wouldn't it, my lord?" Quincy pointed at the mountain of mail teetering between them on the desk. "If I were in prison, I wouldn't be able to save you from all that dull paperwork. You should be out tending your properties or attending balls and such, not here signing every little thing."

"Little things such as bank drafts?"

He watched as Quincy glanced around the room, at the thick Turkish carpet and two floor-to-ceiling bookcases overflowing with leather-bound books. Quincy stood, and stepped over the debris as he walked past the red-striped armchair that clashed wonderfully with the burgundy leather wing chair, to the mahogany side table supporting a silver tea service. "Judging by this room, I would wager bank drafts are never 'little' where you are concerned, my lord." He wiped one gloved finger through the dust on the table. "Though perhaps you should find a replacement for the downstairs maid before you go off to your properties."

Sinclair allowed one side of his mouth to curve up. Intrigued by the cheeky lad, he rummaged through one of the piles on his desk. "Here's an invitation I don't wish to accept. Let's see how you handle it."

"Certainly, my lord." Quincy took the invitation, read it, then unearthed the inkwell and a pen while Sinclair searched the desk drawers for a clean sheet of paper. A few moments later, Quincy handed over a neatly penned missive. It bore Sinclair's signature at the bottom.

Sinclair frowned as he studied the note. "Very diplomatic refusal. As it happens, I do have another engagement that evening. But the body of the note is written in a different hand than the signature."

"Of course. My writing, your signature. Your own mother could not tell it's not by your hand."

"Damned if you aren't right." Sinclair glanced from the mountain of newspapers and ledgers to the young man, then to the clock striking the hour, and grimaced. Late again. He shuffled a few folios together, casting another look at the lad. Quincy held Sinclair's gaze, unblinking.

Sinclair never had been able to resist a puzzle, and the impertinent pup intrigued him. Five years as a cavalry officer had trained him to make decisions quickly and follow his instincts, and those instincts shouted at him to keep the young man around. All was not as it seemed. "I think you bear watching, Mr. Quincy. Let's see what you can do with this mess by the time I get back."

Moments later, Sinclair called for his hat, gloves and walking stick, and exited the house, leaving Quincy to tackle the mounds of correspondence and books that littered his office. He was already late for a meeting with his solicitor. Much as he wished to stay and supervise the lad, Sinclair settled for posting one of the downstairs footmen outside the library. Let the lad sink or swim. Even on such short acquaintance, Sinclair would wager a year's income that Quincy was a strong swimmer.

Hoping he could still rely on his staff to keep things under control—though this morning had been more chaotic than usual—Sinclair pushed aside thoughts of his new secretary as he trudged down the street. Keeping his strides even and steady despite leaning on his walking stick required his full concentration. For him, the ebony cane was no fashionable affectation, and he had grown heartily sick of needing it.

After months of struggle, he had left his crutches behind and worked up to three long walks per week, and two short walks that ended with fencing lessons at Henry Angelo's. It galled him that he could not yet box, as he used to study with Gentleman Jackson. The last time Sinclair had stripped to fight, the blows he'd received from being slow on his feet had been inconsequential—until his mother saw the bruises. For her sake, he would wait before trying again.

But he could wield a foil. Each session with Angelo, Sinclair forced himself to do one more lunge than the time before, no matter how much his leg muscles screamed in protest.

Today, however, he would play truant from his self-directed regimen, so he could get back to checking on Mr. Quincy's progress. Sinclair walked straight home from the meeting with his solicitor, intent on going directly to the library. Plans changed, however, when he was waylaid by the butler with a request to meet his mother in her salon. At least Grimshaw, the footman, was at his post and assured him Quincy was still inside the library. By the time Sinclair calmed Mama and helped her deal with various household crises, four hours had passed since he'd left Quincy alone. Blast.

With some trepidation, Sinclair opened the door to his library, expecting to see his new secretary seated behind his desk, up to his elbows in paperwork. It had been three weeks since his last secretary had married the downstairs maid and sailed for America, and Sinclair had more important things to do than paperwork, such as relearning to walk.

But the secretary was not in sight.

The top of Sinclair's massive desk was visible, however, for the first time in weeks. Papers were arranged in neat piles and ledgers put away. Even the dirty tea service was gone, replaced by, of all things, a vase filled with fresh daffodils. He finally spotted Quincy perched on the bookcase ladder, stacking books.

"Well done, lad!" Sinclair said.

Quincy jumped down to the floor. "My lord!" he said, reaching for his spectacles on a shelf. "I didn't expect you yet." He put the spectacles on and began unrolling his shirt sleeves.

Sinclair sat down and looked at his polished desk, marred only by four neat stacks of papers. "What is the order to these?"

Quincy shrugged into his coat and hurried over, still buttoning it up. "These are invitations you should accept, these I've declined for you, these are correspondence from your stewards—I believe they require your personal attention—and these are bills that you—"

"Enough! By Juno, I can't believe you did all this in the short time I was gone. Have you a genie in your pocket?"

"If I did, my lord, I would not be seeking this position." He adjusted his spectacles. "Is everything satisfactory?"

"Fine, fine." Sinclair propped his boot heels on the desk corner. Nothing fell to the floor. That clinched it. He had to hire Quincy, despite the lad's shortage of experience or references. Perhaps providence had sent Sinclair just the person he needed to put his chaotic life in order. Or at least his library—the entire room had been set to rights. Even the slippers and balled-up stockings were gone from under his armchair by the fire.

He watched Quincy straighten his cuffs, and noted that his coat, though clean, had been mended at the elbow. Perhaps providence had also set Sinclair in Quincy's path, as the lad was obviously in need of a well-paying position.

There was a brief knock, then Mrs. Hammond peeked into the room. "Will you be needing anything else, Mr. Qui—Oh, my lord, I didn't know you had returned."

Sinclair glanced at his housekeeper. "No, Mrs. Hammond, Mr. Quincy won't be needing anything else. You might check with him tomorrow, though."

"Yes, my lord, thank you." Mrs. Hammond winked at Quincy before she bobbed a curtsy and closed the door again.

"I trust tomorrow morning at nine is agreeable?" Sinclair said, rising to shake his new secretary's hand.

"Yes. However, I shall need Sundays off, and every other Saturday. I also need an advance on my wages. Half the first quarter's salary should do."

Sinclair raised both eyebrows. "Whatever for?"

"To pay my landlady. She's quite adamant about receiving rent payments and I'm afraid I've fallen behind."

"You can have a room on the third floor. I'll send a footman to help collect your things."

"Thank you, but no." Quincy pushed up his spectacles.

"Why not? It would be convenient and save you money."

"Convenient for you, yes, but not for me. May I have the advance now? Ten shillings would suffice."

"Cheeky bugger," Sinclair muttered, opening the middle drawer of his desk to search for the cashbox. He stopped. "Did you tidy all of the drawers this way?"

"Yes. 'Twas impossible to put things away otherwise."

Sinclair lifted the unlocked cashbox lid and stared at the money inside.

"Yes, I could have," Quincy said, as though reading Sinclair's thoughts. Quincy let out a small sigh. "The list of applicants from the employment agency is in the top left drawer. I suggest you re-interview some of them. Good day, my lord." He jammed his hat on his head and reached for the door.

"Where are you going?"

Quincy slowly turned to face him. "Do you wish me to turn out my pockets?"

"No," Sinclair said, rubbing his chin. "I don't believe that will be necessary." Quincy's reaction had told Sinclair all he needed to know of the lad's character.

"Good. I wouldn't do it if you asked."

Sinclair bit back a smile. "I thought as much. But I still don't know why you're leaving."

The secretary's chest rose and fell with a deep breath. "I realize it takes time to build respect and trust, but I will not work for someone who *dis*trusts me from the beginning. Good day, my lord."

"Wait!" Sinclair limped across the room and blocked the door. Quincy trembled slightly when Sinclair clapped him on one slender shoulder. "I have decided I like your impertinence. I want you to stay."

"No." Quincy flashed a grin. "At least, not this afternoon. I will return in the morning, however."

"Good lad. Take the ten shillings and pay your landlady, then go see my tailor. These clothes are dreadful."

"Your tailor, my lord?" Quincy's cheeks flushed to the roots of his pomaded brown hair. "If you don't mind, I already have a, um, tailor, though it's been a while since I visited . . . him."

"Whatever pleases you. Just replace your coat and trousers. They're ready for the rag merchants." Sinclair stepped back and surveyed Quincy from his battered hat to the paper-thin soles of his shoes, until it appeared the rest of his blood had rushed to his face. "Good lord, man, your last employer must have been a first rate pinchpenny. When's the last time you had new shoes? Or a good meal? You're thinner than a half-pay corporal. Never mind." He continued before the embarrassed youth could speak. "Visit your tailor if you prefer, but see that you stop off at my cobbler on your way here tomorrow." He scribbled an address on the back of a calling card before handing it over.

"Th-thank you, my lord." Quincy bowed stiffly and hurried out of the room.

"Harper!" Sinclair shouted when he heard the front door close.

The butler entered the library. "Yes, my lord?"

"Congratulate me. I've filled half the vacancies in the staff."

"I believe that calls for a toast, my lord. Does this mean you'll soon be interviewing maids?"

"Yes, brandy should do nicely. And no, not just yet. I don't think interviewing maids would be half as entertaining as interviewing Mr. Quincy was."

The butler sighed. "As you wish, my lord."

Hurrying home in the gathering dusk, head bent low against the stiff March wind and rain, Quincy stopped to purchase lengths of fabric for a day coat, trousers, and two shirts. Quincy also selected a length of sprigged muslin, and stopped a few more times for potatoes, cheese, and a leg of mutton.

Quincy had barely stepped through the door of the third-floor flat when a brunette in braids grabbed one of the parcels.

"You got the job! You got the job!" she said, hooking her

arm through Quincy's and spinning them until her skirts and hair fluttered out.

"Yes, Melinda, I got the job. Now stop dancing before you start coughing again. You're making me dizzy. And it means work for you, too. His lordship doesn't want to see me in rags again. Can you finish a coat by morning, if I help you?" Quincy set the bolt of dark blue wool on the table.

"If you help? Impossible. Without your help, however . . ."

"Jo, is that you?" a voice called from the other room of the flat.

"Yes, Grandmère."

"Come here, child. I've been waiting all day."

Quincy and Melinda grinned at each other, then Melinda took the remainder of the parcels while Quincy went to the other room.

"Sit, sit, and tell me all about it," the old woman said, patting the bed beside her.

"I knew acting as Papa's secretary would help you get us out of the suds someday," Melinda said, following Quincy into the room, having dropped the parcels on the table.

"Is Lord Sinclair all we thought he would be?" Grandmère asked, pulling Quincy down beside her.

"Yes, and you were absolutely right. I think he enjoyed my impertinence more than I did."

Grandmère chuckled. "Knew that would get him. He hates toadeaters almost as much as his grandfather did. Now, *that* was a man who appreciated a pretty ankle!" She turned serious again. "I still wish there was another solution, but I am glad everything is working out just as you planned. Do you think he suspects anything?"

"No, I'm sure he doesn't," Quincy said.

Grandmère pulled Quincy close for a hug. "Good girl."

Chapter 2

"Excellent, Mr. Quincy, excellent." Sinclair slid his booted feet from his desk and rose to walk around his new secretary when he entered the library the next morning.

"I'm sorry I'm late, my lord, but your cobbler—"

"Do be quiet, Mr. Quincy." Sinclair stepped back and rubbed his chin. "Your tailor does fine work, lad."

"Th-thank you, my lord. The cobbler insisted I put these shoes on your bill, but they were frightfully expensive. I don't—"

"I said be quiet, Quincy." Sinclair lifted the lad's trouser-leg with one thumb and forefinger to get a better look at the sturdy black shoes. Quincy flushed to his roots. "They're just what you should wear, working for me. If you feel guilty about the expense, you can tackle that stack of bills over there and make sure no one is cheating me."

He waited until Quincy seated himself at the drop-leaf desk by the window, then handed him the accounting ledgers. "Start with the household accounts, then we'll move on to my other properties."

"Yes, my lord."

The library door opened and the housekeeper bustled in

with a tray of scones, jelly and tea. "Good morning, my lord, Mr. Quincy."

Startled, Sinclair stared at Mrs. Hammond. He couldn't remember the last time she'd personally brought a tea tray to anyone but his mother. This one hadn't even been sent for. He turned his attention to Quincy, who smiled at Mrs. Hammond when she poured two cups for them before she left.

"Do you intend to wrap all of my staff around your finger, Mr. Quincy?"

Quincy walked over to the tray and took a sip before answering. "Housekeepers are valuable allies, whether you're the lord of the house, the scullery maid, or anyone in between."

Sinclair grunted. "Just don't run off and marry the downstairs maid."

"You haven't replaced her yet, my lord." His eyes twinkled. "Do you wish me to handle that, or will you leave the hiring up to Harper or Mrs. Hammond?"

"Leave you to hire a young, pretty maid? I think not. That would be as bad as letting Harper do it." Sinclair leaned close to Quincy, pleasantly surprised to note that he smelled only of lemon soap and rain-dampened wool. With Johnson, his previous secretary, he'd often needed to open the windows, especially in warmer weather. He couldn't help noticing Quincy's porcelain-smooth jaw. "You don't have even a hint of whiskers yet. How old are you, anyway?"

"Nineteen, my lord, but we already established that shaving was not a requirement for this position. How old are *you*?"

Sinclair blinked, then gave a faint smile. "Far too old for a man of my years. Carry on, Mr. Quincy." He drank the tea Mrs. Hammond had poured, then picked up his hat, gloves, and stick, and left for his walk.

Quincy sat down before her knees gave out. "Everything is fine," she whispered. "Everything is just fine. Lord Sinclair doesn't suspect a thing." She had never counted on her employer getting so, well, so . . . *close*. Whiskers? She could bind her bosom and insert a rolled-up stocking in her trousers, but she knew no way to fake having whiskers.

But Sinclair didn't suspect a thing. She could do this. Everything was fine. After a few more deep breaths, she pocketed her spectacles and set to work.

Soon the figures in the account books began to swim before her eyes. Johnson's handwriting was even worse than her father's had been, and the Earl of Sinclair's holdings were far more extensive. No matter how many times she added the columns, she never came up with the same figures Johnson had. She threw her pencil down in disgust.

"I can hear the earl now," she muttered. "Terminated on the first day. What will Grandmère say?" She shoved her spectacles back on and stepped out into the hall.

"Mr. Harper, do you mind if I send one of the footmen on an errand? It may take him a while to find what I need."

"I have just the man in mind," the butler said. "Thompson's post is near the top of the stairs, but we usually find him near whichever room the maids are cleaning."

"Harper, I insist you do something about that buffoon upstairs!" A man no taller than Quincy appeared behind them, holding an armful of limp cravats. "His tongue fairly hangs to the floor whenever one of the female servants walk past. It is positively disgusting."

"I heard it's something else that fairly hangs to the floor, but I may be mistaken." Harper stepped aside. Quincy felt her ears burning but kept her expression bland. "Mr. Quincy, have you met Broderick, his lordship's valet?"

They had barely exchanged greetings when a giant in Sinclair's livery with shoulder-length blond curls crossed the hall, following a maid toward the back stairs. "Thompson, Mr. Quincy has an errand for you," Harper called.

Quincy got a crick in her neck looking up at Thompson while she described what she needed him to buy, and gratefully leaned against the wall when she returned to the library.

When she had devised her plan, she hadn't considered how many other people she'd be dealing with in addition to her employer. But no one suspected a thing. She could do this. Everything was fine. "Keep saying that," she muttered, "and it'll be true." She went back to work, and had just finished sorting the morning's mail when Mrs. Hammond knocked.

"Sorry to disturb you, Mr. Quincy, but her ladyship requests you join her in the drawing room."

Her ladyship? What could Sinclair's mother possibly want with her? Once again she pushed her spectacles on and left the library. She followed the housekeeper upstairs, down a hallway wider than her entire flat, and into a room decorated in yellow with green and orange accents, reminding Quincy of daffodils.

In the center of the daffodil sat Lady Sinclair, an older, more delicate version of her son, with silver streaks in her chestnut hair and the faint scent of jasmine floating around her. Knowing from her research that the former earl had passed away nearly six years ago, Quincy was surprised to see Lady Sinclair wearing a half-mourning gown of gray, trimmed with lavender.

"I am pleased to make your acquaintance, Mr. Quincy," she said, raising one hand. Quincy remembered to bow over it, then stood stiffly with her arms at her sides.

"Please, sit down. Would you care for tea?"

"No, thank you." Quincy sat on the edge of the cushion.

"Well, let's get right to the point, then. How do you like your new position?"

Alarm skittered up her spine, and Quincy forced herself to breathe. Terminated already? Could Lady Sinclair do that? "Fine, my lady."

"Good." She tilted her head to one side, studying Quincy's face.

Quincy fought to keep her expression neutral, to hide her growing unease.

"Have we met somewhere? Perhaps I know your father or a brother."

"No, my lady, I don't believe so. My brother died at birth, and my father passed away a year ago."

"I am sorry to hear that." She studied Quincy for what felt like a century. Quincy pressed her palms flat to her knees to keep from fidgeting. The mantel clock chimed the hour. Lady Sinclair's eyes widened, but her expression cleared again so quickly, Quincy thought she might have imagined it.

Lady Sinclair cleared her throat and leaned toward Quincy. "Now, about your job. You handle my son's correspondence, know which affairs he's invited to?"

"That is part of what I do, yes."

"Good." Lady Sinclair refilled her teacup and settled back on the cushions, again studying Quincy.

This was getting right to the point? "Is there something specific you wish to know, my lady?"

"Hmm? Oh, yes. Yes, I—I would like you to keep me informed as to which affairs my son is invited to, and which invitations he accepts." She took another sip of her tea and set the cup and saucer on the table at her side. "Has anyone ever told you that you have honest eyes, Mr. Quincy?"

"No, my lady, I don't believe so." Quincy resisted the urge to squirm.

"Well, you do. I feel as though I can tell you anything and it will be kept in strictest confidence." She leaned forward and lowered her voice. "You seem like someone who is comfortable with secrets."

Quincy involuntarily leaned back. "Thank you—I think—but I should remind you that my first allegiance is to Lord Sinclair. I am sure he would not have hired me if he did not think my activities would be in his best interest."

Lady Sinclair straightened. "That's as it should be. I'm not asking for anything that would betray his trust in you. I'm simply concerned that, well . . ." She rested her hand on Quincy's sleeve. "Benjamin has always been very private, keeping his own counsel. But he's becoming downright reclusive, especially since Anthony returned to Oxford. Anthony is my younger son." Lady Sinclair beamed with motherly pride for a moment, then her expression turned grave again. "Benjamin insisted there was no further need to disrupt Tony's studies. But I know Benjamin is not nearly as recovered as he would like everyone to think. His wounds were too . . . grievous."

Lady Sinclair quickly took another sip of tea. "And after that nasty bit of business last fall, I fear he's quite turned off the idea of marrying."

"Last fall?" Quincy tried to project the right tone of polite boredom to mask her curiosity.

"During the Little Season. Benjamin was pleased with how quickly he mastered getting about on crutches, and started going out in Society a bit. Some of the ladies quite doted on him. Wounded hero, and all that. He was smitten with a raven-haired miss, and I think he may even have asked for her hand. But he came home one night and smashed all the crockery in his room. When I quizzed him about it, he would only say that her heart was as black as her hair."

Quincy tried to think of a suitable response, but none was forthcoming.

"Whatever she said or did, he still needs a wife, a helpmate. I know he spends a great deal of time at his club, but that's with other former soldiers, and I'm sure all they discuss is politics and games of chance. I ask you, how is he to find a suitable wife in St. James's Street?"

"I'm sure I do not know."

"That's why I want you to let me know which balls and such he is invited to, where there will be young ladies of quality. I can apply a little motherly pressure on him to accept, and then who knows what might happen? And if he should mention any miss in particular, you will let me know, won't you? Then I can make certain she's invited to tea, and to the soiree I'm hosting in a few weeks."

Quincy furrowed her brow. Sinclair might consider this spying, but she had no wish to offend the lady of the house, either. "I think I can do that without breaching any confidence."

"Good lad! I knew I could count on you." Before Quincy could react, Lady Sinclair enveloped her in a brief hug, then moved to the pianoforte. Lady Sinclair seemed different than when their strange little interview began, but Quincy couldn't quite put her finger on the change. Perhaps she just imagined it.

Quincy walked back to the library, listening to the strains of a Mozart sonata. What wounds had Lady Sinclair alluded to? A leg injury—that would explain why Sinclair was forever propping his feet up, and often limped or walked with a stiff gait. She stifled her curiosity, however, instinctively knowing Sinclair would not welcome inquiries into the subject. And heaven forbid he ever discover his mother had just shared such private information with his secretary on such short acquaintance.

Her thoughts as to why Lady Sinclair had told her these things were interrupted by Thompson, who met her in the hall. She relieved him of his package and returned to work on the account books. She was making such great progress, she didn't hear Sinclair enter a few hours later.

"Good Lord, what is that monstrosity?"

She jumped, nearly bumping into his chest. He was leaning over her, his hand on the back of her chair. Her shoulder brushed his fingers as she moved.

He sniffed and looked around the room. "Has my mother been in here?"

"No, my lord. I joined her in the drawing room, at her request."

He stepped back to allow Quincy room to rise. "Wrapped her around your finger, too, I suppose?"

Quincy tilted her chin up to meet his gaze. "She said she was pleased to make my acquaintance and she . . . she—"

"She what?"

"Hugged me."

Sinclair's mouth opened, but no sound emerged. He raised both eyebrows. "You still haven't told me what that monstrosity is on your desk." He reached around her to flick one of the colored balls strung on rows of wires in a wooden frame.

"It's an abacus." She flicked back the ball he had moved. "My last employer had one, and I found it quite helpful. It might blend in better if you had a Chinese decorating scheme."

"Bah. This is *my* room, and its decorating scheme is that it has none." He sank into the sofa and put his feet up on the

ottoman. "So, report. What did you learn about the household accounts this morning?"

"I'd rather not say yet, my lord. I found some confusing
entries, and I'd prefer to look into them more carefully before discussing the matter."

"Commendable. Get cracking, then." He opened the folio he'd carried under one arm and began reading.

Quincy nodded and went back to work, trying not to
think about Lord Sinclair sitting just a few feet away. She
risked a peek at him through her lashes. It took all her pow-
ers of concentration to turn her attention back to the account books instead of his profile, to gaze at the figures on
the page and not the figure seated in the chair.

The deeper she delved into the entries, the easier it became to concentrate. When she finally caught on to the pattern taking shape in the books, she would have shouted in
triumph if it didn't mean such bad news for Sinclair. The
abacus proved her figures were correct, not Johnson's. She
gathered proof from paid bills, ledger books, and correspondence files, spreading them out across the desk and
even onto the floor as she worked.

Sinclair peered at Quincy over the top of the document
he was pretending to read, and considered their interview
yesterday. Though he was still sure he'd made the right
choice, all sorts of questions nagged at him. It was too soon
to know for certain that Quincy was a man of his word, and
would only use his forgery skill for his employer's benefit
rather than detriment, but Sinclair felt confident things
would turn out for the best. His instincts were always right.

Quincy had apparently gotten over his initial discomfort
of this morning, and made himself at ease at Sinclair's
desk, using every square inch of its surface. Sinclair hadn't
noticed before how slight of stature the lad was, dwarfed by
the leather chair and oak desk, his heels not even reaching
the floor. Quincy squinted as he tried to make out Johnson's
indecipherable scrawl. His expression soon cleared, as he
must have learned the secret cipher.

He even began humming under his breath and swinging

his crossed ankles above the carpet, looking more like a child playing make-believe than a young man at work. But it was no child's intellect with whom Sinclair had crossed verbal swords earlier.

Time for a little reconnaissance. Sinclair rose from the sofa and settled in the chair across from Quincy. It took the lad several seconds to notice him, but he finally looked up with a start.

"My lord?"

Sinclair leaned his elbows on the desk, chin resting on one palm. "Tell me how you learned to forge."

Quincy's jaw worked for a moment, then he crossed his arms. "Have you changed your mind about Newgate?"

"No."

Quincy just looked at him. Sinclair was beginning to think the lad would refuse to answer, but he stayed still, silently awaiting a reply.

"It was by accident," Quincy said at last. He picked up the pencil, toying with it. "My . . . last employer was ill for a long time. His hands would tremble, which made it hard to write. One day I copied his signature on a letter." He shrugged one shoulder. "After a little practice, he couldn't tell my version from his."

"You had his permission?"

Quincy looked insulted that Sinclair would even suggest otherwise. "Baron Bradwell didn't want others to know how far his illness had progressed."

"Proud man."

Quincy looked up from the pencil. "Aren't we all?"

Sinclair examined his fingernails for a moment. "I don't recall giving you permission to learn *my* signature, or a letter from which to copy it."

Quincy lowered his gaze. "I needed this job. Notes to merchants or agencies are easy to intercept."

Sinclair straightened. "You stole a note from one of my footmen?"

"Borrowed. I did deliver it." He glanced at Sinclair over the top of his spectacles. "Eventually."

Pieces of the puzzle fell into place, giving him an entirely different picture. Sinclair wasn't certain whether he felt angry or impressed. And he'd thought Quincy audacious before. "The employment agency didn't send you, did they?"

Before Quincy could reply, Harper knocked on the door. "Beg pardon, my lord, but Lady Sinclair requests your presence," the butler intoned.

Sinclair stood. "We'll finish this later," he warned, and faced the butler. "Where is she? The drawing room?"

"Her bedchamber, actually."

Sinclair's eyebrows raised. The butler gave a slight nod. Odd, indeed. Sinclair shot one last look at Quincy, who had gone back to organizing stacks of papers, and headed upstairs.

Hannah, his mother's maid, opened the door before Sinclair could even knock. "It's a miracle, my lord," she whispered, "a bleedin' miracle!"

Sinclair stepped inside the door, and froze. His mother was in front of the mirror, performing a girlish pirouette, her skirts flaring out. Her *yellow* skirts. Not black, not gray, not even lavender. Soft, sunny yellow. A color she hadn't worn in over five years.

"Is something amiss with my appearance, Benjamin?" Lady Sinclair looked at him in the reflection. "Your father used to tell me this dress was flattering on my figure."

"It was. It is! It's just that, ah . . ."

His mother smiled. "You have been after me for ages to put away my widow's weeds. Now that I've decided to do so, you can't string together a coherent sentence?" She clucked her tongue, then turned to her maid. "Hannah, I think I'll wear the dark blue. It would only shock everyone senseless if I were to wear bright yellow to Lady Fitzwater's card party tonight."

"Yes, m'lady." The maid sprang forward, gathering up the yards of dresses and fabric strewn across his mother's bed, setting aside a dark blue mass.

Lady Sinclair nodded. "Now, Benjamin, which ball are you going to squire me to tomorrow night?"

"Ball?" He swallowed.

"You haven't forgotten our agreement, have you? You promised to attend balls—yes, yes, I know you still can't dance yet—and look about for a wife, and I promised to dance with at least one gentleman each time we go. Have you picked someone out for me yet? What's his name?"

Sinclair sank into the delicate-looking chair at the dressing table, grateful it didn't collapse the way his knees threatened to, and watched his mother walk toward him, hands on her hips. "You spend your days dreaming up ways to set me back on my heels, don't you?"

His mother laughed.

After a stunned moment, Sinclair chuckled too, from the sheer delight of hearing her laughter. It had been absent so long.

In the dark months following his father's suicide, Sinclair had often wondered if his mother would suffocate under the weight of her grief and humiliation. She had switched to half-mourning only last fall, at his request, when Sinclair had been brought home to recover from his injuries. He'd suffered nary a twinge of guilt when telling her that seeing her in black made him feel his own death was imminent.

He'd meant the comment as a jest, but quickly realized he'd found a way to bring her back to life, to make her give up her isolation and go about in society again. Hence their agreement. He agreed to do things he'd planned to do anyway, but dragged his feet about them, until she agreed to do things she hadn't done since becoming a widow.

This was the first time she'd followed through—planning to attend her first ball. He'd have to sort through his invitations, and older gentleman acquaintances, and find someone suitable for the occasion.

"Well, Benjamin? Whose ball?"

He stood up and kissed her cheek. "It's a surprise, Mama."

His mother gave an inelegant snort. "You haven't the least idea whose yet. Why don't you have your new secretary sort through the mail and pick one?"

"Have Mr. Quincy pick one?"

"Yes, Mr. Quincy. Had a nice chat with him this afternoon. Charming young fellow. I like him much better than Johnson."

"Well, he certainly smells better than Johnson."

Lady Sinclair smiled. "I think you chose well, Benjamin."

Quincy the forger had had a nice chat with Lady Sinclair . . . and wrapped her around his little finger, too.

Before Sinclair could form a reply, his mother spun him by the shoulder toward the doorway. "Now, shoo! I have to get ready for Fitzy's card party."

"Yes, Mama." He bussed her on the cheek again and set off back to the library. As he struggled to limp down the stairs, he thought back on their conversation, and the sudden changes in his mother. The spring in her step, the sparkle in her eye—if he'd seen that in anyone else, he'd expect mischief.

Sinclair paused to rest on the landing. His mother had seemed her usual self—usual since Papa's death—at breakfast this morning. She hadn't gone out, and no callers had come in, either. The only thing that made today different from any other day had been . . . had been her chat with Quincy.

Quincy?

He remembered his mother's words. *Charming young fellow.*

Had Quincy managed to charm his mother out of the blue devils? In one afternoon? When Sinclair had been struggling to do just that for years? Years!

But how?

His own words came back to him. *I think you bear watching, Mr. Quincy.*

Indeed.

He entered the library, noting that Quincy barely looked up as Sinclair sat on the sofa. He grabbed the folio with the latest report from his solicitor and again pretended to read it as he studied his new secretary. He had every intention of continuing their earlier discussion, but first he wanted more time to think about his conversation with Mama.

The lad was so absorbed in his work that he moved from

the desk and knelt on the floor, organizing papers and stacking ledgers. Still kneeling, his back to Sinclair, Quincy stretched to reach another pile, the tails of his coat falling to either side. Quincy was wearing new trousers in addition to a new coat, as Sinclair had requested. The tailor had done fine work, despite any misgivings Sinclair might have had.

But something was wrong.

Quincy sat back on his heels, studying a piece of paper. Then he leaned forward to drop it onto a pile of receipts, his trousers stretched taut across his backside. Normally Sinclair paid little attention to other men's clothing, other than to confirm that his own attire was appropriate to the occasion. But he couldn't take his eyes off Quincy.

And then Sinclair recognized what was wrong. Though very circumspect, Sinclair was no monk. His last dalliance had been long before Waterloo, but he hadn't lost his appreciation for a fine female derrière . . . and that's exactly what he was staring at.

Mr. Quincy was actually a Miss.

Without thinking, Sinclair sprang forward, kneeling on the floor beside Quincy, and grabbed her wrist as she set down a receipt. The spasm of pain in his leg made his voice harsher than he'd intended. "What the hell do you think you're doing, *Miss* Quincy?"

Chapter 3

Sinclair heard Quincy gasp. She stared back at him, frozen.

"I ask again, what the hell do you think you're doing, *Miss* Quincy?"

The fire popped and crackled.

Sinclair made to rise, but realized his leg wouldn't cooperate. He couldn't get up without first releasing Miss Quincy, and he had no intention of letting go until he had answers from her.

At last Quincy glanced at her wrist, still held firmly in Sinclair's grasp, and back up at him. Perhaps a part of him had realized all along that her smooth alto voice was that of a woman, not a young man, but now it was as steely as her gaze when she spoke. "I am doing exactly what you hired me to do, Lord Sinclair."

"I hired—"

"You hired a secretary." Her words were clear and slow, as though she spoke to a child. A not-very-bright child. "I am performing the duties of a secretary. Is there a problem?"

Sinclair blinked in shock. "A problem?" He realized he was gaping like a fish just hauled onto the dock, and closed his mouth. She continued to stare at him, the picture of calm, while he tried to gather his scrambled thoughts. "She asks if there's a problem," he said, speaking in the direction of the fireplace.

"Because I don't see that there is one."

Oh, she had bottom, he'd give her that. And not just the shapely one shielded by her coattails. "How about, for starters, the fact that you lied to me?"

"About what? Everything I've told you is true."

"True? *Mister* Quincy?"

"I never claimed to be a Mister."

Sinclair felt his jaw fall open again, and closed it.

"I stated my name as J. Quincy. It is. It's just that it's Josephine, not Joseph. And I did not give myself a courtesy title. *You* did that."

"You just didn't bother to correct my misconception?" He raked her up and down with a glance. "An understandable misconception, given your attire," he touched the soft, silky strands beside her ear, "short hair," he used one finger to lift the top of her waistcoat away from her shirt, "and lack of bosom."

At last he had the satisfaction of seeing her blush. It stole up from below her cravat until it covered her entire face in a delightful shade of pink.

Delightful? Bosom? What the hell was he thinking?

"The clothes fit better this way." She swallowed, turning even more pink. "And this is appropriate attire for a secretary."

When he didn't reply or release her, she pointedly looked down at her wrist again. "Do you intend to hold me all day?"

Abruptly he let go, inwardly wincing at the red imprints he'd left on her pale skin. He half expected Quincy to rise and leave, but she pushed up her spectacles and sat back. Papers rustled beneath her as she crossed her legs.

Guiding his weak leg with both hands, he assumed the same position. Blood began to flow back into the limb. Another minute or two and he'd be able to rise with his dignity intact. Angry, but dignified.

"What now?" She calmly waited. No tears. No wailing.

Damn. He was more disturbed than she was. Well, hell, he was the one who'd been shocked, not her—she knew about her disguise.

Quincy entwined her trembling fingers, the first sign of nervousness he'd observed.

Maybe he had disturbed her after all. He sat up straighter. "What now? Now you collect your things, miss, and leave. Before I send for the Watch."

She inhaled, intent on arguing, he was sure, but suddenly let it out on a sigh. A sigh of defeat. Now, why did that sting? He should be glad.

"Very well." Her cheeks suddenly flushed again. "I've already spent the ten-shilling advance. You'll have to wait until I secure another position before I can pay you back. Minus the prorated portion for yesterday and today's work, of course."

"Work?" He glanced around the room. In two days, all Quincy had done was sort through his mail. And rearrange his library, organize papers into who-knows-what-for piles, coerce his housekeeper into doing tasks she hadn't done in years, and . . .

And make his mother wear yellow. Make her laugh.

Some of his righteous anger melted away, despite his efforts to draw it back around him like a cloak. Quincy had tricked him, had lied by omission.

But she had also made his mother smile. And ask to go dancing.

Damn.

"Yes, my work. I was just about to tell you what I had found. The confusing entries that I mentioned earlier? I solved the puzzle. Well, part of it. We're sitting on the evidence."

Sinclair glanced at the piles around them on the floor, and back at Quincy. "Evidence of what?"

"Johnson, your previous secretary, handled all of your accounting?"

"Yes. What of it?"

"He embezzled from you."

Breath left Sinclair's chest in a rush. "Embezzled?" The

anger returned in full force, centering him, clearing his thoughts. He leaned forward, his voice a growl. "Prove it."

Quincy didn't even flinch. "He did it in small increments, so you wouldn't be as likely to catch on." She grabbed the top sheet from a nearby stack, and opened a ledger. "Here's one example. See this receipt for brandy? Monsieur Beauvais delivered two cases, but the ledger shows payment for four."

"Didn't Beauvais simply deliver two more cases?"

"There's no receipt indicating that. How long has Harper worked for you? Is he reliable?"

"He's been our butler since I was in short coats. Of course he's reliable." Sinclair struggled to his feet, needing to move, to do something. "But I thought Johnson reliable, too. No wonder he and his bride were in such a bloody hurry to join his cousin in America."

Quincy rose, as well. "They've left the country?"

Sinclair looked at her sharply. "How much is missing? More than this petty theft?" He gestured at the receipt in her hand.

Quincy paused, obviously choosing her words carefully. "My lord, if I were willing to steal from you in this manner, knowing this 'petty theft' was enough to get me hanged if caught, then I certainly wouldn't hesitate to steal on a grander scale. Hung for a sheep, and all that."

"Damn!" Sinclair stalked to the door and yanked it open. "Harper!" he shouted. "I want an inventory of—"

"My lord, wait," Quincy interrupted. "Any items Johnson might have taken would have been discovered by now."

"Not him, Miss Quincy. The maid, his bride! She had access to the silver, to the entire household." He finished giving instructions to the butler, then closed the door and began to pace. "Misbegotten son of a—"

"I was thinking more along the lines of your properties, your investments, rather than your household. Johnson had access to your entire fortune, did he not?"

Sinclair stopped. He glared at Quincy.

She stared back. "You need me."

He shook his head. "How much is missing?"

"So far? I can prove at least ten thousand pounds is gone."

"Ten . . . thou—?"

"At least. Probably more."

Sinclair rubbed his hands over his eyes. This was not happening. Not to him. Not now. Not when he needed his money for . . . Sinclair lowered his hands. The brazen miss was still staring at him. From across the room, and with her spectacles in the way, it was hard to discern the emotion reflected in her eyes. Pity? No. Desperation? Probably. Determination, certainly.

"You need me," she said again. "It will take time to go through the rest of Johnson's records and determine the extent of the damage."

Sinclair shook his head. Again.

"How long did he work for you?"

"Five years. He worked for my father before that." Sinclair suddenly felt drained. His physical reserves were still low to begin with, and after today—changes in Mama, the old secretary had stolen from him, the new secretary had tricked him—he just wasn't up to it. He slumped on the sofa and lifted his right leg onto the ottoman. "A man can do a lot of stealing in that much time."

"Don't enact a Cheltenham tragedy for my benefit," Quincy said, her tone aloof.

Sinclair almost laughed, despite himself. She had bottom, right up to the end.

End?

Absently rubbing his thigh, Sinclair watched her pick up the various piles from the floor and stack them crisscross on his desk, then reach for her coat and hat. She was leaving.

That's what he wanted, right? Quincy gone. He'd told her to go. Not just once, but three times. His life was chaotic enough without having to deal with a female secretary. And if word got out, it would be disastrous.

A loose paper fluttered to the floor as she pulled on her coat, and Quincy bent over to retrieve it. Her coattails separated, revealing her very feminine backside. Again.

Sinclair raised his gaze to the ceiling, exasperated with

himself. He had no business staring at her derrière. Regardless of how shapely it was.

To be fair, Sinclair conceded that she was good at what she did. Bookkeeping, that is. How long might the embezzlement have gone unnoticed, if not for Quincy? He certainly hadn't figured it out in the three weeks since Johnson had left. And the changes in Mama, those had occurred in just one day. If the two women were to, say, have tea together once a week or so, what other changes might come about?

Quincy buttoned her coat. Pulled threadbare gloves out of a pocket and tugged them on. Started walking for the door, her spine rigid.

"How much time to go through all of Johnson's records?" Sinclair said, calling himself a thousand kinds of fool even as the words left his mouth.

Quincy stopped, her hand on the knob. "I don't know. Days. Weeks, possibly."

Sinclair turned on the sofa toward Quincy, making sure her attention was centered on him before he spoke. "Then that is your top priority. You can begin first thing in the morning."

"Morning?" For the first time, she looked truly startled.

There was a knock on the door, and Quincy jumped back.

Mrs. Hammond poked her head in. "I was just taking some tea up to her ladyship, my lord, and wanted to know if you'd care for a spot as well?"

Changes, indeed. "Yes, Mrs. Hammond, thank you."

The housekeeper nodded, smiled at Quincy, and spun on her heel, leaving the door open.

Quincy cleared her throat.

He interrupted before she could speak. "You've earned the right to solve the rest of the puzzle. After that," he rose from the sofa, drawing himself to his full height, "you're done." Her eyebrows lifted. "Do we understand one another, *Mister* Quincy?"

She raised her chin, eyes narrowed. Footsteps sounded in the hall, coming closer. For a moment he thought Quincy was going to fling his offer back in his face. But then she nodded, once. "Yes, my lord, I believe we do."

Grimshaw, the downstairs footman, entered with a bucket of coal, preventing any more candid conversation.

"See you in the morning, then, Mr. Quincy."

Quincy adjusted her hat. "Yes, my lord."

He saw her smile, just before she walked out the door.

Sinclair poured himself a brandy and sat down again, his foot propped on the ottoman. It might prove awkward working with a female secretary, but Quincy would certainly continue having a positive influence on his mother. And Quincy's position was by no means permanent—how long could it take her to finish going through the books? For Mama's sake, he would just have to make the best of the situation.

And make sure Quincy kept her coat on.

Quincy stepped out the door, nodding a greeting to all the staff she passed, and made it two houses down the street before her knees buckled. She sat down, or rather fell down, at the foot of a statue guarding another town house. Her hands shook, her head spun, her stomach tried to take flight.

He knew.

He'd fired her.

And then he'd un-fired her.

At least temporarily.

She buried her face in her hands, her stores of impudence and bravado utterly depleted, used up in her brazen confrontation with the earl.

So much for her brilliant plan. At least the part about passing herself off as a Mister with no one the wiser. Quincy snorted.

The part about getting a job as Sinclair's secretary, well that part was still intact. Somewhat. Yes, he knew, but he was letting her stay on, anyway. At least until she found out how much her predecessor had stolen.

Why?

Why had Sinclair un-fired her? Any reasonably competent secretary could go through the records and find the extent of the theft, now that she had pointed it out.

A little detail of their conversation suddenly came back to her. Why was he willing, no, insisting, on still calling her *Mister* Quincy?

Was he embarrassed to let anyone know she had fooled him, even for such a brief time? Quincy raised her head, her breathing returning to normal. Perhaps he was so impressed with her skills, he was willing to go along with her charade? Or was he simply reluctant to risk the scandal of anyone knowing he had a female secretary?

They would be working together closely.

Very closely.

A shiver tiptoed up her spine. A shiver, not of fear, but of anticipation. She cradled her wrist, where he had held her in his firm grip. He had long, strong fingers. Calluses. Small white marks from old and not-so-old scars. Powerful hands.

Powerful man.

And she worked for him. At least temporarily.

And they shared a secret.

If he wasn't going to reveal her deception, then she certainly would not. Her sister and grandmother didn't need to know that Sinclair knew. Not telling them wouldn't be lying. Not exactly. Their knowing that he knew would only cause them undue stress and concern. Right?

Quincy's head began to swim.

Whatever Sinclair's true reason for letting her stay, she would find out soon enough. She needed this job, or more specifically, the wages from it, too much to quibble. She dusted off the seat of her trousers and headed for home.

As she traversed the streets alone, she was again grateful for her father's pragmatic, flexible nature that had let her adopt "Joseph" and leave Josephine behind, irrevocably, when their family moved five years ago. Papa's failing health had made it impossible for him to care for a household of women. Under society's ever watchful eyes, "Joseph" handled matters Josephine could not, relieving Papa's burdens.

A few snips of the scissors to her hair, a few tucks to secondhand trousers and coats, and the transition was complete. Final. Giving up any girlish dreams about her future had been worth the peace of mind her new role gave her. She hardly ever imagined herself wearing a gown, and instead enjoyed the freedom of movement allowed by wearing trousers.

She had to focus on the positive, on the gains. Because the losses were just too great to bear.

Living in a small cottage and leasing out their manor house had generated enough money to pay bills and keep food on the table. Everything had been fine until Papa's death last spring. With no male heirs, by law his title and entailed property—everything—had reverted back to the crown. Stupid laws.

Quincy kicked a pebble, watched it career off a lamppost, then with grim satisfaction saw it squashed under the wheels of a passing hackney into a pile of horse droppings.

To distract herself from her own problems, she thought about the earl's. Surely Johnson could not have done too much damage? Not enough to beggar the earl. Not enough for him to exercise strict economies, like cutting back on his staff. Not when she was so close to getting her family out of dun territory, and moving her sister out of the city.

"Jo, you'll never guess what Madame Chantel gave me today!" Melinda greeted Quincy when she walked in the door.

Quincy pasted a smile on her face. "What did she give you?"

Melinda held out her upturned palm, showing a shiny new guinea. "A bonus! She said Lady M was so pleased with the embroidery on her ballgown, she paid her a bonus, so Chantel gave us a bonus, too!"

"I'll wager Lady M paid Chantel a great deal more than a guinea."

"Don't cavil! Every penny helps, you said so yourself."

Quincy exhaled. "I did indeed."

"Haven't you put that away yet, Mel?" Grandmère called from her chair by the window.

"I'm doing it now. How much have we got, Jo? You know I have no head for sums."

Quincy picked up a jar from the top shelf without disturbing the gray cat sleeping there, took out the paper twist of tea on top, and poured the coins onto the table. "Give me a moment, please. I can't think with someone leaning over my shoulder." The image of the handsome earl, as he towered over her this afternoon, rose in her mind. Even when sitting on the floor, he had been formidable. Their knees had touched, and for several seconds she'd been unable to move, stunned by the unexpected intimacy.

Melinda sat at the other side of the table, her hands demurely folded, and watched Quincy stack the coins.

"I've already paid Mrs. Linley the rent, so I think we have enough to buy food and coal until next quarter day," Quincy said at last. "I just hope summer comes early, so we can cut back on the coal soon."

"You really didn't need to buy this length of muslin," Grandmère said. The fabric lay across her lap as she transformed it into a dress.

"Yes, I did. Now that she's getting better, Melinda is growing so much her gowns are almost indecent." She looked at Mel. "I've seen Mrs. Linley's son watching you get water from the pump. The way he follows you around, he should at least offer to help you up the stairs with the bucket."

Mel blushed. "He does, sometimes. Sometimes he walks behind me up the stairs, to catch me should I fall."

Quincy and Grandmère exchanged glances.

"See that he doesn't 'catch' you *before* you fall, miss."

"Yes, Grandmère."

"With my salary and the wages you two earn from Madame Chantel, barring anything unexpected, this summer we should finally be able to start saving to buy our cottage." And barring her un-firing being only temporary, she silently amended. She would just have to make herself indispensable to the earl. Make him need her. Make him keep paying her a salary.

Even with her new job, if they relied on savings alone,

she'd die of old age before they had enough money to buy a cottage. Quincy needed to scrape up enough to get back into the Exchange. Buying and selling investments on the 'Change was their only hope. She scooped the money back into the jar and covered it with the tea.

"Our own cottage? You really think so, Jo? Sometimes I can't remember what it was like to live in the country."

Quincy's heart twisted at the wistful expression on her sister's face. "We'll get there yet, Mel." Just so long as a certain prior secretary hadn't beggared the earl.

She fervently hoped they wouldn't need to repeat the process of finding a new employer. Grandmère had agreed to Quincy's scheme only after Melinda nearly succumbed to lung fever during the winter. Though they'd never say it aloud, neither of them thought Mel would survive another winter in the city. The cost of the apothecary and medicines had depleted their meager savings until Quincy had to sell the last of Grandmère's silver plate to buy coal. And this was after she'd been forced to sell out her investments at their lowest last summer, after rumors hit that Wellington had lost at Waterloo. If only she'd been able to hold out a few more days—stock prices went back up with the news that he had in fact been victorious.

She and Grandmère had spent the last month poring over newspapers and *Debrett's Peerage*. Grandmère tried to remember anything about the families that would help determine the character of Quincy's potential employer, and who would also be likely to kick up less dust should he discover Joseph Quincy was actually Joseph*ine*.

Well, they'd guessed right on *that* point. So far.

Their list had shrunk until only one acceptable peer was left who hadn't been killed, lost his fortune, or left for an extended tour of the Continent now that Bonaparte was incarcerated on St. Helena. And he'd had a thieving secretary.

Not anymore. Tomorrow she would perform her duties, discover the extent of the damage, and become indispensable to the earl. Her sister's life depended on it.

Chapter 4

Quincy followed the butler into Sinclair's library the next morning, breathing deeply to calm her nerves. Aristocrats were much like large dogs—best not to let them see one's fear.

"Ah, good morning, Mr. Quincy," Sinclair said from his seat on the sofa, surrounded by folios and papers. Her papers—those she'd stacked on his desk the day before—had not moved.

"Good morning, my lord." She accepted Harper's offer to take her coat and hat, then tugged her waistcoat back into place. Adjusted her cravat. Had she tied it too tight? Realizing she was fidgeting, she locked her elbows to her sides.

Harper shut the door as he left, leaving Quincy alone with Sinclair. She swallowed.

"Sleep well, Miss Quincy?" Sinclair stood, gesturing for her to be seated at the desk.

"Yes, thank you. And you?" The impertinent words were out before she could stop them.

Sinclair raised one eyebrow. "Like the dead, thank you." He shook his head when she tried to sit at the smaller, drop-leaf desk. "Your stacks are here, and won't fit over there. You don't want to spend another day on the floor, do you?"

Ignoring her flushed cheeks, he pointed at the leather chair behind his own desk. "Sit."

"But—"

"Sit."

She sat. Her initial refusal had only been a token protest. From sitting here yesterday, she completely understood why he liked this chair. Butter-soft leather. Cradling her. If only her feet could reach the floor.

"We should get something clear right from the start, Miss Quincy," Sinclair began.

"Yes, my lord. You have to choose."

He started to speak, stopped, then spoke. "Choose?"

She nodded. "Whether you are going to address me as Mister or Miss. You can't do one in private and the other in public. Too easy to use the wrong term. Or be overheard."

Sinclair folded his arms. "I see your point. Wouldn't want to make a faux pas." He propped his chin on one fist and studied her in silence so long she felt the urge to squirm. "Why not drop the courtesy title altogether? I'll just address you as Quincy."

"That would be most improper, my lord."

Their gazes met, an ironic smile curving Sinclair's mouth.

Quincy felt herself flush. "That is, it would imply a, ah, familiarity that does not exist."

Still studying her, Sinclair tilted his head. At last he spoke. "I hired *Mister* Quincy."

She squashed an unexpected, illogical stab of disappointment. "Then the matter is settled." Quincy pushed her spectacles up, pulled a pencil out of the top drawer, and reached for the top ledger.

Sinclair's hand pinned hers to the book. "And as I was saying before you interrupted me, Mr. Quincy," Sinclair leaned toward her, close enough for her to note, before she stopped breathing, his warm scent of bay rum, "you may stay in my employ only so long as you adequately perform the duties for which you were hired—namely, discovering how much Johnson stole."

Quincy opened her mouth to correct him, since he'd known about the embezzlement only *after* he'd hired her. But with her hand still trapped beneath his—his very large, very powerful hand—she decided to let the matter rest. For now.

A knock on the door was followed by the appearance of Mrs. Hammond, carrying a tray of tea, scones and jelly.

Sinclair straightened, surreptitiously releasing her hand. Not a mark on it. Circulation hadn't even been interrupted, though she'd felt enough heat from his touch to leave a burn. She opened the ledger and went to work. After the intimacy of their earlier exchange, Quincy didn't trust her knees enough to stand and get a cup of tea. She ignored Mrs. Hammond's idle chatter and Sinclair's monosyllabic responses.

She was startled a few moments later to realize Sinclair was addressing her. Mrs. Hammond was gone. They were alone again.

"I said, milk or sugar, Mr. Quincy?" Sinclair held up a cup.

"Yes, please."

She thought he muttered "should have known," but couldn't be certain. She was too surprised that he was waiting on her. She thanked him when he set the cup and saucer on the desk, but his only reply was a grunt as he limped back to the sofa, to the folios he'd been reading before she entered. Someday she'd get a peek at those papers he was always studying.

He shuffled papers for a moment, but abruptly dropped them to his lap and stared at her. "Mr. Quincy?"

Her stomach knotted. "Yes?"

"Why?" He waved his hand, his gesture encompassing a great deal beyond just her short hair and masculine clothes.

Quincy pushed her spectacles up. "I had no other choice." When he looked ready to press her further, she cut him off. "Which is more important for you to know—my life history, or how much money Johnson stole?"

At first Sinclair looked like he was going to argue, but then he nodded and picked up his papers. His expression, however, left no doubt the topic was not closed. Merely delayed.

After a few tense minutes, Quincy's nerves began to settle. Her awareness of Sinclair eased just enough to let her work. She felt in her element, deciphering the entries, making the numbers tell their story, creating a picture of Sinclair's finances. Time passed unnoticed.

Until Lady Sinclair entered the library.

"Benjamin, dear," she called out, sailing into the room in a swirl of russet skirts and jasmine scent.

"Yes, Mama," Sinclair said, rising stiffly.

Lady Sinclair paused, looking around the library, smiling at Quincy. She took her son's hand and made him sit beside her.

Quincy tried to keep her attention on the books, but couldn't help overhearing.

"I met the most charming gentleman at Hookham's. Lord Graham. Oh, don't frown like that. He's an acquaintance of Fitzy's and she introduced us. Anyway, he's coming to call in, oh, a few minutes, and you're going to join us for tea. He's bringing his daughter, Cecilia. She's making her come-out this Season."

Was that sound Sinclair groaning? Quincy turned the page.

"And Mr. Quincy?"

Quincy looked up, meeting Lady Sinclair's dazzling smile.

"Lady Cecilia will be bringing her companion, Miss Ogilvie, so you'll join us too, won't you? Just to keep the numbers even."

"I don't think—"

"Mr. Quincy will be delighted to join us," Sinclair interrupted her, his look clearly conveying that if he was going to suffer through this, then so was she.

"Excellent!" Lady Sinclair clapped her hands once and left.

After a moment, Quincy found her voice. "I'd like to point out that socializing is not part of the job duties for which—"

"It is now." Sinclair's tone brooked no argument.

Quincy grimaced. At the prospect of having tea with his mother, an aging Romeo, a simpering debutante and her companion, Sinclair looked even less thrilled than Quincy felt.

Then it hit her. Lord Sinclair's mother was matchmaking, and Quincy was going to have a front row seat. The simpering debutante would practice her feminine wiles on the earl, and Quincy would get to watch him try to fend her off.

This could be fun.

Accompanying Grandmère to the tooth drawer last year had been more fun than this.

After the introductions were made, everyone sat, and Lady Sinclair poured. Quincy was squished on a tiny settee next to Miss Ogilvie and her voluminous skirts. The skirts were so full, Quincy was half surprised there were no panniers beneath the woefully out-of-date gown. Obviously the clothing budget was all used up on Lady Cecilia.

Sinclair looked to be faring no better, seated across from Quincy, on another tiny settee next to Lady Cecilia. Her skirts were so narrow and thin they left little to the imagination about her figure, which was, essentially, narrow and thin.

Lady Cecilia's lips were full and pouting, however. She was staring at Sinclair as intently as Quincy's cat stared at a mouse. And yes, the little hussy was even batting her long lashes at Sinclair, too. He smiled at the fluttering lashes.

Hmph.

"Are you all right, Mr. Quincy?" Miss Ogilvie whispered.

Quincy hadn't realized she'd made a sound. "Perfectly, Miss Ogilvie. And yourself?"

"Yes, thank you. Very kind of you to join us. I, ah, I usually end up sitting by myself." Miss Ogilvie blushed.

"My, um, pleasure. Cake?" Quincy passed the plate of cakes. Miss Ogilvie took the plate, and Quincy took a sip of tea. The clock ticked. Another minute gone.

It had been so long since Quincy had made or received a social call. Had forgotten how mind-numbingly boring they could be. How long did these things last? Grandmère or Mel would know. Over the last few years, Quincy had learned a great deal about impersonating a Mister. But as Lady Sinclair chatted with Lord Graham, Quincy realized with regret that she'd forgotten much of what she had been taught about being a Miss.

As Sinclair glanced at her over the rim of his teacup, she reminded herself she had made peace with her self-imposed station in life a long time ago. Sinclair put down his cup and gave his attention back to Lady Cecilia.

Odd, though, that it had never caused her a twinge like this before.

The last time she'd sat sipping tea across from a handsome young man, there had been a different twinge. That man had been a suitor, someone she'd known since childhood, had considered a friend. Until he'd come to retract his marriage proposal.

The polite chatter faded to the background as Quincy recalled Nigel, in his fine tailcoat, explaining how he'd realized they just wouldn't suit. It wasn't even her short hair or even her trousers he'd objected to so much, but her business activities. He wanted a wife who could sew and cook, and the only stock Quincy could manage came not in a cooking pot but on paper.

Quincy shoved away the memory. She had made peace with that a long time ago, too. In fact, she should be grateful to Nigel. He'd taught her a valuable lesson, one she would never forget. In taking on a man's role, she had made herself unsuitable to be a man's wife. Ever.

The fact that marriage was impossible for her was a small price to pay, she reminded herself, for being able to save her sister's life. Quincy pasted a smile on her face and glanced at Miss Ogilvie, who smiled back. Quincy's face began to ache.

Lady Cecilia laughed at something her father said, and glanced from beneath her eyelashes to check Sinclair's reaction. Sinclair bared his teeth in a semblance of a smile.

"They make a charming couple, do you not agree?" Miss Ogilvie whispered, her nose almost in Quincy's ear.

Quincy mimicked Sinclair's bared-teeth grimace. "Charming."

Sinclair replied to a question from Lady Cecilia, and the hussy placed her hand on the earl's knee. He dropped his walking stick, and in leaning to reach it, slid his knee out from beneath her hand. Strategic retreat, no confrontation. Impressive.

"May I confess something to you, Mr. Quincy?" Miss Ogilvie's nose was almost in Quincy's ear again, reminding her of an overgrown puppy. Without waiting for a response, Miss Ogilvie continued. "I have hopes of finding a match for myself. I cannot remain Lady Cecilia's companion forever, perhaps not even to the end of this Season. She is quite intent on becoming betrothed. Soon."

Quincy had been only half listening, absorbed in trying not to stare at Sinclair's interactions with Lady Hussy. Miss Ogilvie earned her full attention, though, when Quincy realized it was not just the companion's full skirts that were encroaching on her half of the settee, and on her person. Miss Ogilvie had placed her hand on Quincy's knee.

Quincy choked on her tea.

Sinclair glanced over. Raised his eyebrows in silent question.

"Miss Ogilvie, I—I cannot tell you how flattered I am," Quincy said, setting her cup down and reaching to extricate the woman's hand. Too bad she didn't have a walking stick of her own to drop. "But I must confess I am in no position to be anyone's suitor." She moved the hand, only to have it turn and grasp hers, so that, through threadbare gloves, they held hands.

Quincy felt her cravat constrict, her cheeks flush. Sinclair was still watching.

Miss Ogilvie squeezed her hand. "There's nothing wrong with a little, shall we say, companionship, until circumstances change? I quite fancy you, Mr. Quincy."

Quincy tried to breathe, but the air kept getting stuck in her throat.

"Do you fancy me?" Miss Ogilvie let go of Quincy's hand, to trail her fingers up Quincy's thigh.

Quincy choked, again. On air. No tea required.

"You'll have to excuse the dear boy, Miss Ogilvie," Sinclair said. He'd stood and crossed to their settee, proffering the plate of cakes. "He's dreadfully shy."

"Oh. Thank you, my lord." Miss Ogilvie took another cake, and Sinclair sat back down.

As the companion bent her head to take a bite of cake, Quincy finally managed to meet Sinclair's impassive gaze.

He winked at her.

Quincy smiled back, and saw amusement reflected in Sinclair's eyes. They shared a silent moment, acknowledging the absurdity of the whole situation. She wanted to laugh out loud, especially when she realized Lord Graham was trying the same hand maneuver on Lady Sinclair.

With a flick of her gaze she drew Sinclair's attention to his mother. Lady Sinclair seemed to appreciate Lord Graham's hand on her knee even less than Sinclair had enjoyed Lady Hussy's.

Quincy saw Sinclair's jaw tighten. He rose, plate of cakes in hand, and thrust it in front of Lord Graham. The gentleman fell back against the cushions, hands now on his own lap. He looked up with a guilty start.

"No th-thank you, my lord," Lord Graham said.

"You're right," Sinclair said, so softly Quincy barely heard him. "You have had enough." He stood over Lord Graham.

Lord Graham cleared his throat. Lady Sinclair dusted crumbs from her skirt. Quincy and Miss Ogilvie were finally in accord—neither dared breathe.

Lady Hussy jumped up. "Papa, I am terribly sorry, but I just recalled another appointment. We wouldn't want to disappoint, um, Aunt Meredith."

Sinclair stepped back.

"Who? Oh, er, yes, Aunt Meredith." Lord Graham stood, also brushing crumbs from his lap. "No, wouldn't want to disappoint the old gel." He bowed over Lady Sinclair's hand. "Beg your forgiveness, but we must be off."

Lady Sinclair gave a regal nod.

Lord Graham gave an awkward bow in Sinclair's direction, then held out his arm for his daughter. The two headed for the door, not even looking back to see if Miss Ogilvie followed. She did, but only after a last scaring glance at Quincy.

Harper opened the door and escorted the guests from the room.

"Mama?" Sinclair cupped her cheek.

Quincy examined the pattern in the carpet, biting her bottom lip in debate. Should she get up and leave, too?

Lady Sinclair held still for a moment, then grasped her son's hand, her voice bright. "Wasn't that a refreshing change, Benjamin?"

Sinclair helped his mother rise from her chair. "I've never found encroaching mushrooms to be particularly refreshing."

Lady Sinclair gave a quiet chuckle. "Mr. Quincy?"

She jumped to her feet. "Yes, my lady?"

"Thank you for your help. It would have been rather awkward without your presence."

Quincy hoped the skepticism she felt wasn't visible in her expression. "My pleasure."

Sinclair's mouth tightened and he dropped his gaze, but Quincy thought he was hiding amusement.

"I'll let you lads get back to work then, shall I?" Lady Sinclair gave her son a final pat on the arm, and left the room.

Quincy headed back to the library, Sinclair in step beside her. Though neither spoke, the silence did not feel awkward or uncomfortable. Quite the opposite, actually. The realization surprised her enough to make her steps falter.

"Easy, lad," Sinclair said, grasping her elbow to steady her.

Quincy stared at him in surprise, from the informal address as much as from the contact of his hand around her arm.

Sinclair tilted his head to one side, brows raised, smiling at her. It was a genuine smile, that lit up his warm brown eyes and showed nearly perfect white teeth behind full but utterly masculine lips. A smile that made her insides melt like chocolate.

She swallowed. Sinclair gestured for her to precede him across the hall, and the moment passed.

"You acquitted yourself . . . adequately, Mr. Quincy," Sinclair said as he sat on the sofa in the library, while Quincy settled in the big leather chair at the desk. "But your social skills . . . frankly, they lack polish."

Quincy felt her back stiffen. "You didn't hire me for my social skills." Indeed, there had been scant opportunity to practice social niceties, since Quincy had been engaged in efforts to keep her family fed and sheltered. When most girls her age were learning to play hostess, Quincy was learning to correspond with her father's business associates.

"True." Sinclair stroked his chin. "But if my mother has her way, and she usually does, you'll get ample opportunity to practice those rusty skills."

"Why would Lady Sinclair care about my polish? Or lack thereof?"

"She doesn't." Sinclair grinned and opened a folio. He must have felt her steady gaze boring into him, because he finally put down the papers. "You will simply be present any time we need to even the numbers. I agreed to let Mama parade debutantes before me in a scheme to help me choose a wife, but only if she were to leave off her mourning and face the tabbies. She has apparently decided it is finally time to do so."

Quincy could only reply with a soft "Oh." She picked up a penknife and began to sharpen a quill. The knife slipped as the implications of his words sunk in. She pinched the tiny wound between her teeth. "You intend to marry?"

Sinclair looked at her sharply. Must have heard the squeak in her voice. "Of course. As the eldest son and now the Earl of Sinclair, it is part of my duty." He absently rubbed the heel of his hand over his right thigh. "I would probably have done so last year, if not for," he glanced at his hand, "distractions."

So, Lord Sinclair did not consider himself to be in love with anyone. Why should that suddenly make her feel relieved?

"And Mr. Quincy?"

"Yes, my lord?"

"You really need to work on schooling your expression next time a young miss makes an advance toward you."

"Next time?" Quincy's cheeks burned. "There won't be a next time. Miss Ogilvie was just, ah, fast."

"Oh, I'm certain there will be a next time. For some reason, the ladies seem to find you . . . irresistible."

Her cheeks felt positively aflame as Sinclair chuckled, though she couldn't help a small smile of her own. "Lady. Singular. And Miss Ogilvie is, well, she's nearly desperate. As soon as her companion makes a match, Miss Ogilvie will be cast aside, and Lady Hu—that is, Lady Cecilia is intent on making a match quite soon."

Sinclair leaned forward on the sofa to see behind the desk, his gaze sweeping Quincy from head to toe, making her blush even hotter. He tapped his chin with one finger, studying her. At last he nodded. "Irresistible." She opened her mouth to protest, but he shook one finger at her. "Ah, ah, ah. We shall see who is proven correct at Mama's next matchmaking tea."

Next?

Chapter 5

Sinclair stepped out of Henry Angelo's, still breathing hard from his training session. The pleasant mood from exercising was quickly fading, as his body reminded him of all his aches. Soaked with perspiration, his clothes clung to him, suffocating him. Sweat dripped from his forehead, stinging his eyes, mixing with the big drops of cold rain blowing sideways in the stiff spring breeze.

Precipitation was welcome at the moment—he imagined steam rising from his shirt collar as the droplets fell—though he'd be shivering by the time he reached home. Broderick would use it as an excuse to make him drink one of those foul-tasting tisanes his valet swore by. Sinclair grimaced, adjusted his grip on his walking stick, and started down the steps to the street.

"Sorry 'bout that last *flèche,* old chap," said a voice from behind. The tone conveyed the opposite meaning.

Sinclair waited until he reached the secure footing of the sidewalk before turning to face the speaker, the son of his father's rival. "No apology needed, Twitchell." He forced facial muscles into a smile instead of cracking the man over his skull with the walking stick.

"Thought you'd be more agile by now, though I s'pose

you're lucky to be on your feet at all." Twitchell adjusted his hat.

Sinclair managed a stiff nod, but was spared having to reply, as Twitchell's coach pulled up and the twit wasted no time getting in out of the rain.

The nasty business between their fathers had ended five years ago with both men dead, but Twitchell would likely carry a grudge against the Sinclair family into his own grave.

Sinclair had no time or energy to spare for such foolishness. He continued alone toward home, struggling with each step. He'd been increasing the length of his fencing sessions by a few minutes each week, but since hiring Miss Quincy, he'd felt even more impatient to get back to his former self. Perhaps the extra hour today had been a tad too much.

Perhaps he should set his next goal to be free of the limp by the time he had to let her go. Was that feasible? She would only be around a fortnight longer. A month at most. He nodded. Seemed a reasonable goal.

Thinking of the secretary, he pictured Miss Quincy poring over the ledger books at his desk, nibbling on the end of a pencil as she deciphered Johnson's scrawl. From her perch in his big leather chair, she often crossed her ankles and swung her feet when she was deep in thought—an innocent, carefree gesture so delightfully in contrast to her usual no-nonsense attitude.

He'd teased her once about the pencil-chewing, insinuating she must not get enough to eat. The bleak look in her eyes, though she'd quickly masked it, made him feel like an ass. Passing Mrs. Hammond in the hall that afternoon, he'd oh-so-casually mentioned that Mr. Quincy seemed to enjoy Cook's offerings. Ever since, the housekeeper made regular appearances with food-laden trays, from scones in the morning, luncheons befitting the Queen, to afternoon tea and cakes.

Watching Quincy eat with such enthusiasm—no missish picking at the food for her—Sinclair couldn't help but eat heartily himself. His previous lack of appetite had been a matter of concern to everyone but himself, it seemed. Now Mrs. Hammond beamed at him when she cleared away the tray, the plates empty save for crumbs.

He didn't think Johnson had ever slipped a scone into his coat pocket to take home. He'd only seen Quincy do it once, but he was certain her pockets were often full of crumbs.

Of course Sinclair had fed Johnson, too, but Johnson had taken his meals with the upper servants. Did Miss Quincy realize the uniqueness of the situation? Mrs. Hammond waited on Quincy as though she were, well, part of the family.

His step faltered.

Not only was Quincy most definitely *not* part of his family, she wouldn't even be part of his staff for much longer. She was only going to work for him long enough to determine how much Johnson had embezzled, and get Lady Sinclair securely out of mourning and into Society. After that, Quincy would be gone. His stomach knotted.

Though he might enjoy her company, Sinclair couldn't have a female secretary indefinitely. He couldn't risk the potential scandal. Thanks to Papa and the previous Lord Twitchell, Sinclair and his mother had already lived through enough scandal to last several lifetimes.

A familiar carriage pulled up in the street, breaking Sinclair from his rumination. He hailed the driver. "Elliott?"

"Cap'n. Mr. Harper saw the clouds and thought you might change yer mind about walking." Thunder rumbled overhead and the skies opened up even more. Elliott calmed the horses as the groom let down the step.

"Harper was correct. My compliments on your timing, Elliott."

"Thank you, sir."

Sinclair sank back into the cushions as the carriage rolled down the streets through the pouring rain. The ache in his leg had spread to the entire right side of his body, throbbing in counterpoint to the thunderclaps.

Some days the protective nature of his men annoyed Sinclair, but today was not one of them. As a sergeant, El-

liott had served in Sinclair's regiment, as had half his stable staff. They took excellent care of his horses and
equipage, and sometimes, himself personally. He'd lost
track of the times Elliott had unexpectedly shown up when
he'd tried to walk too far. "Just exercisin' the beasts,
Cap'n," the coachman would say, leaving Sinclair at least
the illusion of dignity.

Sinclair fervently hoped that, with perseverance and
some divine assistance, Elliott's rescues would soon be
unnecessary.

By the time the carriage arrived at the town house, Sinclair was so stiff he could barely scoot forward on the
bench. He cursed his weakness—he should have kept walking. He'd be cold by now, but he'd be able to move. The
groom opened the door and let down the step, then dashed
through the rain to hold the horses' heads.

Sinclair glanced out the door—no one about except a
maid hurrying past on the sidewalk—grabbed his walking
stick, and gingerly shifted his weight. At the same instant,
thunder clapped overhead. The horses jolted forward, and
the groom, watching the buxom maid instead of the horses,
let go.

Sinclair missed the step.

He stumbled on the pavement, then caught himself on his
weak right leg, a move jarring enough to make him see
stars. Taxed beyond its limit, his leg promptly buckled. The
first round of stars had just flickered out when another set
appeared as Sinclair landed on his backside.

The world paused to witness his humiliation.

He heard a woman giggle. His vision cleared, and he saw
the maid stopped in front of his door, laughing. His servants
gaped at him. After an eternity passed, the maid held a hand
to her mouth to hide her humor, ducked her head, and
moved on.

His face burned with shame. He considered, then rejected, the idea of crawling under the carriage. Feigning
unconsciousness was not an option, either. He sat up
straight, shoulders back, daring anyone else to laugh.

Harper opened the town house door, gasped, and gestured for more footmen to come assist. Elliott cursed, whether at the horses or the groom, Sinclair couldn't tell. The groom at the horses' heads became animated again, apologizing profusely as he offered assistance to his lordship.

His lordship, in the street. On his ass.

Where was lightning when it was needed? Just one bolt, and he'd never make a fool of himself again. Damn leg. Perhaps he should feel grateful for the burning in his cheeks, because it distracted from the painful throbbing in his leg. And backside.

The heat of embarrassment began to fade, swept away by the chill breeze. Time to get up. He shifted, but his legs refused to cooperate. He was stuck. That he had fallen was bad enough. With renewed shame, he now realized he was too weak to get up out of the street under his own power.

It required two footmen to raise Sinclair to his feet again. Which two, he couldn't tell, because he couldn't look them in the eye. Bloody hell. Hadn't he left this damned weak-as-a-kitten stage behind months ago? Apparently not long enough, for they lifted him up with the disgusting ease of much practice.

Once Sinclair stopped swaying, Harper shooed away the footmen as he handed Sinclair his walking stick. The butler stayed two steps behind as Sinclair slowly, laboriously, limped into the town house. Not out of deference, Sinclair realized with a grimace, but to catch him.

"Would you like a tray sent to your room, my lord?"

Sinclair made it up the front steps and into the hall without further assistance. Turned and handed his hat, gloves and greatcoat to Harper without losing his balance. He loosened his cravat as he looked up at the stairs. Ten thousand steps, at least, between here and his bedchamber, and Broderick lying in wait with a tisane.

"No tray, thank you. I'm not going to my bedchamber." He needed some place quiet in which to lick his wounds, a peaceful haven away from hovering servants and mothers. He knew the perfect spot.

* * *

Quincy looked up from her account books, surprised by Sinclair's entrance. Usually he went straight up to his bed chamber upon returning from Henry Angelo's.

"Don't mind me," Sinclair said, collapsing onto the sofa with a muffled groan. He stretched out flat, his feet hanging over the sofa arm.

Quincy pushed aside her abacus and tried to keep the worry out of her voice. "Is anything wrong?"

"Just don't let Broderick know I'm here." He flung one arm over his eyes and settled into a more comfortable position.

Quincy relaxed, realizing Sinclair's odd behavior meant nothing more than avoiding being fussed over by his valet. "Rough exercise session?"

"Not with Angelo," came the terse reply.

Quincy blinked. She waited for Sinclair to elucidate, but he remained silent. "Do you need a beefsteak, or perhaps a hot brick?"

Sinclair's lips twitched in what might be a smile. "Thank you for your concern, Quincy, but I just need some quiet. Go back to work."

Quincy obediently moved balls across the wires on the abacus, glancing at Sinclair from the corner of her eye. Within a few minutes his arm dropped to his side, though his eyes remained closed and his breathing was deep and steady.

There was a soft knock at the door, and Harper entered. He drew breath to speak, but before he could utter a sound, Quincy cut him off.

"His lordship asked to be left alone," she informed him, quietly but with more force than she'd intended. If she couldn't ease Sinclair's discomfort, at least she could make sure his rest was undisturbed.

The butler glanced at Sinclair, nodded at Quincy, and withdrew, closing the door.

Quincy returned her attention to her work. But the numbers on the page weren't nearly as fascinating as the figure on the sofa. She gave up the pretext of adding. Almost without volition, she soon found herself standing next to him.

She watched Sinclair sleep, transfixed by the rise and fall of his chest and the little tuft of dark hair visible at the open collar of his shirt. He'd stuffed his cravat into his waistcoat pocket, the tail of it just peeping out. The hair framing his face was still damp with perspiration, curling against his razor stubble as it dried. Wouldn't do to let him catch a chill. She picked up the knitted throw from the wing chair. This wasn't fussing over him, was it?

In the week she'd been working for the earl, she'd seen through his façade of toplofty lord. On Tuesday, she had listened to him complain about the dust gathering in the downstairs rooms and how long it took for someone, anyone, to answer the front door these days. The staff had functioned smoothly when his father was alive, and there had been little turnover since those days. What was the problem?

On Wednesday, they'd shared a secret smile as they'd both been forced to fend off advances during another of his mother's matchmaking teas. They relaxed as Lady Sinclair chatted with the debutante's mother, hardly daring to make eye contact with each other again for fear of bursting into laughter.

Thursday, she woke up breathless from a dream in which it was *her* hand upon Sinclair's knee, and he wasn't fending off her advance.

At work, she tried to concentrate on the books, but couldn't help overhear Lady Sinclair's comment about a particular Miss probably bearing beautiful sons and daughters. Nor could she miss the cool tone in Sinclair's voice as he agreed Mama was probably correct, but he would have no part in proving her theory.

Friday, just as Quincy was leaving for the day, he came into the library for a glass of brandy before escorting his mother to a ball, which was in addition to squiring her to a card party and two soirees earlier in the week.

"Forgotten how much I detest all this social folderol," he had said, settling in the wing chair, his legs stretched out toward the fire.

"It's not so bad, is it?" Quincy marked her place in the

ledger and closed the book. She'd never been to a ball, and unless a fairy godmother showed up, wasn't likely to. Life had already proven hers was no fairy tale with a happy ending.

"If I went at all, I used to pop in, say hello to the hosts, then head over to my club for the rest of the evening. Much better company."

"But your mother—"

"Yes. Mama. Now I stay the entire evening." He took another sip of brandy, staring at the flames. "She's got more color in her cheeks now. Hell, more color in her wardrobe." He glanced at Quincy sideways, silently acknowledging her part in his mother's transformation.

She nodded. "Good night, my lord." She grabbed her gloves and hat, headed for the door.

" 'Night, Quincy." He swallowed the last of his brandy. "Thank you."

She paused, hand on the doorknob, warmth spreading through her at his words. "Try to enjoy the ball."

He had saluted her with the empty glass.

Quincy adjusted the knitted throw in her arms. If she was more at ease in Sinclair's company, the reverse must be equally true. Here he was, napping on the sofa while she worked. And he no longer tried to conceal his limp in her presence. He still tried to hide it from his mother, though, and Lady Sinclair pretended not to know any different.

Most telling was the fact that, more often than not, he forgot to address her as Mister. Quincy chose to take that as a sign that he would also forget about her employment being only temporary. Things were definitely moving in the right direction. She could never marry, but she could earn the money needed to save her sister's life.

Lady Sinclair expected her son to marry, and would accept any eligible woman of childbearing age as a daughter-in-law, but if she knew the extent of the financial damage Johnson had inflicted, she would insist on an heiress. Not even Sinclair knew how deeply Johnson had reached into his pockets, and Quincy wasn't about to tell him until she had more proof.

Quincy settled the throw over him, at least resisting the urge to tuck it under his chin, and went back to her desk.

"Don't look at me that way, Quincy." Sinclair had awakened from his nap and settled at his desk with one of his ever-present folios. "You make me think I'll soon be begging on the street."

Quincy bit back a smile. "Sorry, Sincl—my lord. Would you prefer I address your neckcloth?"

She'd have to watch her tongue more carefully. Impertinence was one thing, but being overly familiar would never do—even though he was becoming quite familiar, since she saw him at work every day, and he'd made more appearances in her blasted dreams. That he appeared in her dreams was only to be expected, since her new employer played a major role in her life. Nothing more to it than that.

"Just answer me this," Sinclair said. "Do I need to cancel my standing order for spirits from Monsieur Beauvais?"

"Yes."

Sinclair slammed his glass down on his desk, his third brandy that afternoon.

Quincy hurried on. "Not because you cannot afford it, but because Beauvais is accustomed to cheating you. There are at least three other merchants I would stop patronizing for the same reason. What they have done is nothing out of the ordinary. I would wager most of your friends are or would be in the same situation if they do not pay close attention to their accounts."

"That's a relief. I don't mind telling you, your long face these last couple days has—"

"There's more."

"More?"

"Or less, actually. I'm still investigating. Let me just say that, should you decide on a wife soon, may I suggest she be someone who does not have extravagant tastes?"

Sinclair's face contorted with anger. Quincy started to move away, cursing her flippant remark. Before she could take a second step, Sinclair grabbed her shoulder to spin her back to face him. "Are you saying I'm dished up?"

The sudden movement made them both stagger. Instead of grabbing at his hands, which now clutched her lapels, Quincy grasped Sinclair's shoulders to steady him as much as herself. Beneath his shirt was warm, hard, unyielding bone and muscle. Surely he wouldn't actually harm her. Her pulse hammered in her ears all the same. By sheer force of will she kept her voice level. "If you were dished up, I would have already given notice and begun searching for an employer with deeper pockets."

He stared into her eyes, his unblinking bloodshot gaze searching for a reason to believe her. Their noses were but inches apart. Quincy felt his brandy breath warm on her cheeks. The scent was intoxicating, though she hadn't imbibed any of the drink. Perhaps it was just his nearness that was making her lightheaded. Heat from his body washed over her, from a pleasant warmth in her belly, rising in temperature to nearly burning her hands where they rested on his shoulders.

This would not do, not at all.

"You're going to ruin the theater for me if you keep enacting such melodrama, my lord. And I wish you would advise me when you plan to indulge in more than a bottle by yourself, so I can absent myself. Your breath is wilting my cravat."

Sinclair blinked. He stepped back and smoothed her lapels with exaggerated care. "My most humble apologies, Mis . . . Mr. Quincy." He tried to straighten her cravat but only made it worse. "It was not planned, I assure you," he added softly as he stumbled from the room, his limp more pronounced than usual.

Quincy leaned against the desk, hand over her pounding heart, trying to regain control of her breathing. His anger had been almost as startling as his touch, as he fumbled with her cravat, his fingers brushing her chin. Smoothing her lapels, his palms flat against her chest.

"Would you care for a brandy, Mr. Quincy?" Harper closed the door behind him and poured two drinks. "I've ordered the carriage brought 'round for you, as his lordship requested." The butler handed her one of the glasses, then sat on the sofa. "Drink up, lad. It'll steady your nerves." Quincy was vaguely surprised to see the butler making free with the earl's finest brandy, but shrugged it off.

She took a sip and coughed as it burned its way down her throat, then set the glass on the desk, her hand shaking too much to hold it steady.

Harper swallowed his glassful in two gulps. "Lord knows we all need a drink when he gets like this. Damnable weather." He got up to stare out the window at the pouring rain. "But you'll get used to it, just as we all have."

"Are you saying the rain makes Sinclair drink too much?"

"Well, it doesn't help matters. He missed the step getting out of the carriage this morning. Landed on his bad leg. Broderick is tending to him now, but don't be surprised if he's not quite himself for a few more days. Takes him longer to recover when the weather is cold and wet."

Quincy mouthed a silent "Oh."

Harper let the curtain fall back as the carriage came into view, and handed Quincy her hat and gloves. "Don't judge him too harshly, lad. He did insist the carriage take you home, and pick you up in the morning if it's nasty out." His expression relaxed, a hint of a smile in his eyes. "The way I see it, London streets are always nasty, don't you think?"

"Thank you, Mr. Harper. You're very kind." She smiled at the older man. "And I will reserve judgment, as you suggest." But the truth was, Quincy had already passed judgment on her new employer. Even with this afternoon's outburst, she liked him quite fine.

"Good morning, my lord. How are we feeling this morning?"

"We have a devil of a head, you dolt. Lower your voice." Sinclair opened one eye enough to see daylight peeking between his lashes. Too much. He flung an arm over his face. "Broderick, you idiot, close the curtains."

"They *are* closed, my lord."

Sinclair moved his arm. "Then have them replaced with something more substantial. Tomorrow. Not today. I don't want anyone in here today." He sat up, slowly, so his head could keep up with his shoulders.

Broderick plumped the pillows behind him and thrust a mug filled with a foul-smelling brew into his hand. "It will soon be summer, my lord, and the weather will be warm, and the incessant rain will stop."

"And then it will soon be winter, and we'll go through it all over again. Bah." He tasted the brew and grimaced, then drained the mug.

"Ah, but by then you'll be much better. Think how far you've come already!"

Sinclair glared at the wall while Broderick pulled back the covers, raised his nightshirt, and massaged liniment on his thigh. He could barely tell which throbbed more, his head or his leg.

Definitely his leg. From his hip to his ankle it was one long throbbing ache, deep in the bones, sometimes so intense it made his eyes water.

When he'd come to his senses after Waterloo, in those first dark days when he'd prayed for an angel of mercy to ease his misery, laudanum kept the pain at bay, kept him sane. But soon he needed it even when he felt no pain, and he'd given it up before losing himself to the drug. The only thing left to deaden the pain was alcohol, and he'd developed quite a tolerance for it. Even his mother couldn't tell when he drank more than usual.

But his new secretary knew. Sinclair almost grinned. Quincy had as good as called him on the carpet for it. Impertinent chit. No, make that impertinent pup. He had to call her pup, even in his thoughts. He'd almost slipped up yesterday and called her Miss.

At the memory of how roughly he'd treated her, he cringed. His behavior was inexcusable. Had she taken him in disgust because of it? Ordinarily he might not give a fig what his secretary thought, but Quincy was no ordinary secretary. "Broderick, are you through torturing me yet?"

His valet reached for the jar of liniment again. "Not quite, my lord. Shall I order a light breakfast for you? Tea and toast, perhaps?"

Sinclair held his stomach. "Gad, no. But do find out if Mr. Quincy came to work this morning."

Broderick stepped out into the hall to pass on the request. Sinclair heard the raised voices of another squabble, and Broderick soon returned, his face flushed.

"Really, my lord, Thompson's behavior is unconscionable," Broderick said, shutting the door and coming back into the room. He dribbled more liniment onto Sinclair's leg and began working it in. "I don't know why you tolerate him, even if he is an excellent match to Tanner."

"Two footmen having the same coloring and height is just a coincidence. Why do you care so much, Broderick? Thinking of setting up one of the maids as a flirt for yourself?"

"My lord! I would never—" He broke off as the door opened.

Sinclair grabbed for the sheet to cover his bare leg. Broderick brushed his hand aside and continued the massage.

"You sent for me, my lord?"

Sinclair forgot about the throbbing pain. Quincy stood in the doorway, staring at him, eyes wide, her face flushed to the roots of her hair. Sinclair felt a little heat rise in his own face. Blast Broderick and his conscientious care.

Quincy pushed her spectacles up. "Why did you call me up here?"

Broderick gasped. "You insolent whelp! How dare you—"

"Enough, Broderick. Mr. Quincy is justifiably upset at being interrupted from important work. Aren't you, Quincy?"

"I am employed at your pleasure, my lord."

Her blush intensified, as though she, too, suddenly realized the innocent-sounding words could have other connotations.

Sinclair cleared his throat. "I'm expecting a packet of papers to arrive this morning. When it's delivered, would you send—"

"It's already here." Quincy fled the room without a backward glance.

Sinclair groaned and held his hand to his head. At least she was still speaking to him, and he'd detected no hint of anger. Just a very becoming blush. Later he'd apologize for the misunderstanding. Surely she didn't think he'd intentionally sent for her, to come to his bedchamber?

"I think you had better put some clothes on, my lord, if you don't wish the boy to expire from embarrassment."

Sinclair groaned again.

Though she kept a hand over her still-fluttering stomach, Quincy slowed to a more decorous pace once she reached the first floor, and continued on to the library as though nothing were amiss. She hadn't seen anything truly disturbing, after all. She'd become accustomed to many things in the world of men, first working for her father and now for Sinclair. And of course she had seen the male form before without layers of clothing. She and Melinda had helped care for their father, bedridden the last few months of his life.

But Sinclair was no invalid elder. With his wavy chestnut hair tousled from sleep, his nightshirt unbuttoned to reveal dark curls and a deeply muscled chest, she wanted nothing more than to erase the lines of pain etched around his eyes, and run her fingers through his hair. And get another glimpse of his bare leg . . .

The direction of her thoughts startled her. She'd dealt with and worked around men for many years, but she'd never had thoughts like this before. Not when the squire's son stole a kiss beneath the apple tree when she was thirteen, not even when Nigel had given her a chaste kiss upon their betrothal.

She stumbled a step. Sinclair was not likely to steal a kiss from her anytime soon. Ever. She shook her head. She must focus on the job duties she had been hired to perform, not on her employer's bare leg.

She located the folio that had been delivered moments before she'd received the odd summons, and felt in control again by the time she neared Sinclair's bedchamber.

His bedchamber. If she had managed to keep fooling him

about her gender, she wouldn't be surprised that he'd summoned her there. But he did know, and had sent for her anyway. Was this merely an example of him accepting her presence? Treating her as he would a man? And was it for her benefit, or for the other servants watching their interactions?

Thompson was nowhere in sight, forcing her to open the door herself. She managed to not blush this time. Though he was still in bed, Sinclair had donned a deep green satin dressing gown, and the blankets were pulled up to his waist. She squelched a jolt of disappointment. Sinclair pushed away Broderick and his shaving brush when she entered. "Will you need anything else?" She handed him the papers, fervently hoping none of her previous thoughts were apparent.

Sinclair shook his head. "How goes your investigation?"

"There are bills owed to merchants I'm not familiar with. I think it best for me to pay them in person. If I take your carriage, I should return by lunch."

"Go alone? I don't think—" Sinclair interrupted himself. "Yes, of course." He glanced at his valet. "Care to take Broderick with you? He resembles a mother hen this morning."

"That won't be necessary, my lord," Quincy said as Broderick choked on a reply.

"Do take Thompson with you, though. He may prove useful."

"Thank you, my lord," Broderick and Quincy said in unison.

Quincy settled into the carriage a few minutes later, Thompson riding up top with Elliott, the coachman. Just as she had this morning, she snuggled against the soft squabs and rubbed her bare hands across the smoky gray velvet. Once upon a time, Papa had a fine carriage such as this, pulled by matching bays. She sighed and leaned back to enjoy the ride.

"Is this the place, Mr. Quincy?" Thompson held the door open for her when they arrived.

Quincy glanced at the address on the bill and compared it to the number above the chandler's shop door. "Yes, Thompson, thank you." She started for the shop but stopped.

"Thompson, have you been in his lordship's service very long?"

"Almost six years, sir. He hired me and Tanner afore he went off to fight the bloody Corsican."

"Good. You may hold the purse. I trust you can count without using your fingers and toes?" She looked up at him sideways, grinning.

Thompson chuckled. "Yes, sir. Lady Sinclair insists all her staff learn to read and write and cipher."

"Really? Well, let's get on with spending Lord Sinclair's money, shall we?"

Thompson grinned and opened the shop door. "Yes, sir!"

The chandler closed his mouth with a snap when Thompson gave him his money due, and pumped Quincy's hand, pleased to meet Lord Sinclair's new secretary. "The last one had beady eyes, don't you know," he said with a wink.

It was the same with the baker, the greengrocer, and the tailor. They glanced at Quincy and stared at Thompson. Despite the drizzle, the footman wore a powdered wig, which added another two inches to his already impressive height. Some merchants even reduced their bills for "prompt payment."

The butcher was different. With a barrel chest and hands like hams, he was several inches shorter than Thompson but twice as wide. "What happened to Johnson, eh? Sinclair catch on and tan his sorry hide?"

"I believe Mr. Johnson decided America was more to his liking. What do you mean by 'catch on'?"

He stared at Thompson. "Nothing."

"Please wait for me in the carriage, Thompson." As soon as the footman was out of earshot, Quincy pulled a sovereign from her coat pocket. She held it up so the coin glinted in the sunlight. "You were about to say?"

"I don't write so good."

"I noticed." Quincy pointed to a barely legible bill of sale.

"Johnson said that weren't no problem. He'd write the bills for me. 'Cept he'd add to 'em, like. Whatever I was owed, he'd double it on the bill, then keep most of the extra for his 'fee.' "

"Only most, not all of it?"

"I got six mouths to feed and another on the way."

Quincy handed him the sovereign. "Do you know if Johnson was performing this service for anyone else?" When the butcher hesitated, she pulled out another coin.

"A Frenchie named Beauvais what sells brandy, and a cooper two streets over, that way."

Quincy nodded. "You can't keep doing this. Someone else is bound to catch on. What you did was punishable by law, Mister . . . what is your name, anyway?"

"Sam." Sam narrowed his eyes and stepped closer until Quincy had to strain her neck to see beyond his jaw. "You going to turn me in?"

Quincy gulped. She caught a flash of movement to the right, and realized they'd attracted an audience. The little boy peeking around the shop door couldn't be more than three. He had the same dark hair and green eyes as Sam. Another boy peeked out, a head taller than the first child, and then another. Soon there were five of them, all watching her with avid green eyes.

"No, Sam, I'm not going to turn you in, but only because of those six mouths. I have something else in mind."

Sam appeared not to have heard her. "I sure would hate to mess up a young face like yours."

Quincy ignored the threat to her own safety, imagining the life the five boys would have if their father were in Newgate. "What I propose, Sam, is that you spend two hours per week with me until you can write a legible bill of sale."

Sam stepped back. "Why?"

She thought of what her life had been like since her father's death last year. "Because children shouldn't go hungry, nor should they be deprived of a father. I'm going to teach you to write an honest bill of sale, and you will promise to not 'add to' them. Agreed?"

Sam still looked doubtful. And menacing.

"If you improve your reading and writing, you can make sure no one is cheating *you*."

At that, Sam's expression cleared. He shook hands and

arranged to meet with Quincy after church on Sunday afternoon. Back in the carriage, she checked her hand for broken bones.

The last address on her list was near the docks, a merchant who supplied everything for the stables from hay to bridles. As they traveled closer to it, the fancy carriages in the streets gradually gave way to hacks and carts, and the finely dressed pedestrians disappeared, replaced by streetwalkers and sailors.

Thompson opened the carriage door. "You sure this is the right place, Mr. Quincy?"

"This is the place Johnson sent his lordship's money. Let's find out if it's right." Thompson followed her through the door set in the massive wall of the warehouse. The grimy windows allowed little daylight to illuminate the interior. "Halloo!" she called into the gloom. "Anybody here?"

She heard footsteps behind her, heard Thompson shout "Oi!" As she turned to look back, she caught a fleeting glimpse of something thrown at her. Lights exploded in her head, then everything went black.

Chapter 6

"My lord," Harper said from the bedchamber doorway, his voice unusually tight. "You may want to come downstairs."

Sinclair looked up in time to see the two upstairs maids run, shrieking, past the open door toward the staircase. He set his papers aside. "Is the house on fire?"

"No, my lord. The carriage has returned with Mr. Quincy and Thompson. They've been attacked."

Sinclair's stomach twisted into a cold knot. "The devil you say!" He shoved his feet into slippers, grabbed his walking stick and hurried downstairs.

"They're in the parlor. I've already sent Tanner for the doctor," Harper added, at his heels.

"Good thinking." Wild thoughts assaulted Sinclair as he negotiated the stairs. Who would attack poor Miss Quincy? How badly was she hurt? He should never have let her go out like that, accompanied by just a footman. He was supposed to be keeping her safe!

Sinclair entered the parlor right behind Mrs. Hammond. Two of the maids, Maude and Matilda, hovered over Thompson, who sat by the window holding a piece of beefsteak over his left eye.

He stood up, leaning on the chair's back for support. "I'm sorry, my lord. They snuck up behind us. Got away with the purse too, though there weren't much left in it."

"Don't worry about it. Sit down." Sinclair looked around for Quincy and found her stretched out on the sofa, eyes closed, face pale. Mrs. Hammond knelt beside her, patting her hand, sobbing. Quincy was deathly still. An icy fist closed around Sinclair's throat, choking him. His pulse raced at double-time.

Lady Sinclair entered and clapped her hands. "Maude, fetch my vinaigrette. Matilda, go see if the doctor has arrived yet. Mrs. Hammond, stop that immediately. You are likely frightening the lad."

"Let me have a look, Mrs. Hammond," Sinclair said, moving the housekeeper aside.

Quincy still hadn't moved. Partially hidden by her hairline, a goose egg was forming on her temple. The frames of her spectacles were twisted, the left lens cracked. Sinclair lifted them off and opened one eyelid. The pupil contracted. The knot in Sinclair's stomach loosened a fraction. His hands shook with relief.

"Is he . . . ?" Lady Sinclair peered over his shoulder.

"No, he's just in the arms of Morpheus." He patted Quincy's cheeks. "Can you hear me, lad? Come now, nap time is over."

Maude returned with the silver vinaigrette. Lady Sinclair lifted the lid and waved it under Quincy's nose.

Her eyes fluttered open as she coughed and pushed the silver case away. She squinted. "My lord? What—"

"Easy, lad." The knot in his stomach uncoiled. Sinclair pulled her up and sat beside her on the sofa, barely resisting the sudden urge to hold her close to his side.

The coachman entered and stood by the door, twisting his hat between his hands.

"What happened, Elliott?"

Elliott snapped to attention. "We were at the last stop, a warehouse near the docks. Mr. Quincy and Thompson went inside. A minute later three men ran out. I tied the team to a lamppost and went inside. Thompson and Quincy was conked out on the floor. Thompson woke up when I got to him. We carried Quincy."

"Thank you, Elliott."

"Aye, Cap'n." The coachman tugged his forelock and left.

Sinclair turned to Quincy. "How do you feel?"

She held her hand to her head. "Where are the bricks that fell on me?"

"Sorry," Thompson said, flushing. "That was me."

"Are you injured anywhere aside from your face?" Sinclair asked the footman.

"No, my lord, I don't think so. Quincy, er, broke my fall."

"Glad I could be of service," she said with a faint smile. She touched her face, then patted her pockets. "Has anyone seen my spectacles?"

"They're ruined." Sinclair held them up. "I'll have them replaced tomorrow. Have you a spare pair until then?"

"Thank you, my lord, but it's not necessary for you to—" She broke off as Tanner announced the doctor.

"Good afternoon, Dr. Kimball," Lady Sinclair said, as he bowed in greeting. "Ladies, shall we leave the doctor to his work?"

Quincy tried to rise but Sinclair held firm to her wrist. "The doctor is not necessary, my lord," she said, trying to twist her hand free. "I'm fine. Just had the wind knocked out of me."

His reply was soft, for her ears alone. "I need to know if you're hurt." He raised his voice. "Dr. Kimball, why don't you start with Thompson?"

"I'm *not* hurt, and the doctor doesn't need to know anything," Quincy quietly argued.

"You're not the one who just had ten years scared off his life." Aware of how long he'd been holding her, Sinclair relaxed his grip.

"Nasty bump, but nothing else," the doctor announced a few minutes later, patting Thompson's shoulder. "I would avoid bricks for a few days if I were you." He held out the bits of red brick that had been lodged in Thompson's wig. Sinclair stepped over to have a closer look.

Quincy bolted from the room.

Once out in the hall, she forced herself to take deep breaths and walk, not run, past the footmen stationed outside the dining room. Moving slower also helped keep the floor from tilting so wildly. Where to go? The library was too obvious. Lady Sinclair's drawing room? No, she might also insist the doctor examine her. Perhaps down to the kitchen? Ah, yes, tea was just what she needed for her throbbing headache.

Cook seemed surprised to see a visitor but soon set a pot of tea and a cup on the table. "There's trouble brewing abovestairs, I don't mind telling you," she confided, stirring a pot of soup on the closed stove.

Quincy let her talk. Occasional answers of "Uh-huh" and "Really?" were all the cook needed to keep gossiping about the household members while Quincy drank.

"So this is where you hide."

Quincy shot to her feet, knocking over her chair. "My lord! I thought Dr. Kimball would be some time with Thompson, so I—"

"Missed afternoon tea. I see you rectified matters." Sinclair held out his hand. "Your turn to be examined."

"It is not necessary. I am fine, really."

Sinclair cocked his left eyebrow. "We've had this discussion. Allow—"

"No."

Sinclair tapped his finger on the head of his walking stick. Suddenly his faced relaxed. "You're not *afraid* to be examined, are you . . . lad?"

The scullery maid snickered. Quincy glared at her. "Well, you see, I um . . . Yes." She straightened her shoulders and looked Sinclair square in the eyes. "I don't have much use for doctors."

Sinclair pursed his lips as though pinching back a smile. Quincy had the sneaking suspicion he was teasing her. "Let's discuss it in the library, shall we?"

After a moment of silent debate, Quincy obediently followed him.

Harper came in after them with a tray of two glasses and

a brandy decanter. "I've given Thompson the rest of the day off, my lord," the butler said. "Matilda and Maude promised to look in on him."

Sinclair sighed. "Good. Just don't let Broderick find out, since he disapproves so strongly of fraternization. And please close the door on your way out." Once they were alone, he poured a glass and handed it to Quincy, then poured one for himself. "Thompson's a strapping young man. Suppose he cracked a few of your ribs when he used you for a mattress?"

"I'm sure I would feel some pain if he had." Quincy set her glass on the table, untouched. "Aside from a small bump on my forehead, I feel no aftereffects from this morning."

"That's another thing. Come here by the window. Since we can't let the doctor examine you, at least let me have a look."

Quincy's heart pounded. "That's not—"

"Now."

She swallowed.

"Good lord, Quincy, I'm not going to eat you! I do have some experience at this. We didn't always have a doctor at hand in the army, and we learned to make do." Sinclair's expression softened. "Elliott served under my command for five years. He survived my ministrations just fine, and we don't need to do anything as drastic as extract a pistol ball from your shoulder."

Quincy envisioned the earl on a bloody battlefield, saving his sergeant's life, those magnificent hands deft and sure as he worked, oblivious to the cannon fire and carnage all around. Her stomach fluttered.

"Come here. Now."

Quincy complied. She stood close enough to waltz with him, stared at the stubble on his unshaven jaw, and forced herself to breathe. In, out, in, out. He ran his fingers through her hair, fingertips searching for and finding the extent of the knot on her temple, then checking for other bumps. His touch was tender and thorough, almost a caress. She inhaled his musky scent, blended with a trace of bay rum and something she couldn't quite identify, though it was a pleasant combination. Shivers tiptoed down her spine as he exhaled, his warm breath a gentle puff against her ear. She wanted to lean in, get even closer. Have his warm, solid arms around her, keep her safe.

She tried not to enjoy it. She *shouldn't* enjoy it. It was utterly improper. But no one had ever touched her this way before. Was this a normal reaction? No, just one of those aftereffects from the blow to her head that she'd claimed not to be having. Had to be.

She hadn't thought about the danger she'd been in back at the warehouse, couldn't afford to. But now, in the safety of the library, she did think about it. She'd been utterly defenseless. The brigands could have tossed her body into the Thames, and no one would have known. What would've become of Mel and Grandmère then? Her hands suddenly shook. She clasped them together.

"That seems to be the worst of it," Sinclair said, taking a step back. "You're going to have an impressive bruise by tomorrow. Would you like your souvenirs?" He held out small bits of brick, shiny from the macassar oil in her hair, on his upturned palm.

She tried to smile. "I think not."

"You're trembling." Before she could react, Sinclair pulled her close, wrapping his arms around her. After a startled moment, Quincy gave in, and rested her cheek against his chest, his heartbeat strong and steady beneath her ear. He murmured reassuring words which she felt more than heard, his hand stroking up and down her back in a soothing caress. Her fear forgotten, she twined her arms around his waist and closed her eyes, reveling in the new sensations.

One arm still around her shoulders, Sinclair raised one hand to cradle her head, his thumb stroking her temple. She felt his bristly cheek against her forehead, could almost swear he brushed a kiss there.

A kiss? The ground fell away, and she clung to Sinclair even tighter.

"Not quite the experience you bargained for, eh, my sweet?"

Unable to speak, she shook her head.

Still caressing her, Sinclair gave a little chuckle. "After an ordeal like that, most females would have given in to hysterics long before now."

Better than a bucket of cold water. The ground was back where it belonged, firmly beneath her feet, and Quincy pulled away from Sinclair. "Hysterics?"

"Not that you're . . . that is, just a healthy reaction to . . . any woman, er, *person* would, ah . . ." Sinclair cleared his throat. His gaze darted around the room while Quincy took a step backward, feeling foolish for having displayed such weakness. "Well then. Back to business. Why were you at the docks?"

Quincy ran her fingers through her hair to straighten it and took a deep breath. Right then, back to business, indeed. Distancing herself from Sinclair by sitting at her desk helped even more. She had no business hugging her employer. "I have proof Johnson overpaid merchant bills and pocketed the difference. And I believe he paid several merchants that don't actually exist. That warehouse was listed on a bill of sale from one of them."

Sinclair sank down into the sofa and lifted his foot up onto the ottoman. Quincy tried to ignore how his dressing gown fell open, revealing his bare calves. What would it be like to wrap her arms around his waist, without his dressing gown and nightshirt in the way? When he spoke, she forced her gaze back up to his face. "How much did he dip into my pocket? More than the ten thousand pounds you originally estimated?"

"I'm afraid it's at least double that."

"Damn." He rubbed his thigh. "*One* of the nonexistent merchants? How many more are there?"

"Possibly three."

He leaned his head on the back of the sofa and closed his eyes. Enough time passed that Quincy thought he'd fallen asleep. She was about to ring for Harper when Sinclair finally groaned and stood up. She watched him walk toward her, his gait less steady than usual. He paused beside her desk. "Go home, Quincy." He brushed her cheek with his knuckles, and her eyes fluttered shut of their own accord. "Have Elliott drive you. Mrs. Hammond says the sun will shine tomorrow. If she's right, you and I will dig into this further. If she's wrong, well . . ." He shrugged and limped out of the room.

"Jo! Why are you home so early?" Melinda, carrying a basket of embroidery floss, met Quincy on the steps going up to their flat. She gaped at the departing coach.

"We had a small accident and Lord Sinclair gave me the afternoon off."

"An accident!"

"Dear child, what happened to you?" Grandmère exclaimed when Quincy stepped inside their flat.

"Jo had an accident. Oh, you ripped my coat!"

Quincy shrugged out of the offending garment and held it up to the window. She poked her finger through the rent in the shoulder seam. "Not beyond repair, I hope. I'm unharmed, in case you're interested."

"Of course I know you're unharmed. Do you think I would care about the coat if you weren't? You're the only one who can wear it!"

Quincy laughed and tossed the coat at her sister, then scooped up the gray tabby rubbing against her ankles. "At least Sir Ambrose worries about me," she said, stroking the cat's head. "Don't you, Ambrose? Did you catch another rat for your dinner today to earn your keep?" The cat nuzzled her chin and purred.

"Tell us what happened, dear."

"It was nothing, really." Quincy glanced at her grandmother, then back at the cat in her arms. Grandmère understood the necessity of her disguise, how desperately they needed the steady income afforded by working for the earl. But she would never condone her actions if she knew Sinclair was aware of her true gender. "A footman tripped on the stairs and knocked me down," Quincy fibbed. "A very tall, broad footman. Lord Sinclair felt poorly today anyway, so he sent me home."

"Oh, how romantic!" Mel clasped her hands to her chest. "Is he handsome?"

"Do you think he'll withhold this afternoon from your wages?"

"No. I'm sure he feels responsible for the accident, though it was not his fault." She set the cat down and turned to Mel. "Are you referring to Lord Sinclair or the footman?"

"The footman, silly! The earl is much too old."

"I suppose they're both pleasing to the eye, but I think Thompson may be slightly older than Sinclair."

"How dreadful!" Melinda sat in the chair by the window and set to work fixing Quincy's coat.

Grandmère squinted at Quincy. "Where are your spectacles?"

"My— Oh! Lord Sinclair put them in his dressing gown pocket. I left the room so the doctor couldn't examine me, and I forgot to get them back."

Grandmère moved to the table, tugging Quincy down to sit in the chair next to hers. "Now tell me what you left out," she said softly.

Quincy sighed. Sir Ambrose jumped into her lap and settled across her knees. "I hit my head when the footman fell on top of me and I was senseless for a few moments. Lord Sinclair sent for the doctor to make certain we weren't injured. While he examined Thompson, I left the room. That's all."

"Hmm. And the earl still has your spectacles? This is not good." Grandmère tapped her finger on the table. "You say he's feeling poorly today?"

"He suffered a wound in the war that still pains him. Poor man, it turns him into a bear with a sore paw. The butler says it's worse when the weather is cold and wet. I suppose I will adjust to it like everyone else around him."

"Hmm." Grandmère reached out to take Quincy's hand between her own. "I promise I shall not think you a coward if you decide this charade is too much for you. Doing business with merchants in London is nothing like it was in

Danbury. And working for Sinclair isn't at all like working for your father, is it?"

Quincy stroked Sir Ambrose and stared out the window, remembering how Sinclair had at first frightened her in the library yesterday with his violent behavior. Perhaps violent was too strong a description, but he behaved in ways her father never had. Papa's body had been too weak. Sinclair may still be recovering from his wounds, but he was not weak. All those muscles . . .

She patted her grandmother's hand. "No, this is not like working for Papa, or dealing with merchants in a small village. It's making me think and learn new things. I'd like to believe I can rise to the challenge. I'm actually enjoying it."

Grandmère narrowed her eyes and stared at Quincy. "You aren't forming a *tendre* for the earl, are you?"

"Of course not!" Quincy removed her hat and ran her fingers through her hair. No, of course she wasn't. Couldn't. That would ruin all of her plans.

And besides, she'd made herself unsuitable to be a wife, so there was no point in developing feelings when nothing could ever possibly come of them. She would never bring down scandal on Sinclair or his mother. She would leave before anyone else discovered her secret. She squelched a stab of pain at the thought. "I do like working for him, though. He's generally very even-tempered."

"As you say, *ma chère*." Grandmère gave her a strange little smile, and went back to sewing.

Chapter 7

66$\mathbf{L}$ie down, my lord, and I'll rub more liniment on your leg."

"Damn it, Broderick, forget the liniment. Where's the brandy?" Sinclair flopped onto his bed, weary beyond belief. Something poked him in the hip. He rolled over and searched under the covers, then in his dressing gown pocket. Quincy's spectacles.

He held them up to the window. The frames were hopelessly bent, but the right lens was still intact.

Broderick handed him a glass of brandy, then pulled the dressing gown and nightshirt back to expose his leg. "A compromise, my lord."

"Get on with it, then." While Broderick attacked him with liniment, Sinclair downed his drink and stared through the spectacles at the perfectly clear image of the wallpaper pattern. He sat upright. "It's plain glass."

"Beg pardon, my lord?"

"What? Oh. Bring me another glass, please." Sinclair studied the bent spectacles. Just another part of Quincy's disguise. It wasn't her vision of the world that Quincy needed to alter, but the world's vision of her.

Today's incident was all his fault. He never would have

allowed Mrs. Hammond or another woman in his employ to go near the docks, yet he'd allowed Quincy. Perhaps always trying to think of her as Mr. Quincy was not a good thing. He couldn't risk her coming to any harm.

Working together so closely, he'd come to enjoy her pleasant company, her forthright speech, the quality of her work. She was so organized and efficient. Perhaps women made the best secretaries.

He recalled the moments in the library by the window. He'd known with the first touch that her skull wasn't cracked, but standing so close to her felt so good, breathing in her faint lemon scent. Touching her. Holding her. Comforting her. He'd wanted to tilt her chin up and see if she tasted of lemon.

Perhaps women did not make the best secretaries, after all.

"How are you feeling, dear?"

Sinclair hurriedly threw the covers over his lap and slipped the spectacles back into his pocket. "Mama, even the servants have the manners to knock before entering my chambers."

"Yes, I know. But sometimes my only entertainment of the day is discomfiting you." She sat on the bed and brushed a lock of hair from his forehead.

"Surely that's not the case today?" He adjusted the covers and sat up straighter. "Broderick, don't forget to shut the door on your way out."

"Yes, my lord."

Lady Sinclair leaned against the bedpost. "If you had a wife, she could tend to you instead of Broderick." She patted his knee. "Wouldn't you rather have a beautiful young woman give you a massage?"

"Mama!" He dropped her hand in her lap, trying to set aside the image of Quincy massaging his leg, draped in silk and lace. Or perhaps just a warm ray of sunshine, and nothing else . . . "Please, not today. I have enough to worry about besides getting leg-shackled."

"Yes. Poor Thompson. And Quincy! Such a nice young man. I wonder why anyone would want to hurt him?"

Harper opened the door. "My lord? Elliott has returned."

"Good. Send him up." He kissed his mother on the cheek and slid out of bed. "I don't think anyone intended to hurt Quincy. He was in my carriage, after all."

Lady Sinclair gasped. "But why would anyone want to hurt you?"

Sinclair sat back on the edge of the bed and held his mother's hand. "Quincy discovered discrepancies in the account books. Johnson embezzled from me." Before she could question him, Sinclair hurried on. "Nothing significant, but Quincy's been investigating where the funds went. That warehouse was one of the places Johnson sent money. My money. Of course, the incident was probably just an unfortunate coincidence. In that part of town, it's possible Quincy and Thompson merely stumbled into a den of thieves who didn't appreciate the intrusion."

"Yes, I suppose." Lady Sinclair didn't look convinced. "I never did like Johnson. But your father hired him, and then with everything that happened you were too busy to replace him. I'm glad he's finally gone."

Fortunately Sinclair didn't have time to think about 'everything that happened' as Elliott tapped on the door and stepped in. "You took Quincy home?"

"Aye, Cap'n." He grinned. "He met a sweet young lass in pigtails on the steps and they went up the stairs arm in arm. Beg pardon, my lady."

Lady Sinclair chuckled.

"Thank you, Elliott. That will be all." As the coachman left, Sinclair reached for the belt on his dressing gown, intent on getting dressed.

"You'll let me know if I can help in any way?"

"Of course, Mama."

She kissed him on his forehead. "Try to rest and not be such a beast. Mrs. Hammond predicts it will be sunny tomorrow."

Alone again, Sinclair pulled out Quincy's bent spectacles. *Such a nice young man,* his mother's words echoed.

Young. Why did a nice young *miss* need to work as a secretary, in disguise? The question had plagued him all week. Perhaps supporting a younger sister? How long did she intend to keep up the masquerade?

And how long could he keep up his part in it?

Several times he'd almost slipped up. If anyone had opened the library door when he'd had Quincy in his arms . . . Life as he knew it would be over. He'd have to admit that he'd compromised Miss Quincy and then they'd be forced to marry. Courting Quincy would be courting scandal, and he'd already been through enough scandal to last two lifetimes. He wouldn't risk it, not now when his mother was finally coming out of isolation and rejoining society.

Remembering how good it had felt to hold her, marriage to Quincy wouldn't really be a hardship, but she deserved so much more than a crippled, scarred ex-soldier. She'd resent being trapped into marrying him. He enjoyed her companionship too much to risk it.

As for this afternoon's events, although he thought it most likely that Quincy and Thompson had indeed stumbled into a thieves' den, it was worth hiring a Bow Street Runner to investigate. He sent one of the downstairs footmen to make the arrangements.

The sun did shine the next morning, piercing Sinclair's head with its bright rays. His head throbbed, but thankfully his leg did not.

"And how are we feeling this morning, my lord?"

"Must you ask that every day, Broderick?" Sinclair sat up slowly, his head easily keeping pace. Last night he'd downed only half a bottle of brandy.

Broderick harrumphed. "I take it you're not nearly as cup shot as usual. That's a good sign. Yes, a very good sign." He began fussing with the shaving accoutrements, mumbling to himself.

Later, Sinclair stepped out of his bath in time to hear a screeching fight in the hall.

"I'll see what's happening, my lord. It's probably just Maude and Matilda at it again."

Sinclair tied the sash around his dressing gown and stepped into the hall. The upstairs staff had gathered, gawking at the two maids wrestling on the floor.

"I insist you cease this display immediately!" Broderick shouted. Tanner and Thompson stood at their posts farther down the hall, watching the show and grinning from ear to ear. Maude and Matilda slapped each other and pulled hair, both shrieking.

Sinclair frowned. Why wasn't Harper putting a halt to this? Or Mrs. Hammond? Both were conspicuous by their absence.

Quincy quietly threaded her way through the group, threw her arms around the maids, and drew them together. The maids held still. Quincy briefly whispered in their ears, then let go.

Maude and Matilda blushed and stood up. To Sinclair's astonishment, they apologized to Quincy, curtsied to himself, and immediately returned to work at opposite ends of the hall.

Thompson winked at Quincy, and Quincy hurried down the stairs, back toward the library.

Sinclair shook his head. "Lad's got the whole staff wrapped around his finger."

"Beg pardon, my lord?"

"Nothing, Broderick."

An hour later, Quincy looked up from her work, startled to see Sinclair downstairs. He was lounging against the doorframe, shaved and dressed, looking fine enough to turn a woman's senses to porridge.

"Cataloging Johnson's sins, are you?"

"G-good morning, my lord." Quincy settled the bottle of ink she'd almost tipped over. She straightened papers on her desk, glancing at him from the corner of her eye, vainly trying not to think of their embrace in the library yesterday. He appeared his usual charming self this morning. Gone were the lines of pain around his mouth and bruises under his eyes. "Still trying to assess the extent of the damage. I thought—"

"Good. I know for a fact Johnson got on the ship before it sailed for America, so he can inflict no further damage. But I do find myself curious as to how deeply he dipped into my pocket." He pushed off from the doorjamb. "Grab your hat and gloves, and let's go."

"Go?" She stared at him blankly.

"Yes. We'll visit those three mystery merchants, see if they really exist."

"We?" She shook her head, then rose and gathered the appropriate receipts.

Sinclair called Harper for his own hat and gloves and walking stick. "Should my mother ask, you may tell her I've gone out but will return by"— he glanced at Quincy— "supper. Yes, we should return by supper. Come along, Mr. Quincy."

They stepped out into the sunshine and Sinclair took a deep breath. "Ah, what a lovely morning. Mrs. Hammond was correct, as usual." He clapped Quincy on the shoulder and they set off walking at Sinclair's slow but steady pace.

His limp was no more pronounced than usual, but he was using his walking stick as a cane. After a few blocks, she could no longer contain her concern. "I'm surprised you didn't want to take the carriage, my lord."

He remained silent for so long, she thought he hadn't heard her. Or was ignoring her. Had she offended him?

She barely heard his quiet reply. "Leg stiffens up too much if I don't walk." He glanced at her. "A spare pair?"

Quincy self-consciously touched the rim of her grandmother's old-fashioned spectacles and nodded. The lenses gave her a headache, but she couldn't risk being seen bare-faced.

Sinclair dug in his pocket and handed over the ruined pair. "Don't forget to have these repaired. Have the bill sent to me."

Quincy tucked them away, and they discussed how they'd deal with the three merchants until they reached the first address. Or rather, where it would have been, had the merchant actually existed. The building was an ancient burned-out husk, inhabited only by rodents that scurried out of sight when Quincy peeked through the doorway.

The second and third businesses turned out to be equally fictitious, though at least the false addresses were in a better part of town. By now they were only a few blocks from Sinclair's home.

"Well, that's that," she said, eager to return to the library and the delicious luncheon she knew Mrs. Hammond was waiting to serve. Quincy's stomach growled.

"Fakes, every damn one of them. That thieving son of a—" Sinclair cut himself off as Quincy started walking again. "Where are you going?" he called after her.

"My lord?"

"This way." He pointed over his left shoulder, the opposite direction from his home.

She stifled a sigh and fell into step with him. Her feet ached. Surely his must, too? Not to mention his leg. Her stomach growled again. "Might I ask where we're going, my lord?"

"Of course you can ask."

There was a long silence.

"Where are we going?" Quincy said at last.

"To luncheon."

"I asked where, not why."

Sinclair glanced at her, a spark of humor in his eyes. "So you did, lad, so you did. Ever been to Gunter's?"

"The confectioner famous for his ices?"

"The very same."

"Why?"

"They also make the most mouth-watering sandwiches."

"But why are *we* going there?"

"The food is excellent, the company exceptional, and," he lowered his voice, "there are no screeching maids." They shared a smile as they crossed the street. "Besides, I thought you deserved a treat after your fine bit of negotiating this morning. I'm curious what you said to the maids."

Her cheeks heated at the praise. "I merely reminded them that the footmen were watching and getting a good look at their ankles, and then some."

Sinclair chuckled.

Quincy admired his profile for a moment. He looked years younger when he laughed, handsome and carefree, the way he must have looked before his injury. "Do you often treat your secretaries to lunch?"

"Only those who are attacked." Sinclair turned serious

as they sidestepped a vendor with a cart of oranges. "Are you certain you're all right? No headache, no bruised ribs or anything?"

"Just the bump on my head. I'm fine, really."

Sinclair rested his hand on her shoulder, a comfortable and comforting weight. "You must sometimes do things that Miss Quincy would never consider, but I would hope they are never foolhardy risks." He gave her shoulder a squeeze before letting go. "In some ways, Mr. Quincy is in even greater danger."

Quincy swallowed hard, touched by his concern. "I never indulge in impulsive behavior, my lord." She was scrambling for a topic to steer the conversation into shallower waters when they heard his name called out.

"Sinclair, well met!"

"Leland, Palmer," Sinclair greeted two gentlemen, his posture relaxed. Quincy tried to relax, too.

Former soldiers, like Sinclair, she guessed. Of an age with Sinclair, one was missing his right arm, and the other wore a patch over his left eye, a scar extending both above and below the patch.

"What excellent timing," the one-armed man said. "We were just on our way to luncheon."

"As were we," Sinclair replied. "We—"

"Then it's settled!" the one-eyed man exclaimed. "Off we go!" He clapped his hand to Sinclair's shoulder, spinning the earl around until they were all headed the way Sinclair and Quincy had just come. Since that was the direction of Sinclair's house, Quincy happily fell into step behind the three gentlemen.

"Haven't seen you in ages!" the one-eyed man continued. "Leg been bothering you?"

"No, no, nothing of the sort. Just been, ah, busy."

"Busy?" the one-armed man repeated, dropping back a pace, even with Quincy.

She kept her eyes forward, refusing to meet his frank, assessing gaze. Her cravat suddenly felt too tight.

Sinclair cleared his throat. "Lord Palmer, Sir Leland,

this is Quincy. My new secretary." The three exchanged greetings.

"Ah, this explains your absence of late," the one-armed man, Lord Palmer, said.

Quincy and Sinclair both raised their eyebrows, her surprise mirrored on his face as they looked at each other.

"How so?" Leland said.

"You saw the disaster that was Sinclair's library soon after Johnson left," Palmer said. "By now it's a wonder this unfortunate lad hasn't been lost forever amidst all the debris."

Sinclair tilted his chin up. "Are you implying, sirrah, that my library is a mess?"

"No, good sir, I am not *implying* anything. It is a direct statement."

Quincy stared at the sidewalk to hide her grin. When she looked up again, they had turned a corner, onto St. James's Street.

"I'll have you know my library is neat as a pin. Not so much as a receipt out of place."

Leland and Palmer gaped at Quincy. She looked down again, this time to hide her blush.

"Ah, so that's why you are taking the lad to luncheon!" Leland said. "Good show, old chap, but if the lad's managed to work such a miracle, he deserves more than just lunch at your club—"

"Actually we were headed to Gunter's," Sinclair said.

"—Though Brook's is a good place to start."

"Brook's?" Sinclair looked shocked. "No, we can't—"

"Well, it's not like we can take you to White's anymore, is it?" Leland said jovially.

"Was that a lifetime ban, old boy, or just for the remainder of this decade?" Palmer added.

Sinclair looked like he wished for a hole to open up in the sidewalk. Quincy just wished she understood why. Then she remembered—the old scandal. She thought it in poor taste for his friends to joke about the incident at White's.

"Shall we?" Leland gestured for the others to precede him through the doorway.

Palmer stepped through, and waited expectantly.

Sinclair glanced at Quincy, and grimaced before he shrugged and ushered her in.

"Your club, my lord?" Quincy's step faltered. "If Papa could see me now, he'd roll over in his grave."

"What was that?" Palmer said.

She cleared her throat. "I said everyone looks so grave."

"Wait a few hours," Leland said. "They haven't had enough to drink yet!"

Once they were all seated, Sinclair ordered roast beef and claret for the two of them. "Unless you wish something else?"

"Tea instead of wine, if you don't mind. I need to keep a clear head if I'm to accomplish anything this afternoon."

"I'm sure your employer wouldn't mind if you had a glass or two," Leland said. "That library would drive any man to drink."

"It wasn't so bad," Quincy said. "It merely needed—"

All three men leaned forward.

"—Organizing."

They all leaned back.

Quincy tried to blend into the background as the three friends began chatting, catching up on mutual acquaintances, horses for sale, and boxing matches—the male equivalent of gossip. Their conversation faded as she tried to look without gawking at the people and furnishings in this holiest of male sanctuaries. Men smoked cigars, and waiters passed carrying trays laden with bottles and glasses.

Two young men sauntered by, discussing the merits of a particular opera dancer. Quincy swiveled her head to follow their conversation, until she felt a kick to her shin. She glanced up in surprise, and saw Sinclair frowning at her.

He gave a minute shake of his head before he returned his attention to Leland's blow-by-blow boxing story.

Their food arrived. Conversation, except for the "pass the salt" variety, halted while they ate. The roast beef and jam tarts were not as good as Cook's, but Quincy was so hungry it didn't matter.

A few moments later, Sinclair gestured for her to wipe

her mouth, which she did, horrified to be caught in public with food on her face. Apparently she missed the spot, as Sinclair leaned toward her, extending his napkin. "Bit of jam," he murmured.

For a frozen heartbeat, she thought he would wipe her face while Palmer and Leland looked on. Then Sinclair handed her the napkin, and she exhaled. A moment later he nodded that yes, she'd gotten it, and she returned his napkin.

She had realized from the start of their acquaintance that she was more comfortable with her masquerade than Sinclair was, though he'd gamely played along. But he'd almost given her away just now, if the looks exchanged between Palmer and Leland were anything to go by. They seemed to be having an entire conversation, without a word said aloud.

Quincy sipped her tea, trying not to squirm in her chair, trying to calm her racing heart, as the two men glanced her way.

What if someone else did find out? What if someone other than Sinclair learned her secret? Would he cast her out?

Ever since she'd come to her senses on the sofa yesterday, she'd expected to hear that he was no longer willing to go along with her charade. She knew he felt guilty about the incident at the docks, though that was ridiculous. He even winced every time he saw the bruise on her forehead.

She'd also noticed that Thompson now directed odd looks at her when no one else was about. Could the footman have noticed something when he fell on her? Or worse, *felt* something when he carried her?

She wore a linen strip to bind her small breasts, and a snug shirt under a loose-fitting shirt, then a waistcoat and coat. Surely he couldn't have felt anything through all those layers of fabric? And she had no curves to speak of to give her away. At seventeen, Melinda already had a more womanly shape than her older sister.

Abruptly Palmer dropped his napkin on the table and tilted his chair back on two legs, draining the last of his claret. "What say we head over to Gentleman Jackson's? Ever done any boxing, Mr. Quincy?"

She took another sip. "No, my lord, can't say I have."

"Now's as good a time as any to start," Leland said. "Go a few rounds, work up a sweat. Just the thing to put hair on your chest."

Quincy choked on her tea.

Sinclair thumped her on the back. "Perhaps another day." He took his leave of his friends, citing the amount of work to still catch up on when they protested his departure. Quincy followed at his heels.

With the exit in sight, she sighed with relief. She'd had luncheon at a gentlemen's club with no one the wiser, and no harm done.

She nearly bumped into Sinclair when he stopped abruptly just outside the club's door. "Afternoon, Twitchell," Sinclair said, his voice tight. Without waiting for a response he continued on, his back straighter, his stride laboriously even.

She craned her neck to see who could provoke such a reaction from Sinclair. She was shocked by the barely contained anger in the man's face as he returned Sinclair's greeting, and by his gaucherie in staring at Sinclair's leg rather than meeting the earl's eye. She gave him a wide berth as she hurried after Sinclair.

They'd walked a few blocks and turned the corner when she realized Sinclair had slowed down considerably, a fine sheen of perspiration highlighting his upper lip. He ought to rest, but she knew he'd never admit it. She paused in front of a tobacconist's shop. "May we stop a moment?"

"I don't smoke."

"Neither do I." She was actually more interested in stealing a glance at a bonnet in the window display of the shop next door. She was picturing how it would look on Mel, of course. Quincy had given up any plans to wear a bonnet, or anything else even remotely feminine, when she'd adopted her disguise.

An image reflected in the window drew her gaze to a flower girl across the street, who couldn't have been more than sixteen. Quincy flinched as a passing buck draped his arm around the girl and spoke in her ear, his other hand roaming the backside of her threadbare dress. She pushed him away, her face flaming. The buck sauntered on, his cruel laughter ringing in the air.

"Damn jackanapes."

Quincy gaped at Sinclair. He was staring across the street as the scene played out.

"Imagine how often that must happen to her," Quincy said softly. "And what about the men she can't make leave her alone?"

Sinclair's mouth tightened into a grim line.

A plan sprang to mind, fully formed. "I know you detest interviewing, my lord, but we're still short one downstairs maid. I have an idea for replacing staff members that would avoid using an employment agency."

He turned to look at her. "And forgo the opportunity to have prospective maids lined up the length of the hall? Do go on."

"Agencies only send out qualified candidates—people who are trained and experienced, and have character references. Such people shouldn't have much trouble finding employment if they truly desire it."

Sinclair narrowed his eyes. "What is your point?"

Quincy indicated the flower girl with a tilt of her head. "She couldn't get a nice, safe job as a maid. She probably has no reference, and likely no living parents, or at least none sober. She's too young to be out on her own."

Sinclair looked back at the street. "You want me to take her in?" Both of his brows raised into his hairline.

"Her, and others like her." Seeing Sinclair cross his arms over his chest, Quincy spoke faster. "I know Elliott served with you, as did most of the stable lads. And a dozen groundskeepers and footmen at your other properties, all hired within the last year—how many of them also served in the army?"

Sinclair uncrossed his arms, only to prop his fists on his hips.

"Give her a safe, warm place to sleep, clean clothes, and train her to be a proper maid. Then write her a glowing reference so she can find another employer."

"You're serious!" His brows still hadn't come down. "Quincy, I realize you may have had some rough times, but we can't save every vagrant and orphan in London."

She swallowed past a sudden lump in her throat. "You can save that one." She left the words framed in silence.

Sinclair frowned. "But—"

"Give her room and board, and pay her reduced wages while she's in training. It will save you money. And this kind of project will require extra attention, and not just from Mrs. Hammond." She played her trump card. "You'll need to involve your mother."

Sinclair looked blank. "My mother?"

"Selecting and training the girls will take up much of her time."

He whipped his head around to stare at Quincy. A slow grin spread across his face. "Yes, it will take up much of her time, won't it? She will hardly have any time to worry about *my* social schedule!" He threw back his head and laughed. "Come along, Quincy, we have to set this plan in motion!"

Chapter 8

"You'll be happy to know, Quincy, that after only one week, my staff has now increased by two maids in training, one tweeny, and a stable lad," Sinclair said as he strode into the library, an ironic smile twisting his lips at conveying a status report to his secretary. He started for the sofa as usual, but instead settled in a chair pulled close to her drop-leaf desk.

Quincy closed the account book, giving him her full attention. "I will add them to the payroll immediately."

He'd chosen the chair over the sofa so they didn't have to shout, he told himself, not so he could catch a whiff of her lemon scent as she moved, or be close enough to see those expressive eyes behind her newly repaired spectacles. Her look of open approval and admiration made his chest swell.

"And they are . . . ?" she prompted.

Details, details. "Ned is a six-year-old who ran away from the chimney sweep he'd been apprenticed to, smack into Mama's silk skirts as she walked out of Hookham's Lending Library. After climbing down hot, sooty chimneys, he seems delighted to muck out stalls in the stables."

Quincy scribbled information into the appropriate ledger.

"Celia is about eleven. Cook found her weeping over her dead mother in a doorway. She hasn't spoken a word or smiled, but I think she's pleased with her new circumstances."

Quincy nodded. "She carries the message platter between floors like it's the Ark of the Covenant."

"Yes. All my staff seems to be quite dedicated." Well, most of them. Most of the time. "I found Irene in the shadows outside the theater, being beaten for not 'performing' properly." Sinclair rubbed his fist over his thigh. "I whacked the pimp with my walking stick and brought her home in the carriage. Between sobs, she explained her father had sold her in exchange for several bottles of gin. She's seventeen." He stared at his fist. If he should ever come across her reprobate of a father . . .

Quincy scribbled more notes in the ledger. "And the other maid in training?"

"Daisy, an orphan. The flower girl we saw." Quincy's sudden, grateful smile was dazzling, shooting through him, holding him in place as he soaked up the warmth in her gaze, like a cat soaking up the sun on a windowsill. He needed to find ways to coax that from her, often.

His reaction caught him utterly off-guard. He cleared his throat. "She's helping Mama tend the plants in the conservatory, when she's not working with Mrs. Hammond." He leaned back to prop his boots up on one corner of the desk. "Their inexperienced efforts are adding to the household chaos, not easing it, but since Mama's attention is now focused on them, rather than me, I don't mind." As if to punctuate his sentence, they heard a tray crash to the floor out in the hall. "I think afternoon tea will be late again."

They shared a grin as Quincy went back to work.

"She's gone!"

Quincy had just stepped into Sinclair's town house early one morning a week later when she heard the commotion upstairs.

"What do you mean, gone? Who's gone?" Harper demanded, climbing the stairs. He joined Celia, Daisy, Irene and Mrs. Hammond clustered on the first-floor landing. Curious, Quincy followed.

"When I woke up she weren't there," Daisy sobbed. "Her clothes is gone, her shoes is gone, and everything!"

"Who's gone?" Mrs. Hammond asked. "Is it Matilda? Maude?"

"Right here, Mrs. H.," Matilda called from the end of the hallway.

"Where did Maude go? Did she leave a note?" Mrs. Hammond directed at Daisy. Since joining the household, Daisy shared Maude's room.

Matilda joined the group and snorted. "A note? She couldn't do no more than write her name. Always too busy flirting with the footmen to pay attention to Lady S's lessons."

"The footmen!" Harper shouted. "Where are Thompson and Tanner? I knew something like this would happen. Broderick warned me, but I—"

"Oh, shut your clack," Mrs. Hammond snapped.

"Celia, why don't you and Irene go see if Cook needs help with breakfast?" Quincy broke in. "Do you know if the other servants are accounted for?" she asked, looking from Harper to Mrs. Hammond.

"All the females but Maude are here."

"Tanner is in the wine cellar, and I just passed Grimshaw and Finlay at their posts downstairs." Harper scowled. "But I haven't seen Thompson all morning!"

"We'll check his quarters next," Quincy said. "Daisy, will you show us to Maude's room? Perhaps she left a clue as to where she went or why."

The group stepped away from the landing, but stopped when they heard the front door open and shut.

"Thompson?" Harper said incredulously.

"Yes, Mr. Harper?" The footman looked up at the group with a guilty start, his eyes wide.

"Do you know where Maude is?" Mrs. Hammond called down to him.

"No, ma'am. Haven't see her since last night, when she was talking to Broderick."

"Broderick!" Sinclair roared from behind his closed bedchamber door. They heard more mutterings from Sinclair, but no response from the valet.

"Broderick?" they all repeated. "Broderick!" Harper chuckled. Mrs. Hammond tittered. They all started laughing. After a few moments, Mrs. Hammond wiped her eyes with the corner of her starched apron and shooed the girls back to work. Harper went downstairs, tsking.

Quincy stood alone, still chuckling, when Sinclair jerked his door open a moment later. He stepped barefoot into the hall, holding his dressing gown closed with one hand, clutching a sheet of paper with the other.

"Did you know about this?" he demanded, waving the paper at Quincy.

"That depends." She stopped smiling and stared at his sleep-mussed hair and darkened jaw, suddenly realizing that not only was she quite comfortable seeing him in dishabille, she rather enjoyed it. "To what are you referring?"

"Read this."

She reached for the paper, resisting the urge to smooth his hair, to straighten the collar of his nightshirt. She unfolded the note and read the valet's spidery handwriting:

Lord Sinclair,

While I have thoroughly enjoyed working for you (such a fine figure!) I regret I must leave you now (and so urgently, too!). I learned yesterday that my mother in Manchester is quite ill and needs me more than you. I do apologize for leaving so abruptly, but I am assured you will be fine, as you are nearly fully recovered from your injuries.

Please wish me happy, as I am soon to be married.

B

PS: Maude (my intended!) leaves with regret also, as we cannot bear to be parted.

"Maude and Broderick?" Quincy started to chuckle but forced a straight face when she saw Sinclair's thunderous expression. "No, my lord, I knew nothing of this. Maude and Thompson, perhaps, but not . . . not—" She broke into laughter anyway. Sinclair's expression relaxed, and after a moment, he joined in.

"Well, at least we aren't shorthanded when it comes to maids, are we?" Sinclair retrieved the note from her hand, their fingers touching, lingering too long for the contact to be an accident. He ran his hand through his hair, and Quincy took a step back. "But I am warning you now, Quincy, I refuse to hire a valet off the street, so don't even ask."

"Of course not, my lord. We wouldn't want to risk him letting the razor slip when he shaves you." She drew her finger across her throat, drawing a chuckle from Sinclair, and went back to work in the library.

"Damnable timing," Sinclair announced without preamble two hours later. He crossed to the armchair and stuck his feet out toward the low fire in the grate. "Just last night I had decided I would escort Mama to Lady Stanhope's ball after all. Now, of course, it is out of the question."

Quincy closed the account book she'd been working in. "Unless you were planning to also take Maude or Broderick with you to the ball, I don't see what one has to do with the other."

"No, I don't suppose you would." He tossed a scoop of coal on the fire.

"Thompson or Tanner or even Harper can help you dress. Besides, you owe it to your mother to go."

Sinclair leaned forward to stare at Quincy. "What does she have to do with anything?"

"She threw herself whole-heartedly into your plan, working with the girls—"

"Your plan, you mean."

"And she has exercised remarkable restraint this last week, has she not? Has she said a word to you about grandchildren, or wedding invitations, or required your presence at another matchmaking tea?"

"No," Sinclair mumbled into his cravat.

"I didn't quite hear you."

"No, damn your hide!" He glared at Quincy.

She smiled serenely back. "Then it's settled. You will grace the Stanhopes with your presence this evening, squire your mother, charm the girls silly, and come home with a clear conscience."

Sinclair groaned. "You're no help, no help at all." He called Harper for his hat, gloves and walking stick, and went out for his walk.

Quincy wiped the silly grin off her face and went back to work.

At his club, Sinclair found Leland staring morosely into his wineglass in a corner, his eye patch askew. "Mind some company?" Sinclair said, sitting down.

Leland waved agreement without looking up, and swirled the wine in his glass. Suddenly his head snapped up. "Sinclair! Jolly good to see you!"

Sinclair's eye's narrowed. "How many glasses have you had?"

"This is the first." He tossed back half of it in one swallow, and leaned across the table toward Sinclair. "You and I, we've been good friends for what, ten, eleven years now?"

"Twelve, I believe." He motioned for a footman to bring him a glass and refill Leland's.

"Might I move in with you? Not for long, mind you. Just until my mother dies or I find an heiress willing to wed me."

Sinclair grinned. "Things that bad?"

Leland sighed. "I know we've been at low water for some time, and I've learned to live with it, really I have. I don't mind having only four courses at dinner. I don't even mind not being able to keep a mistress. But Mama's gone too far with her purse-pinching ways this time, too bloody damn far." He took another swallow of wine and lowered his voice when he spoke again. "She's renting out rooms in the house."

"She's taken in boarders? How ingenious."

"Ingenious! I have three strangers living under my roof!"

"Strangers paying you rent, you mean. Be practical. You have a source of income without going into trade."

"A prune-faced retired governess, a pious cleric, and a half-pay lieutenant with one leg."

"All respectable citizens. Think of it as your civic duty."

Leland stared at his glass a moment. "It could just as easily have been you or me, couldn't it?" He adjusted his eye patch and stroked the scar that curved from above his left eyebrow to his upper lip. "We're only charging him half as much as the others."

Sinclair rubbed his right thigh, feeling the rough scar tissue beneath the smooth fabric of his trousers. What youthful foolishness had convinced him that running off to war would quiet the gossips after his father's scandal-shrouded death? At least Sinclair had come home relatively intact, which was more than could be said of many of the men he'd served with. He'd stopped trying to remember those who had fallen. He'd had to, to stop the nightmares.

Instead he concentrated on the survivors from his unit less fortunate than himself. He'd hired several of them, as Quincy had pointed out, but he also had other plans. Working to better their lot had banished the bad dreams. So far only his solicitor knew of his efforts, and he preferred to keep it that way. Even Quincy didn't know, and he worked on the plans under her very nose. Johnson's thievery had thrown a wrench in the works, but with any luck it would prove to be an insignificant setback.

Sinclair cleared his throat. "Enough dwelling on the past." He held up his glass. "A toast. To Broderick and Maude and their marital bliss."

Leland clinked glasses with him. "Your valet? And who's Maude?"

"An upstairs maid." Sinclair sighed. "Stop laughing, you dolt."

"I'm sorry, I can't . . . help myself." Leland covered his face, but his shoulders shook with silent mirth. "I'm sorry, old chap. This is the second pairing in less than a month, isn't it? What a matchmaker you are!"

"It's no laughing matter. The only trained staff I've managed to replace so far is my secretary. It's a damn nuisance."

Leland stopped laughing, though he seemed on the verge of starting again at any moment. "Mr. Quincy seems a nice enough chap. Certainly smells better than Johnson did."

"I paid dearly for keeping Johnson on when I was not at my best, believe me. And Quincy is nothing like Johnson." Sinclair briefly imagined what Leland's reaction would be were he to share just *how* different Quincy was from Johnson.

"Seems awfully young, though. Why'd you hire him?"

Sinclair stroked his chin. Because Quincy aroused his protective instincts. Because she stimulated his intellect. Because she made him laugh, and it had been a long time since he'd seen the humor in anything. "Quincy is very efficient. And . . . I enjoy having him around."

Leland gave him a puzzled look, but said nothing.

Quincy was destined to accomplish little today, for she had just settled back to work when Lady Sinclair requested she join her for luncheon, then asked her to participate in a discussion with Mrs. Hammond about the household staff. Lady Sinclair shared her ultimate goal, which was to convince society matrons to take in and train other girls like Daisy and Irene. Their conversation lasted well into the afternoon. It was nearly time to go home, yet Quincy had finished little of her work. She had no choice but to stay late to catch up.

She was still bent over the books when she heard Sinclair come home and trudge upstairs to get ready for the evening. Lord and Lady Stanhope had invited him and Lady Sinclair to dinner prior to the ball.

Daisy had just cleared Quincy's supper tray when Tanner poked his head around the door.

"His lordship asks you bring his ruby stickpin to him. Says you know where he left it."

Quincy nodded and Tanner left. Stickpin? Ruby? When Mrs. Hammond had helped her clean the library her first day, she'd seen many of Sinclair's personal effects strewn about the room, under the furniture and stuffed between the cushions. But she hadn't seen any jewelry. She'd gone through every drawer, file, shelf—ah, there was one place she had looked only briefly.

The cashbox.

She opened the lid—still unlocked, she noted with a faint smile—and removed the bank notes. A handful of gold shirt studs, two rings, and a half dozen stickpins were left among the coins. She smiled and sorted through the pins. Emerald, sapphire, diamond—oh yes, ruby, too. She grabbed them all, then paused. He was asking her to bring jewelry to complete his ensemble, on his way out for the evening, possibly to woo a potential bride.

She squeezed the pins within her fist, until they dug into her palm. She'd known he was planning to select a bride. It shouldn't matter to her. She put the box away, then headed upstairs to Lord Sinclair's bedchamber.

Picturing him in the process of getting dressed, her steps faltered. Her heart thudded in her chest but she kept walking. Surely he'd be dressed by now if he'd asked for his jewelry.

"Quincy?" Sinclair looked startled when she knocked and stepped into his room. "But I asked Tanner to bring . . . Ah, good, you found it."

She intended to leave the pins and exit quickly, but she was mesmerized by the sight of him. He stood before his mirror in his shirtsleeves, tying his cravat. His lawn shirt molded to his form, and muscles in his back tensed and shifted as he moved his arms. Broderick had been right. Such a fine form! All the exercising he did to strengthen his leg benefited the rest of his body, too. Distantly she realized he'd spoken to her. "Beg pardon, my lord?"

"I said I see you found the ruby stickpin. That is why you're here, isn't it?" He pulled on his waistcoat of black silk. Thompson stepped forward to help him into his evening coat of black velvet, then stepped back again. Sinclair's trousers were black, as were his boots. His white shirt and cravat were the only relief.

She wanted to run her hands over the soft velvet coat, to feel his hard muscles ripple beneath her fingers. Her mouth went dry. She tore her gaze away from his body and looked at his eyes. "Yes. But ruby? And wearing all black is so . . . unoriginal."

Sinclair cocked one brow. "You are now an arbiter of fashion?"

"Of course not. But I thought you were above such banality. At least wear the emerald instead of the ruby." She advanced into the room and dropped all the jewelry but the emerald pin on the dressing table. No longer able to resist the urge to touch him, she reached up to straighten his cravat.

"Damn nuisance."

She dropped her arms and jumped back. "I'm sorry." Her cheeks heated at his reaction to her forward behavior.

"Not you, Quincy." Sinclair grinned. Her stomach flipped over on itself. "This dinner, the balls, selecting a wife—I'm tired of the whole thing. If it weren't for the changes in Mama . . ." He lowered his voice, so quiet Quincy barely heard him. "And my leg already aches." He untied the cravat and pulled it off. "Thank you, Thompson, that will be all."

The footman bowed and left the room, leaving the door open.

"You can't give up," Quincy said. "It will set your mother back weeks, perhaps months." Having spent so much time in Lady Sinclair's company, Quincy knew how important her lighter spirits were to Sinclair. She grabbed another cravat from the stack on the dresser and stretched to loop it around his neck. "I have a plan."

"Another plan?" Sinclair raised his chin to allow Quincy to tie the cravat.

"A cunning plan." She started tying the material into a knot that she recalled her father wearing.

"Tell me about your cunning plan." He bent his knees a bit to make it easier for Quincy to reach him, bringing them almost nose to nose. Amusement danced in his warm brown eyes.

"A strategy, actually. You must attend balls regularly. And not just as your mother's escort."

Sinclair groaned. "But I don't want—"

"You haven't heard the strategy yet." She tried to keep her tone light. "Can you dance yet?"

Sinclair froze. The clock on the mantel seemed extraordinarily loud. "I believe I could," he answered at last. His face was impassive, but at least his jaw wasn't clenched.

"Good." Quincy let out the breath she'd been holding. "Dance the waltzes, but nothing else. Never dance with the same lady twice at the same function. And you must dance with the wallflowers as well as the diamonds. Your hostesses will love you for it."

"Why only waltzes?" He eyed her handiwork in the mirror and, to her surprise, nodded approval.

Quincy positioned the emerald pin as she spoke. "It will set you apart. It will give you charm, and make you more enigmatic. But most importantly, you will have a chance to converse with your prospective brides without chaperones hanging on every word, and not be interrupted by changing partners."

"But I want a wife, not a conversationalist."

Quincy flushed. "Eventually you'll have to deal with her, ah, outside the bedchamber. Wouldn't you prefer someone whose company does not grate on your nerves?"

Sinclair stroked his chin. "I suppose. But why the wallflowers?"

Quincy poked him in the chest. "You conceited fop! Do you think because they are shy or not the easiest on the eye that they would make poor spouses? And have you never seen a swan only a few weeks old?"

"Really, Quincy, you're too easy to tease." He chucked her on the arm and moved her to the side, holding her shoulders until she was steady on her feet again, then turned this way and that, inspecting his reflection. "Wonderful, wonderful." He gave a last tug on his cravat. "You wouldn't be interested in taking Broderick's place, would you?" He peered at her coat, and plucked several gray cat hairs from her sleeve. "No, I suppose not." He grinned at her blush.

"I don't believe I have even half the patience Broderick did." Quincy spun on her heel and headed for the door. "Good night, my lord."

Sinclair chuckled. "Impertinent pup."

Chapter 9

~~~⚜~~~

Dinner was as bad as Sinclair feared. The food was fine, but the company was tedious. Lady Stanhope seated him between two simpering misses. No one within earshot was worth conversing with, unless he wanted to join in a discussion of fashion. He grit his teeth, his grimace mistaken for a smile by the ladies and his hosts. At least Mama appeared content, conversing with the elderly viscount seated next to her.

How he wished he had Quincy nearby to banter with and trade barbs. Had she ever been able to attend supper parties or balls? Certainly her company would be more interesting. He tried to picture her in a gown instead of trousers. Didn't work. Those legs shouldn't be hidden by skirts. Trousers, pulled taut across her shapely backside, now *that* he could picture all too clearly.

Finally the meal was over, the receiving line dealt with, and the dancing begun. Sinclair prowled the edge of the room, debating whose dance card to sign.

Miss Mary Marsden, perhaps. The little brunette was being completely ignored by the fawning bucks swarming around her beautiful older sister. Lady Louisa, definitely. A stunning blonde in her first Season, she wasn't full of herself yet.

Miss Prescott, too. Supremely self-conscious, she nearly fainted when Sinclair approached where she sat with the chaperones. Her freckles, which matched her riot of red curls, stood out in relief on her pale cheeks when she stood before him, her wide green eyes nearly level with his own. "You—you wish to d-dance with me, my lord?"

"I'm not too late to sign your card for a waltz, am I?" he said, raising her hand and dropping a kiss in the air just above her fingers.

"N-not at all, my lord." She flashed him a simple, genuine smile, the first he'd seen all night. Perhaps Quincy's plan had merit after all.

Sinclair scanned the room again as a Scottish reel started, reminding himself he was only committing to a few minutes of dancing, not a lifetime. Not yet, anyway.

Town was still thin of company this early in the Season, and Lady Stanhope's entertainment was the better for not being so crowded. He managed to sign some eligible lady's card for every waltz of the evening, and nothing more. Quincy's strategy was little more than common sense. Another of her many talents—pointing out the obvious that he had missed.

Leading Lady Louisa onto the dance floor, he drew several startled glances. Twitchell had to jab his wife in the ribs before she closed her mouth in surprise. Lady Louisa seemed not to notice. She was likely still in the schoolroom last fall, and missed his ignominious return to Society when he had walked with crutches.

He acquitted himself quite well, he thought with a touch of pride. He performed his duty during each of the waltzes, even taking his mother out on the floor once despite her laughing protests, and hovered near the gaming rooms or on the balcony in between, resting his leg. He tried to converse with his partners, he really did, but he had little patience when it came to discussing bonnet styles or the weather. At least Miss Prescott was interested in other topics, though she directed all her comments at his cravat.

The last waltz over, he made to leave, his conscience clear just as Quincy promised. He said his farewells to his hosts and headed for the door, where Mama was already waiting. The crowd surged and swirled like ocean currents, and pushed him into a woman with a thick coil of hair as black as a raven's wing. "Terribly sorry, my lady—" He felt the color drain from his face. "Lady Serena," he finished.

"Lord Sinclair, what a delightful surprise," she said, holding on to his arm longer than necessary to steady herself. She patted one of her curls into place. "I'm the Duchess of Warwick, now."

"Of course." Sinclair stared into her deceitful blue eyes, resisting the impulse to wring her delicate neck. "How is your husband the duke?"

"Not so well, I am afraid." Her full lower lip protruded and she batted her kohl-rimmed lashes. "He tires easily these days, and often retires for the night at sunset. And he is such a sound sleeper, too."

Sinclair blinked at her blatant invitation. "Sorry to hear that. Do give His Grace my regards."

"I thought you had removed to the country," Serena said, taking his arm again when he tried to move away. "I must say, you seem to have made a remarkable recovery since I saw you last." She let her gaze travel down the length of his body and back up to his eyes.

He swallowed the bile that rose in his throat. "Thank you. You must excuse me. I'm late for another appointment." He brushed her off without another word and strode for the door. Sending Mama home in the carriage, Sinclair didn't stop walking until he reached his club.

Lord Palmer and Sir Leland were already at his favorite table, with a young gentleman he didn't recognize.

"Ahoy there, Sinclair," Palmer called. "Do join us. Have you met my wife's nephew?"

"Here, here," Leland added, raising his empty glass. "You must help Alfred celebrate his birthday."

"Well, happy birthday, lad," Sinclair said, sitting down.

"Thank you, sir."

Alfred passed the bottle to him, a glass appeared at Sinclair's elbow, and he joined them in toasting Alfred's new majority status. Drowning out the image of Serena's face was a bonus.

Quincy raised her head with a start. The candles had burned low while she dozed, her head pillowed on an account book. She heard a thump again, out in the hall. She tiptoed to the door and opened it a crack. Sinclair leaned against the front door, holding his head.

"Are you all right, my lord?" she said softly, stepping into the hall.

He looked around and squinted at her in surprise. "Fine, fine," he said in a stage whisper, and waved her off. He straightened and walked toward the stairs but took two steps to the side for every three steps forward.

"Do you want me to get Harper or one of the footmen?"

"No, don't bother 'em. Brod'rick will—Oh." He sat on the third stair, his chin in his hand, with such a crestfallen look Quincy wanted to laugh. Or cry.

"Come, my lord, we can't have one of the maids finding you here in the morning." She tugged on his arm and he stood up.

"Go on with you, Quincy. I can get myself to bed." He waved her off again. The motion made him sway, and he fell backward.

Quincy caught him with a grunt. "Oh no you don't. If you fall and break your neck, I'm out of a job." His lopsided grin confirmed that she'd hidden her concern with just the right tone of impertinence. She pulled one of his arms around her shoulders, wrapped her arm around his waist, and helped him maneuver up the stairs.

She briefly wondered who was assigned front hall duty this time of night, for they should be the one allowed to help Sinclair, not her. Just then a feminine giggle reached her ears from the region of the back stairs, followed by a masculine grunt. Sinclair swayed. His body was pleasantly warm and solid against hers. Quincy gave silent thanks to the couple fooling around backstairs, wrapped her arm more firmly about Sinclair's waist, and tried not to let on how much she was enjoying the situation.

She left him leaning against the doorjamb in his room while she searched for a candle in the faint light from the fire. Before she could find one, she heard a crash behind her. Sinclair was holding the water pitcher, the washstand on its side, the basin in a dozen pieces on the floor.

"Sit, before you fall and break something else," she muttered, pushing him onto his bed.

He clutched the ewer to his chest. "I wanna wash. Feel dirty."

"That's not all you're going to feel, come morning." She pried off his left boot.

"Did you know that shame—shameless little wench had the audac—gall to invite me to her bed after she called me a cripple?"

Quincy dropped his boot with a thud. Her heart pounded. How dare someone hurt Sinclair? "Cripple?"

Sinclair nodded vigorously. "Said so last fall after I asked her to ma-marry me. Now that I can walk again, seems I'm not so un-unappealing compared to the dried-up old duke she ma-married."

Quincy closed her eyes. She wanted to gather him in her arms, cradle him to her, blot out his pain. She clenched her fists to keep from touching him. "Sounds like the shameless little wench got what she deserved." She reached for the ewer, but Sinclair grasped it tighter.

"Wash."

She sighed with mock exasperation. "All right, but I am *not* getting you a bath." She found a cloth under the washstand, dipped it in the ewer, and wrung it out. Sinclair tipped his face up, eyes closed.

Quincy's breath caught in her throat. She stared at him, his handsome features relaxed and vulnerable, painted with the soft gold light cast by the fire. She shook her head. *He's your employer, you silly twit!* She stroked the cloth over one elegant cheekbone, down to his strong jaw, across his chin. Before she could touch his full lower lip, he toppled backward. Water sloshed over his chest and the ewer rolled off to the side. She squeezed her eyes shut, taking a moment to collect herself.

"Now look what you've done," she grumbled, setting the ewer on the floor. "Probably catch your death from a chill." With the experience from tending her invalid father, she wrestled Sinclair out of his coat and waistcoat and untied the cravat she had tied just hours before.

Though the actions may have been the same as when she helped her father, her reaction to Sinclair's body was quite different. Her hands had never shaken like this, nor had her pulse been this erratic. Beneath her concern for the man and his pain lurked something deeper, stronger, more intense, than she'd ever felt before. She firmly tamped it down.

The bed sheets were dry, but Sinclair's shirt was not. Her hands still shook, but she undid the buttons and rolled him out of that, too. If her hands lingered over his warm bare skin, drifted over the corded muscles of his arms as she did so, who would know? She tossed the garments over a chair.

"Sure you don't want Brod'rick's job?"

She jumped. She raised her guilty gaze from his broad, naked chest to his face, his eyes still closed. "Quite sure. I much prefer account books to drunken lords."

He chuckled. "A hit! Tell me, Quincy, do you ever fence?"

"Only with words. Now give me your other foot."

Sinclair raised his left foot.

"Your *other* foot. I've already pulled off that boot."

"Stocking."

Quincy groaned and rested his heel against her hip while she peeled the silk stocking down his leg. Sinclair wiggled his toes, tickling her ribs. "Stop that or I'll—I'll—" Laughing, she stepped back and let his foot drop to the floor.

"You'll what?"

"I'll leave right now and make you fend for yourself, you drunken lout." Laughter softened her words.

"All right, you win. For now." He sat up. "At least pull off the other boot before you desert me."

She gripped the boot and tugged, but nothing happened.

"It's easier if you turn around." He grinned in the semi-darkness.

"Anything to get this over with." She turned around, stepped over his leg so his boot was between her knees, and tugged. Sinclair planted his bare foot on her backside and shoved. Quincy staggered forward several steps, nearly losing her balance. "Of all the dirty, rotten, low-down tricks . . ." She tossed the boot at him.

Sinclair batted it aside, laughing. "I re-rescin—take back my offer for you to replace Brod'rick." He suddenly frowned and held his stomach. "Ooh. I think I'm going to—"

Quincy yanked the chamber pot out from under the bed, but it wasn't needed. Sinclair's stomach gave a loud growl. His befuddled expression almost made her laugh. "You're not sick. Just hungry. But the kitchen staff are asleep, so you'll have to wait until morning."

Sinclair nodded and patted the bed, searching for the washcloth. Quincy retrieved it from where she'd draped it over the ewer and held it out to him. Sinclair tilted his face up, leaving his hands in his lap.

Quincy hesitated a moment, then wiped his face with the cloth, trying to make it seem impersonal, failing miserably. Realizing she was turning it into a caress, she moved on to wash his hands. His large, powerful hands, pliant and accommodating, his fingers tangling with hers.

"You being nice so I'll give you a raise in pay?" he said after several moments of quiet.

"Yes, that's it," she said brusquely. She wanted to touch him without the cloth, to do much more than hold his hand. She let it fall to the covers and tossed the cloth over her shoulder. "I'm only nice to you if I think I can gain from it. Now give me your right foot."

He raised his right leg. "How much you want?"

She thought of a suitably ridiculous figure. "Oh, fifty pounds a quarter would be nice." She peeled off his stocking.

"Done. Add it to your next pay."

Quincy snorted. "I hope you don't conduct much business in this condition." She pulled back the covers. "If you want your trousers off, you are on your own."

"This is . . . fine," Sinclair said, scooting over and lying on his side. He tucked up his legs so Quincy could cover him with the blankets, then stretched out again. "I feel much better now. Thank . . . you." His eyes closed.

"You're welcome, Benjamin," she whispered.

He snored.

Before she could stop herself, Quincy leaned over and gave him a soft kiss on his forehead.

The clock struck three. She didn't have the heart to wake the coachman, and she certainly wasn't going to walk home at this hour. Hoping Melissa and Grandmère weren't too worried, she grabbed a blanket from Broderick's cot and curled up on the library sofa.

Despite his aching head the next day, Sinclair agreed to accompany his mother on morning calls. Feigning interest in the hen party conversations, he wracked his brain to put the blurry images of last night in some semblance of order. He clearly recalled that Quincy had helped him to bed, but mixed in with the memories of her barbed comments were vague images of soft curves and gentle hands touching him. And he could swear Quincy had kissed him on the forehead, just as he was falling asleep.

Had he touched *her*? A horrible thought froze his hand with the teacup halfway to his mouth. Had he gone too far?

Thinking back, he realized he always seized every opportunity to touch her—in an avuncular, man-to-man, employer-to-employee way, of course—but he'd never crossed the line to inappropriate. His entire relationship with Quincy was inappropriate, a little voice whispered. He ignored it.

Then he remembered her derrière. At his suggestion, she'd turned around to pull his boot off, and he'd planted his foot on her backside. Just to help. Nothing unusual in that. His bare foot, on her firm, round, oh-so-feminine derrière. And he'd enjoyed it. Immensely.

Had he done anything else improper?

"Damn!"

"Benjamin!"

"Beg pardon, Mama, ladies." After an awkward pause, the chattering in Lady Bigglesworth's front parlor resumed. Lady Fitzwater and Sir Leland arrived moments later, and Sinclair had to set aside his speculations and participate in the conversation.

It seemed hours before they set home again. Once there, he headed directly for the library and took up a position on the sofa. Quincy greeted him politely, then went back to work, alternating between moving balls on the abacus and scratching in the account books. Sinclair pretended to read while he covertly observed her. She paid little attention to him, with no indication she felt uncomfortable in his presence.

Sinclair heaved a sigh of relief. He hadn't disgraced himself as a gentleman last night, fortunately. Unfortunately, he'd also been too drunk to fully appreciate the opportunity. He vaguely remembered the feel, but it had been too dark to see . . .

Sinclair strolled over to the desk and reached for a pencil, startling Quincy. He leaned a little closer to his secretary than absolutely necessary, and watched the blush stain her cheeks and disappear below her collar. She turned a delightful shade of pink as she smiled uncertainly at him.

Dazzled by her smile, he accidentally dropped the pencil, and it rolled several feet away. "Would you please get that?"

"Of course, my lord." Quincy scooted sideways from him before standing up, then walked over to the pencil and bent over to pick it up. Giving in to an imp of mischief, Sinclair unabashedly paid close attention as Quincy's coattails separated, revealing her subtly rounded, distinctly feminine, backside.

He quickly raised his gaze when she turned around. Her blush deepened even further, but she gamely held out the pencil to him. He almost forgot to take it. Sinclair opened his mouth to speak, changed his mind, and returned to the sofa.

He watched her frown as she deciphered a poorly written bill of sale, her concentration focused on her work once more. He could have sat and watched her all day if Mama had not summoned him upstairs to consult on household matters.

Later that afternoon, Harper tapped on his bedchamber door. "Come in," Sinclair said, eyeing the butler's reflection in the mirror as he tied a fresh cravat.

Harper cleared his throat. "I don't know quite how to say this, my lord. I have the highest respect for him, I assure you, but, ah . . ."

"Spit it out, man," Sinclair said, ripping off his wrinkled cravat and reaching for another.

"Well. It being quarter day and all, Mr. Quincy paid the staff this morning, but, ah . . ."

"Yes?" The ends of his cravat dangling, Sinclair faced the butler.

"I'm afraid he overpaid everyone," Harper finished in a rush.

Sinclair cocked one eyebrow. "Overpaid?"

"Yes. Mrs. Hammond and Matilda seemed surprised when they came from the library, as well."

"Thank you, Harper. I'll look into the matter." Sinclair returned to tying his cravat, and frowned at his reflection.

An hour later he strode into the library. "I understand that yours is a generous nature, but I wish you would have asked my permission first."

"Permission for what?" Quincy replied, looking up from the stack of mail.

"Harper told me you overpaid the staff this morning. I hadn't planned to give them another raise until Michaelmas."

"Raise?" Quincy shook her head. "I paid no one any additional salary, only what was recorded in the . . ." Their gaze locked.

"Johnson!" they said in unison.

"Blast that embezzling snake!" Sinclair slammed his fist on the desk. "Last year I instructed him to raise everyone's pay, and he recorded it in the account books."

"And pocketed the difference." Quincy chewed on the tip

of her pencil. Sinclair dropped onto the sofa. Several minutes passed as he fumed.

"Such a deception had not occurred to me," Quincy interrupted the silence. "But now that it has, I can think of several other ways he might have dipped into your pockets. I've started examining the books for your other properties, and—"

"Beg pardon," Harper said, opening the door. "There's a young woman insisting she speak to Mr. Quincy. She says it's urgent, so I—"

Quincy darted out the door before he finished the sentence.

A few seconds later, she dashed back in and grabbed her coat and hat. She paused at the door to look back at Sinclair. "My grand . . . um . . . that is—I have to go." She dashed out again before Sinclair could say a word, leaving the earl and the butler staring, dumbstruck.

Chapter 10

Quincy and Melinda ran through the streets toward their flat.

"I'm sorry, Jo, but I didn't know what else to do," Melinda said, wiping away a tear.

"It's all right, Mel, you did the right thing." Quincy bounded up the stairs two at a time. "Mrs. Linley?" she called, entering the flat.

Their landlady looked up from her needlework by the window. "She'll be fine, lad. The apothecary is with her now." She pointed at the closed bedchamber door with her needle.

Quincy paced. Melinda arrived, breathless and coughing, and fell into step with her. Finally the door opened.

"Your grandmum's lucky she didn't break her bloomin' neck instead of just her ankle," the apothecary said, stepping out. He gave a series of instructions, handed Quincy a bottle of laudanum, and collected his fee. "I'll stop back in a se'nnight. She should be able to walk about with a cane in a few weeks. See that she stays off her feet 'til then." He tipped his hat and left.

Quincy had barely absorbed the instructions when Mrs. Linley stood up. "You two will be all right, won't you?" she said, gathering up her work. "I left some bread baking."

"Fine, fine," Quincy said absently as she headed to her grandmother's bedside.

Quincy was struck by how frail her grandmother appeared. The old woman who barely raised the blankets had been her anchor through the years as Quincy had lost first her mother and newborn brother, then her father. Grandmère was all the family she and Melinda had left. After glancing at the heavily bandaged right foot, she knelt beside the bed and clasped a wrinkled hand.

"Jo? About time you came home. Where have you been?"

Quincy gave a watery smile. "I'll forego asking how you feel." She stared at the rapidly coloring bruise on Grandmère's temple, and touched the fading bruise on her own forehead.

"Oh, no, you cannot do that. You must give me a valid excuse to catalog my aches and pains. Which at the moment are fading quickly, I might add. That whippersnapper may have cold hands, but he was generous with the laudanum." She wiped a tear from Quincy's cheek. "Now, while I'm still sensible, I want to know where you were all night, miss."

Quincy cleared her throat, seeing an image of Sinclair's face in his bedchamber last night, first when he'd tilted it up to her, then as he fell asleep. "At Sinclair's town house. All day, and all night. I slept on the sofa in the library."

"I did not think the earl was a harsh taskmaster."

She shook her head. "That's not it at all. There were several commotions that prevented me from getting my work done, so I stayed late to catch up. I fell asleep at my desk."

"And does the earl know of your dedication?" Grandmère hid a yawn behind her hand.

"I doubt he remembers." She was spared having to explain the cryptic remark, as Grandmère exhaled on a gentle snore.

With the crisis past, Quincy's hands began to tremble, and she indulged in a brief moment of abject fear. How could she and Mel survive without Grandmère? They needed her affection, her guidance, her connection to their past. So much had already been taken from them. Another loss would shatter them.

But this was no time to indulge in hysterics. She took deep, calming breaths, in time with Grandmère's snores, and soon regained her composure. She had to be strong.

"How is she?" Melinda crept into the room behind her.

"Sleeping." Quincy rose and lead her sister to the hearth. She filled the kettle for tea. "How did this happen?"

"I'm not sure." Melinda toyed with the fringe on her shawl. "We were going to take some finished work to Madame Chantel's, then go to market. I reached the bottom of the stairs first and stopped to say good day to Hubert— Mrs. Linley's son—when I heard thumps and groans and suddenly there was Grandmère, at the bottom of the stairs." Her face went white at the memory. "At first I thought she was . . . but then she—she . . ."

"What?"

"She cursed."

Quincy chuckled.

"Hubert and Mrs. Linley helped me carry her upstairs, then I ran to fetch the apothecary, and then you." Her hands trembled.

Quincy reached out to cover her sister's hands with her own. "You did just fine, Mel."

"I was so frightened!" Mel flung herself into Quincy's arms. "We've lost so much already, I don't think I could bear it if anything happened to you or Grandmère."

Quincy held her sister as she sobbed, and stroked her back and shoulders. "Yes, you could. You're stronger than you know. God willing, though, you won't have to prove it anytime soon."

They stood that way for several moments, waiting for Mel's breathing to return to normal. While Quincy gladly provided the shoulder for Mel to cry on, she wondered if she'd ever have someone to offer that comfort to her.

She banished the foolish notion. Quincy cried on no one's shoulder. Not since the day her mother died after giving birth to a still-born boy. Papa had been too bereft to offer comfort, and Quincy had not wanted to add to Grandmère's burden.

She brewed a pot of chamomile tea, and they sat down to discuss practical matters. Sir Ambrose stirred from his bed by the fire and jumped onto her lap. His warm, soft purring body was even more soothing than the tea, and helped her gather her scrambled thoughts. She scratched behind his ears, feeling more in control again as she and Mel considered their options.

First they needed to reorganize the division of household chores. Melinda usually washed clothes and fetched water, but Grandmère had done the food shopping. Until her broken ankle healed, getting her up and down two flights of stairs would be a major undertaking.

"Maybe we should find a ground-floor flat?"

Quincy glanced around at the heavy oak table, mahogany bureau and wardrobe, all leftovers from better times, and shook her head. "We can't afford to hire a carter again, and there's no way we can move these pieces by ourselves. If they didn't mean so much to Grandmère, I'd have sold them, too."

Mel reluctantly agreed. "Keeping them is more important to her than a few months of inconvenience." She took a deep breath. "There's still the problem of getting her to church."

Quincy groaned.

"Maybe we could get the vicar to come here for services?"

Quincy swallowed the last of her tea. "She's going to feel like a prisoner up here."

"Can we spare enough money to buy a Bath chair? Then she could at least move about the flat on her own."

"Possibly." Her stomach grumbled. "I take it since the two of you were on your way to market, there's nothing here for dinner?" Melinda nodded. Quincy sighed. "Fetch me the basket, and I'll drop off your work at Madame Chantel's, and go to market. And look for a chair."

After dinner, they took turns sitting up with Grandmère through the night. Once she woke up from a nightmare about her fall, feeling guilty and worried about almost leaving Mel and Jo alone in the world. Her ankle pained her so she took another dose of laudanum—not enough to put her to sleep but enough to make her maudlin.

Reluctantly, Quincy reminisced with Grandmère in the early morning hours, delving into painful memories, re-opening old wounds. How many more times would they discuss her mother and newborn brother, wondering if anything could have been done to prevent their deaths? Might Papa still be alive if his weak heart had not been dealt such a harsh blow? Would have, could have, should have.

Quincy must have dozed off, for she suddenly found Grandmère staring at her, her eyes bright.

"Life is precious, *ma chère*. Have I taught you that?"

"*Oui*, Grandmère." She patted her grandmother's hand, as much to reassure the old woman as to make certain she wasn't dreaming.

"Precious, and sometimes much too short. You must wring as much joy from it as you can."

Quincy blinked.

"Fate conspired against my son, against my family, but gave me one as strong as you. I know what you sacrificed for us, *ma chère*." She reached up to stroke Quincy's hair. "These men, these English fops, they would condemn you for what you've done, but I understand. Josephine became Joseph. With your sacrifice, you saved us."

Her gnarled hand gripped Quincy's, surprisingly firm, her gaze unwavering, adding a dose of reality to the strange conversation.

"But you don't have to give up everything, *ma chère*. Just remember what I've taught you. You take whatever bit of happiness you can find. *Carpe diem*. Do you understand?" She reached one shaking hand to cup Quincy's cheek. "I won't condemn you for getting what you need."

Quincy could only stare in stupefaction. Grandmère had just given her carte blanche . . . for something. Before she could ask for clarification, Grandmère snored.

"That's it on the left, my lord," Elliott said as the coach stopped, pointing to a three-story structure that tilted like the Tower of Pisa. "I seen him go up the stairs, but I ain't sure which one Mr. Quincy lives in."

Sinclair exited the coach and stared around him in dismay. The neighborhood was a step above squalor, but barely. His worry about Quincy's abrupt departure yesterday had increased tenfold when she hadn't shown up for work this morning. And this is what she came home to every night? He straightened his shoulders and swung his walking stick. "Walk the horses, Elliott." Ignoring the stares of the children playing in the street and the men sitting in the doorways, he strode to the indicated building.

A blowzy woman on the ground floor, hanging laundry from the underside of the steps, gave him directions. Breathing through his mouth, Sinclair climbed the stairs, skipping a step here and there where slop buckets had spilled.

The third-floor landing was swept clean. He knocked on the door of number seven, then bent down to scratch behind the ears of an enormous gray tabby stretched out in the doorway. It purred its appreciation.

"Yes?" The young woman with brown pigtails who answered the door looked down at him in surprise and suddenly went pale.

"I'm here to see Mr. Quincy." Sinclair straightened and took off his hat.

She gulped and bobbed a curtsy, then stepped aside to let him in. "Please be seated, my lord," she said, pointing to the table and chairs. She started across the room, looked back at him over her shoulder, grinned, and ran to the bedchamber door. "Jo!" she called softly. "You're never going to believe who's here . . ." The rest was lost as she closed the door behind her.

Sinclair sat on a chair at the table, noticing the faint aroma of lemon. He glanced around the tidy, tiny room. One wall was dominated by a heavy wardrobe and bureau, similar to his mother's at home. A gilt-framed portrait of a young couple in wedding attire hung above the fireplace. Crude shelves and wooden crates stacked near the hearth held cooking utensils and food stuffs, and an overflowing work basket leaned against a leather wingback chair by the window. Just how far had Quincy and her family fallen? His thoughts were rudely interrupted as a large ball of fur hurled itself onto his lap.

"Sir Ambrose! Get down!" Quincy said, emerging from the bedchamber. The cat on Sinclair's lap flipped his tail in reply and settled more comfortably across the earl's knees. Sinclair bit back a grin as his secretary stared at him and the cat in horror, a blush staining her cheeks. Quincy cleared her throat. "Good morning, my lord." She stole a glance at the clock on the mantel and gasped. "Terribly sorry. Had no idea it was so late."

"Rough night?" Sinclair said pleasantly, stroking the cat. Its purr vibrated through his thighs, a delightful sensation in a limb more accustomed to feeling pain. He watched Quincy roll down her sleeves. Except for her missing coat and cravat, she wore the same clothes as when she bolted from the library the previous afternoon. But yesterday there hadn't been dark shadows under her eyes. Today they were puffy and red.

Quincy nodded and sat across from him at the table, buttoning her cuffs with trembling fingers. "My grandmother fell down the stairs. That's why Mel came to fetch me."

Sinclair quickly covered Quincy's hands with one of his own. "She survived?"

"Yes, thank heaven. I don't know how we'd go on without her." Quincy stared at their enjoined hands. Sinclair gave her fingers a reassuring squeeze before reluctantly pulling free. "She sustained a few bruises and broke her right ankle. She's sleeping now, after being awake most of the night. If you give me a few moments to wash and change clothes, I can be ready to—"

"You must have a low opinion of me indeed if you think I expect you to work today." Sinclair winced as Sir Ambrose dug in his claws for purchase and rearranged himself into a more comfortable position. "I'm here because of a mistake you made with the payroll." He bit back another grin as Quincy went pale.

"Mistake?"

Sinclair pulled a large, heavy purse out of his pocket and set it on the table with a satisfying *clink*. "You didn't pay yourself your fifty-pound raise."

Quincy's jaw dropped. A muffled gasp behind the bedchamber door reminded him they had an audience.

"I was not serious about the raise, and I certainly did not believe you were. Indeed, I imagined you wouldn't even—"

"Remember agreeing to it? I'm shocked. You underestimate my capacity for conducting business under, shall we say, less than ideal conditions."

"You were disguised." Quincy folded her arms.

"A trifle castaway."

She rolled her eyes. "Foxed."

Sinclair shrugged. "I've developed quite a tolerance for drink in the past year or so. You'd be surprised."

"Regardless, I cannot accept this. It's—"

"Well deserved," Sinclair interrupted. "You've saved me many times this amount in the few weeks you've worked for me. If not for yourself, accept it for your family. Buy your sister a new frock and have a surgeon examine your grandmother's ankle. Who did you have in already, an apothecary?"

Quincy took a deep breath and let it out slowly. "Yes, but I'm sure—"

"We would be happy to accept it," Melinda said, closing the bedchamber door. She snatched the purse from the table and dropped it into her apron pocket. "Thank you, my lord. You cannot know how much this means to us, especially now that we need to buy a Bath chair."

Quincy sighed. "I suppose the matter is settled." She suddenly sat up straight. "Where are my manners? Lord Sinclair, my sister, Melinda."

Melinda bobbed another curtsy. Sinclair nodded. "Pleased to make your acquaintance, Miss Quincy." She blushed. "We're agreed, then." Sinclair stood up, released Sir Ambrose's grip on his trousers and set the cat on the floor, and futilely tried to brush the cat hair from his lap. "I'll expect you back on Monday. Unless you need more time with your grandmother?"

"Thank you, my lord, that should be more than enough, I think," Quincy said, rising to walk with him to the door. "I appreciate your kindness."

Sinclair clapped her on the shoulder. "Nonsense. I'm only kind when I think I can benefit from it." With a chuckle and a wink, he left.

Any qualms or doubts Sinclair might have harbored about keeping Josephine Quincy on as his secretary vanished as soon as he'd crossed the threshold. With this new crisis, it would be nothing short of outright cruelty to send her packing now.

Nothing need change as long as no one else knew her real identity. They'd continue working together, just as any other employer and employee. Sinclair descended the steps, his spirits light.

Melinda stared at the closed door, her hand wrapped around the coin purse, and chewed her bottom lip. Quincy rummaged through the crates for something to eat. She unwrapped the towel from last night's bread, ripped off a chunk and spread jelly on it. She froze when Mel spoke.

"Jo, he knows who you are."

Quincy frowned. "What do you mean . . ." Her eyes widened. "Oh, heavens, no." She sat down heavily in the chair. Sir Ambrose jumped up on the table and began to lick the jelly off the bread in her limp hand. She had dreaded something like this. It was one thing to omit the little detail that Sinclair knew her secret, but to outright *lie* to her family? If Mel knew, soon Grandmère would, too. Grandmère would insist she leave Sinclair. Her stomach clenched.

"It's all right, though, because I think he likes you."

Perhaps she wouldn't be forced to choose to lie. Quincy tore off little pieces and fed it to the purring feline, glancing at her sister from the corner of her eye. "Of course he likes me. Otherwise he would have fired me."

"No, I mean he *likes* you." Melinda poured tea for both of them and sat down.

Quincy froze. "What makes you think that?"

"He touched you. Not just once, but twice." Mel sipped

her tea. "Perhaps I'm wrong and he doesn't know." Quincy brightened. "Then that means he likes *Joseph*."

Quincy groaned and dropped her head to the table. The clock struck the hour, and Quincy sat up. "What a coil." She swept Sir Ambrose into her arms and hugged him to her chest.

"But if he likes *you*—Josephine, that is—then there is no problem at all. Marry him, and Grandmère and I can live at one of his estates in the country." Melinda smiled over the rim of her teacup. "You can go back to being a girl, and won't have to dress and work like a man to take care of us, ever again."

Quincy's heart fluttered. "Now you're being absurd." Sinclair could never be interested in marrying her. Even if he did want to court her, which was impossible, it would cause a ruinous scandal. Lady Sinclair would go back to being a recluse, and as for Sinclair . . . Quincy couldn't allow that to happen. She wouldn't.

She let Sir Ambrose climb up and drape himself over her shoulder. "Besides, I think you're rushing your fences. Sinclair is very busy, and his younger brother has been at Oxford since the Christmas holidays. Perhaps he's just lonely." She sipped her tea. "Yes, that must be it. I don't pressure him to marry, as his mother does. I don't ask him for advice or favors, like his friends, or break the china, like the servants. I am simply there, doing whatever needs to be done. I tell him when he's being kind, like with the maids-in-training. Or when he's being an ass."

"Jo!"

"Pardon. But you know what I mean. It's simply . . . friendship. Yes, friendship. That's all you saw, Mel." That's all it could be. Her sister still didn't look convinced. Quincy shrugged and yawned. "It's your turn to sit with Grandmère. I'm going to take a nap. Wake me after two o'clock, and I'll start shopping for a Bath chair. We're going to need one soon, if we're to preserve Grandmère's sanity. Not to mention our own."

The remainder of the week dragged by for Sinclair. He was loathe to admit it, but he missed his no-nonsense secretary's company. In the short time they'd been acquainted, he'd come to rely on Quincy's opinion more than anyone else's, even over his friends of long-standing, Sir Leland and Lord Palmer.

Though correspondence piled up and tradesmen's bills arrived uninterrupted, Sinclair left them stacked on his desk, untouched. It would take Quincy days to catch up, but Sinclair needed to concentrate on the papers sent over by his solicitor. Perhaps he'd offer her a treat to make up for the unexpected workload. She already had a full dish, as head of her family. Twice Sinclair thought about going over to see how they got on, but could think of no excuses that didn't sound flimsy even to his own ears.

One bit of business he did attend to was meeting with Mr. Wooten, the Bow Street Runner. The group of thieves had since abandoned the warehouse where Quincy and Thompson had been assaulted, but Wooten had caught up to them. Six men now awaited trial on various charges. Sinclair gladly paid the runner's fee. Much as he wished he could bash the thieves in the head for having hurt Quincy, he'd have to rely on the courts for justice.

At least the pleasant weather held, and Sinclair's leg ached less than usual. He suffered through two more balls, and vowed never to attend two in a row again. They weren't total disasters, however. He decided to further his acquaintance with Miss Mary and Lady Louisa, and with Miss Prescott. She offered the most intelligent conversation of the three, but still couldn't look up past his neckcloth. It seemed absurd to converse with the rosebuds or pearls threaded through her red curls, but no one else appeared to notice.

The tedium of the social schedule was eased by the progress Mama was making. The viscount who'd been her dinner companion at the Stanhopes was also her dance partner at least once at each event they both attended. And Mama had worn a green gown to the last ball.

Monday morning dawned at last. Sinclair found himself awake earlier than usual, eager to breakfast and head to his library. Quincy was already hard at work when he entered.

"Good morning, my lord," she offered, her pencil scratching in a ledger.

"Isn't it, though?" Sinclair said, throwing open the window by Quincy's desk. "The birds are chirping, the sun is shining, my mother is occupied with someone's business other than mine . . ."

Quincy chuckled. "Just so long as you don't burst into song."

"Never that." He took a deep breath of the crisp air. "Unless of course I'm three sheets to the wind, or in the company of those who are." He patted her shoulder before he sank into his leather chair and propped his feet on one corner of the desk. "How is your grandmother?"

Quincy put her pencil down and reached for the abacus. "Much improved. She refuses any more laudanum, so she's awake and alert, and chafing at her inactivity. Who would have guessed she'd miss arguing with the butcher and greengrocer?"

It was Sinclair's turn to chuckle. He sorted through the morning mail, listening to the *chlock, chlock* of Quincy adding figures on the abacus. "Are you free Wednesday evening?" Sinclair asked when she stopped to record a figure.

She raised her brows, then quickly schooled her features to a neutral expression. "Yes."

"Good. I'll need you to stay late, and help me with a special project." Knowing curiosity was going to drive Quincy fair to distraction, Sinclair smiled, settled back in his chair, and said not another word about it for two days.

By Wednesday afternoon, Quincy was ready to strangle Sinclair. The obnoxious man had said nothing more about the mysterious special project, and this morning had not even bothered to confirm that she'd stay late as he'd asked.

Oh, who was she fooling? Of course she'd stay. She'd do anything he asked. Drat him.

Late in the day, when she would normally clear her desk prior to going home, Sinclair rose from the sofa and headed for the door. "Stay," was all he said, waving his finger at her.

"Woof," she muttered as soon as the door closed behind

him. She could continue trying to catch up, but her thoughts kept drifting to wondering what the earl had in mind for this evening. Her palms grew damp.

Better to distract herself by thinking of other ways Johnson might have stolen money. Sinclair's holdings were extensive, with a country estate, smaller properties scattered around the kingdom, and a large portfolio of investments in the Exchange. If she were Johnson, how might she go about trying to line her pockets with the earl's coin?

She looked up with a guilty start as the library door swung open and Grimshaw entered, pushing a cart laden with covered dishes. Sinclair was right behind, practically vibrating with energy as the footman fidgeted with arranging the silverware and removing the covers.

"Thank you, Grimshaw, we'll serve ourselves," Sinclair said.

The footman bowed and left.

Quincy could only gape at Sinclair.

He pulled two chairs up to the cart. "Dinner is served, my lady," he said with a courtly bow. Warmth surged through her at his words, and gesture. Mouth-watering aromas reached her. "It's getting cold," he prompted.

She couldn't resist a smile as she took the indicated chair. He sat down across from her and they filled their plates. Roast chicken, cod, potatoes, asparagus, peas with tiny onions . . . more food than she usually saw in a week. She dug in.

As Mr. Quincy, she didn't have to pretend to have the birdlike appetite of a debutante, but she didn't want to make a pig of herself. After a taste of everything, her thoughts drifted back to the plans for the evening. "About your special project, my lord . . ."

"First we must fortify ourselves." He ate another forkful of fish.

That did nothing to ease her trepidation. "Aren't you concerned the staff will think this odd?" Her gesture encompassed the cart, the two of them, and the lit candles, as twilight cast shadows in the room.

He sipped his wine. "How often have they served you in here?"

She cocked her head to one side. "True, but you're not usually present. Except when they bring the tea tray."

"Yes, been eating entirely too many biscuits since hiring you." He patted her hand. "At ease. They think Mr. Quincy is staying late to catch up after being absent a few days. Ogre that I am, I'm overseeing your progress." He picked up his fork and gestured for her to do the same.

She obediently ate another bite. "Don't you have to escort your mother somewhere?"

He shot her an exasperated look. "She's spending the evening with friends. I wished her good night and personally helped her into the carriage before I summoned dinner. Now will you hush up and eat?"

She ducked her head to hide her smile, and returned to the food before it got cold. They chatted about inconsequential topics, like the respite from the rain, the delicious food, how Sinclair had lured the cook away from Palmer's household with the bait of a new closed stove.

Lulled by his boyish charm, Quincy relaxed and let him refill her wineglass. She shouldn't let him fill it again, but watching his hand curve around the bottle, she couldn't remember why.

At last she sat back, patting her mouth with the napkin. How could just the two of them have possibly eaten all that food? Sinclair retrieved a tray from under the cart. With a flourish, he removed the cover to reveal a platter of apple puffs.

She groaned. "How did you know I can resist any temptation but apple puffs?"

He flashed her a wicked smile. "I'll remember that for future reference."

She refused to eat a whole puff by herself, so Sinclair cut one in half while she searched the cart for clean dessert plates. There was only one. Just as Quincy was going to ring for a servant to bring more, Sinclair shook his head. He scooted his chair around the corner of the cart, closer to hers. She did the same, until they sat so close their knees touched.

"We'll just have to make do," he said, sliding both halves of the puff onto one plate. They each ate their half of the dessert, sharing the plate and an intimate smile.

When there was nothing left but crumbs, Sinclair replaced the covers. "I could never do this with Miss Quincy, you know."

She smoothed the napkin over her lap. "I expected to be her again by now." Had she actually said that out loud? She sat up straight.

"What happened?" He rested his arm along the back of her chair, turning toward her. "Or should I say, what didn't happen?"

"What didn't happen was my wedding. On June nineteen." That was it—no more wine for her.

"The day after Waterloo? Was he killed?"

She shook her head and pushed up her spectacles. "Nigel and I had an understanding, since I was ten and he fourteen. If nobody came along who made our hearts flutter, we'd marry each other when I came of age and he completed his schooling."

He topped off their wineglasses. "So it was an arrangement, not love."

"Hardly love at first sight when one drops a frog down the other's neck at their first meeting."

"That was uncalled for."

"What else could I do? He had insulted Mel."

Sinclair choked on his wine. "Should have seen that one coming," he murmured. Louder, he continued, "So you progressed from assault with a frog to planning to get leg-shackled?"

Quincy nodded. "We became co-conspirators for all the mischief in the neighborhood, and exchanged letters when he was sent off to Harrow and then Oxford." She took another sip. "I'm very forward, you know," she confided as an aside. "Last May, he secured a position as a clerk at the Home Office, and came to visit me in Danbury. It was the first time he'd seen me since I cut my hair short and gave up wearing dresses. He was . . . taken aback." He'd actually stared at her in horror for a full five minutes, but Quincy didn't think Sinclair needed to know that. "Of course I had told him in my letters what I'd done, but—"

"Seeing the reality was something else entirely." Sinclair leaned one elbow on the cart, no hint of judgment in his posture or expression.

She could get accustomed to being the center of Sinclair's attention. "Nigel tried to adjust, to adapt, and I think he would have, in time, but he was so new on the job. I told him I had planned all along to go back to being a girl, but he worried he'd lose his position if word got out about what I'd done before we married. He's the fourth son of a viscount, has to make his own way in the world. He couldn't afford a scandalous wife."

"Bastard."

She couldn't have heard him right. "This is why I drink tea instead of wine," she said, pointing an accusing finger at him. "Even Grandmère and Mel don't know about Nigel." She gave him a playful jab to the shoulder. "It's only fair that you confess something."

His brow furrowed in a frown while he thought. He scanned the room, now shrouded in deep shadows, the sun having set while they ate. "Hiring you was the second most impulsive act of my life."

She was stunned by the intense expression in his brown eyes, the honesty she saw there. She toyed with her napkin. "Which begs the question, what was the first?"

He hesitated long enough, she doubted he'd answer. "Buying my colors to join the army."

She leaned toward him. "I've often wondered about that, since you did so *after* inheriting the title."

He shrugged. "I couldn't fight the gossips, so I ran off to fight Napoleon." He tossed his napkin on the cart.

It seemed that was the extent of the confession he was willing to make. No, she wouldn't let him get away with that, not after she'd spilled her guts about Nigel. She waved her hand in an "and so . . ." gesture, made encouraging noises.

Sinclair grimaced, but then relented. "Ancient history.

There was a bit of a scandal after Papa's death. Gossips said I killed his rival, the previous Lord Twitchell. With my bare hands." He shot her a look that dared her to be frightened.

A shiver coursed through her, but it had nothing to do with fear. "When has gossip ever been accurate?"

Sinclair seemed pleased with her response. The mantel clock chimed the hour. He stood. "Carriage should be here any moment. Do you have a pair of white gloves?"

"No." She stood also. They were close enough she had to tilt her head back to see him.

"Thought not. I'll loan you one of mine." He held his hand up to Quincy's, touching his larger, calloused palm to her smaller hand. "They'll be loose, but will serve propriety."

Quincy raised her gaze from where their palms touched, up to his face. The air around them seemed to crackle, like just before a lightning storm. He curled his fingers over hers. His lips were parted, his head tilted toward hers. For one heart-stopping moment she thought he would bend down and kiss her. She could tug on his hand, pull him down to her. Or he could pull her off balance, make her fall into his arms. She couldn't breathe.

They heard a knock on the door. They sprang apart, hands dropping to their sides.

"The carriage is ready, my lord," Harper said.

Sinclair nodded, and the butler retreated. "Here," he said, pulling a pair of white gloves out of his coat pocket. "You'd better put these on now."

She felt the weight of his hand against the small of her back as he guided her toward the door. She couldn't see his face, but felt sure her own was bright red. If they wanted to avoid scandal, letting the butler catch the earl kissing his secretary was not the way to go about it.

She tugged the gloves on, still warm from being in Sinclair's pocket, and was almost breathing normally again by the time they stepped out into the hall.

Chapter 11

Quincy followed Sinclair out to his waiting carriage and climbed into the dim interior. She fell back against the squabs next to Sinclair as Elliott started the horses. She ought to move to the empty seat. The evening was already cool, and she felt the warmth radiating from his body only a few inches from her own. She ought to move.

She stayed. Though having his bulk beside her held an element of risk, of the forbidden, it was just too pleasant to pass up. Couldn't she just enjoy the moment, with no thought for what the future might hold?

She glanced out the window. Carriages drove past in the opposite direction, streetlamps alternately revealing and hiding the crests on the doors. Sinclair's carriage door bore his family crest, too. Here she sat, beside an earl of the realm. What business did she have going with him?

In the intimacy of the dark carriage, Quincy struggled not to fidget. Finally she could stand the quiet no more. "Now can we discuss your special project?"

Sinclair scratched his jaw. "Tonight actually has two purposes. One, I wanted to offer you a treat. You've worked very hard, doubly so since your grandmother's accident. And two . . ." He shifted his walking stick to his other hand.

"Yes?"

He moved his stick back to its original position. "As I said Monday, I want your help with a special project. I need someone to give me an intelligent, forthright opinion. Someone who doesn't have anything at stake to color their view."

"Sounds intriguing. Opinion on what?"

"Selecting my wife."

Quincy drew a quick, deep breath. He wanted her to help him choose a wife? A simple intellectual exercise in logic. An intelligent, forthright opinion, he said. Simple. So why did her stomach suddenly twist into knots?

"I've shocked you speechless? You disappoint me, Quincy."

She cleared her throat. "Not at all. I was just, ah, considering suitable candidates."

"Good. I knew I could count on you."

The carriage rolled on in the darkness.

"You still have not told me where we're going."

"That's because I want it to be a surprise." He sat back against the cushions and hummed a tune.

Quincy folded her hands in her lap to diminish the temptation to wrap them around his throat. When he started whistling, she grit her teeth. Her jaw ached by the time the carriage stopped again. She glanced out the window, and her mouth dropped open. "Drury Lane!" she exclaimed when she'd recovered. "Oh, Sinclair, this is marvelous! I take back all the horrible things I've been wishing on your head for the past half hour."

Sinclair chuckled. "I remember what you said about not wanting me to ruin the theater for you. Will this suffice, do you think?"

"Perfect." After the steps were let down and she stood on the sidewalk, she stuffed her hands in her pockets to keep from throwing her arms around the earl. "Very practical, too. We can satisfy my curiosity about the performing arts, *and* look about for your wife." Some sweet to go with the bitter.

"Just as I planned."

Quincy followed Sinclair in, eyeing the throng of brightly dressed ladies with their escorts littering the lobby. A glance at the low-cut gowns that threatened to spill feminine charms gave Quincy new appreciation for her own multilayered clothing. Seeing several gentlemen wearing coats similar to hers, she realized Melissa had unerringly patterned her clothes after the ton's more conservative styles.

Relaxing in the knowledge that she didn't look out of place, and confident in her masculine mannerisms and disguise, Quincy resolved to enjoy the evening to the fullest. She paid close attention to everyone Sinclair stopped to greet or who stopped him, particularly the females.

Some were pretty, most were prettily behaved, and a few showed enough obvious wealth to cancel out any losses caused by Sinclair's previous secretary. But none seemed quite right. None of them deserved to be Sinclair's countess.

Quincy almost stumbled as the enormity of that last thought struck her. How could she come to that ridiculous conclusion? Her employer had asked for her help with an important project. She couldn't let him down.

At last they reached Sinclair's box.

"Mama, I did not know you were coming tonight!"

"Obviously." Lady Sinclair smiled at them, not quite hiding her surprise at seeing Quincy. A silver-haired gentleman sat beside her, and two other couples filled the remaining chairs in the box.

Quincy glanced about, realizing there was no place left to sit. They'd have to leave. She held her chin high, determined not to reveal her disappointment.

"Sinclair, well met!" called out a voice.

The earl turned toward the entrance. "Leland, what marvelous timing. I was just trying to figure out how to seat all of us, and now you can save me the trouble. Or do you have a box full of guests, too?"

"Not at all, come right along. Evening, Lady Sinclair, ladies, gentlemen." He sketched a brief bow and hurried out as the curtain lifted on the beginning of the farce on stage.

Sinclair left without another word. Quincy glanced back

at Lady Sinclair, who gave her a small, private smile. She bowed toward her and ran after Sinclair and his one-eyed friend.

Sir Leland did have other guests, as it turned out. She exchanged greetings with Lord Palmer, and was introduced to Lord Alfred, a quiet redhead. Alfred immediately returned his attention to the stage, but Leland and Palmer both shot her sidelong glances throughout the evening, making her stomach flutter. Had she or Sinclair said or done something to give them away at lunch the other day, after all?

The farce on stage was a farce within itself. Actors stumbled over their lines, tripped over stage props, and bumped into each other. After several tedious minutes, Quincy shifted her attention to the audience, especially those seated in the boxes across the way.

"See anyone who catches your fancy?" Sinclair whispered in her ear.

Gooseflesh raised all over her. "For me or for you?" she whispered back, feeling bold in the semi-darkness.

Sinclair laughed heartily. Fortunately, so did the rest of the audience just then. "See the blond miss in pink directly across from us?"

"The one who keeps patting her curls?"

"Yes. She's Lady Louisa. What do you think?"

"Vain."

"Probably right. How about the brunette three boxes over to the right? That's Miss Mary."

Quincy squinted. "Seated between the two giants?"

"Her parents."

"Mousy. Once away from those behemoths, she will probably overcompensate. Not a good bet."

"That leaves Miss Prescott. Ah, there she is, two boxes over to the left."

"Very equitable of you, selecting a blonde, a brunette and a redhead."

"I thought it only appropriate. Miss Prescott has you to thank for being included on the list, by the way. A wallflower, you know." He paused, waiting for the crowd's burst of laughter to die down. "Well, do you think she'll do?"

"Do? I can't tell. I haven't even met the chit yet."

"You were certainly quick to dismiss the other two without meeting them!"

"That was different."

"Hush!" Sir Leland glared at them.

Quincy lowered her voice, and Sinclair bent closer to her ear. "They had obvious flaws. I'll have to meet Miss Prescott to determine hers."

His lips brushed her ear when he spoke. "You mean determine *if* she has flaws, don't you?"

Quincy blinked. "Yes, of course that's what I meant." Miss Prescott would probably make an ideal countess, as would the other two she'd dismissed so quickly. Admirable countesses, in fact. But for some other earl.

· Another woman near Miss Prescott caught Quincy's attention. She seemed familiar, but in the poor light Quincy couldn't place where she knew her from. "Who is the raven-haired lady in the box next to Miss Prescott? She keeps trying to catch your eye."

Sinclair stiffened. "Lady Serena, now Duchess of Warwick. Pay her no attention. God knows I try not to."

She couldn't stop herself from touching his arm in a gesture of sympathy. "The 'shameless little wench'?"

Sinclair looked shocked, then relaxed. "The very same."

They settled back as the curtain rose on *Much Ado About Nothing*. The actors performed well, allowing her to enjoy the Bard's work. Being able to share smiles with Sinclair at the funny bits made it even better.

At the conclusion, Sinclair and Quincy parted company with the other gentlemen in the box and threaded their way through the crowd in the lobby. Still chuckling from the performance on stage, they made slow progress, and frequently halted altogether as acquaintances greeted the earl. Quincy stayed close behind him, almost grabbing his coattails as the surging crowd threatened to separate them.

"Lord Sinclair, we meet again," a female voice declared. Sinclair stopped so abruptly, Quincy bumped her nose against his back. He stood ramrod straight, exuding all the haughtiness of an old title.

"Good evening, Duchess," he said, his voice cold.

A chance to see the shameless wench up close! The foolish woman who spurned Sinclair's proposal.

Rubbing her sore nose, Quincy peeked over his shoulder . . . and stifled a shriek. She quickly ducked her head, her heart pounding.

Blast! Of all the cursed times to run into someone who knew her as Josephine Quincy. Since no hole opened up in the floor to swallow her, she bent her knees, the better to stay hidden behind Sinclair. The surging crowd, which had annoyed her earlier, was a godsend as the press of bodies shielded her from discovery.

Quincy forced herself to breathe. The "shameless wench" might now be Serena, the Duchess of Warwick, but Quincy had known her as Rena, an earl's daughter who wouldn't deign to play with the offspring of a mere baron. A bothersome child, she had delighted in bearing tales to their elders when Quincy and neighboring boys rode the parson's horse without permission, or picked green apples from the squire's orchard.

Why should it surprise her that little Rena had grown up and married an old duke, then invited an earl to her bed? Hadn't Quincy caught Rena, at the age of five, showing her silk drawers to Tommy Simpson, age six, after he agreed to give her a shiny penny?

As soon as the duchess was distracted by another gentleman, Sinclair plowed into the crowd and out of the theater, with Quincy in tow.

Several silent minutes passed in the carriage. Her heartbeat had almost returned to normal when Sinclair finally spoke. "Have you found a Bath chair for your grandmother yet?"

Ah, they were ignoring the encounter with the duchess. Suited Quincy just fine. Serena had already caused her enough anxiety. "Friday I found a used one that was reasonably priced. She can get around the flat just fine, and out onto the landing. She misses being able to go farther afield, though."

"Perhaps if you moved to a ground-floor flat?"

If only . . . "I tried to find one to start with when we came to town last year, but the rents were higher. We all agreed moving now isn't worth dipping into the money we've saved for our cottage. A few more weeks, and this will just be a memory."

"I'm sure you're right." The earl was quiet the rest of the trip home. He stared out the window until Elliott stopped the coach in front of Quincy's building. "I'll arrange some way for you to meet Miss Prescott, and any others we may add to the list."

"Excellent." Quincy scooted forward on the bench while the tiger opened the door and let down the steps. Her knee brushed Sinclair's. "Thank you for a pleasant evening, my lord." She got up, headed for the door, when the horses snorted and the carriage rocked. The sudden motion made her lose her balance. Sinclair caught her about the waist, and instead of the floor or pavement, she landed on his lap. Breath left her lungs in a rush.

His chest was warm and solid against her back, his arms snug around her waist. "Are you injured?" His voice, warm and deep, full of concern, whispered against her ear. Stubble on his jaw grazed her cheek.

"No," was all she could manage. She tilted her head back, resting it on his shoulder. Enveloped in his embrace, bathed in his scent, an enticing blend of bay rum, liniment and Sinclair, his face mere inches from her own, she was just able to make out his glittering eyes in the darkness.

Injured, no, but she'd never be the same.

She felt him shift beneath her. His leg! She must be causing him great pain. She struggled to get up, flailing in a tangle of their arms and legs before finding her balance again, his hands on her hips to help lift her to her feet, and she scrambled out of the coach to the pavement. She straightened her coat and pushed up her spectacles. The whole incident had lasted only a few seconds, but would be imprinted on her mind forever. "Thank you again, Sinclair. My first trip to the theater was quite memorable."

Sinclair waved. "Go on with you."

She waved and went up the stairs, preparing herself for a

rash of questions about the evening from Mel and Grand-mère, treasuring the feeling of being held in Sinclair's arms, however unintentional the circumstances. Knowing it would never be repeated, regretting that's the way it had to be. She had to be satisfied with the little bits of joy that came her way, because that's all she would get.

The carriage rocked into motion. Sinclair banged his head against the cushion. Twice. How could he be so stupid? Hadn't he *any* control over rude male instincts that made him haul Quincy onto his lap?

Tonight could have been a disaster in so many ways, so many times. It was probably a mistake to have taken her to the theater, though he'd meant well. After their private dinner, even running into Serena couldn't erase all the fun from the evening. Though if he ever got his hands on Nigel, the cowardly bastard wouldn't be long for this world.

Sinclair had set out to give Quincy a taste of freedom, to give her a chance to lessen the weight of responsibilities she carried like a cloak, if only for a short time. Instead, she had made *him* feel differently—younger, more alive. Lighter in spirit than he had felt since before buying his commission five years ago, certainly better than he had felt since a French soldier sliced open his thigh with a bayonet near a tiny village called Waterloo.

He enjoyed their time together—seeing the outrageous dandy costumes through Quincy's unjaded eyes, bantering with her in the dark of the theater. He arranged his schedule so they spent more time in each other's company than he ever had with Johnson or Broderick. In fact, the only other person he had ever spent this much time with, at least willingly, was Tony. His younger brother, now in his second year at Oxford, wasn't due home for a visit for several weeks yet, at the end of Hilary Term.

This was ridiculous. How could he want to spend so much time with his secretary? While Quincy was unquestionably of gentle birth, they were far from social equals. Not to mention the niggling detail of her masculine charade. No wonder his mother and friends had looked shocked this evening. How could he explain? He knew of several matrons known for their eccentric habit of taking their pugs everywhere with them. Instead of a pet pug, he dragged along his secretary?

He might pawn off his behavior to others as eccentricity or a simple affectation, but not to himself. Being near Quincy was pleasant, but touching her in public, even in the most casual manner, could bring disaster. He delighted in the freedom of clapping her on the shoulder, and other incidental contacts which would never be allowed if she were dressed as Miss Quincy. But in the box, he had been shocked by the temptation to kiss her cheek when he'd whispered in her ear. The temptation to kiss her after dinner, and when she'd sat on his lap . . .

If anyone discovered their deception, the world would come crashing down around their ears. And if anyone caught him kissing "Mister" Quincy, well . . . He'd just have to see to it that didn't happen. No more touching.

He thought back to the moment in Leland's box at the theater, and he shivered just as he had when Quincy touched his arm in sympathy. She understood his pain and mortification at Serena's hands, and it had nearly undone him.

One night last winter, he and Leland had consumed so much brandy they passed beyond the realm of maudlin into another territory. They cried in each other's arms—Leland mourning the loss of his left eye, Sinclair afraid he might never again walk without the aid of crutches. After the worst hangover of their lives, they had never mentioned the incident again.

Since that one moment of weakness, he had not felt the desire to seek comfort from another human—until tonight.

Until Quincy.

Sinclair frowned. Bad enough his lips had brushed her ear whispering to her in the darkness of the theater. He'd almost crossed the line, when she literally fell into his lap. If she had turned her head just a little farther, brought that luscious mouth of hers just a fraction of an inch closer . . . Granted, he had saved Quincy from a tumble to the floor, so she hadn't suspected him of any dastardly intentions. Until an armful, not to mention lapful, of Quincy had started to have an effect on other parts of his anatomy. Then she couldn't get away from him fast enough, and he, base creature that he was, couldn't resist assisting her up if it meant the chance to cup her derrière with his hands.

He slammed his fist against his knee. He was supposed to be finding a wife, not fondling his secretary.

This would never do. If Quincy thought she was in any danger from him, stubborn as she was, she would quit, regardless of the hardship it would cause her family. He couldn't risk that. He had to see that her family was well-cared for. Had to keep Quincy close.

Besides, another employer would certainly discover her secret just as he had, and the next gentleman might forget he was a gentleman. Especially if Quincy bent over to retrieve a pencil. Or fell into his lap.

No, she was much safer right where she was. Close to him.

"We should visit your estate at Brentwood as soon as possible," Quincy informed him the next morning when Sinclair joined her in the library.

At the thought of being alone with Quincy in the country, his pulse leaped. He imagined the two of them settling in front of the fire for a quiet game of chess, taking their meals alone, feeding her bites of apple puff . . . just the two of them. After a full day of showing her around his estate, he would teach her to play billiards, wrapping his arms around her to show her how to hold the cue stick just so. Or they could read aloud to each other, side by side on the sofa, so he could hear the breathless quality her voice took on whenever he was near. When they would say good night, she'd be just down the hall from him, instead of across town.

Just the two of them. Alone.

He settled into his leather chair and propped his feet on the desk, carefully schooling his expression before peering at Quincy over the toes of his boots. "Why is that?"

She pushed her spectacles higher on her nose. "There's an excellent chance Johnson did similar tricks with the books at Brentwood. Showing debits for paying people he didn't actually hire, that sort of thing."

Sinclair crossed his ankles. "Agreed. What are my social commitments for the next few days? Anything to keep me from traveling while this fine weather holds?"

Before Quincy could reply, Harper tapped on the door. "Lord Palmer and Sir Le—"

"Sinclair old chap, so good to see you again," Palmer announced, stepping around the butler. Leland shot Harper an apologetic glance as he entered the library.

"You too, Palmer, but it's only been a few hours since you last clapped eyes on me." Sinclair nodded agreement when Harper gestured for a tea tray.

"Hope we're not disturbing anything," Leland said, settling in the wingback chair.

"I'll come back in a little while, my lord," Quincy said, edging toward the door.

"Stay," Sinclair said, waving her back into the room. "We won't be long. You and I need to finish looking over those accounts. Do you have them ready yet?" Quincy shook her head and returned to her desk.

"I told you we should not have come so early," Leland said to Palmer.

"Not at all," Sinclair said, joining them by the fireplace. "Paperwork is like swallowing a live toad. Get it over with first thing in the morning, and nothing worse can happen all day. I assure you, I do not mind the interruption. Now then, what brings you two here?"

Palmer crossed one ankle over his knee and stretched his arm along the back of the sofa. "I've had my eye on a filly at Tattersall's, and was wondering if you'd give your opinion on her?"

They discussed horses at length, Sinclair pleased that his friends still sought his equine advice even though he hadn't been able to sit a horse for more than a few minutes since his injury.

After a brief knock, Harper held the door open as Mrs. Hammond entered with the tea tray, followed by Lady Sinclair. The three men jumped up. As they exchanged greetings, Sinclair braced himself for whatever his mother had up her sleeve. He could count on one hand the number of times she'd ventured into his library.

She sat down and poured the tea. "Lord Palmer, you're looking quite well these days," she said as she handed him a cup.

"Thank you, Lady Sinclair," Palmer said. "May I return the compliment?"

"I think marriage quite agrees with him, wouldn't you say, Benjamin?"

Sinclair choked on a swallow of tea. Quincy buried her face in the account book, but not before Sinclair saw her smile. Unfazed, Lady Sinclair turned her attention to Leland, who had jumped up from the sofa at the word "marriage" and walked over to the bookcase, putting the large desk between himself and Lady Sinclair.

"And you, Sir Leland," Lady Sinclair began. Even from across the room, Sinclair felt the fear radiating from Leland, as his gaze frantically darted from his mother to Sinclair, pleading for help. Sinclair shook his head. Leland was on his own. "How is your mother? I haven't had a chance to see her since your guests settled in."

Leland exhaled and leaned one hip against the desk. Quincy peeked at Lady Sinclair, and Sinclair could swear he saw his mother wink at his secretary. A wink? The hair stood on the back of his neck. This did not bode well, not at all. Quincy turned her attention back to the ledger without batting an eyelash. "Quite well, thank you," Leland said. "She seems to really enjoy having, er, guests in the house."

"Is she still thinking of renting out the ground floor back parlor?"

"I suppose so. We already have three boarders, but Mama thinks there's room for more."

"I know someone in need of lodgings in a suitable neighborhood, something with no stairs."

"Really? Who?"

"Mr. Quincy."

Quincy's head popped up at the same moment Sinclair glanced at her. Mama had quizzed him over breakfast about last night's activities, and he'd mentioned the injury to Quincy's grandmother only to avoid dwelling on his un-gentlemanly conduct at the end of the evening. He thought of Quincy living in Leland's house, and his gut clenched. What was Mama trying to do?

"Your grandmother has a broken ankle, does she not, Mr. Quincy?" Lady Sinclair continued. "And ground-floor lodgings would simplify matters while she recovers?"

"Yes, but—"

"Mama likes to meet with her prospective boarders. Shall we arrange for you to meet her this evening?"

Quincy started to shake her head, just as Lady Sinclair declared it a marvelous idea. The secretary took a deep breath. "That would be agreeable."

Sinclair rubbed his temples. Quincy, living under Le-land's roof? With servants about, and other boarders nearby? Could she maintain her masculine persona well enough to avoid giving herself away? She'd have to stay "in character" at all times, even in sleep. No frilly, feminine nightgowns. She probably wore a nightshirt anyway.

Egads, what was he doing, imagining Quincy's bed attire?

And Leland's mother, Lady Fitzwater. What if she should notice something different about Mr. Quincy? Women had the reputation of sometimes noticing things that men did not.

The one bright spot was that Leland's town house was in a neighborhood infinitely better than the slum where the Quincy family currently resided. Physically, they'd all be much safer.

Thinking of safety, another realization slammed home. There was no way Quincy could accompany him to his country estate. Not if he wanted to consider himself a gen-tleman. If their secret got out, she'd be ruined, regardless of his behavior. She had already placed herself in jeopardy in so many ways, but this was one risk he would not allow her to take.

He swallowed his disappointment.

Chapter 12

❦

"**A**nother match made in the household," Sinclair announced later that afternoon, striding into the library. He dropped onto the sofa with a sigh and propped his feet up.

Quincy set down the mail. "Who is it this time?"

"Tanner and Irene. Apparently he recently discovered he is heir to a freehold farm, and the current owner, a distant cousin, is in poor health. Tanner felt the need for a wife before he went to learn the running of the farm. Irene, it turns out, came to us already pregnant and was concerned about her child not having a father. They left this morning, without giving notice."

"How rude."

Sinclair grunted. "Do I look like a bloody matchmaker to you, Quincy?" He crossed one ankle over his knee. "No, I did not think so. But try explaining that to Mama. According to her, this is all my fault. They're all atwitter upstairs figuring out the new division of duties." He let out a long-suffering sigh.

"I was unaware you had thrust Irene and Tanner into each other's company, and plunged them into situations where they both suddenly felt the need for a spouse." Quincy grinned at the earl as she opened the ledger book once more.

"My point exactly." Sinclair roused himself from the sofa and dropped into his leather desk chair with a grunt. "You realize, of course, we will have to find someone to replace them both, quickly." He groaned again and ran his fingers through his hair. "It might take days, or weeks, to find suitable candidates. Inspecting Brentwood will have to wait."

Quincy bent over the ledger to hide her disappointment. Canceling the trip was probably for the best, however. She was enjoying Sinclair's solitary company far too much. Last night she had almost kissed him when he held her on his lap.

"As long as everything is in upheaval upstairs, you might as well make the most of it," Sinclair said, reaching back and flipping her ledger book closed. "Go meet with Leland's mother. If you both agree on arrangements, take tomorrow and the weekend to move. I think your grandmother would be much happier there."

"Undoubtedly easier to live with, at any rate," Quincy said, rising. "Thank you, Sinclair."

"Umm." Sinclair waved her off, staring into the middle distance.

Quincy was halfway home when the solution to her employer's staffing problems hit her. Or rather, it was a boot that hit her, thrown by an angry landlord. She ducked as he tossed another boot, then flung a chair out to the pavement.

A sobbing woman tugged on the man's arm. "We'll have the rent by Monday, I swear!"

"Bugger off, wench," he growled, and tossed more of their belongings into the street. He threw her off his arm with such force she tripped down the stairs and sprawled on the pavement.

"You can't treat my sister that way!" a man yelled, appearing in the doorway.

"Who's going to stop me, *you*?" the landlord sneered. "You can bugger off, too, you stupid cripple." The landlord shoved him down the steps and threw a long stick after him.

As the young man tried to stand, the landlord threw a wooden crate at him. It landed a foot away, sending up a spray of broken pottery. Shaking off his sister's hand, he grabbed the wooden stick and headed up the stairs. The landlord slammed the door in his face.

"Jack, what are we to do?" The young woman dabbed at her face where shards of pottery had drawn blood.

"Oh, poppet, don't cry. I can't bear it when you cry." Jack hopped down the stairs to his sister and wrapped his arms around her.

Only then did Quincy realize his unusual gait was because his left leg extended just six inches below his hip.

"I believe this is yours," Quincy said, stepping toward the pair and holding out a boot.

They turned identical startled gazes on her. Of nearly the same height, they shared the same black hair, blue eyes, and delicate bone structure.

"Thank you," he said, taking the boot. He let go of his sister and hopped over to the other boot, tossed it toward the crate, and started gathering up their other belongings in the same manner.

"I'm Quincy," she said, extending her hand to the woman, whose sobbing had eased to the occasional hiccup.

"Jill," she said, shaking Quincy's hand.

"No!" Quincy bit back a smile.

"Afraid so," Jill said, with a watery grin. "Papa was quite cupshot when we were born, and Mama was too exhausted to argue."

Quincy grinned, too, and they watched Jack gather up the pair's few belongings, moving quickly with his crutch and one leg. "Have you anywhere to go, anyone to help you?"

"We'll be fine, thank you very much," Jack said. He held the back of the rickety chair and gestured for Jill to sit down.

"I meant no insult," Quincy said quickly. "I may be in a position to help you. Do you mind if I ask what skills you possess?"

"We worked for a modiste," Jill said. "Jack made deliveries, while I sewed. But she returned to France last month, and we haven't been able to find other work since."

"Would you be interested in learning to be a maid, or," Quincy turned her gaze to Jack, "a footman?"

"Your attic's to let. Who'd hire me as a footman?"

"You might be surprised. Will you wait here?" She didn't wait for a reply, but spun on her heel and raced the few blocks back to Sinclair.

She found him still in the library, staring unseeing at a folio on his desk. "I may have found a solution to your staff shortage," she said, breathless from running.

"How's that?"

"Will you promise to keep an open mind while I show you? It's a few streets over."

"I don't think I like the sound of that," he said, but followed her out of the house.

They paused just out of earshot.

"You can't be serious!" Sinclair looked from the twins back to Quincy. "Have you bats in your belfry? You want to hire him as a footman?"

"The position is called footman, not *feet*man. He seems qualified." She grinned, drawing a reluctant smile from the earl. "And you haven't seen him move yet. I would wager Thompson would have trouble keeping up with him." She raised her voice. "Jack! Would you join us, please?"

Jack stared at the earl, exchanged glances with his sister, and headed over.

"Notice how well his clothes are made. His sister Jill is a seamstress. She could easily find work if she were willing to leave her brother behind."

"Jack and Jill?" Sinclair chuckled. "How can you be sure they're really siblings? I don't want anything havey-cavey going on under my roof."

"Trust me, you can be sure." Quincy stepped aside as the twins neared.

Sinclair stared at the two, then cleared his throat. "I am the Earl of Sinclair," he announced. "My secretary tells me you are in need of employment. As it happens, I have need of—" he glanced at Quincy, closed his eyes, and briefly shook his head. "I have two staff openings in my household. Are you interested?"

"Yes, my lord," they answered in unison.

The earl looked from one to the other. "Then we are

agreed. I'll send Elliot back with the cart in a few minutes to collect your things. You can work out the details with my butler."

"Thank you, my lord," they said. Jill curtsied and Jack bowed.

"*I* am the one with bats in the belfry," Sinclair muttered as he passed Quincy, heading home again.

"Glad you agree, my lord," Quincy said.

"Impertinent pup."

The rest of the day passed in a blur for Quincy. Lady Fitzwater, Leland's mother, pronounced herself delighted to rent the ground-floor back parlor to the Quincy family. She asked for one month's rent in advance, naming a sum Quincy thought more than reasonable, especially given the improved neighborhood.

She wouldn't have to worry about Mel's safety nearly as much, and her sister could finally put her hair up, as befitted her age. With such cheery prospects, Quincy didn't even begrudge the funds it would cost to move their belongings. Any misgivings she had about renting space in Sir Leland's house were forgotten.

Later she met with Sam, the butcher, to reschedule his weekly reading and writing lesson, explaining she had to arrange for a carter for the next morning.

"Nonsense!" Sam boomed. "What time shall I bring my cart 'round to your flat?"

"Please, dearie," Sam's wife said when Quincy started to refuse. "I'll even see to it he puts down fresh straw. Did you tell him about your new contracts?" she said to her husband.

Sam's barrel chest puffed out even farther. "That's right, laddie. I got *written* contracts with two nobs in Mayfair! Supply them with all their meat now!"

Quincy congratulated him, then headed home to share her own good news.

"I know, Mama, but he's a footman, not a *feet*man," Sinclair said with a grin, standing before his mother in the drawing room.

"Really, Benjamin! What do you suggest we do now, go out and find a man missing his *right* leg, so we'll have a matched set?"

Sinclair's humor vanished. "That wouldn't be difficult."

She jumped up from the sofa and hugged him. "I know," she said softly, resting her cheek against his shoulder. She squeezed his arms and stepped back. "You say his sister Jill is a skilled seamstress? It would be a waste to put her to turning mattresses or dusting. The maids need new uniforms, and I believe I need a new gown or three. I wonder if I could set her up with her own shop, in time?"

Lady Sinclair barely nodded when Sinclair excused himself and headed for his library.

It was empty. He knew it would be, remembered giving Quincy time off, but hadn't realized before how empty the room felt without her. It would be three long days before she returned.

He sat at Quincy's drop-leaf desk, behind and to the side of his own massive oak desk. Moved a few balls on her abacus, then slid them back. Didn't want to upset her calculations. He took a deep breath, expecting only to smell ink and paper and leather, but was shocked to detect the scent of lemon. Faint, but he definitely smelled lemons.

Quincy's soap. It certainly wasn't her aftershave, Sinclair thought with a chuckle.

He grew serious, thinking of himself at Quincy's age. At school then, his biggest worries were about tests he hadn't studied for, and avoiding getting caned while still getting into mischief with his friends. He hadn't been responsible for the well-being of anyone save himself, and even that hadn't been a major concern.

Most females of Quincy's age were attending balls and other social functions, in the pursuit of finding a husband. Like Miss Mary, and shy Miss Prescott. What would Quincy look like, dressed for a ball? For that matter, when was the last time she had worn a gown of any kind?

Trapped in her masculine disguise, Quincy would never dance at a ball. She'd never have a Season. Would never be able to marry. Never have children. And there was nothing he could do about it.

He suddenly couldn't bear to remain in the library.

He rang for Harper and requested his black mare be saddled. The conversation with Palmer this morning had reminded him how much he missed riding, and he had the perfect destination in mind to test his leg's improvement.

Twenty minutes later he reined in a few doors down from Quincy's flat. He handed a shilling and the reins to a street urchin, and promised him a half-crown if he and his horse were still there when he returned.

He found Melinda halfway up the first flight of stairs, an overflowing shopping basket in one hand, the other covering her eyes. "I can't bear to look, Jo. Did you drop her?"

"No, we did not drop her, you ninny," Quincy muttered from the shadows farther above, gasping for breath.

"You would have heard me fall, goose. Now run up ahead and open the door. Watch where you put your hands, Hubert!"

"Sorry, Mrs. Quincy," a strange voice mumbled.

Sinclair started up the stairs, watching Quincy and a young man make a chair with their arms for Quincy's grandmother. "May I be of assistance?" he said, reaching the landing.

Staring at Sinclair in surprise, the unknown youth dropped his jaw and his side of Mrs. Quincy.

Sinclair caught her and easily swung her up in his arms.

Quincy stooped to catch the crutches before they slid down the steps. "Grandmère, this is Lord Sinclair," she said, when she realized both adults looked at her expectantly.

"So you're my Jo's employer," she said, wrapping one arm around Sinclair's neck to keep from slipping.

"Yes, ma'am. Do you mind if we continue this upstairs?" Small as she was, the unaccustomed weight and recent horseback ride was making his bad leg throb. And they were drawing a crowd at the foot of the stairs.

Mrs. Quincy followed his glance. "Whatever you say, young man." She leaned her gray head against his shoulder, making it easier for him to see where he stepped. "I'm sorry I caused such a fuss," she added, not sounding the least bit sorry. "I thought I could hop up the stairs as easily as I hopped down them."

Melinda had already opened the door and scooped up Sir Ambrose, guarding the threshold. "This way, my lord," she said, opening the bedchamber door. Quincy darted inside, pulled back the covers on the four-poster bed, and grabbed a pillow from the cot to put at the foot of the four-poster. The massive piece of furniture left barely enough room to walk between it and the cot on the other side.

"Thank you, my lord," Quincy said.

"My pleasure," he replied, gently setting his burden on the bed, making sure her foot was atop the pillow.

"No, 'twas *my* pleasure," Mrs. Quincy said, winking at him.

Sinclair didn't think he could still blush, but he felt his cheeks grow warm. He cleared his throat. "I trust everything is satisfactory at Sir Leland's house?" he asked Quincy.

"Yes, thank you, my lord. We are moving in the morning."

"Melinda, don't just stand there, set some water on for tea." Mrs. Quincy shifted over on the bed and patted the edge of the mattress. "Won't you join us for a few moments, Lord Sinclair?"

"I, um . . ." He cleared his throat again and decided to take pity on poor Quincy, who stood with her back against the wall, looking like she wished the floor would open up and swallow her. "I would like nothing better, ma'am, but I only stopped by to tell Quincy here that I have decided to visit Brentwood, after all." Was that disappointment he saw on Quincy's face? He stepped aside as Melinda returned to the tiny room. "I shall be leaving tomorrow morning, and won't return until late Monday, so you can have an extra day off. Get settled."

"But you can't go without me!" Quincy appeared as shocked as her sister and grandmother once the words had left her mouth. "I mean . . . the whole point of going to

Brentwood is to inspect the books, talk to the merchants, see if Johnson also played his tricks there, right?"

"Of course." Did the little minx *have* to remind him of his failure? In front of witnesses?

"Would you know what to look for?"

"I think so, since you've pointed out his methods."

Quincy shook her head. "But what if he did things differently there?"

Now it was Sinclair's turn to feel trapped. He was trying to be a gentleman, but Quincy was making that impossible. She was right about the books, and they both knew it. Sinclair might recognize some tricks, but what if he missed something?

Faced with her damning logic, if he refused, Grandmère and Melinda might become suspicious of him. Should he risk possible damage to her reputation later, or reveal that he was aware of her deception now?

The little imp of mischief returned, reminding him how much he'd enjoy the time alone with Quincy. And how miserable he'd be if she left his employ, which she'd have to if her family found out that he knew her true identity.

Unthinkable.

He ran his fingers through his hair, hoping to come up with an alternative tactic. Nothing.

Mrs. Quincy kept looking from him to Quincy and back. She was assessing him, assessing his relationship with Quincy, he felt sure. Any other employer, any other secretary, and there'd be no question of them taking the trip together.

He sighed. "You're right. I'd like to travel while the weather is still dry. Can you be ready by Saturday morning?"

Quincy nodded.

"I promise to have Quincy back by Monday night, ma'am."

"Three days?" Mrs. Quincy said. "Yes, that should be enough time."

"His lordship is taking Jo for three days?" Melinda said from the foot of the bed, disbelief in her voice and on her face.

"That will be fine," Quincy said quickly. "We should be settled in our new home by then."

"Good. I'll call for you at Leland's, then. Good day, ma'am, Miss Quincy." He bowed quickly and headed for the door, escaping the undercurrents in the tiny flat.

They were right to be concerned about Josephine going with him to the country, and under any other circumstances he would never even consider it. But Quincy had forced him into a corner.

Besides, it was quite proper to take his secretary to inspect his country estate. And they did share the goal of protecting Quincy's secret. What could go wrong?

"Are you serious, Jo?" Grandmère said as soon as the door shut behind the earl.

"Why not? We can reach his estate in one day, spend a day inspecting the account books and talking to merchants, and travel back in a day. Nothing scandalous in that, is there?"

Grandmère fell back on the bed, her arm draped over her eyes.

"He wants to get Josephine alone," Melinda said solemnly.

"He wants nothing of the sort!" Quincy shot back. "I'm perfectly safe with Sinclair. He is a gentleman." He had resisted any temptation to kiss her when they were alone in his library after dinner. Even when she was on his lap, practically begging him to kiss her, he had been a perfect gentleman. He had no interest in her, at least not in that regard.

Melinda looked horrified. "Maybe he wants to get *Joseph* alone."

Quincy tossed a pillow at her.

Grandmère sat up. "Jo, why did he not simply send a servant with a note to tell you he was leaving? Why did he deliver the message in person?"

Quincy shrugged. "He was probably just out on one of his walks."

"Not unless he was walking his horse, too," Grandmère said. "He has a pleasant scent, but he's definitely been on a horse since he bathed this morning."

Mel giggled.

Quincy squeezed her eyes shut. She didn't need to think about Sinclair in his bath. "His leg is getting stronger. He must have gone for a ride, and while out he decided to go to Brentwood after all."

Grandmère narrowed her eyes. "Are you sure he does not suspect anything?"

"Did he seem suspicious to you?" Both women opened their mouth to speak, and Quincy raised her hand to cut them off. "Oh, never mind."

"Mel, please go see if the tea is ready," Grandmère said.

Quincy flopped onto the little cot. Three whole days, alone with Sinclair! She covered her face with her arms to hide her grin.

"The earl is a handsome man," Grandmère said. *"Très virile."*

Quincy silently agreed.

"A man of the world."

Undoubtedly. He'd traveled to France and Belgium, probably farther.

"A very open-minded man, would you not agree?"

Quincy moved her arms so she could see. Grandmère was propped up on one elbow, staring at her, her eyes bright.

"Do you remember what I told you, *ma chère*? Such an open-minded man would give you what you want, what you need. A few moments of joy, with no consequences." She smiled. "Perhaps many moments, depending on his stamina, *n'est-ce pas?"*

Quincy's cheeks heated. At last she understood what Grandmère had given her carte blanche for. Good thing she was already lying down, for she felt decidedly weak in the knees.

Chapter 13

❦◦◦◦◦◦◦

"**S**inclair, so good to see you," Sir Leland called as Sinclair strolled, unannounced, into his study the next morning. "Care for some sherry?"

"No, thank you. Just need a respite. I hoped your household might be a little less topsy-turvy than mine at the moment." He settled on a sofa that looked a little worse for wear. The Turkish carpet beneath his feet was threadbare in placcs, but it was a carpet. The only floor covering in Quincy's flat had been a scrap before the fireplace, covered with cat hair.

At Leland's raised eyebrow, Sinclair told him about the latest changes in his staff.

"Another match! Oh, this is wonderful! And twins, you say! Wait until I tell Palmer!"

"It's not that funny, damn it!" Sinclair grinned in spite of himself. He started to speak again, but heard what sounded like a small army marching through the back of the house.

"Mama's new tenants must have arrived," Leland said, rising.

Grateful he wouldn't have to be crass enough to suggest they go have a look, Sinclair followed his host's lead.

"Do please bring your grandmother in here, Mr. Quincy,"

Lady Fitzwater called from the front parlor doorway. She smiled politely at her son and Sinclair, then returned her attention to the activity in the hall.

Sinclair stared at the line of people marching up the hall. Quincy pushed her grandmother in her Bath chair, their gray tabby perched on Mrs. Quincy's lap like a king on his throne. They were followed by two fellows with bloodstained aprons, obviously father and son, carrying the mahogany wardrobe. Behind them came four boys of varying ages, carrying pieces of furniture and belongings. Melinda trailed at the end of the column, her arms full with a small crate.

Quincy directed the troop into the appropriate room, while wheeling her grandmother close to Lady Fitzwater.

"One more trip should empty the cart, Mr. Quincy," the big man boomed. "You stay here with your womenfolk."

"Thank you, Sam. I don't know what we would have done without your help. Or your boys."

Sinclair coughed to hide his smile. Quincy's ability to wrap people around her finger was not limited to his household.

"Yes, thank you," Melinda said. The eldest boy blushed. His father gave him a playful punch that almost knocked him off his feet, and they set out for another load.

"Lady Bradwell!" Lady Fitzwater gushed to Quincy's grandmother. "It's so good to see you again!"

Bradwell? That name seemed familiar, but he couldn't place it. Sinclair looked at the two older women, then across to Quincy. It took a moment to recognize the expression in her eyes.

Panic.

"My goodness, is that you, Fitzy? When Jo said—I never imagined!"

Lady Fitzwater bent down to kiss Mrs. Quincy, no *Lady Bradwell's,* cheek. They clasped hands. Quincy looked torn between the desire to flee and for a hole to open up in the floor. *You're not going anywhere, my dear. This is just getting interesting.*

"I haven't seen you since . . . goodness, since before your confinement, Fitzy."

Lady Fitzwater beamed, and gestured for her son to come near. Leland left Sinclair's side and submitted to a kiss from his mother. "Leland, Lady Bradwell introduced me to your father. Such a matchmaker you were in those days, Dominique!"

Quincy's panic eased enough to show surprise at the revelation about her grandmother.

Leland bowed over Lady Bradwell's hand, and they exchanged greetings.

"You already know my Jo," Lady Bradwell said, patting Quincy's hand where it rested, white-knuckled, on the back of the Bath chair. "Allow me to present my granddaughter, Melinda Quincy."

Quincy's grandmother continued the charade without actually lying. Nicely done.

Melinda came forward and curtsied. Leland's mouth fell open. His mother had to nudge him in the ribs before he performed the niceties.

Lady Fitzwater suggested they move into the parlor to catch up. Quincy pushed her grandmother's chair into place beside the sofa, then excused herself, saying she had to check on her helpers. Already deep in conversation, the ladies paid scant attention to her departure.

"Until tomorrow, Mr. Quincy?" Sinclair called as she dashed out of the room.

"Tomorrow," Quincy repeated.

With a thoughtful glance at Lady Fitzwater and "Lady Bradwell," Sinclair invited Leland to be his guest for an early luncheon at their club, and they left the ladies to their coze.

"Who's here already?" Quincy sat up despite her aching body's protest, forced her other eye open, and tried to bring Mel's face into focus.

It must have been after midnight before she finally dropped onto her straw pallet, exhausted from a day of packing, carrying, and unpacking. Now, living in Sir Leland's house, she had to keep up appearances even in sleep, for it would spell disaster if anyone discovered Melinda and "Joe" shared a bed, as they had in their old flat. Their private flat, where no coal-carrying maids came and went unannounced.

With the money Sam had saved her by not having to hire a carter, she'd buy another bed as soon as she returned from—"Sinclair's here? Now?" She threw back the covers, jumped up as fast as her aching muscles allowed, and yanked her nightshirt over her head. "Go make him some tea or something. I'll be right there."

Melinda nodded and closed the door behind her.

Quincy dressed and tied her cravat with all the speed she could muster. She ran the brush through her short hair and tossed it in the portmanteau she'd packed the night before, and opened the partition door that led to the main section of the parlor. Grandmère's and Mel's bedchambers were on the far side, also separated by partitions that could slide back to reveal an area large enough for a modest ball.

"Good morning," Sinclair said, sitting at their pitifully small table in the big room, Sir Ambrose draped over his lap. Sinclair scratched behind the cat's ears and took a sip of tea.

"Sorry I'm late. The clock stopped yesterday, and this street is much more quiet than—"

"You're not late. I'm early." Sinclair pulled out his watch and showed her it was only half past six. "Sit. Eat. Your sister makes wonderful scones."

Dreaming. Yes, she must still be in her bed, thinking the Earl of Sinclair sat in their quarters, sipping tea, stroking her cat, with her sister looking on, wearing her night rail and dressing gown. Quincy lowered herself into a chair and held up the cup Mel set on the table. Hot tea splashed on her wrist as Mel poured.

No, not dreaming. Blast.

"I confess to finding myself eager for the ride out to Brentwood," Sinclair said with a sheepish grin. Mel flashed her a triumphant look over his head. "Leland and I have run tame in each other's houses for years, so the cook thought nothing of letting me in. I was prepared to wait in the front parlor, until the most delicious scent of freshly baked scones reached me, and your sister took pity on me."

Quincy sipped her tea. "Yes, Mel's quite good at cooking up things," she said. Mel glared at her.

As if sensing undercurrents, Sinclair set Ambrose on the floor and rose. "I'll leave you to your breakfast and good-byes. The horses are in the mews; I'll wait for you there."

"Horses?" she said blankly.

"Yes. You do ride, don't you?"

"Of course. Just not, um, recently." Not since she was thirteen, and never astride, at least not with a saddle. "I'll be along shortly."

"Good. And thank you again, Miss Quincy." The earl bowed and let himself out before he could see Mel blush.

"Well, does this prove to you he has no nefarious plans in mind?" Quincy asked her sister, while they searched through the stacked crates for boots.

"How do you mean?" Mel dug Papa's worn leather boots out from the back of the wardrobe.

Quincy stuffed a stocking in the toe of each boot. "He could hardly have his wicked way with me if we're both on horseback, instead of riding in a closed carriage."

Mel chewed on her bottom lip. "I don't know. In some of the Minerva Press novels I've read, the villain—"

Quincy threw a scone at her. After changing footgear, stowing her shoes in her portmanteau and saying a quick good-bye to her sleepy grandmother, she headed out for the mews.

"I thought it may have been a while since you rode, so I chose a gentle mount," Sinclair said, holding the reins of a gray gelding. "Meet Clarence."

Quincy grinned and stepped forward to stroke the horse's forehead. "Hello, Clarence." The horse whickered and raised his head to nibble on her hat brim. "Hey, I need that!" When Quincy pulled her hat out of his reach, he sniffed around her neck, his long whiskers and warm breath tickling her, then moved on to nuzzle her pockets.

"Here," Sinclair said, pulling several lumps of sugar from his pocket. "He has a bit of a sweet tooth. My mother has spoiled him horribly."

Quincy chuckled as she took the sugar, and was careful to hold her fingers flat while Clarence inhaled the lump from her palm.

"Climb up, and we can be on our way before the rest of the city is out of bed." Sinclair swung up into the saddle of his bay mare with a grace and ease Quincy enjoyed watching.

It was his movement she admired, she told herself, not his form. Not the way sitting astride made his trousers hug his muscular thighs. With a sigh of pleasure, she turned back to her own horse before Sinclair noticed her staring at him.

The saddle was a long way up from the ground. The stirrup barely reached down to her hip. She couldn't possibly get her foot in it, let alone use it to jump up into the saddle. As a child, when she'd ridden the neighbor's horses running loose in the pasture, she hadn't needed saddle or stirrups to get up on those enormous creatures. And now she wasn't even hampered by skirts.

While Sinclair spoke to Sir Leland's only groom, Quincy patted Clarence once more and took a few steps back. With a last glance to make sure no one observed her, she hopped up, bracing her hands on the horse's back. She forgot to keep her arms stiff and almost went too far, and ended up slung over Clarence's back. The pommel dug into her ribs, knocking the breath from her lungs.

Muffled noises told her she had an audience. She raised herself up and swung her leg over. At least she faced the horse's head and not his tail.

She glanced over at Sinclair, who was valiantly trying not to smile. The groom bent over to brush dirt off his boot, his shoulders shaking with silent laughter. "I did say it has been a while since I rode," she said stiffly. She thought of the absurd picture she must have made and grinned. "Now that I've provided you with your laugh for the day, would you hand me my bag, please?" she asked the groom.

"Yes sir," he said, his grin nearly splitting his face. He

helped her tie the portmanteau to the pommel, and she and Sinclair trotted out into the street.

She let Sinclair lead the way, weaving between the farmers' carts and dodging the street vendors. They soon left the city behind and he nudged his mare into a canter. Quincy kept Clarence to the side and a little behind, the better to watch how Sinclair rode and controlled his horse. She mimicked Sinclair's motions, moving in rhythm with her horse's stride, and soon stopped feeling like a sack of potatoes jouncing along in the saddle.

Once she was no longer in imminent danger of falling off, she relaxed and began to enjoy the ride. She felt the horse's power between her knees, his muscles flexing and shifting with each stride, carrying her swiftly, high above the ground. The wind whistled past, its chill bite dispelling any traces of fatigue, stinging her cheeks and ears, leaving her exhilarated.

Sinclair set the paces, from a walk to a canter to a gallop, then down again, preventing the need to change horses at any of the inns they rode past. Quincy easily kept up, thanks more to Clarence following the mare's lead than to her own skill.

A mail coach passed them, three boys riding on top whistling and cheering as the coach left them in a cloud of dust. Not long after, the coach reached a mail stop and Sinclair whistled at the boys as they overtook the coach. They galloped for several minutes. For the first time that day, they were alone on the road, with no traffic visible in either direction. Sinclair slowed the horses down to a walk.

"So your grandmother is Lady Bradwell," Sinclair said without preamble.

Quincy almost fell out of the saddle. Clarence whickered in protest as she pulled on the reins, righting herself. She'd been hoping Sinclair hadn't paid attention yesterday. Drat the man.

"That would make Baron Bradwell your previous employer, as well as . . . ?"

"Father."

Sinclair nudged his horse to the other side of the road, away from a muddy rut. She couldn't read his expression.

Quincy followed suit. How bad could this be? He already knew her biggest secret, and had kept her on anyway. He wouldn't use this latest information as grounds to terminate her employment, would he? They were getting along so well. She hadn't discovered the full extent of Johnson's thievery yet, and Sinclair had promised she could stay on at least until then.

And she was making progress on her main goal. Even with moving, they still had funds saved toward their cottage. Every day in Sinclair's employ meant the chance to set more money aside. She had to get Mel out of the city before winter came again.

Practical considerations aside, she liked working for Sinclair. Liked Sinclair.

"So Baron Bradwell, the man who signed your reference, was your father."

They rode side by side now. She nodded.

"A *glowing* reference, by the way." Sinclair looked at her sideways.

"He did say those things about my skills. I just wrote them down for him." She tried to keep her tone light, but heard the defensive note creeping in.

"After he died?"

Quincy shrugged.

"And his signature?"

"I never said it was *not* a forgery."

Sinclair tilted his head to one side. "True."

She took his wry grin as a good sign. When he pointed out a clump of tulips blooming beside the stone wall bordering the road, she tried to relax and enjoy the ride again. She didn't realize how far they'd traveled or how much time had passed until her stomach growled.

Luckily Sinclair soon reined in his mare under a chestnut tree on the edge of a pasture. "Let's see what Cook packed, shall we?" He swung one leg over and jumped down, staggering slightly on his bad leg. He tied the reins to a low branch and rummaged in one saddle bag.

Again mimicking his actions, Quincy swung one leg over and jumped down. She bent her knees to lessen the jarring impact with the ground, but instead of straightening up, they continued to bend until she knelt in the grass. Somewhere along the road, jelly had replaced her leg muscles.

"It's best if you walk around a bit," Sinclair said, his back to her. He must have heard her muffled groan as she stood up. "Perhaps we should take you to Gentleman Jackson's after all," he said, still not looking at her while he pulled sandwiches and a flask from his saddle bag. "Toughen you up a bit more." He held out a sandwich, his warm brown eyes sparkling with laughter.

"I *know* Grandmère would not approve of that," she said, taking the sandwich.

"I didn't think she'd approve of this." They sat on the low rock wall in the sun-dappled shade beneath the tree, shoulder to shoulder, and unwrapped their lunch.

"She had no choice. Since she agreed that I was the one who had to inspect the books at Brentwood, she couldn't very well not let me go and do just that." Quincy took a bite. "Besides, I reminded her that you're a gentleman, and I'd be safe with you."

Sinclair chewed and swallowed. "Of course."

She thought his agreement was reluctant, but she must be mistaken. Of course she was safe with Sinclair.

While they ate, Quincy stared across the pasture at a cottage with a copse of woods behind it. The house was in dire need of fresh paint and new thatch on the roof, but it was ringed by daffodils, blue bells, and a few early tulips. A rose trellis climbed up one side.

It looked much like the cottage they used to live in, before Papa died. Like the cottage she intended to have again, someday soon. Three women worked in the kitchen garden beside it, hoeing, pulling weeds, and from the way one wore a kerchief over her face, spreading fertilizer. Quincy never thought she'd miss getting dirt under her nails.

"Something wrong?" Sinclair asked, handing her the flask.

She took a swallow and gave it back. "Just thinking. I

need to bring Mel back to the countryside, someplace like this. Last year I didn't know the pollution in London would affect her so badly." She took another bite of her sandwich. "This is the first spring we haven't had a garden to plant. Mel and I used to be up to our elbows in dirt this time of year, like them." She pointed at the women in the garden.

Sinclair chuckled. "And with your grandmother directing every step, I imagine."

"Oh, no, she worked right beside us. She's very particular about what she cooks, and it starts with how it's grown. She has never trusted English shopkeepers."

He took a drink. "Does she distrust English secretaries?"

Quincy chewed a little longer than necessary. "It was never a matter of trust, just . . . finances. Papa had some setbacks with his investments. One after another. After another." Sinclair gestured for her to continue. "When we moved from the manor house to the cottage in Danbury, working for Papa was just another economy. Besides, I had often seen Mr. Stephens at work in Papa's study, and there was nothing he did that I couldn't do."

Sinclair turned to face her, straddling the rock wall. She swung her leg over the wall and mirrored his position. All of his attention was focused on her, as though she were the most fascinating, most important person on earth. His steady, attentive gaze was more intoxicating than wine. No wonder she was revealing too much of herself to him.

"Josephine stayed at the manor, and Joseph moved into the cottage?" He retrieved an apple and folding knife from of his pocket.

"Seemed the most logical way to make the change." She was transfixed by his hands as he opened the knife, then sliced the fruit in one swift thrust.

"And your family didn't mind?"

"Grandmère was furious at first, Papa was already blue-deviled, and Mel thought it high adventure."

"Is it an adventure?" He held out half of the apple.

She took it, their fingers brushing. "It is now."

The only sound was a raven calling from the tree

branches above, and the crunch of apple as they each bit into the juicy, tart fruit.

"Why'd you leave the cottage?"

Stupid male-biased laws. "Since Papa died with no heirs, the king's men came and took everything away. We were all right through the spring, and in the summer we had the garden, but after the harvest was complete, we realized we wouldn't make it through the winter with what we'd been able to set aside. London seemed to hold the most opportunity for work."

She might have rambled on, but Sinclair's steady gaze had shifted to her mouth. Nonplussed, she watched, mesmerized, as he reached out and cupped her cheek in his calloused palm, so warm against her skin. His thumb brushed the corner of her mouth. Her lips parted in surprise. Her heart stuttered as he wiped a drop of apple juice from her bottom lip, then licked the drop from his thumb, his eyes never leaving her face.

"I'm not your first, then."

First? A dozen images flashed through her mind, but she could form no coherent words.

"Employer. Since your father." He bit into his apple again. She couldn't stop staring at his lips, his mouth, his jaw.

He was still awaiting a reply. She gave a slight shake to her head and dragged her gaze back up to his eyes, which were crinkled with humor at discomfiting her. "I worked for a few shopkeepers, helping with inventory, clerking, but nothing paid well enough or lasted very long. Until you."

She couldn't even blame it on wine this time. How could one man get her to reveal so much of herself, in such a short time? Her role as Mr. Quincy required subterfuge and reticence, even with her own family. With Sinclair, she just melted. He breached all her defenses without a single volley fired.

He inched closer on the rock wall, until their knees touched. Her heart sped faster when he rested one large, powerful hand atop her thigh. "You're a resourceful woman, Miss Quincy." His voice was rich and deep, a caress to her senses as much as his hand on her leg.

He leaned forward, slowly enough that she could retreat if she wanted, closer until his breath mingled with hers, and brushed her lips with his. The touch was light and tender as a summer breeze, sweeping the breath from her lungs. She leaned into him, returning the kiss, tasting the apple they'd shared, tasting Sinclair, feeling enveloped by his warmth and scent and coiled strength.

The stubble on his chin contrasted with the softness of his lips, gentle but firm. She felt his admiration and affection for her, so much conveyed with the simple touch of lips. She was awed by the wonder of it, wanted it to go on forever.

He caressed her cheek, his fingers brushing back her hair. Her senses reeled, and she steadied herself with a hand on his shoulder, such a strong, broad shoulder, her other hand on his chest. A small part of her, the part not in shock at the pleasure of the kiss, was pleased to feel his heart pounding just as hard as hers. She could hear their beating hearts, feel his beneath her hand, through the layers of fabric, the heat and pounding.

Sinclair pulled back. Quincy almost fell over at the loss of contact, but Sinclair reached a hand to steady her. She realized the pounding was the approaching mail coach. The boys on top hooted and hollered at them as the coach thundered past on the road.

He adjusted her hat, a smile crinkling the corners of his eyes. Another carriage approached from the opposite direction. The moment was over.

"We should get going," Sinclair said, standing up and dusting off his trousers. "It's still another five hours at this pace, and we want to arrive before dark."

Quincy mutely nodded and tried to rise. Sinclair helped her up with a hand under her elbow, a knowing smile teasing his lips as she rose to her feet, a little shaky. Her eyes narrowed, but she couldn't resist returning his smile. Letting his chest swell with pride at flustering her with just a kiss, well, who was she to deny him?

They untied their horses. Quincy took a step back,

preparing to jump up, but bumped into Sinclair, standing behind her.

"Allow me." He bent over and cupped his hands. Resting her hand on his shoulder, purely for balance, she placed her foot in his hands. Looking up at her through his lashes, he licked his lips. She shivered, but not from cold.

With a grin, Sinclair tossed her into the saddle. A moment later she heard the creak of leather as Sinclair swung into his saddle, and they set off.

The day continued warm and dry, the sky clear of all but a few puffy clouds. In midafternoon they stopped at the Three Soldiers Inn to water the horses and eat a hot meal. While Sinclair arranged for their horses' care, she had a few moments to chat with the innkeeper, and asked about the inn's name.

Soon she and Sinclair were seated in the tap room, enjoying a hearty beef stew and crusty bread. "Did you know the head groom is blind?" she said between mouthfuls.

Sinclair glanced up before taking a big bite, but said nothing.

"The cook has a wooden leg. And the innkeeper's arm isn't broken, it's paralyzed."

"Better eat up. We need to get going again."

Quincy ate another spoonful. "All three of them served in Belgium. That's where they got hurt. Didn't you serve in Belgium, too?"

Sinclair grunted.

"The inn was a gift to them, but they don't know who their benefactor is. He still sends a solicitor over once a month to help them with the business. They were each down to their last shilling, but now they can take care of their families again." Quincy gazed around the room as another group of travelers entered and were attended to by the innkeeper. "I wonder who would do such a thing, put men into business like this?"

Sinclair drained his mug of ale. "Some great looby with more pounds than sense, no doubt." His gaze skittered away from hers. "We need to go. Clouds are moving in. Here, pay the innkeeper and I'll get our horses."

Within minutes they were on the road again. By late afternoon the clouds multiplied and filled the sky, scudding past on a quickening breeze.

"Not to worry," Sinclair said, following her stare at the ominous sky. "Brentwood Hall is just over that rise. Less than two miles to go."

A mile farther, Clarence began to limp. Quincy jumped down, holding her knees stiff so she didn't sink to the ground. Her teeth rattled in her skull. "Which foot is it, Clarence?" she said, patting his neck. "Hoof, I mean." He tilted his left rear hoof as though preparing to sleep. "Clever boy," she said, squatting down to take a look.

"What's amiss?" Sinclair said, riding back to her and dismounting.

"My kingdom for a nail," she replied. Still squatting, she stared back down the road. "His shoe is back there somewhere."

"Blast. Well, it's not far. We'll just walk the rest of the way. Work some of your soreness out." He grinned and helped pull her up again.

Leading the horses, they had walked only a few yards when a thunderclap resounded nearby. Sinclair's mare reared, pawing the air only inches from his shoulders. Clarence pinned his ears back, but kept all four hooves on the ground.

Sinclair had just calmed the mare when the clouds opened up. He threw his head back and laughed. "You wanted a little adventure, didn't you, Quincy?" he said, wiping raindrops from his eyes. He swung up into his saddle and held out his hand to her. "Hold tight to Clarence's reins. I don't fancy chasing after him in this downpour."

She took his hand, grasping his wrist as he gripped hers, and he swung her up. He let go before he nudged the mare and they set off. She nearly toppled off the horse's backside before she reached with her free hand and grabbed on to Sinclair's waist. Clarence didn't need any instruction, and kept close enough to the mare that Quincy could hold his reins and still hold Sinclair with both hands.

At first she just held on to his hips, for that is what *Mr.*

Quincy would do. Then she realized there was no one about to witness their ride. She wrapped her arms around his waist, feeling much more secure, not to mention warm, enjoying the illicit feel of his legs resting against the inside of her thighs.

Sinclair patted her clasped hands and threw a grin at her over his shoulder, approving her position.

Cold rain continued to pelt down. The wind drove drops under her hat brim and down her collar, raising goose bumps in their wake. She clung even closer to Sinclair, drawing comfort from his warmth and solid bulk. All too soon he reined in before a large manor that appeared out of the mists.

A butler opened the huge oak front door. "May I be of assistance, sir?" He squinted at them. "Good Lord, it's you, my lord!" He stepped back and ushered them inside.

"Have someone see to our horses, Bentley," Sinclair said, shrugging out of his soaked coat. "This is Quincy, my new secretary. We'll need the farrier for his gelding. How have you been, old chap?"

"Quite fine, my lord. I am relieved to see you hale and hearty. We heard such rumors since you returned from France!" He gestured and servants came running. The hall became abuzz with bodies moving about, taking their soggy belongings.

Quincy soon found herself standing before a roaring fire in the drawing room, a glass of brandy in her hand. Deprived of the warmth of Sinclair's body next to hers, the fire was most welcome. Odd that she felt more chilled indoors than she had out in the wind and rain.

"With any luck, this will blow through by morning, and we can inspect the property without getting soaked," Sinclair said, standing next to her. He downed his brandy in one gulp and held his hands out to the flames. "I'm anxious to see the new seed drill I ordered last fall. There should be any number of changes since I was last here."

Drawn by the fire, the cold seeped from her bones and she no longer fought the urge to shiver. She set her full glass on the mantel beside his empty one. "How long has it been?"

"Over five years, since before I bought my colors." He stared at the fire.

How could one own an estate in the country, yet choose to live in the noisy, dirty city? Quincy saw Sinclair shift his weight, off his bad leg. How foolish of her to forget. He'd had no choice in the matter—he'd been brought to the London town house last fall to recover from his injury. Now that he was almost healed, he was staying for the Season. To search for a wife.

She needed to sit down. The stew they'd eaten a few hours earlier suddenly felt like lead in her stomach.

Bentley's quiet cough brought her thoughts back. "I've had hot water sent to your rooms, my lord. I am afraid your things are quite soaked, Mr. Quincy. I have one of the maids tending to them now, so they should be ready by morning."

Quincy felt the blood drain from her face. Someone had gone through her things? Well, of course they would. In a household like the earl's, guests didn't lay out their own belongings, even if the guest was an employee. Had she packed anything that would give her away? "Thank you."

Sinclair made a choking sound. "He's about Anthony's size, wouldn't you say, Bentley? See if you can find one of his nightshirts and a dressing gown. I doubt Quincy fancies sleeping in the altogether."

"Yes, my lord."

As soon as the butler left, Quincy pinned Sinclair with a glare. He looked unapologetic for discussing her bed attire. Or lack thereof.

"Well, we don't want the bath water getting cold, do we?" Sinclair slapped her on the back and, with an arm draped heavily across her shoulders, led her from the drawing room.

For the first time today she realized he hadn't brought his walking stick. If she was stiff and sore after spending the day in the saddle, she could only imagine the pain Sinclair was feeling. He must be holding on to her for support.

Heedless of any observing servants, she tightened her grip around his waist when they reached the stairs, taking more of his weight as they climbed. Neither spoke. Quincy didn't want him to mistake her concern for pity, and lines of concentration creased Sinclair's brow. She was breathing heavily herself by the time they reached the top.

He didn't let go until they reached her room. He slid his arm from her shoulders, briefly cupping her cheek before dropping his hand to his side. "Good night, Quincy," he whispered.

By the soft candlelight in the hall, she read a multitude of emotions in his eyes—apology for her soaked clothes and servants going through her things, acknowledgment of her assistance, discomfort at needing such help. She swallowed, realizing she'd happily hold on to him all night. *He's your employer.* "Go soak in the tub before the water cools."

He quirked one eyebrow, then smiled and limped to his own room, two doors down from hers. She felt bereft without him. She shook her head and entered her room.

The fire had been lit just after their arrival, and was only beginning to remove the chill from the room. The red and black Chinese decor was perfectly coordinated, down to the silk screen in one corner. She moved it closer to the tub, blocking in more of the fire's heat. Now that she considered it, every room she'd seen in the magnificent house was perfectly coordinated. Nothing like the mismatched pieces in Sinclair's library or his bedchamber. His rooms were comfortable, yes, but not conforming.

She had removed her waistcoat and cravat and was reaching for the buttons on her shirt when she heard a short knock, and the door opened.

"Good evening, sir," said a footman, closing the door behind him. "I am Wilford." He bowed, careful to keep the garments draped over his arm off the floor. "Since you came unattended, Bentley has assigned me to assist you during your stay. May I help you with your shirt?"

Chapter 14

Quincy stared at the footman, dumbstruck.

"Have I given offense, sir?"

"No!" She cleared her throat. "That is, I am grateful for your offer, Wilford. I am just used to making do for myself."

"I see. Of course, sir." He shook out the nightshirt and dressing gown hanging over his arm and spread them on the bed. "These belong to Master Anthony, the earl's brother. I trust they'll do until your own clothing is dry." He gave her a frank look, his gaze traveling from head to toe. "You seem to be of a size."

She fought the urge to snatch up her coat and cover herself. "Thank you, Wilford. That will be all, I think."

The footman turned to leave but stopped with his hand on the knob. "His lordship has requested supper in one hour. I shall return to help you dress after you bathe."

"No!" Quincy heard the squeak in her voice, hoped Wilford did not. "If it is not too much trouble, I would prefer a tray in my room. Please extend my apologies to Lord Sinclair, but I find I am . . . quite fatigued."

Wilford nodded and at last left her in peace.

While she waited impatiently for the tray to be brought, Quincy sat on the edge of the bed, watching the steam rise from the tub. Her stomach growled. She longed to undress and slip into the bath—a hot-water-up-to-her-chin soak was a luxury she hadn't been able to indulge in for quite some time—but didn't dare. Not yet.

After what seemed hours, a maid delivered the tray and bobbed a curtsy on her way out. Quincy glanced between the two objects of her desire, debating. Hot food, cold bath? She decided both were better lukewarm. She stripped and stepped into the tub, bringing the tray within reach, and ate while washing.

After the rigors of the past two days, and a warm bath and full stomach, she barely had the strength to climb into bed and pull the covers up to her chin before she fell fast asleep.

A familiar, throbbing ache in his thigh woke Sinclair just before dawn the next morning. He threw back the covers, stretched his sore muscles, dressed, and limped downstairs. A little coffee with his brandy took the edge off the ache, and he prowled through the house. Not much had changed in the years he'd been away.

How was it possible for him to experience such cataclysmic changes in his life, yet his home appear the same as the day he left?

Since returning to England, he had stayed in London only to ease his mother's anxiety. Feeling guilt for the strain and worry he'd caused her, he'd allowed her to bring in an endless parade of doctors to consult about his leg. His patience just stretched so far, however. Dr. Kimball had been the only one not to chastise him for fighting off the sawbones after he'd been injured, and so Sinclair had not sent him packing as he had the other quacks.

Quincy's question about his choice of residence last night had started him thinking. Now that he was fully recovered, he could move back to Brentwood. The thought made his steps light, until he remembered a tiny complication. It was one thing to have Quincy work for him in London, going home to her family every evening. Living at his estate, that wouldn't be possible.

Her grandmother and sister wouldn't allow Quincy to follow him to Brentwood permanently. He shouldn't even consider it.

He would find a way.

He entered the study and skimmed through the steward's books. Good thing he'd brought Quincy, because he found nothing to indicate Johnson had pulled his tricks here. What secrets might the ledger yield to Quincy's trained eye? He set the books aside and stared out the window.

How could she sleep through a glorious morning such as this? Gone were the rain clouds. The sun shone brightly, showing everything clean and refreshed. He longed to saddle his mare and go riding, to explore his property. He wanted to show it to Quincy, to see it through her eyes. Wanted to spend the day in her company, relaxed.

Wanted to kiss her again. Wanted to taste her again, feel her lush mouth against his, wanted to discover what feminine charms were hidden beneath her masculine disguise.

He rushed up the stairs, the ache in his leg forgotten, and stopped outside Quincy's door to listen. All was quiet within. If she hadn't thrown the footman out last night, Wilford would be hovering nearby, waiting to assist her.

That had been a damn close call. Sinclair had become so used to his chaotic town house that he'd forgotten what a well-trained staff was like. It hadn't occurred to him that Bentley would take it upon himself to assign a footman to their "gentleman" guest. Not until Bentley had shocked him with the news that Wilford said "the boy nearly fainted at the suggestion of help with his bath." Sinclair winced at the near disaster.

He had brought Quincy on this trip so she could enjoy a little freedom, not be embarrassed or hopelessly compromised. She thought she was here merely to further investigate Johnson's embezzlement. Sinclair had other ideas.

If she was denied the ability to participate in feminine activities, he was going to make sure she enjoyed some of the masculine pursuits. Well, some of the more tame pursuits, at any rate. Like a carefree jaunt about the countryside on horseback. Away from her sister and grandmother, and his own mother.

All three women were much too bright to be fooled easily, and he feared letting something slip that would reveal he knew of Quincy's little deception. Then everything would be over, and he'd come to enjoy her company far too much to let it end.

Sinclair knocked on Quincy's door. No response. The beautiful day was wasting. No telling when the rain would return. And they only had today before they must head back to London. How much of their precious time together would she waste in sleep?

He tried the doorknob, expecting resistance. It opened easily. The foolish chit hadn't even locked her door! It was beyond the bounds of propriety for him to enter, but better him than the footman. He locked the door behind him.

"Good morning," he announced loudly. The figure on the bed didn't stir.

The sun bathed her face in a warm glow, highlighting her delicately carved features, her adorably dainty nose. Her short hair was tousled from sleep, revealing a reddish-brown without its usual coat of pomade.

He hesitated a moment longer, then strode into the room and plopped down on the edge of the mattress, bouncing once. The ancient bed creaked in protest.

Quincy slept on, lying on her side, her arms wrapped around the pillow, the blankets slipped halfway down to her waist. He'd never before seen her with so few layers of clothing. The thin cotton nightshirt was barely decent, revealing freckles on her ribcage, the dusky edge of one nipple. The tantalizing hint made his mouth suddenly dry. He had often imagined her clothed in nothing but a ray of sunshine. His imagination was a poor thing.

Sinclair could do naught but gaze at her, for several minutes. No one seeing Quincy should be fooled for even an instant into thinking she was anything but a young woman. Striking, strong, yet achingly vulnerable. A lock of hair curled over her brow, crying out to be tucked back into place. If he were Prince Charming, he'd awaken Sleeping

Beauty with a kiss. He caught himself reaching toward her, and flattened his palms to his thighs. He cleared his throat to clear his unruly thoughts.

"How can you sleep through a stunning day like this?"

"Go 'way, Mel," Quincy said without opening her eyes, her voice slurred with sleep.

"I am not Mel, and I am most certainly not going away."

One eyelid slowly raised to half-mast. A moment later both eyes flew wide open. The pillow muffled what sounded suspiciously like "Good Lord!"

"Now that I have your attention," Sinclair said, folding his arms, "I wish to know when you intend to get up."

Quincy continued to stare at him.

"Are you actually awake, or just dreaming with your eyes open? I am not leaving until I'm certain it's the former."

She suddenly scrambled back on the bed, tugging the blankets up to her chin. "I am quite awake, my lord."

"Are you feeling all right? You look pale. You did not catch a chill from our soaking last night, did you?" He rested his palm on her forehead. It felt warm, but not unduly so. Without thinking, he brushed the lock of hair away from her face. The silky strands were even softer than he'd imagined. A shame she always wore it slicked back, though it did help her disguise.

"I feel fine, my lord. Just a little . . . surprised . . . to see my employer in my bedchamber. That is all."

Sinclair realized he was gazing at her like a besotted fool, his hand cupping her cheek. He cleared his throat again and stood up. "Better me than Wilford, though, eh? Which it easily could have been, since you didn't lock your door last night."

Her eyes widened. "I meant to. Must have fallen asleep."

He crossed to the window and flung open the drapes. "We have a lot of work waiting for us. Let's cover as much territory as possible while the weather holds, shall we? I'll meet you in the stables as soon as you've eaten."

He closed the door on his way out and walked a few steps down the hall, then leaned against the wall. For the love of Juno! What had he been thinking, touching Quincy like that? It was one thing to kiss her at lunch, when they were both fully awake and dressed. But when she was still in bed, wearing nothing but a nightshirt?

A thought chilled him. What would *she* think of his caress? However unintentional, that's what his touch upon her cheek had been, a caress. Would she consider it brotherly? He'd often awakened his younger brother, sat on his bed, ruffled his hair. That was the direction he could aim for—acting as her elder brother.

Then again, after that kiss yesterday, perhaps not.

All right, friends then. Friends who kissed. He wanted her to rely on him, confide in him. Trust him. The warmth he felt, the protectiveness, the desire for her company—all were the hallmark of friendship. Surely? It was unconventional for a man in his position to count a woman among his friends, but Quincy was far from conventional.

To be honest, though, after seeing her face relaxed in sleep, with the sweep of her long lashes and soft curve of her mouth, his feelings weren't limited to friendship. He'd had a sudden image of her waking up beside him in *his* bed. And falling asleep in his arms at night, exhausted and sated after their lovemaking.

Wincing at his foolishness, Sinclair went downstairs and out to the stable.

How could he have ever thought her to be male? And having seen though her disguise, seen the feminine side she tried to hide, how could he ever look at her the same again?

Quincy gaped at the closed door. Yes, Sinclair had sat right down on the edge of her bed. He'd watched her sleep. For how long? He'd touched her. She'd leaned into his hand when he brushed hair away from her eyes, then let his fingers trail down her cheek, his touch gentle and confident. She'd been surprised by his caress, but not by how much she'd enjoyed it.

Did he think her wanton? It was one thing for him to have kissed her yesterday, out of doors, in a moment of camaraderie. But this morning, in such an intimate setting, was something else entirely. Perhaps he believed as Grandmère did, and was simply taking a moment of joy where and when he found it.

Touching her gave Sinclair joy?

He did seem to take any and every opportunity to touch her. Until yesterday, she had always accepted them as friendly, platonic gestures.

Did he see her as a woman, despite her role of Mr. Quincy? Her heart beat faster.

She wouldn't find out sitting up here all day.

She slid out of bed and gasped in pain. Giant pincers grabbed her legs, mercilessly squeezing sore muscles. Stretching toward the ceiling and touching her toes a few times eased their grip enough for her to walk to the door and lock it before she dressed. Wilford might be stubborn enough to offer his assistance again. First the footman walking in, then Sinclair. She'd never again forget to lock the door.

Just as she was ready to head downstairs, a maid delivered her portmanteau and dry clothes. Quincy decided to save the clean clothes for after their ride, but did retrieve the list of local merchants she'd brought from town. She found her way downstairs to the dining room and stopped long enough to grab two scones and a cup of tea, which she drank on her way out the kitchen door.

"The farrier will re-shoe both our horses, but he won't arrive until this afternoon," Sinclair said when she arrived at the stable. "Think you can handle Beauregard?"

Quincy eyed the enormous black gelding with trepidation. Three stalls down, she saw one of the grooms elbow another, and they both snickered. Her chin went up. "Easily." She vaulted into the saddle and walked Beauregard a few steps while Sinclair swung up on to a gray gelding he called Zoltan. Then they were off, Sinclair giving her a tour of his property on their way to town.

How did he manage to look so at ease in the saddle when her muscles were screaming in protest? She felt bounced like a sack of potatoes on Beauregard's back, nothing like the gentle rhythm she'd established with Clarence.

It quickly became apparent Sinclair truly loved his land,

as he greeted tenants by name, pointed out each landmark and told its history. He also knew most of the merchants by name, who greeted him in return. In short order, Quincy was able to confirm that all of Brentwood's merchants were legitimate, and not party to Johnson's thievery.

On the ride, they covered the south and west parts of Sinclair's land, past the tenant cottages and fields being prepared for planting, back to the manor house for luncheon. Sinclair promised they'd go to the north and east after they ate, where there would be sheep pastures and excellent fishing spots.

"If we are to return when you promised my grandmother, I had better start looking over the account books instead of riding with you," she said as Bentley ladled mulligatawny soup into her dish.

"But . . . Yes, I suppose you're right."

Was she mistaken, or did Sinclair sound disappointed?

Her stiff muscles didn't regret staying behind, though she missed Sinclair's cheerful company as he rode off down the drive without her. She settled into the deep leather chair in his study, account books open and strewn about the desk to compare notes with her books from London. Certain she wouldn't be disturbed, she tossed her spectacles onto the desk, snuggled deep in the chair, and delved into the books.

Everything was perfect. Every penny paid out had been for a legitimate expense. Every merchant had delivered the goods for which he'd been paid. When Bentley brought tea, he confirmed the wages received by the staff matched those listed in the books.

Johnson's sticky fingers had not reached this far. His thefts were limited to the London household, and Quincy was certain she'd already uncovered the extent of the missing funds there.

She had solved the puzzle, had fulfilled the task for which Sinclair had hired her. With a sick feeling in the pit of her stomach, she realized Sinclair didn't need her anymore.

But she still needed him.

She needed the wages from this job to save for her cottage in the country. More importantly, she needed to see Sinclair every day.

Grandmère had told her to seize every moment of joy that came her way. Spending time with Sinclair certainly fell into that category. She wouldn't let go easily.

Perhaps she had missed something. Perhaps Johnson had simply hidden his efforts more carefully. She dug back into the books, double checking every entry, adding every column again.

Absorbed in trying to find something, anything, Quincy was oblivious to her surroundings. She barely stirred when thunder rumbled in the distance. The afternoon passed swiftly until Bentley opened the study door, his face ashen.

Quincy's stomach knotted with apprehension when she saw his expression.

"Zoltan has returned to the stable, sir," he said stiffly. "Alone."

Quincy dropped the ledger. "Sinclair's horse?" Her heart pounded.

The butler nodded. "The saddle is still firmly cinched on. Several of the grooms have already set out to search for his lordship. I thought you would like to know."

"Thank you." Her mind raced. "Has Clarence been shoed yet?"

"I believe so."

She spared a glance out the window, and noticed for the first time rain pouring down. "Please have him saddled. I'll join in the search." She ran to her room to exchange her comfortable shoes for Papa's boots, her whole body shaking as disturbing images crowded into her mind. She pushed those thoughts aside and grabbed her hat and coat from Bentley, who waited for her in the hall.

"Here, sir," he said, handing her a length of oilcloth. "It's not much, but 'tis all I could find, and will keep you drier than your coat alone."

She flashed him a smile of gratitude, then ran out the door and climbed onto Clarence's back.

The trail of hooves in the mud was easy to follow, too

easy. No point in going where the grooms had already gone. She directed Clarence farther up the drive before moving into the pasture and across the undulating hills and valleys.

Ducking low against the gelding's neck, she checked under each tree and stared along the edge of every stone wall, searching for Sinclair's inert form. The wind picked up, blowing away the clouds. For a moment the rain stopped and she saw patches of blue sky. She glanced back the way she'd come, then swept the horizon. Nothing looked familiar.

"Bloody hell, I'm lost," she muttered. She patted her horse's neck. "Some rescuers we are, hey Clarence?" After debating possible actions, the only logical decision was to keep looking for the earl. Maybe she'd stumble on to the manor house as well.

The respite from the rain was brief. New clouds quickly moved in, varying shades of dark gray to almost black. Rain fell in a torrent, reducing her vision to less than fifty yards at best.

Clarence slogged through the mud, walking no faster than Quincy could have on her own. Even at his snail's pace, she almost lost her seat when he abruptly stopped at the edge of a stream. Usually little more than a drainage ditch, water gushed past and over its banks, carrying tree limbs and other debris.

Something black bobbed near the edge, caught on a rock. Quincy jumped down and grabbed it before the current could snatch it again.

Sinclair's hat. Inside the crown was fresh blood.

She gasped and dropped it, then immediately picked it up again. With a roaring in her ears that had nothing to do with the rushing water, she held her hand up to shield her eyes from the rain and peered along the edge of the ditch. Afraid she'd find Sinclair's inert form, she searched in both directions, both sides. The water wasn't deep or swift enough to have carried away a large adult male.

No body. Farther upstream the mud looked different. Clarence followed at her shoulder as she made her way to the spot that caught her eye.

Deep marks in the mud showed where Zoltan must have dug in. Rocks rimmed the edge of the stream, any number of which could do serious harm to a human skull. Sinclair was nowhere in sight. Tracks in the mud on the opposite bank gave her hope he had staggered away, and was not lying at the bottom of the stream.

"Well, Clarence," she said, raising her voice to hear herself above the pounding of the rain and the fast-moving water, "if we back up to get a running start, do you think you can leap this mighty chasm?" Clarence snorted. "I'll take that as a yes." She remounted him and urged him back from the ditch. "We have to find him," she said against his neck. She shivered, already chilled. "Soon." She gripped the reins with her rain-soaked gloves, whispered a fervent prayer for her own safety as well as Sinclair's, and nudged the horse.

Not only did she keep her seat, her teeth didn't even rattle when Clarence touched down on the other side. "Good boy!" she shouted, patting him on the neck. "Now let's find the earl."

They plodded on, searching for any sign of a creature moving on two legs. Twice she thought she spotted grooms on horseback in the distance, though her eyes could have been playing tricks on her in the downpour. She found no more human footprints, but the grass grew in thick clumps, and the sheep had mucked up any prints that might have been in the bare spots.

"At this rate, they'll have to send out a search party for *me*," Quincy said with a sigh of disgust. The rain eased off to a drizzle and she stood in the stirrups to get a better look across the fields. Darkness was fast approaching, adding to the urgency of the task.

"Look, Clarence!" she said, sitting down and nudging him forward again. "That's either a tall, thin sheep, or we've found him!" The gelding responded to the excitement in her voice and broke into a trot toward the dark shape at the far end of the pasture.

"Sinclair!" she called a few moments later, reining in Clarence beside the earl. She was so relieved to find him, she forgot about being cold and wet.

Sinclair kept moving, limping badly, eyes squinted nearly shut against the rain in his face.

"Sinclair!" she shouted again, reaching for his shoulder.

He glanced at her, then in one swift motion jumped back a step, turned to the side, and raised his fists.

She jerked back the hand she'd reached out to him and stared at him. Just how hard had he hit his head?

He blinked. "Oh. It's you." Several heartbeats later he dropped his fists.

"Sinclair? Do you know the way back to the house? I found you but I lost myself."

"House?" His brows snapped together as he frowned in concentration. He turned in a slow circle, scanning the horizon, swaying so much Quincy reached out to steady him. "N-no house. Shepherd's hut. That way." He pointed the way he'd been walking, then reached up to swipe rain from his eyes.

It wasn't rain trickling down from his hair into his right eye, but blood. Tamping down a fresh wave of panic, Quincy ignored the goose bumps that suddenly rose on her flesh. She fished a handkerchief from her waistcoat pocket and handed it to Sinclair, who only stared at it. "Wipe your forehead," she ordered, hoping he didn't hear the tremble in her voice.

"Oh. Y-yes. Yes, o' course." He dabbed the linen, now soggy from the rain, at his forehead. He stared at the blood on it when he drew it away.

"My lord!" she said briskly. "We need to find shelter. Are you sure you don't know the way back to the house?"

"Sh-shepherd's hut over there," he repeated, raising his chin. The movement unbalanced him and he grabbed at Quincy's leg. He wrapped one hand around her ankle, and reached up with the other.

Quincy gripped the pommel with her left and pulled him up with her right hand when he jumped. How her arm remained attached to her shoulder was a mystery, but he landed on Clarence's rump. And almost slid off. He grabbed her left thigh and right hip before he righted himself.

"S-sorry," he mumbled, swaying forward until his chin

rested on her shoulder. He heaved a deep sigh and silently raised his arm, pointing in the direction he'd been headed.

Quincy struggled to stay upright under his weight, until she nudged Clarence forward and Sinclair leaned back again. Too far back. He grabbed at her hips, then wrapped his arms around her waist and locked his fingers.

She stared at his mud-streaked hands, so big and so close, held snug to her belly. Despite the drizzling rain, something uncoiled in her stomach, something warm and fluttery, and spread through her whole being.

It froze, however, when she felt a shiver wrack Sinclair's body. She removed one glove to touch his hands. "You're like ice!"

"Mmm."

While Quincy chafed Sinclair's hands with one of her own, Clarence plodded through the mud across the pasture. She fervently hoped they were close to the shepherd's hut. Sinclair needed to get warm and dry, quickly.

Several minutes later she looked up in the fading twilight and saw the outline of a small cottage, barely bigger than the barn behind it. She guided the horse to the front door. "We're here, my lord," she said, patting his laced fingers.

He let go and promptly slid to the ground. With a *splat,* he landed on his backside in the mud. "D-damn," he muttered between blue lips.

"Are you hurt?" Quincy slid out of the saddle and unintentionally dropped to her knees.

"J-just my dignity." He groaned and heaved himself up to his knees. They stood up together, hands on each other's shoulders. Quincy's ungloved hand slid off his coat onto his lawn shirt.

"You're soaked to the skin!"

"A dip in the stream will do that," Sinclair said, swaying.

Quincy grabbed his elbow. "Stay here, Clarence," she said, then wrapped her arm around Sinclair's waist and helped him to the hut. The door squealed on its hinges when she opened it, allowing the rain-washed wind to replace the musty air inside.

They stood on the threshold a moment while her eyes adjusted to the gloom. A river rock fireplace dominated the left wall, and crude plank shelves lined the right. A small bed was tucked against the far wall, and a table missing one leg and two equally rickety-looking chairs blocked the path to the shelves. There was just enough room to walk around the furniture without bumping into the coat hooks on the wall beside the door.

"Any wood or coal?" Sinclair leaned toward the fireplace, squinting. He stumbled forward, and stubbed his toe on the bedstead.

Quincy ignored his curse and pushed him onto the bed. "Sit down. I don't have the strength to pick you up off the floor." She easily fell into the welcome pattern of disguising her concern and relief with a sharp tongue. Sinclair was alive, she'd found him, and they'd reached shelter. Now she just had to get him warm and dry.

She knelt before him and tugged off his boots. As the second boot came off, his ankle was cradled in her hand. She felt a tremor, different from his shivering. Sinclair's laugh grew louder.

"This seems f-familiar, somehow."

She smiled, remembering the night she'd put him to bed when he'd been three sheets to the wind. She tried to think of a suitable reply, but her mind went blank when she saw Sinclair wrap his arms around his stomach. Now sober, he stared at a spot beyond her shoulder, his eyes glazed.

"Sinclair?" He didn't respond. She snapped her fingers a few inches from his nose.

He slowly turned his head toward her. "Quincy? Good. Ring for Harper, won't you? The f-fire's burned down."

Quincy shut her mouth with a snap. "Undress."

Sinclair gave her a blank stare.

She swallowed hard. "You have to get out of those wet clothes, and Harper isn't here to help."

"Mmm." He nodded and reached up with his hands, but his numb fingers wouldn't grip the fabric. "Can't find the buttons," he said, surprised.

Quincy grasped his icy hands and lowered them to his lap. "Lift your chin," she ordered. She untied his soaked cravat and pulled it off, then undid the buttons on his waistcoat and shirt, reminding herself she'd performed the same service for her father hundreds of times. This was no different.

She licked suddenly dry lips. Oh, but it *was* different. "Lean back on your elbows, my lord."

Sinclair missed his elbows, and flopped onto his back.

Her fingers shaking almost as badly as Sinclair's with the audacity of her actions, she undid his trouser buttons. "Can you manage the rest while I start a fire?"

He held out his hand and she pulled him up. "Thank you, Sergeant," he said. "You may go now."

Quincy raised her eyebrows at the non sequitur, but turned toward the fireplace as Sinclair began stripping off his coat. There was wood stacked by the hearth, and a tinderbox on the mantel. She coaxed a flame and blew gently on it, trying to ignore the sound of wet garments sliding over skin and hitting the floor. She turned around when Sinclair cursed again.

He stood beside the bed wearing only goose bumps and damp linen drawers that concealed almost nothing. He was struggling with the tape that held them on his hips.

She gulped. She stumbled back a step, tripping over the hearthstone, and had to grab the mantel to steady herself before she fell into the fire. Hot. It was suddenly much too hot in the hut. The flames cast a golden glow over Sinclair's skin, all hard planes and muscular curves. The brief glimpses she'd previously had of his chest and leg did nothing to soften the blow of seeing him now, standing in all his masculine glory. A fine figure, indeed.

He blew on his fingers, tried the knot again. "Blast."

She tried to speak, cleared her throat. "Let me help." He dropped his hands to his side to allow her to grasp the tape. Acutely conscious of the large, powerful, nearly nude male body before her, she tried to focus on just the knot. Warm breath ruffled her hair as she fought the wet fabric.

She squeezed her eyes shut. "Stop. I can't concentrate when you do that."

"Do what?"

"Breathe."

He chuckled, and the muscles in his flat abdomen contracted. She felt the vibration all the way to her toes. She tugged on the knot, and her fingers brushed some of the crisp, dark hair that lay in tight curls, feathering down his torso. Purely accidental contact. She bent over to get a closer look in the dim light, wishing that her nails were longer, anything that would help pry the knot loose. Quickly. Her hands were beginning to shake.

Sinclair's hands brushed her hair back from her face. She closed her eyes, absurdly wanting to purr like her gray tabby. Another shiver wracked him. With his hands still smoothing her hair, she trembled, too. One more try, and then she was going to just rip the wet garment off him.

"Ah," he said as the knot burst free. Without warning, gravity took over and his drawers dropped to the floor.

Breath left her as though she'd been struck. The view was even better close up. Dear lord, what an exquisite work of art. She should move, avert her eyes, but she could only stare. He was all broad shoulders and acres of smooth skin over well-defined muscles. The jagged scar on Sinclair's right thigh only added to, rather than distracted from, the overall image.

He shivered, head to toe. A *cold* work of art.

Tearing her gaze away from the bounty before her, she pushed on one solid shoulder, urging him down to the bed. Despite the chill in his skin, or maybe because of it, her fingers burned at the contact. She flung the blanket over him.

"I have to take care of Clarence," she said, and darted out the door. The rain cooled her cheeks as she led Clarence to the tiny barn. She found straw to rub him down, but instead of the horse's flank, she saw Sinclair's. The image of his magnificent nude body was forever burned into her mind's eye.

Deep breaths. Lots of deep breaths.

She discovered the barrel of oats in the corner hadn't been invaded by mice yet. She settled Clarence with a pile of oats and a bucket of rainwater, determined to keep her mind on the business at hand, survival. She couldn't dwell on the impossible, like exploring those dark curls, feeling his skin like silk over steel. She gave herself a mental shake. Concentrate. Just survive the night.

After stoking the fire to a blaze, she checked on Sinclair. He lay huddled under the moth-eaten quilt, his eyes shut, but his chest rose and fell in a steady rhythm. His skin felt clammy when she touched his forehead and cheek.

"You're still cold," she whispered.

"D-damn right." His teeth chattered.

She jumped back, then gave a nervous laugh. "Let's see what your shepherd left behind that might help warm you up." Nothing she found on the shelves looked edible. There were two opened jars of preserves, each with a thick crust of green mold. A tin box held the aroma of tea but no leaves. The teakettle seemed sound and clean, so she filled it from the rain barrel outside and set it on the hearth to heat.

Only then did she realize how cold she was herself. Despite the oilcloth, her coat was damp, and rain had seeped down her collar. With stiff limbs, she peeled off her outer garments and hung them on hooks. Sinclair's clothes would never dry by morning if she hung them up near the door. She pulled the rickety chairs close to the fire, then shook out his clothing and draped it over the chair backs. Water dripped on the floor as she wrung out both their cravats. She set their boots and stockings before the fire.

The teakettle whistled. She pulled it back from the flames, poured a little into the cracked earthenware mug she'd found, and took it to Sinclair.

"N-not now, Sergeant," he muttered, pushing her hand away.

She was taken aback for a moment. Should she go along with his delusion, or try to bring him back to the present? He shivered. "You need to get warm, Captain. Drink it."

"*I* give the orders around here," he said in a slow, deliberate voice. A dangerous voice. "Go away."

Quincy bit her lip. "Captain Sinclair! You will drink this, *now*! Do you hear me?"

Sinclair's eyes fluttered open. He stared at her for a frozen moment, then reached a trembling hand for the mug.

"You'll spill it," she said, holding it away from him. She knelt beside the bed and lifted his head, holding the mug while he sipped.

"What the hell do you think this is, Sergeant? 'Tis nought but water!"

"What do you care? It's hot!" She held the cup to his mouth again. "Drink!"

He muttered another curse, but drank the rest of the water. He refused a second cupful, and when she'd turned back from setting down the mug, his eyes were closed again.

"Sinclair?" No response. "Captain!" He didn't move.

The ice in her limbs spread, twisted around her heart. Hot tears pricked at her eyelids. She swiped at them with an impatient hand. This was no time to fall apart. Sinclair needed her.

She leaned nearer, and felt as well as heard his slow, even breathing. With trembling fingers she pushed away damp hanks of hair from his forehead and touched the knot forming at his temple. The gash had stopped bleeding, but his skin was still clammy, and his lips had a disturbing blue cast. The bed shook with his shivering.

Fear and desperation lent her strength, and she tugged the bed closer to the fire, then added more wood. It wasn't enough. But there were no more blankets or even a towel with which to rub him.

Ah, but there was something else. Quincy stepped to the far corner, her back to the earl, and unbuttoned her shirt.

The linen strip she used to bind her breasts was tolerable for about eight hours, and suffocating after twelve. She'd now had it on for sixteen. Her nerveless fingers made the task difficult, but she managed to unwind the linen and rebutton her shirt.

Sinclair hadn't moved. She ripped off a length to use as a bandage, then rubbed his hair with the remainder of the linen. His thick hair slid between her fingers like wet silk, curling at the sides and nape as it dried. She wound the binding over the knot on his temple, doubling the cloth where it covered the open wound.

Was his head injury serious? She had no way of knowing, and chafed at not being able to do more for him. Was there anything she *could* do?

His shivering. She must find some way to stop his shivering, get him warm. But there were no quilts to wrap him in, no more blankets to pile on. Melinda had almost died from pneumonia. She'd contracted the illness after being caught in a rainstorm, cold and wet for only an hour. Sinclair had now been shivering all evening and most of the afternoon.

Except for his leg injury, Sinclair was a strong, healthy man, whereas Melinda had always been sickly. Surely nothing would come of this other than a sniffle? She glanced over as he rolled to his side, curling into a ball. His teeth were chattering, his lips still blue.

This was all her fault. If not for her insistence on inspecting the Brentwood books, he'd be home in London now, warm and dry as toast. What if he contracted pneumonia and died? Lady Sinclair would never forgive her. Quincy would never forgive herself. Thinking of losing him, an icy fist closed around her heart and squeezed so hard she could barely breathe.

She stared out the tiny window, at the blackness of night beyond, listened to the rain pounding on the roof. They were utterly alone. There was no one to call on for help. Even if the grooms found them in the morning, it might be too late.

She remembered how she'd helped her sister get warm. What if she did the same for the earl? Her cheeks flooded with heat, and it had nothing to do with sitting close to the fire. But under the circumstances, there was no other practical way to warm him. It had to be done. She tossed another chunk of wood onto the flames and climbed into bed with Sinclair.

She curled up behind him, breathing on his neck. She tucked her knees behind his and plastered herself to him, chafing his arms, chest, shoulder, every shivering body part she could reach.

Decorum be damned, he wasn't going to die on her watch.

Besides, it was what any sergeant would do for her captain.

Chapter 15

Heaven.

He'd died and was on his way to heaven, carried in the arms of an angel. A soft-spoken angel who told him everything would be fine. He wanted to tell her everything was already fine. While they flew, she cradled him in her arms, surrounding him in a warm cocoon, his face pillowed on her breast, breathing in her faint lemon scent.

Angels wore no corsets, he was delighted to discover. Her breast shifted slightly under his cheek when he moved. He reached up his free hand to feel the round, firm flesh, rubbed his thumb over the nipple until it pebbled under his touch.

Better stop, or she might turn around instead of taking him the rest of the way up to heaven. He sighed and went back to sleep.

Sinclair awoke with a splitting headache and a weight pinning down his entire body. It was a pleasant weight, though, not the least bit painful. Quite comfortable, actually. Warm.

He cracked one eye open. Didn't recognize the surroundings. Opened both eyes. Took a moment to adjust to the light spilling through the dusty, single window. It hurt to move his eyes; he certainly wasn't going to risk moving his head just yet. He stared at the rough-hewn lumber ceiling. Where the hell was he?

Ah, shepherd's hut. Rainstorm. Damn horse.

Quincy. Where the hell was Quincy? His secretary had ridden up on her gray gelding in the storm, brought him to the hut. Where was she now?

The weight pinning him down shifted. Snored. A soft, gentle, female snore. He'd heard his share of them before, though it had been a long time. But it was usually the morning after a night of—

What the hell?

He risked splitting his head open, and lifted it. Looked down.

He froze, breath caught in his throat.

Quincy lay across him in a boneless sprawl, a human blanket. Her head was pillowed on his chest, a hand over his heart, one arm wrapped about his waist, one leg tucked intimately between his.

Oh, bloody hell.

"Mmm." She shifted, her silky hair brushing his chest.

He groaned. Dropped his head back.

Cold air hit his chest as she looked up. He met her sleepy green gaze with his.

"G'morning," he croaked. Cleared his throat.

She blinked at him owlishly. Her hair was tousled, her cheek creased. Reminded him of yesterday—was it only one day ago?—when she'd woken up while he sat on her bed. He'd imagined waking up with her, never dreaming it would happen so soon.

And he'd imagined waking up *beside* her, not beneath her.

She shifted again, the soft wool of her trousers sliding against his bare skin. Against his bare leg, and other bare parts of him. Shifting her weight brought more of her into contact with more of him, and suddenly all his blood rushed south.

That woke her up. Awareness flared in her eyes, like a

new flame. Just as quickly, she schooled her expression, nonchalant. Like this was an everyday occurrence.

Sinclair groaned. Chimney sweeps. Mining shares. Boxing matches. Anything that would get the blood circulating to other parts of his anatomy, and away from thoughts of Quincy's anatomy. He flattened his palms to the mattress to keep from grasping her hips.

Was ever a man so tempted, buck naked, in bed with a beautiful woman stretched out on top of him? *You're a gentleman,* she'd said under the shade of a tree. *I'll be safe with you.* He tightened his hands into fists. If God moved in mysterious ways, He also had a wicked sense of humor.

"Sleep well?" He winced at his husky tone. He was suddenly reminded of a conversation early in their acquaintance. He certainly hadn't slept like the dead this time.

"Once your feet stopped feeling like blocks of ice, yes." Quincy reached up, pressing her hand to his forehead, his cheek. "You feel much warmer now." She frowned. "Perhaps too warm."

He quirked one brow.

She ducked her chin. When she looked up again, she was a bit flushed as well. He manfully refrained from pointing this out.

The moment stretched, her heart beating next to his. He watched Quincy watching him, silently debating, her brow furrowed in concentration as though he was an account book to be reconciled, a puzzle to solve, a decision to be reached. Morning light was unflattering to many women, but his Quincy was stunning in it. Her skin glowed with health, her eyes blazed with intelligence. She worried her bottom lip with her teeth. He wanted to trace the heightened color with his finger, with his own lips.

"Bentley had half the staff out looking for you yesterday. I thought I'd lost you."

He was about to retort that *she* was the one who had been lost, since he had known where he was all along, but then her quiet admission, and her unspoken meaning, sunk in. She thought she'd lost him, as though he were hers to lose.

As though he belonged to her. His heart swelled. It seemed only fair that he belonged to her, since she most definitely belonged to him.

"If you'd hit your head on that rock with just a little more force, or if your skull wasn't quite so thick—"

He stopped her with a finger to her lips. "I didn't survive Napoleon's best only to be done in by a skittish horse and an ill-placed rock."

She kissed his finger. His heart skipped a beat and blood pounded through his veins. Perhaps they should continue this conversation after they were vertical. He rested his hands at his sides, where they couldn't misbehave.

Quincy shifted again, a full body caress, eliciting his groan as her leg slid over his bare skin.

Her brow furrowed. "Are you hurt?" She began running her hands over him, testing his bones, testing his willpower.

"Stop," he said between clenched teeth. Her hands stilled as he took deep breaths, trying to stifle the dizzying current of desire coursing through his veins. He inhaled her warm scent, a hint of lemon, a touch of musk. He groaned again. "Quincy, darling, you have no idea what you're doing to me."

Her weight resting on one elbow, she traced the curve of his ear with one finger, while the palm of her other hand flattened against his chest and slowly began sliding down his torso.

He watched her hand disappear beneath the blanket, felt the caress as she continued to trace a path southward, skimming his ribs, massaging a small circle over his abdomen, heading ever closer until he couldn't resist the urge to raise his hips in an attempt to meet her hand. He dragged his gaze up to her face, stunned by the purposeful look shining in her green eyes. "Maybe you *do* know."

She dropped her gaze, just as she skimmed her hand across the top of his thigh, back and forth, her forearm grazing his hip, torturing him, so close, yet not nearly close enough. "I want to touch you."

He opened his mouth to speak, to protest, but it turned into a gasp as she stroked her palm in a circle from his thigh, over his hip, up to his navel, down and around to his other thigh, ever nearer, but not quite touching him where he wanted, needed it most. "Quincy," he moaned, twisting the sheet in his fingers. "Trying my damnedest here to be a gentleman."

"Forget the gentle," she whispered, her lips brushing his ear, her warm breath sending jolts of desire racing through his body. "I want the man." Her hand closed over his erection.

The sensation was so intense his vision turned black for a moment. She swallowed his gasp, her mouth closing over his, soft and warm. He could drown in her kiss, drown in sensation. He released his vise-like grip on the sheet to wrap his arm around her waist, cup the cheek of his innocent seductress. "This really isn't the place or time—"

"This is the only time." She slid her hand up and down his length, threatening to finish things before they'd properly started.

A man could only resist so much temptation, and Quincy was more than he could deny. He rolled them, putting Quincy on her back. The room spun. Her hand was still pressed between them, making spots dance before his eyes. He grasped her wrist and raised both of her hands above her head, and kissed her luscious mouth.

Quincy pressed her head back into the pillow, breaking the kiss. "But I want to touch you. Feel you." Her cheeks were flushed, eyes dark.

Blood surged through his veins. Sinclair let go of her wrists so he could slip a shirt button free and drop a kiss on the newly exposed, creamy flesh at the base of her throat. "You can, you will." Another button, another kiss. "But later." Button, kiss. "Otherwise this is going to be embarrassingly brief." He held still as the earth spun too fast for a moment, then resumed freeing Quincy from her shirt. He slid another button free, this one in the middle of her belly, and slipped his hand inside, delighted there was no cloth binding blocking his way to the smooth silk of her bare skin. He cupped one breast and rubbed his thumb across her nipple, felt it harden beneath his touch. So much better than in his dream. "It's my turn to touch." He pushed her shirt aside so he could kiss the dusky nipple.

"Oh." Quincy arched her back as he licked and nibbled his way across to her other breast. "I suppose that's . . . oh! . . . only fair."

He spread the sides of her shirt apart, raising up on one elbow to gaze upon the feast before him. The silky skin was marred only by the slightest markings left behind by her binding cloth. His gut clenched. He understood the need for abusing her flesh in such a manner, but he swore it wouldn't have to be that way for much longer. He'd see to it. Personally. He kissed along the faint red lines, smoothing them with his tongue.

He saw Quincy open her mouth to speak, but the first syllable stuck in the back of her throat, and emerged as a moan.

The freckles he'd caught a glimpse of the day before were sprinkled across her shoulders, chest and stomach. He wanted to kiss each one. Sunlight slanted across the bed, bathing Quincy in soft light, accenting her every curve and plane. "Beautiful," he murmured.

Seeing her eyes widen in surprise, Sinclair nodded and leaned down for another kiss. "My beautiful angel," he whispered. She should never again have to question the way she looked in his eyes, if it took him the rest of their lives to convince her.

"But I'm not—"

He silenced her protest with a kiss. "You are. Never doubt that." He kissed his way along her stubborn jaw, down her slender throat, feeling her pulse quicken. "Didn't anyone ever teach you not to argue with a naked man?" He felt as much as heard her bubble of laughter, and she brought one hand to stroke along his bare shoulder, twining her fingers in his hair.

He lingered over her breasts, but soon the sensation of her wool trousers rubbing against his erection was too much. "Someone's overdressed," he growled against her neck. He stroked her breasts and abdomen, moving his hand in slow circles, lower and lower, subjecting her to the same exquisite torture she had given him, until he could slip his hand beneath the waistband of her trousers . . . and encountered a firm, warm length. "Ah, Quincy?"

"Hmm?" She raised her head, her eyes glazed. "Oh, careful with that," she said, retrieving what turned out to be a rolled-up stocking. "Took a lot of experimenting to get it the right size and shape." She tucked it beside the pillow, then turned to meet his questioning gaze, a smile tugging at the corners of her mouth.

He chuckled. "Someday you'll have to share with me just how you determined the correct proportions for Mr. Quincy," he said, undoing the flap of her trousers and sliding his hand inside. He found the tie to her drawers, and soon was sliding them and her trousers down, past her hips, his hands skimming over her warm flesh. Breath caught in his throat at the sight, Quincy warm and pliant in his arms, moaning his name.

He swung one leg across hers, careful not to crush her, keeping his weight on his knees and arms. They stretched out together, flesh on flesh, from chest to knee. He was going to burst. He reached one hand down to her curls to prepare her, make sure she was ready. One finger slipped between the damp folds, mirroring the action of his tongue while they kissed.

Quincy pushed against his shoulders. He raised his head, stayed perfectly still while the room spun again. "Did I hurt you?"

"No, no. Stop." She turned her face aside, her fingers digging into his upper arms.

"It's all right, I—"

She shook her head, killing him. "This isn't what I meant to happen."

Blood had been pounding through his veins like molten lava, but now it all froze solid. "You . . . touched me like that, and didn't expect to . . . ?"

"I just wanted to touch you, to know what it was like . . . to pleasure you." He was dying, but the distress in her voice was even more painful.

It took a moment for her words to penetrate the fog in his brain. "You thought I would just lay here and let you—"

"You were fairly accommodating last night." That might be true—he had only the haziest of recollections after being thrown by his horse. "I didn't intend for you to . . . That is, you can't, um . . . Inside me." She blinked up at him.

He squeezed his eyes shut. Not all of him was frozen. Parts were solid, yes, but certainly not cold. *Painful* parts.

She slid one hand down his back, wiggled it under his hip, her fingers searching. "Today is the thirteenth day," she said, as if that explained everything.

"And that means, what? Bad luck?" He groaned as her fingers neared her target.

"Grandmère taught me how to count." Her tongue darted out and licked her bottom lip.

He couldn't resist a quick kiss and lick to her bottom lip, too. "I'm sure she taught you a great many things. What does that have to do—"

"Count the days . . . of my cycle. On the thirteenth day, there's a high chance of, um, consequences. Permanent consequences."

Understanding dawned. Bless practical French grandmothers. Sinclair leaned down for another kiss.

"So since we can't, um, . . . I just wanted to . . ." Quincy's fingers reached their destination. Breath left him in a rush as her hand wrapped around him once more. "With my hand."

Lava melted and moved again, flowing. Surging. She didn't want to thwart his ardor, just divert it. He might live after all. "Hands can be good." Was there anything more erotic than Quincy's delicate, ink-stained fingers holding him? He nuzzled her neck, his hand drifting back down to her curls. "We can do hands."

Quincy tried to squeeze her other arm under him.

"Oh, no. Ladies first." After he'd raised her arms above her head, relaxed around the pillow, he set to work. Time to make *her* see stars.

He couldn't remember the last time he'd had a woman in his bed, but Sinclair was gratified to know he hadn't forgotten anything important, judging by Quincy's glazed eyes and breathy moans of approval. He ministered to her with his mouth and hands, fingers and tongue, gentle nips and slow strokes, reveling in the reactions his touch evoked, gusty sighs and low moans that emanated from deep in her throat.

The other women before had meant little, a means to scratch each other's itch. Now that he was here with Quincy, her head pushed back, her throat arching up for his kiss, he wanted only Quincy. Ever more.

He found two especially sensitive spots, one with his mouth, the other with finger and thumb, and returned to them over and over, laving them with attention, until her breath came in harsh gasps and her fingers clawed against his back.

"Oh, yes, that's . . . oh." She broke off with a strangled cry, her eyes squeezed shut, mouth open, her short nails piercing his skin, quivering in his embrace.

Sinclair nuzzled her neck and held her close until her shuddering stopped, breathing slowed, and fingers unclenched.

Her eyes drifted open. "Oh. My."

He couldn't hold back a satisfied grin. His normally unflappable Quincy looked so . . . flapped. Loose-limbed and breathless, her face and other parts of her flushed from exertion as well as from his beard stubble. There was a spot or two on her neck that might prove to be a bruise, but she hadn't objected while he made them, marking her as his. In fact, she'd held his head in place.

Her gaze slowly focused on him, a look of wonder in her eyes. "I never knew that was possible."

"Only with me, Quincy," he whispered. "No one but me." He leaned down to claim her kiss-swollen lips.

The room spun again, but this time it was because Quincy had rolled them over. "My turn now." Her eyes glittered with a feral light as she swooped in for a kiss, her hand snaking down his belly, her touch leaving flames in its wake.

He was going to die. He carded his fingers through her silky hair, holding her close while letting her hands roam across his body, before she finally closed in on the most needy part of him. His hips raised off the bed of their own accord, thrusting into her hand. Just as he thought he would explode, she let go. He sucked in deep breaths as she slid her hands between his legs, up, down, over, around, across his torso, as though cataloguing every texture and contour of his body. He stopped breathing when her hand skimmed over the scar above his right knee.

"Hurt?" She stared into his eyes, all worry and concern, no trace of self-consciousness.

He could only shake his head, and urge her hand to continue its exploration. He'd never experienced such craving to be touched like this before, the need to feel her, to have her feel him, so intense that his vision blurred. But there was nothing wrong with his other senses whatsodamnever. He stroked down her back, caressing the soft skin over a spine of steel.

One question had been nagging at him, and finally pushed to the fore of his thoughts. Most of Quincy's tender ministrations repeated what he had done to her. But not all. "You seem to know what you're doing. Not that I'm complaining, mind you, I just wondered how . . ."

"Raised in the country," she replied, her voice muffled against his neck.

"Farm. Yes. That still doesn't explain—"

Quincy sat up, her hand roaming over him in lazy circles. "I was playing with a litter of kittens up in the barn loft one day when a groom came in to play with the dairy maid."

"You peeked." He couldn't help but grin.

"She would sneak us cream for strawberries in the summer. I thought he was hurting her."

"So you were going to defend her? Taking care of people even at the tender age of . . . what?"

"Ten."

He chuckled.

"Before I could climb down the ladder, though, they became, shall we say, vocal. They were quite specific. I realized she was enjoying what he did to her. And vice versa."

"So you filed this knowledge away."

"Until today." She bent down to kiss him, and he stopped

worrying about how she knew what to do, was just damn grateful she was doing it. She trailed kisses down his jaw and throat, returning to the sensitive spot she'd discovered where his neck joined his shoulder, and bit him.

He heard raspy moans, realized they came from himself. She reacted to his every sigh and groan, adjusting her grip, her touch, the pressure, the speed, driving him mad, seeking out other sensitive areas, torturing him with her clever hands. He wished she'd hurry up, wished this would last forever.

She slid her hand back to his groin. She leaned over to claim his mouth in a kiss, and thrust her tongue against his at the same instant she gripped his erection.

His hips bucked twice, three times. Then everything went black.

Seconds or hours later, he opened his eyes. Quincy stared down at him, her worried frown easing as his vision cleared. She snuggled against his side, her arm draped across his waist. He pulled her closer, stroked her shoulder with his thumb.

"Well. That's never happened before." He coughed to clear his throat.

"Really?" Quincy gave him such a smug, self-satisfied look, probably the same way he had looked at her earlier. She moved her hand, and he felt the rapidly cooling evidence of their activity slick across his belly.

"Of course *that* has happened, but not . . . Never mind." He closed his eyes. Seeing the walls waver was just too disconcerting. This way he could concentrate on the woman beside him, drink in her scent, memorize every detail.

His woman.

His eminently practical woman, who saw the goose bumps rise on his naked body before he even realized he was cold, and left his embrace to do something about it. A moment later she rested one knee on the cot, naked herself except for her open shirt hanging off one shoulder. It was the most erotic sight he'd ever seen.

She reached for him, a cloth in her hand. Halfway there, she paused, gave him a sidelong glance from beneath her lashes, and bit her bottom lip. He nodded, though he wasn't certain she'd been seeking permission. She reached for him again, her hands steady now, and wiped him clean. Quintessential Quincy, never let a little detail like uncertainty or inexperience keep her from acting as though she knew perfectly well what she was doing. He felt himself stirring again. She was being quite thorough.

Her unskilled but enthusiastic efforts were far more arousing than the most practiced courtesan, and with blinding clarity he realized why.

He hadn't loved any of the women he'd been with before. That innocuous, four-letter word made all the difference. He loved Quincy.

She was a walking contradiction—a beautiful woman's body hidden by masculine clothes; the heart of a warrior, the soul of a romantic, ruled by a pragmatic mind—and he loved every aspect, every inch.

He snagged her wrist as she pulled back, and kissed her palm. He had to blink. Must be some dust in his eye.

Must have dust in her eye, too, because she blinked several times, then gathered up the blanket that had been kicked to the floor in their exertions and covered him. "We should probably get back to the manor house as quickly as possible," she said, smoothing the blanket over his chest, tucking it under his chin.

He heard the regret in her words, and briefly panicked that she felt guilty about what they had done. But she licked her lips as she touched him, and he knew she regretted only that the moment had to end.

"Bentley was beside himself with worry about you yesterday." She stroked one finger down his cheek.

He heard the rasp of his beard, and thought of letting her shave him, sitting in his lap, dressed the same as she was now. "Perhaps you should help me get warm again before I have to put on damp clothes," he said, trailing his fingers up her bare thigh.

She laughed and swatted his hand away. "You'll get warm by getting up and moving around." She retrieved her clothes and began to dress. He openly watched her don her drawers and trousers, stared at her ink-stained fingers as they did up the buttons of her shirt, remembering the feel of those fingers on his flesh. Only when she reached for her waistcoat did she look back at him, a blush stealing across her cheeks when she realized his scrutiny. "Do you intend to ride back to the manor wrapped in the blanket?"

He groaned, swung his legs over the side, and sat up. And then gripped the edge of the cot as the floor and ceiling threatened to swap places.

Quincy was beside him in an instant, bracing his shoulders, keeping the earth on its axis.

"I don't understand," he mumbled against her. He reached up to quiet the demented carpenter hammering at the inside of his forehead, and felt cloth wrapped around his brow.

"Don't," she said, lowering his hand. "You'll dislodge the bandage." She murmured soothing nonsense as he waited for the laws of gravity to be reinstated. "You must have hit your head harder than we thought. Perhaps I should take Clarence alone and bring back a doctor."

He risked opening one eye, saw that all the parts of the hut were where they should be, and opened the other eye as well. "Do you know the way back?" He started to shake his head, but stopped himself in time. "I'll be fine. Just pretend to be Broderick for a few minutes."

"Can't do that," she said, stepping away to gather his clothes. "Broderick would take one look at these grubby, mud-stained garments, and expire on the spot." She held out his drawers and a smile.

It took far longer than usual for him to dress, and required much of his body to come into contact with much of hers in the process, repeatedly, but they were soon both decent. She tied his wrinkled, muddy cravat, and he returned the favor, savoring the last few moments of intimacy. Soon they'd have to return to their public roles of lord and employee, but in the meantime he took advantage of the solitude to thoroughly kiss her.

She pulled back, her eyes sparkling, mouth reddened. Damn, he'd forgotten about the whisker burn. "I'll go fetch Clarence," she said, backing away.

No, that was wrong. *He* should be taking care of *her*. "I will—"

"Fall on your face. You're still wobbly. Stay here. I'll be back in a moment." She had almost reached the door when she darted back, kissed him, then dashed outside.

Sinclair leaned against the wall by the door and let out a sigh. Overshadowing the pleasant lassitude from this morning's activity was an overwhelming fatigue. Felt like he'd spent the night carousing and fighting, rather than taking a simple tumble from the saddle. The dip in the stream probably hadn't helped.

Footsteps nearing the door had him standing straight, shoulders back, before Quincy stepped inside. He headed to the hearth. Tea was too much to hope for as he poured from the kettle into a chipped mug. He forced down a swallow of water, but it didn't ease the parched condition of his throat. The water felt gritty. He threw the rest of it on the ashes in the hearth with a sigh of disgust. "Let's get back to the house and have a decent breakfast, shall we?"

"One last thing." Quincy straightened the bedclothes and tucked the length of soiled cloth in her pocket, leaving no trace of their passing the night in the hut. She draped his arm over her shoulders and helped him limp outside.

The horse whickered. Sinclair mounted the gray gelding and held out a hand to Quincy.

She looked different this morning. It wasn't just because of their intimacy, or the lack of spectacles. It was as though her clothes didn't fit as well. The linen . . . ?

The bandage around his forehead, the cloth she'd used to clean him, both were from the cloth she used to bind her breasts, to look the part of Mr. Quincy. He'd have to replace it as soon as they returned to the house.

"Sinclair?"

Her voice brought him back to his senses. "Just admiring the view." He gave her a wolfish grin, which she returned with a shy smile. She gripped his hand and swung up behind him, grasping his shoulder to steady herself.

"Settled?" He reached behind him, patting her back, until she leaned against him.

"Ready." Her warm breath in his ear made him sit up straight. Did she torture him, test his willpower, on purpose? He contented himself with tangling their fingers together, her hands clasped at his belly.

It took over an hour to reach the house, riding around obstacles instead of jumping them. He'd wanted to show off the rest of his property to Quincy, but he barely managed to hold the reins, never mind the strain of talking. His head felt ready to explode, and his chest ached from the effort of breathing. That must have been some fall he took yesterday.

The only bright spot was the close contact with Quincy. Her arms around his waist, her legs pressed against his, as they'd been during their ride to Brentwood the other day. Tangled up with his, as they'd been this morning, nothing between them. . . .

Dear Lord, how could he go back to just an occasional hand to her shoulder after this?

Ah, but he didn't have to. As soon as they were married, he could touch her as often, as intimately, as he wanted. He could show her the rest of his property, give her a tour of the house. Make love to her in each of its fifteen bedchambers.

After they were married. He wouldn't risk "consequences" until after they were properly, formally pledged to each other. He had resisted temptation this morning, but the need to make Quincy his in the most elemental way, to bury himself inside her, might overtake his good senses next time. He had to get her back to her family, before he did something they'd both regret.

"My lord!" Bentley exclaimed when they at last rode up to the house.

"Hot food, hot bath, and brandy, Bentley, in whatever order you can produce them," Sinclair said as Quincy slid off Clarence.

"And a doctor, my lord?"

"What? Oh." Sinclair swiped the bandage off his head and tucked it into a pocket. "No need. Just a bump."

"Of course, my lord," Bentley said. The butler stepped aside as Quincy slipped past, not meeting anyone's eye.

Damn. Self-assured Quincy, feeling guilty? Sinclair hurried after her, cursing the limp that slowed him down. "Wait," he called when she started up the stairs two at a time.

"Yes, my lord?" In a gesture befitting a duchess, Quincy stopped with her hand on the rail and turned only slightly.

"It has occurred to me—" Sinclair waited until he reached the riser where Quincy stood, then realized he was too winded to speak. Besides, the servants in the downstairs hall could overhear. He rested his hand on Quincy's shoulder until they reached the landing. "It has occurred to me that I have yet to thank you for what you did. Last night."

More gasping for air, and after only one flight. Could he have caught a chill from his brief soaking? Impossible. He'd better start making trips to Henry Angelo's more often. "I would have reached the hut on my own eventually and waited out the storm, but I . . . I appreciate your efforts on my behalf." Quincy's right eyebrow raised. Damn, this wasn't going at all the way he planned. "And I'm sorry for any, ah, discomfort I may have caused you last night."

Quincy's lips twitched. "You're welcome, my lord." She folded her arms over her chest, and at last he understood. Not guilty, just self-conscious about missing a vital piece of wardrobe.

Servants approached, carrying buckets of hot water. With one last glance, they each entered their respective room.

Quincy locked the door after the departing maid, stripped, and reluctantly slipped into the tub. Her muscles still ached, but she didn't want to wash. Didn't want to wash away the feel, the scent of Sinclair from her body.

Carpe diem. She'd seized the day all right, and made memories to last a lifetime. She'd warned Sinclair she was forward. He hadn't seemed to mind. As Grandmère said, he was a man of the world. By Juno, what the man could do with his hands, that mouth! Long, strong fingers, soft lips, rough stubble . . . He evoked sensations she'd never experienced before, had never even dreamed were possible.

Ah, her dreams. Sometime last night, she and Sinclair had changed positions, changed roles. Instead of her holding him, he had cradled her. He caressed her, reactions rippling through her, a prelude to what was to come when they awoke. Her dreams would have more substance from now on. Blessing, or curse? Time would tell.

She dipped the washcloth in the water and lathered the soap. A small consolation—it was the same spicy scented soap that Sinclair used. She inhaled deeply and began to wash. Water dripped between her breasts. She had a sudden memory of Sinclair touching her there this morning, kissing, licking.

She'd always known the practical purpose for the female bosom, but had no idea it could also produce so much pleasure. Overhearing the groom and dairy maid all those years ago had not prepared her for the reality, the intensity.

She rested her head against the edge of the tub, letting warm water slide over her skin.

Years ago Grandmère had taken her aside for a private conversation, telling her what to expect of her growing body, what it meant to be a woman. How babies were made, how to prevent them. Consequences, and how to avoid them.

Nothing she'd done with Sinclair this morning would have consequences. Nothing was irreversible. Just memories that would have to last her a lifetime, because her time with Sinclair was growing short. Days, at the most. Today, in fact, might be her last with him.

As soon as she made her report about Johnson's embezzlement, he could let her go.

Perhaps he wouldn't do that. Perhaps he'd grown fond enough of her company to keep her on. Keep her near, while he returned to the task of selecting his wife. Select a woman of breeding and stature and wealth, a wife who would not cause a scandal. Quincy grabbed the washcloth, began scrubbing furiously.

Keep her near, while he married, and held another woman in his arms at night.

Quincy jumped out of the bath.

She quickly dressed, but was missing an important item. How could she replace her binding cloth? Ripping the bed sheet would cause speculation. Do without? No, no, her figure was slight but not nonexistent, even with all her other layers of fabric. Would a cravat be long enough?

A scratch on the door interrupted her pacing. She opened the door a crack and peered around the edge. Sinclair stood in the hall.

"I believe you dropped this, Mr. Quincy," he said, handing her a folded length of cloth. He looked both ways down the hall, then ducked inside, kissed her on the cheek, and was gone.

She leaned against the closed door, holding the cloth to her face. It smelled of Sinclair. It was almost identical in size and shape to the one she'd ripped in half last night, though the edges were not hemmed. A man of the world, and a smart one, too. She used the cloth to dry her eyes.

As soon as she was dressed decently, she opened the door for servants to remove the tub. Wilford knocked while she was tying her cravat.

"Lord Sinclair wishes you to join him in the breakfast parlor when you're ready, sir."

Startled since she hadn't heard his approach, she tugged the ruined knot loose. "Thank you, Wilford." She pulled the ends together and tried again.

"Allow me, sir," Wilford said. He stepped behind her, reached around and tied the cravat neatly and efficiently in a simple knot, without touching her at all.

She watched his face in the mirror while he worked, easily visible since his tucked chin was still an inch above her head. Finished, he nodded at his handiwork. Just before he turned away, he winked at her in the mirror, then left the room.

It was over so quickly, and his expression never altered. Had she only imagined it?

Her hands fluttered to the knot at her throat that he'd just tied for her. Of course. Her Adam's apple, or lack thereof. She smacked her forehead. Blast.

She'd never appeared in public without a properly tied cravat, but had merely considered it part of her costume, not part of a disguise. In the future, she would be more diligent about her cravat, in private as well as public. She headed to the door.

A footman knew her secret now. Her step faltered. If Wilford told anyone, her cravat and rolled-up stocking would be pointless.

"Wilford?" she called out. "Thank you for your, ah, assistance."

The footman came back to the room. "Think nothing of it, Mr. Quincy." He placed emphasis on the "mister." His gaze bored into hers. "Lord Sinclair has always been a right one to work for, even when he's not present. The staff has heard how it was you who found him after his mishap. We're all beholden to you." Wilford raised his eyebrows.

Quincy nodded. Message received and understood.

"This way, sir."

She followed Wilford downstairs to the breakfast parlor, her heart rate gradually returning to normal.

A footman topped off the coffee in Sinclair's cup, then silently withdrew from the room. Sinclair took a deep drink.

"One hundred proof coffee?" she asked, sitting down. Another footman appeared and set a heaping plate in front of her. She let him pour a cup of coffee for her, then he left, too.

Sinclair flashed a faint smile and drained his cup. "Eat up. We're leaving as soon as you've filled your belly."

"Leaving?" No, their time alone, just the two of them, couldn't end so soon. "But you—"

"Promised your grandmother, and I always keep my promises. You did find all you needed to in the account books and talking to merchants yesterday, didn't you?"

"Yes, but shouldn't you rest? Neither of us slept well last night." Jumping Jupiter, did she actually just say that out loud?

"Your grandmother—"

"Will understand." Grandmère had practically *ordered*

her to be with Sinclair. "No one keeps all their promises, especially when they're ill."

"I am not ill. And I keep all my promises. I'm taking you
back to your grandmother, where you'll be safe." He tossed
his napkin beside his untouched plate before limping from
the room.

Safe from what? Or whom? Quincy shut her mouth on
the useless words she'd been about to utter, and wolfed
down her meal. Sinclair would never admit to needing a day
of rest, especially if it meant breaking his word. No man
liked to be bested by a horse. And no man she had ever met
would willingly admit to feeling poorly, at least none with
less than fifty years in his dish. Sinclair even disliked any
reference to his lingering war wound.

She wrapped a couple scones in a napkin and dropped
them in her pocket. Leaving this late, they had no chance of
reaching London before dark, and if they stopped for
meals, they wouldn't arrive until after midnight. She
grabbed her books and spectacles from the library, collected her packed bag from Wilford, and hurried out to the
stables.

A cloud seemed to hover over Sinclair during the entire
journey. He responded to her conversational sallies with little more than grunts or a nod of his head. When he did
speak, his voice was more husky than when he'd called her
darling this morning.

Her body protested the bone-jarring ride and lack of
sleep the night before, but she did not complain. If Sinclair
could doggedly ride on through the misting rain, as miserable as he must feel, than so could she. Her rising suspi-
cions about his state of health were confirmed when he
headed straight to his own town house, and not to take her
home to Grandmère as he'd promised.

He bumped against her as they dismounted, and she
reached to steady him. The action allowed her to look
closely at his face in the light from the gas lamps. His
cheeks were flushed, his eyes bright from fever.

She reached a hand toward his forehead, but saw a groom
watching them. She swerved and brushed a fleck of mud

from his shoulder instead. "May I recommend an early night, my lord?"

They started toward the house. "Of course. Go home, Quincy."

"I meant for you, not me."

He snorted. "Been gone three days. Got things to check on." He climbed three steps to the back door, took a deep breath, and doubled over with a coughing fit.

She waited for it to pass, helped him upright, and pressed her palm to his forehead. "Sinclair, you're burning up with fever. Go to bed."

He shook his head and swayed against her. "Things to do."

She grabbed him by his elbows and stared into his blood-shot eyes. "Go to bed now, or I'll hoist you over my shoulder and carry you there myself."

He blinked at her, then gave a bark of laughter that ended in another coughing fit. "That would make an interesting picture for Mama and the maids, wouldn't it?" He sighed. "All right, you win. Bed sounds wonderful." He gave her a sidelong glance as he opened the door. "Going to come up and help me with my . . . boots . . . again?"

Fortunately the darkness hid her blush. She should go home, but couldn't leave him. Not yet.

As thcy made their way to his bedchamber, she encouraged him to lean on her, perhaps a little more than necessary. She was becoming accustomed to his warmth and solid form against her, his arm a comforting weight across her shoulders. She liked it.

Perhaps too much.

Thompson was at his post, for once, and sprang forward when they neared. "Is aught amiss?"

"Nothing a few days in bed won't cure," Quincy replied. She ignored Sinclair's snort. "I'm afraid you'll have to pretend you're a valet, Thompson."

Sinclair stared at her. "You're leaving me?"

Quincy gaped at the naked plea in Sinclair's tone, and face. She resisted the urge to cup his cheek, draw him into her embrace, kiss him. Now that she knew what it was like to hold each other all night, give each other indescribable pleasure, she longed to hold him again, whatever length of time, whatever opportunity. But, knowing Thompson was watching, she kept her hands at her sides. "Grandmère, remember? I'll be back in the morning." She cleared her throat. "Good night, my lord. Thompson will see to your needs."

The sound of Sinclair coughing followed her down the stairs.

He was home now, warm and dry. He would be fine.

Chapter 16

Grandmère and Melinda had been busy in Quincy's absence. Paintings hung on the walls, packing crates were gone. Several rugs and unfamiliar pieces of furniture graced their sitting room, kitchen, and bedrooms. A stain here, a nick there, what did it matter? Their home was more cozy than since they left the little cottage behind. Best of all was a bed, an actual bed with a down-filled mattress, mismatched sheets and all, awaiting her in her tiny, private room.

Since it was after nine, Mel and Grandmère were sound asleep. Sir Ambrose flipped his tail in greeting from his rug before the fire, but didn't stir himself any further. Quincy flung herself on her soft new bed, not even bothering to undress, and quickly fell into a deep sleep.

"How was your journey, dear?" Grandmère asked the next morning over tea and scones, after they'd finally roused Quincy by waving a rasher of bacon under her nose.

Meat for breakfast? Such spendthrift ways. Her employment may end any day. Every extra penny still needed to be saved toward their cottage. After Melinda explained it was a gift from Sam the butcher and his eldest son, who had continued their reading lessons with Melinda in Quincy's absence, Quincy savored each bite.

"Our journey?" she said finally, sitting back with a full stomach and a second cup of tea. "It was very, um, educational." Grandmère gave her a sharp look, but Quincy evaded her gaze, concentrating on buttering another scone. Her description of the estate was punctuated by sighs of pleasure from Melinda, and Sinclair's unplanned dunking in the ditch was met by appropriate noises of concern. Omitting any mention of the overnight delay in their return to the house was not lying. Not exactly.

"Poor man probably has an abominable head cold by now," Grandmère said, clucking her tongue. She hobbled over to the kitchen wardrobe. "If his throat is sore, see that he drinks warm lemonade with honey. And get him to drink willowbark tea. It will help him recover from the cold faster."

"Oh, yes," Melinda added fervently. "But be sure to sugar the tea, or he'll object to it being too bitter. Assure him it'll make him feel better. It did for me, anyway." The two sisters shared a brief hug at the reminder of how ill Melinda had recently been.

Ignoring the rain, Quincy ran the short distance to Sinclair's house, leaping over mud puddles and dodging the spray sent up by carriages passing in the street.

"Might I suggest a different plan than usual, Mr. Quincy?" Harper said, taking her hat, coat, and gloves.

She raised her eyebrows. Rough barking, reminiscent of seals she had heard on a long ago journey to the seaside, floated downstairs.

"Your presence may be more welcome in the earl's chamber than in the library."

"If not welcome by the earl, then certainly by Thompson, eh?" she said with a grin.

"The night did seem unusually long." Harper's butler mask was firmly in place, but his eyes twinkled.

Thompson met her in the doorway to Sinclair's chamber, dark circles under his puffy eyes. "What the devil happened between you two while you were gone? Kept saying your name all night. I couldn't decide whether he wanted to throttle you or k—"

"Kill me? I imagine he'd be of a mind to cause injury to almost anyone if he feels as poorly as I think he does." She stepped past him but halted at the sight of Sinclair.

He lay sprawled on the bed, the bedclothes in a tangle around his waist. He sighed and was wracked by a coughing fit, then lay back with a groan.

"Good morning, Sinclair," she said softly, stepping closer.

"What's good about it?" he said, his voice a croak. He squinted and turned away as she drew one curtain aside, admitting enough light to see him better.

The red and purple bruise on his temple sharply contrasted against the pallor of his face. She pressed her palm against his forehead, ignoring the need to caress him. "Just as I thought," she said brightly. "You are undoubtedly feeling miserable, my lord, but your fever is slight. Nothing serious."

Sinclair snorted. "Of course it's nothing serious. I'm fine." He sat up and swung his legs over the edge of the bed.

With a footman in the room, it was easier to keep her reaction in check at seeing his bare feet and legs. Her gaze lingered on the deep, puckered scars that started just above his right knee and disappeared under his twisted nightshirt. Raw scars that announced he'd been to hell and back, and lived to tell the tale. Scars that she had traced with her fingertips only yesterday. "I should amend that to say it is nothing serious *yet*. If you stay in bed for a few days, then curtail your activities for another week or so, you should be fine."

"I've spent enough damn time bedridden." He tried to stand up.

She pushed him back. "If, however, you prefer to be foolish and allow this cold to develop into pneumonia, I can describe in great detail the misery you will endure for weeks, if not months, to come."

"What—" Sinclair broke off, caught in another coughing fit. "What makes you a bloody expert? Oh, that's right, you've nursed two patients. One of them you put to bed with a shovel, didn't you? That makes the odds just about even for me, doesn't it?"

Quincy felt the blood drain from her face. She stumbled back a step. "There was nothing I could do about my father's weak heart, and you know it." Her voice rose with her anger, the words nearly choking her before they tumbled out, filled with all the frustration and fury of the last year. "If I can bring my sister through a bout with pneumonia in the dead of winter with little money for food or coal, let alone medicine, then with all of your wealth available I can certainly cure your sorry hide!"

Sinclair sat, frozen in place, staring at her feet. The fire crackled, the only sound in the deafening quiet.

Quincy averted her eyes to dig through her pockets, as much to search for the packet Grandmère had sent along as to hide the tears that threatened to spill. She unwrapped the oilcloth and handed a twist of paper to Thompson. At least her voice didn't shake. "Please ask Irene to—No, she's gone. Ask Jill to brew this, and make sure there's sugar but not milk on the tea tray she brings up."

"Yes, sir." Thompson shut the door behind him.

"I'm sorry." Sinclair's rough voice was almost a whisper.

Unable to look at him, Quincy stared out the window, watching raindrops slide down the pane.

Sinclair reached up, engulfing her icy hand in his warm clasp. "You didn't deserve that. My behavior is inexcusable."

She looked down at their enjoined hands, warmth spreading through her. "Yes. Well." She cleared her throat. "I don't suppose you deserved that either."

"Oh, my poor, sweet poppet!"

They both started at Lady Sinclair's entrance, their hands dropping to their sides.

"Has the doctor been sent for?" Quincy asked, taking a step away from the bed. She sniffed back tears and straightened her shoulders.

"Yes, he should be here soon, dear," she said, gliding closer. "Whatever are you doing, trying to get out of bed?"

"My wits must have gone begging," Sinclair muttered, lying down.

"If they have, there's no need for you to go chasing after them."

Assured that Lady Sinclair had noticed nothing out of the ordinary, and feeling mostly in charity with Sinclair once more, Quincy couldn't resist an I-told-you-so look as she tugged the covers up to his chin. He stuck his tongue out at her.

"What's this I hear the lad decided to go swimming, eh?" Dr. Kimball said, striding into the room.

Quincy and Lady Sinclair left as Dr. Kimball began his examination. When Quincy headed for the stairs, Lady Sinclair invited her for a cup of tea in her sitting room.

They settled on the sofa, Quincy's mind still on Sinclair, barely aware of his mother's chatter.

"I haven't thanked you yet for being with my son."

Quincy sloshed her tea. "My lady?"

"You were the one who helped Benjamin after his fall, stayed with him through the night. Or did I misunderstand his ramblings?"

Oh dear heaven, what had the man said in his ramblings? To his *mother*? "I joined in the search when Lord Sinclair's horse came back without him. I simply assisted him in finding shelter, and we waited out the storm in a shepherd's hut. It was nothing." She wished Lady Sinclair would look elsewhere. Her steady gaze was making Quincy's cheeks flush. The little smile at the corner of her mouth reminded her uneasily of Grandmère.

"Belittle your actions if you wish, Mr. Quincy, but I know you went above and beyond the call of duty to make my son feel better, and I appreciate it."

Quincy choked. Lady Sinclair patted her on the arm.

The housekeeper opened the door. "The doctor has finished and would like to speak with you before he leaves, my lady."

"Thank you, Mrs. Hammond." With one last beaming smile at Quincy, Lady Sinclair rose, and Quincy followed. They joined the doctor in the hall.

"A week's rest in bed should do the trick," he said, handing Quincy a bottle of Godfrey's Cordial. "Give him a dose of this tonic if his coughing gets worse, or laudanum if his leg bothers him. And send for me if his fever increases or does not go down in a day or two." He bowed before Lady Sinclair and left.

"Quack," Quincy muttered, reading the label on the tonic bottle. This would do nothing more for Sinclair than his favorite brandy would.

Sinclair was young and strong, she reminded herself. Even if he contracted the same illness Melinda had, he should recover much quicker than her sister. She gave the tonic bottle to Jill and took the tea tray from her, then knocked and entered Sinclair's chamber. Lady Sinclair followed at her heels.

Sinclair was just settling back under the covers, being helped by Thompson and Jack. When finished, they stood on opposite sides of the bed, Jack tall and straight with his blue livery and new crutch, Thompson several inches taller than Jack but listing to one side.

Quincy poured a cup of willowbark tea and handed it to Sinclair. "I know it's not the best-tasting, but it will help you feel better."

He took a sip and contorted his features as though it was straight lemon juice. "You don't seriously expect me to drink this vile concoction, this—"

"Hush, poppet, and drink up." Lady Sinclair sat on the edge of the bed and brushed strands of hair from his eyes.

"Mama!"

"Sorry, dear." She didn't look the least repentant as she stood and winked at Quincy before exiting the room.

Quincy didn't know quite what to make of Lady Sinclair. But this was no time to ponder mysteries. She ordered Thompson to go to bed before he collapsed. Then she set the twins scurrying, to request Grandmère's chicken soup recipe for luncheon, collect sturdy linen handkerchiefs and a second chamber pot, and a dozen other things she remembered needing or wanting in the sickroom.

"Done?" she asked Sinclair a few minutes later when they were alone. He nodded meekly and held up his empty cup. "You drank it all?" She raised her eyebrows in disbelief. Sinclair shrugged and slid down in the bed until the covers reached his chin.

"You should have another cup every two hours. I'll remind Jill and Jack, in case you forget."

"Where you going?" came Sinclair's muffled, hoarse voice as she reached the door.

"Downstairs. I have a lot of work waiting for me, and you need to sleep." If she stayed, she'd give in to the urge to sit on the bed and hold his hand. She forced herself to go.

She planned to catch up on the earl's correspondence, then bring the account books up to date. She had done no more than break open all the seals when Harper knocked and entered the library.

"You are needed upstairs." He cleared his throat at the alarmed expression on Quincy's face. "I believe his lordship merely wants to give you instructions."

She pushed aside the stack of mail and went upstairs. Yes, she answered Sinclair, she'd bring the account books up to date, and answer his correspondence. The urge to roll her eyes was stronger than the desire to hold his hand, but she resisted both.

She returned to the library, set to work, and just sanded the first letter when Sinclair sent for her again. After the third such request, with the message passed from Jack the upstairs footman, to Celia the tweeny, to Grimshaw the downstairs footman, and then to the butler, Quincy tossed her pen in the air and sighed. She wiped up the ink blots, then enlisted Harper's aid in carrying the account books, correspondence, paper, pens, inkwell and abacus up to Sinclair's sitting room.

"What's going on in there?" Sinclair barked through the connecting doorway.

Harper and Jack helped her tug Sinclair's writing desk from its place by the window to a spot against the far wall, where she could work at his desk and see through the doorway to Sinclair in bed—and where he could see her.

"In the interests of efficiency, I shall work from here for the next few days," she announced, arranging her workspace. "Running between floors all day is Celia's job, not mine."

"Cheeky bugger," Sinclair muttered.

"Yes. Now I shall go back to work, and you should go to sleep. If not for yourself, then to give *us* some rest."

Harper gave Jack a stern glance when the footman's shoulders shook with silent laughter, but she noticed the butler's shoulders twitched as he left the room.

An hour later, Quincy stretched and went to pour Sinclair another cup of willowbark tea. "You'll get used to the taste after a while," she told him, handing him the cup.

He raised one brow in disbelief, and squeezed his eyes shut as he sipped. "Open the drapes. It's a dreary enough day without blocking out what little sun the clouds let through."

She quickly did as he asked, her steps light with the hope his illness wasn't as bad as she'd first thought. When she turned back, he held out his cup, upside down.

" 'Tis best done quickly," he said with a grimace.

She nodded agreement and went back to work.

Jill brought a luncheon tray at noon, laden with bread, cheese, ham, and chicken soup.

"You're not having any soup?" Sinclair asked suspiciously.

She sat in the chair opposite him next to the window, where he'd been sitting for the past hour despite her protests for him to stay in bed. "We had it so much when Melinda was ill, now I can't eat it without thinking *I* am ill. And one of us in the sickroom is quite enough."

Sinclair flashed her a grin and went back to his soup. He leaned back a short time later after eating distressingly little. "Think I'll lie down for a bit," he said, pushing away the tray. "Chilly here by the window."

Quincy opened her mouth to tell him she thought it was actually a bit warm with the sun breaking through the clouds, but thought better of it. Frowning, she watched him limp to the bed. "Would you like me to build up the fire?"

"No. You'll get coal dust all over my account books. Have Jack do it." He sighed, coughed, and settled under the covers. She went back to work.

Lady Sinclair dropped in to see him after her morning calls.

"Mama, what is wrong?"

"Nothing, dear. I just came in to see how you were doing."

Even without being able to see her, Quincy knew from her too-bright tone that Lady Sinclair was hiding something.

"Fustian, Mama. Something has upset you."

There was a pause, before Sinclair growled, "Mama . . ."

"I was at Lady Barbour's when Dowager Lady Twitchell called. She still blames me for ruining her marriage. She tried to stir up the old scandal again, saying you killed her husband."

Sinclair coughed. "He did drop dead while I was clutching his lapels. There were plenty of witnesses in White's when I confronted him about his marked cards."

Quincy dropped her pen. She had known of the scandal before choosing to work for Sinclair, but only knew the public version. She shouldn't eavesdrop, but couldn't stop.

"But you didn't kill Twitchell, anymore than Twitchell killed your father."

"The bastard cheated Papa—"

"Benjamin!"

"And may as well have held the pistol to Papa's head and pulled the trigger himself. And the bas—blighter thought you'd run into his arms after Papa's funeral."

"I did love Durwin once, long ago. Long before you were born. But I was happy with your father. You do know I loved your father very much?" She must have touched Sinclair, because Quincy heard him kiss his mother's hand.

"Yes, Mama. I know."

"Durwin never forgave my father for rejecting his suit."

"Some loves you never get over."

A moment of silence. Quincy stayed still.

"Young Twitchell hasn't forgiven you for what he perceives as your role in Durwin's death. Promise me you won't do anything foolish, like fight a duel. I couldn't bear to lose you, too."

He coughed again. "At the moment I doubt I could defend myself against a ten-year-old." Lady Sinclair must not have appreciated his attempt at humor. "I made that promise to you over five years ago, Mama. I haven't forgotten."

"I know. Just making certain." She kissed him on the forehead. "Try not to be such a beast to your secretary. I feel certain Quincy has your best interests at heart."

The door to the hall opened and closed. A few moments later, Sinclair began snoring.

So. The private version of the scandal wasn't so different from the public one. How Sinclair must hate having everyone know his business. And poor Lady Sinclair had worn mourning until just a few weeks ago.

Whether Sinclair let her go or not, Quincy would have to leave. Soon. She wouldn't risk putting them through another scandal. If one footman had seen through her disguise, so could another. Or someone else. She had to leave. She swallowed the sudden lump in her throat.

Except for Jack popping his head in the door to see if she or the earl needed anything, Quincy worked uninterrupted. She soon finished all the correspondence, signing Sinclair's name where necessary, and declined all his invitations for the next two weeks. His search for a wife would just have to wait.

Maybe it would wait until after she'd gone. Then she wouldn't have to witness it.

Sinclair slept through Jill bringing a tea tray. Not wanting it to go to waste, Quincy indulged in a cup and several biscuits. While she ate, she sat by the window, alternating between watching the rain slide down the windowpane and the steady rise and fall of Sinclair's chest.

She knew what it was like to feel that rise and fall, feel his heartbeat beneath her cheek. She refused to dwell on the fact it would never happen again, that some other woman would be able to do what she could not. She had her moment of joy to remember, to hold close.

By late afternoon she felt caught up enough to read the business section of the newspaper. It was time to return to something she'd dabbled in back when Papa had extra blunt to give her and Mel pin money—investments. Papa had humored her by investing her funds as she directed, and was disappointed but not surprised when she insisted he reinvest her profits rather than spend the money on herself. Lucky for Mel she had been so stubborn—after Papa's death, Quincy had gradually sold those investments to pay for Mel's medicine and doctor bills.

If only Papa had listened to her advice regarding his own investments. Everything her family had been through this past year and more, everything that had been taken away from them, or they'd had to give up . . .

No. She refused to blame Papa for their predicament. Now, thanks to the earl, she had enough money set aside that she could invest some of their funds again. She would have to. Since she was leaving soon, she couldn't rely on savings alone to buy the cottage.

"Quincy, you still here?" Sinclair's voice was thick and raspy.

"How do you feel?" she asked, stepping close to his bed.

He pulled himself up and leaned against the headboard. "Damn. Haven't felt burnt to the socket like this since . . ."

"Waterloo?" she finished for him.

He nodded. "Few days after, actually. I remember dancing at the Duchess of Richmond's ball. Had a skirmish with the French the next morning, and damn near lost my leg. A few days later I woke up in a peasant's cottage." He rubbed his right thigh as he spoke. "Sort of woke up, that is. Needed so much laudanum, the days blurred together. Just as well. Damned embarrassing to have a strange Belgian tending to all your needs, and you barely have the strength to blink your eyes."

With no one else about, she sat on the edge of the bed and took Sinclair's hand in hers.

"Only thing that made it tolerable was they didn't speak any English, and didn't think I spoke any French." He turned their hands over and raised them, dropped a kiss on her wrist.

Quincy had trouble following the thread of the conversation, what with Sinclair rubbing circles over the back of her hand with his thumb. "Must have made for some interesting eavesdropping. How long did you stay with them?"

Sinclair drank from the glass on his bedside table. "Most of the summer. Regiment had to leave me behind. The leaves were turning color before I could ride in a wagon without passing out. Spilt too much claret on the battlefield."

Quincy's stomach did an odd flip at realizing how close Sinclair had come to dying. She'd seen the scar, of course, but hearing about it . . . She'd add the Belgian peasants to her prayers, to her list of things for which she was grateful.

He patted her hand. "Enough reminiscing. Go home, Jo."

She faltered in the act of reaching for the bell pull. Warmth suffused her at his use of her pet name. She wiped the sudden idiotic grin from her face and rang for Jill. "Not until you eat more soup, and drink another cup of tea." She poured a cup and handed it to him.

"You're a firm believer in this tea for someone who does not have to drink the foul stuff."

"I have seen it work. Drink." She answered Jill's scratch on the door a short time later and set the dinner tray across Sinclair's lap. "I realize you have no appetite, but you know as well as I you have to eat." She grinned at him. "Otherwise you'll waste away and we'll have to send for that Belgian."

He saluted her with the spoon, but ate only one mouthful.

Perhaps he'd be more interested in the apple on the tray. She sat sideways on the bed beside Sinclair and sliced the apple into sections, pausing every so often in the task to urge Sinclair to eat more soup. She picked up an apple wedge, intending to offer it to him, until she caught a whiff of its scent, juice glistening at one edge. Her mouth watered. She licked her lips and took a bite. Sinclair's avid gaze darted from the fruit to her mouth. The last time she'd eaten an apple had been the first time they kissed. Heat spread through her at the memory. She bit into the apple again, slowly, and watched as Sinclair's mouth fell open. The hunger in his eyes had nothing to do with food.

A tiny thrill coursed through her.

She picked up another wedge, viewed it from all angles, and looked at Sinclair from beneath her lashes. His breath came faster, and his mouth was still open. She took advantage of this and held the fruit to his lips. He took a bite, eyes still on her as he chewed and swallowed, but he made no move to take the apple. She held it for him again, and this time his tongue swiped the juice from her finger before he ate.

Oh, my.

They exchanged not a word. The only sound was the crunch of apple as she fed it to him, one slice at a time. Sinclair seemed to not want to break the spell, and she wanted to make sure he ate as much as possible.

He swallowed the last bite. "Anything more?" Congestion in his chest alone could not account for his deep, husky tone.

Quincy didn't mistake his meaning for more food. Her stomach fluttered at the memory of the "more" they'd shared at the shepherd's hut. Tempted as she was by the offer, now was not the time. With greater strength of will than she'd known she possessed, she shook her head. "How about you finish the tea?" Their fingers brushed as she passed him the cup.

He took a sip, reaching his free hand to grasp hers where it rested on her knee. "This isn't so bad," he said.

No, not bad at all. With her thumb, she stroked small circles on the back of his hand.

A knock on the door made Quincy jump up. Sinclair squeezed his eyes shut. She was tugging her coat and waistcoat back into position as a maid came in to build up the fire.

Quincy went back to her account books while the maid tidied Sinclair's room, and soon after she went home, needing cool outdoor air on her flushed cheeks.

She still wasn't satisfied with the amount Sinclair had eaten, but at least he'd been drinking the willowbark tea. His fever, slight as it was, should break by morning. Thompson had arrived to relieve Jack, so there was someone to watch over the earl through the night. His mother had wanted to stay, but Sinclair accused her of wanting to wrap him in cotton wool, and sent her away.

Grandmère and Mel were sewing Mel's new gowns when Quincy entered their quarters. She would have offered to help, but since she had a knack for tangling their threads just by being near, she sat on the far side of the room and tried to distract Sir Ambrose by dangling a string.

"I didn't realize how little I have been here since we moved," she said, plucking the cat out of the sewing basket. "Where did all these pictures and such come from?"

"Lady Fitzwater has been very kind to us," Grandmère said. "She claims these were items just gathering dust in the attic, and may as well be put to good use."

"She has invited us to tea every day," Mel said, cutting a thread. "James pushes Grandmère's chair to the front parlor so they can do needlework together in the mornings."

"James?"

Mel blushed. "Sir Leland's footman."

"Sir Leland often joins us for tea, as well," Grandmère said. "He has asked about you. I believe he thinks you work too hard."

Sir Leland asked about her? Quincy covered up her frisson of alarm by picking up Sir Ambrose. It was just Sinclair's friend asking about her. There was no cause for concern. "I think I'll make an early night of it," she said, heading for her bedchamber.

"Wrung out from all the activity of the last few days, *ma chère*?"

Quincy couldn't meet Grandmère's eyes.

She changed into her nightshirt and stretched out on her feather bed, Sir Ambrose purring beside her, and tried to plan for the future.

Sinclair would recover within a week, two or three at the most, and then she would have to seek another position. She squeezed her eyes shut at the sudden pain of not seeing him anymore. Not working for him was unthinkable. So she wouldn't think about it. Leaving, awful as it was, would be the less painful option than staying on, watching as he selected a wife.

Thinking of matrimony, there was another problem to consider. If her search for steady work took even half as long as the first one had, it would delay Mel yet again in putting up her hair and seeking a husband. Blast. Away from Hubert, their former landlady's revolting son, Mel was beginning to notice the men around her. Quincy had even caught her exchanging a wink with Sir Leland's handsome footman. Papa would never approve of such a match.

But she had to get Mel out of the city before winter returned, or they'd likely be attending Mel's funeral, not her wedding. While Quincy rarely suffered from more than an occasional sniffle, Mel seemed to catch every illness that came along. This last winter had been her worst ever, including two interminable weeks when her very survival had been in doubt. Quincy clenched her fists. She would get her family out of the city. Somehow.

She would find a husband for Mel, and would not dwell on the fact that she'd never have a husband of her own. Nor would she dwell on the fact that the man she wanted would have someone else for a wife.

She rolled over and buried her face in Sir Ambrose's fur.

What seemed like only a few minutes passed before she awoke. Her room was still shrouded in darkness when she heard a faint tapping at the hall door.

Sir Leland's footman was poised to tap again when she opened the door.

"Beg pardon, sir," the footman whispered. "But there's a one-legged man in livery at the kitchen door what says Lord Sinclair sent 'im. He says he's to wait for you."

"Tell him I'll be right there," Quincy whispered back, and turned to go dress.

Five frantic minutes later, she hurried through the dark streets with Jack, dodging late-night revelers returning home. "Did Sinclair also send for Dr. Kimball?"

"No, sir. Thompson said you would know what to do."

"Thompson sent you, not Sinclair?"

"Rolled me out of bed, he did. Sir."

Quincy ran.

Chapter 17

Quincy darted around to the kitchen door, past the startled scullery maids, up the back stairs, and skidded to a halt on the rug outside Sinclair's door. She reached up to adjust her spectacles, and realized she'd left them behind. Just as she debated whether to knock, the door swung open and Thompson stuck his head out.

"Oh good, you've come," he said, and pulled her inside, quickly but silently shutting the door behind them.

"Quincy . . . No, Quincy . . ." Sinclair's raspy voice died on a moan.

Forgetting Thompson, she strode to the bed. Sinclair lay tangled in the sheets, tossing his head back and forth on the pillow. She sat on the edge and caught his hands between her own.

"Been doing that for over an hour," Thompson said, standing behind her. "Thought for sure he'd wake up Lady Sinclair and the rest of the house by now, between calling for you and shouting what I think is French swear words. What did you do to him?"

"Sinclair?" she whispered.

The earl stopped thrashing. His fingers, hot and clammy,

curled around her hand. He squeezed once, then went limp as he drifted into sleep.

"Why did you send for me, and not his mother or the doctor?"

"I don't trust doctors no more than you do, and Lady S has enough gray hair from the last time he was sick."

"The last time?" She brushed a lock of hair from Sinclair's sweaty forehead.

"In France, after the last big battle. Surgeon tried to cut off Sinclair's leg, but the earl drew the sawbones' cork and dragged hisself out of the tent, and no one could find him for more'n a week." Thompson tugged the bedsheets back up to Sinclair's shoulders. "Lady S didn't have a single gray hair until she read the casualty lists and saw his name among the missing and presumed dead." He lowered his voice even further. "You don't think he's going to cock up his toes now, do you?"

"I most certainly am not," Sinclair rasped.

Quincy smiled in relief, then frowned. "I don't understand, Sinclair. You were doing so much better. The tea should have—"

"Horrid stuff."

She narrowed her eyes. "You didn't drink it, did you? How did you dispose of it, then?"

Sinclair dropped his free arm over the side of the bed, and Quincy heard a faint sloshing sound. "Chamber pot."

"Ooh, you stubborn creature!" She dropped his hand and stood up. "Thompson, you and I should seek our own beds. Since his lordship knows what's best for his care, there is no need for us to disturb our sleep."

Thompson raised his eyebrows, then shrugged. "Whatever you think best, sir." Both headed for the door.

"You're leaving? Just like that?"

Quincy didn't even look back.

"Wait!" Sinclair reached out for her. "Before you go, would you . . . would you bring me a cup of that damn tea?"

Thompson and Quincy shared a brief grin, then Thompson grabbed the empty teapot from the hearth and left.

Quincy wrung out a cloth in the basin and wiped Sinclair's face. "You only made things worse by traveling so far in the rain in your condition. You should have stayed at Brentwood."

"No." He coughed for several moments, a hard, deep, wet cough that made Quincy's chest ache just to hear it. "Your grandmother would have worried if I didn't get you home on time. I gave my word." He fell back against the pillows.

He had also given his word, if only to himself, that he would not be with her until she was his, legally. But that didn't mean he wanted to be without her until then.

Thompson returned a short time later, carrying the foul-tasting brew. Sinclair struggled to sit up, grimaced when Thompson and Quincy both had to give him a hand. He nodded a dismissal, and the footman retreated to his post in the hall.

Quincy sat on the edge of the bed and handed him the cup of tea. "I'm not turning my back this time."

She had no need to worry. After asking for the tea, it would have been foolish to tip it out. "Cheers." He took a sip. Maybe he was getting used to it, or Quincy had added more sugar this time. It was only mildly awful. He downed the rest of it as quickly as he could. He squinted toward the fireplace, but couldn't read the clock on the mantel in the darkness.

He pushed the bedclothes down to his lap. The fire cast far too much heat, it felt like a boulder rested on his chest, and that demented carpenter in his head was still at it. But he was alone with Quincy, and that was all that mattered.

She traded the empty cup for a cool damp cloth, and soothed it over his brow. Ah, even better. He reached up to pat her hand.

"I should leave, and you should go back to sleep."

Her voice had that hitch in it, that breathless quality it took on every time he touched her, whenever he stood close enough to inhale her scent. Good to know he still had that effect on her, even when he was far from his best. "Not sleepy."

"It's the middle of the night, and you're exhausted. Of course you're sleepy."

"Not sleepy," he repeated, lazily reaching for her hand.

"Well, we can't get you a glass of warm milk. That would make you cough even more. Wonder if there's any chamomile tea in the kitchen?"

He stroked his thumb over her hand. Her voice was more soothing than any tonic. He didn't want to sleep, he wanted to hear her. But talking required too much effort. "Tell me a story."

She laughed. "A what?"

"You want me to sleep, tell me a bedtime story."

"You're being silly."

He nodded. "Story."

"All right, let me think." She took the cloth away, wrung it out, and replaced it on his forehead. "Once upon a time . . . This is ridiculous."

He settled against the pillows, taking her hand in his again. "Keep going."

She sighed. "Once upon a time, there lived a handsome young man named Randolph."

Sinclair opened one eye. Quincy blushed. "I used to tell this to my sister. You want me to continue or not?"

With his free hand, Sinclair waved her on.

Quincy cleared her throat. "Randolph came from a good family, but he was the younger son of a younger son, and had to make his own way in the world. When he finished his schooling, he became the curate at a parish in a small fishing village. He was as poor as his parishioners, but he tried to help them as much as he could. If one of them was sick, he would take their place on the fishing boat, so they would not miss a day's wages."

Sinclair smiled as Quincy got into the spirit of telling a bedtime story, probably falling into old habits. He pictured her as a lass of ten or so, tucking in her little sister with this tale.

"One day, a squall came up in the Channel, and the fishing boat nearly rammed the hull of a capsized yacht. Its crew was thrashing about in the water, battered by the waves. None of the fishermen would risk themselves by jumping in to the rough sea, but they did throw ropes. One of the people in the water was the owner of the yacht, a French aristocrat. His daughter was also in the water, just beyond the reach of the ropes. She tried to swim toward the boat, but her panniers and skirts were dragging her under. She was going to drown.

"Randolph saw the young woman in peril, and jumped into the storm-tossed waters to save her, and saved her father as well. The fishermen pulled the rest of the crew to safety. Everyone on the yacht was saved. The aristocrat was a friend of our king, coming to England to seek refuge from the Revolution. King George was so grateful to Randolph for saving his friend that he granted Randolph a barony. The Frenchman had lost all his riches to the Revolution and the storm, but he wanted to show his thanks as well, and gave Randolph his most precious possession—his daughter Dominique's hand in marriage. Randolph was overjoyed, for he and Dominique had fallen in love at first sight." Quincy's voice trailed off.

"Did you forget how it ends?"

"Thought you'd fallen asleep." She rinsed and replaced the cloth on his forehead.

"So did they live happily ever after?" He gave her back the cloth and pulled the blankets up to his chin. The fire had burned down too low.

"Of course. Well, they did until Randolph died in a carriage accident twenty years ago."

Dominique was her grandmother's name. Sinclair opened his eyes.

She met his level gaze, then leaned forward and dropped a kiss on his brow. "Now be a good lad and go to sleep."

He fell asleep with a grin on his face.

Quincy and Thompson took turns through the night, giving Sinclair more of the willowbark tea between his coughing fits whenever he awoke. Twice she tried to lie down on the valet's cot in the closet, but Sinclair called out for her before her head touched the pillow. She settled for curling up in the chair pulled close to his bed, her hand resting on his shoulder. Thompson gave her a searching look, but she didn't care. There was nothing wrong with touching Sinclair if it gave him some measure of comfort. Exhausted from coughing, he finally fell silent an hour before dawn.

A bleary-eyed Jack came in at seven to relieve Thompson. Quincy stood and stretched, envious of Thompson who headed for his bed in the servants' quarters upstairs. Thinking fondly of her own soft bed, she realized she had left no note for Grandmère and Melinda to explain her absence. She was about to leave when Sinclair called for her again. She ended up scribbling a note for a footman to deliver to Mel, and headed back to Sinclair.

Uncanny. If she tried to leave his side, he became restless and called out for her. If she merely went to her desk to work, he slept soundly. He needed to sleep, so she stayed at her desk. His labored breathing was audible across the room, almost hypnotic.

"Quincy!" Sinclair's raspy voice startled her awake.

She raised her head from her desk and attempted to rub away the imprint of the quill pen from her cheek. "What?" She blinked, bringing the earl into focus.

"What the devil time is it?" He sat up, running his fingers through his mussed hair. "Why didn't you—" He broke off as another coughing fit seized him.

"Good morning to you, too, sunshine," she said under her breath. She rang for the maid, then went to Sinclair's bedside and waited until he fell back against the pillows. "For patients in your condition, Dr. Kimball would recommend weak tea and thin gruel." Sinclair scrunched his face in distaste. "Grandmère, however, recommends any fruit that can be found, toast with orange marmalade, and as much tea as you can drink."

At the mention of fruit, he smiled. "Your grandmother is a wise woman." He started to say more but was seized with another coughing fit.

Quincy poured from a bottle she had concealed under his bedside table, and handed him the cup when he finally stopped. "She also recommends one shot of whiskey every four hours when you are awake."

"I prefer brandy."

"Grandmère was quite specific."

He shrugged and downed the whiskey in one gulp. And promptly coughed for two solid minutes.

When Jill appeared, Quincy requested luncheon for herself and breakfast for the earl, then set to brewing the willowbark tea. By the time she looked back at him, he'd fallen asleep again.

She read the newspaper while she ate, occasionally glancing at the earl. He slept on. She studied the business section, deciding where to invest first. Her only hope was investments. Fortunes, in the modest size she needed, could be won or lost in a matter of months. She really must see about meeting with the earl's solicitor, to check on his portfolio, and to start her own again. Tomorrow, however, was soon enough. Just now she wanted nothing more than to sleep.

"Where'd you hide the bottle, Jo?" Sinclair spoke near her ear.

Quincy jerked her head up, narrowly missing Sinclair's chin. "What are you doing out of bed?" Sinclair stood barefoot beside her, wearing nothing but his nightshirt, which reached only to mid-calf.

"Nature called. Devilish hot under all those blankets. Where's the whiskey?"

She pressed her palm against his forehead. "You're still fevered. Get back into bed, and I'll get the bottle."

He started to grumble but coughed instead. "Can't stop," he muttered, between coughs and gasping for air. "Hate this." He leaned on her shoulder as he limped back to bed.

Quincy winced, seeing the pain on his face as he clutched his hand to his chest. "Hold your breath," she ordered.

Sinclair fell onto the bed rather than actually sitting down, and looked at her, incredulous. "You gone daft?" he squeezed between coughs.

"Trust me. It will help you stop coughing. For a moment, at least."

He clamped his jaw shut. His body jerked twice as he fought back the urge to cough, and then was still. He raised his eyebrows.

Quincy smiled and pulled the whiskey bottle out from

under his bedside table. "Drink it slowly this time," she warned, handing him the cup.

Sinclair's eyes grew wide over the rim of the cup as he watched his mother enter the room, a worried frown on her face. "Don't let on," he whispered. He sat up straight and handed the empty cup back to Quincy.

"Benjamin, dear," Lady Sinclair said, her tone overly bright. She reached to touch his forehead.

Sinclair leaned back, narrowly avoiding her hand. He would have toppled over if not for grabbing Quincy's coattail.

"Good afternoon, Lady Sinclair," Quincy said, moving one foot back to brace herself as Sinclair's sudden tug threatened to pull her down on top of him.

"Quincy." Lady Sinclair gave her a brief nod in greeting, her eyes only for her son. "How are you feeling, dear?"

He nodded, but said nothing. Shielded from his mother's view, his hand still gripped Quincy's coattail to keep himself sitting upright. Quincy felt his slight convulsion as he suppressed another coughing fit.

"His voice is almost gone, my lady," she said, thinking that wasn't completely untrue. She didn't understand Sinclair's reluctance to let his mother know the extent of his illness, but they could discuss that later.

Lady Sinclair frowned. "I think I should send for Dr. Kimball again."

"No!" Sinclair rasped.

"I do not believe he is needed," Quincy quickly added. "I think Lord Sinclair prefers my grandmother's prescription to that of the good doctor's. At this point, he simply needs to rest." She turned to glare at him. "In bed, for one full week."

Lady Sinclair gave a small smile. "Your grandmother has experience in these things? Very well. If anything changes, anything at all, you will be sure to let me know." She gave her son another worried look, then exited the room after a brief backward glance.

When she was sure they were alone again, with Jack stationed outside the door, Quincy spun around to face Sinclair. "What the devil was that about?"

He let go of her coat and fell back. "My youngest brother . . . perished from . . . an inflammation . . . of the lungs."

"Oh." She handed Sinclair another cloth to cough into. He had already soiled all his handkerchiefs, and they weren't coming back with his laundry. Jill had told her the laundress had burned them. She cleared her throat. "You, my lord, are not going to die. Not after what you survived in France. You are going to live to torment your servants and tease your employees for many, many years to come. Now go to sleep."

Sinclair's mouth turned up at the corners as he burrowed under the blankets.

His endless coughing, through the day and another night, was torture. She felt his pain, frustration, and fatigue. As his fever climbed, Quincy bathed his face with a cool cloth. His rapid decline alarmed her, but she kept her panic tamped down. Someone had to remain strong and in charge. Perhaps his recovery would be equally swift.

The maids continued to bring meals on a tray. Except for a quick trip home to change clothes and retrieve her spectacles, Quincy hardly left Sinclair's bedchamber or sitting room. Fortunately, no one seemed to think it odd for the secretary to be tending Sinclair in the absence of a valet.

"Daisy said you didn't hardly touch dinner," Thompson said, entering the room carrying a tray with bread, cheese and cold meats. He set it on the table by the window.

Quincy looked up, surprised to note how low the candles had burned. Sinclair had been restless all evening, muttering in French and English. Her touch no longer calmed him. She had been debating calling for the doctor.

"Let me do that, sir, while you eat." Thompson took the cloth from her hands.

Nodding her thanks, Quincy stood and stretched stiff muscles. She had little appetite, but it would serve no one if she became ill as well. She made a sandwich and had barely taken a bite when the earl grabbed the cloth from the footman's hand and flung it across the room. On its way into the fire, it knocked over the teakettle warming on the hearth, and sizzled on the coals.

Quincy started to mop up the spilled tea, but let it go when she heard grunts from Sinclair, and Thompson called out.

"Here, now, you can't do that." Thompson tried to catch the earl's hands as Sinclair swung at the footman with his fist. Weakened from his illness, there was little strength behind his blows, but Thompson didn't seem inclined to discover how strong he was or not.

"Stop!" Quincy said, rushing to the bed. "You'll hurt him."

"You talking to him or me?" Thompson grunted as Sinclair jabbed him in the ribs.

Still trying to be rid of Thompson, Sinclair pushed and shoved against the oversized footman. His eyes were open but glazed as he thrashed about on the bed, apparently seeing things from long ago and far away.

Quincy reached for one of the earl's flailing arms, but caught his elbow against her nose. Her spectacles flew across the room. "Captain!" she shouted. "Cease and desist this instant!"

Sinclair stopped, stayed still, except for his harsh breathing.

Thompson backed away two steps. The ominous cracking sound beneath his left heel was Quincy's spectacles. Ignoring Quincy's look of dismay, he straightened his wig, which hung over one eye, and pulled his waistcoat down into its proper position.

Sinclair began coughing, the kind of fit Quincy was afraid he would never be able to stop again. He coughed into the cloth Quincy handed him, while she picked his bedclothes off the floor where they'd fallen during the scuffle, and covered him.

Her upper lip felt wet. She licked her lips and tasted the metallic tang of blood.

"Cor blimey, 'e's done drawn your cork!" Thompson darted around the bed to her, pulling a handkerchief from his pocket. He wrapped one arm around Quincy's shoulders and held the handkerchief to her bleeding nose.

Quincy pushed his hand away from her face and looked at the soggy linen. "'Tis not so bad," she said. She put it back against her nose as she felt another drop slide down her upper lip. Only then did she realize Thompson still held her in a one-armed embrace. She looked up, but could see only concern on his features.

And then something else flickered in his eyes. A chill chased up her spine.

Sinclair's coughing had quieted, but now she realized it was more of a gurgling noise. The earl had curled up in a ball against the headboard, his face etched with pain as he fought for air. "He's choking!" Quincy ducked under the footman's arm, toward Sinclair. "Help me move him."

They rolled Sinclair away from the headboard, onto his left side. He did not resist. Quincy climbed up and knelt on the bed beside him. "Grandmère warned me this might happen," she said. "He's drowning inside. Pull the chamber pot out from under the bed."

Thompson did as she bid, and watched in horror as she began hitting Sinclair on his back. "She told you to beat him?"

"In a manner of speaking, yes." With each word, she hit Sinclair between his shoulder blades with her cupped hand. Sinclair did not move. His eyes remained closed. Panic rose in her throat. "I don't understand. She said this would help dislodge the fluid in his lungs."

"Is he supposed to be sitting up, or lying down?" Thompson lit another candle on the bedside table. "Should I hang him upside down over the pot?"

"I don't know!" Quincy blinked back tears of frustration. "Should I fetch Dr. Kimball?"

"There is no time." Quincy bent close to the earl's face. "Cough, Benjamin," she whispered in his ear, still hitting him with her cupped hand. "You must cough. Please, Benjamin, cough for me."

Interminable moments later, Sinclair started to cough. Weakly at first, but he began clearing out his lungs, drawing deeper breaths. He pulled himself closer to the edge of the bed and spit into the chamber pot.

Quincy patted him on the shoulder and sat back on her heels, releasing a sigh of relief. Sinclair, his breathing now almost normal, squinted up at her in the candlelight, and relaxed. "My angel," he murmured. He clutched her hand to his heart, before his eyes fluttered shut.

Thompson's mouth fell open as he stared back and forth between Quincy and Sinclair. "I knew it!" He slapped his palm against his thigh. "I was right all along. Grimshaw owes me a shilling!"

Oh, dear heaven. "Beg pardon?" Kneeling on the bed beside Sinclair wasn't helping her case. She slid to the floor and gave Thompson a wide-eyed stare. "Right about what?"

He stared right back, looking insanely happy. "You. Being a girl."

Her first instinct was to refute his statement, but how would that reflect on Sinclair? And she'd never actively lied—only by omission. "What makes you think that?"

Thompson looked perplexed for a moment, but then his chin came up. "Lord Sinclair ain't the sort to hold another man's hand."

Quincy slumped in the chair pulled close to the bed. "When did you wager with Grimshaw?"

"After the warehouse by the docks, when I carried you out to the coach and into the house. You looked the part and all, but something just weren't right. And you should've seen the earl's face when he saw you conked out on the sofa. Turned whiter than his cravat."

Quincy felt lightheaded. She had gone without sleep too long to deal with this now.

Sinclair moaned. He was still lying sideways across the bed. His hair was plastered to his forehead and his nightshirt clung to him, soaked with sweat.

Quincy got up and flung open the door of Sinclair's wardrobe. "Do you know where his nightshirts are kept? He must have more than one. Ah, here they are." She pulled one out, closed the door, and headed back to the bed.

"You going to dress 'im?"

Already reaching for the buttons at Sinclair's collar, Quincy paused. Right. Help was at hand this time, and no need to add fuel to the servants' gossip. "*You're* going to help him into a clean shirt. I'm going to get fresh bed linens. We have to keep him dry until his fever breaks."

Out in the hall, Quincy found what she needed in the linen closet. Her arms full, she sagged against the neatly piled sheets, wishing it was Sinclair she leaned against, and closed her eyes.

Someone else knew.

Damn, damn, double damn.

What would it take to persuade Thompson to keep his knowledge to himself? Could she trust him not to tell? The scandal she had tried to avoid was poised to erupt.

This was all her fault. She should never have come to work for Sinclair in the first place, never put him in such an untenable position. And his mother! The tabbies would have Lady Sinclair back in mourning, a recluse again. Lady Fitzwater, who had been so kind, and Sinclair's friends . . . So many people close to Sinclair were about to be hurt, and it was all her fault.

She shuffled back into Sinclair's bedchamber. "Thompson, I . . ." She trailed off, not knowing what words should come next.

The footman held his finger to his lips. "I'll roll him over," he whispered, "and you tuck in the sheet."

She complied, and they soon had Sinclair settled with so many pillows propping him he appeared to be sitting up. Thompson gathered up the laundry and headed for the door.

"I'll be at my post if you need anything." He winked at her, and left.

Quincy stared at the closed door, speechless.

With one crisis past and another one inevitable, she could think of nothing but how close she'd come to losing Sinclair this night. She began to shake. Before her knees gave out, and before she could think through her actions, she crawled up onto the bed beside Sinclair.

She needed to touch him, hold him, needed tactile proof

that he still breathed. Sitting with her back against the head-board, legs stretched out, she cupped his cheek and smoothed his hair back from his fevered brow.

His eyes closed, Sinclair reached for her, wrapping his arms around her middle, pillowing his head on her chest. With hot tears coursing down her cheeks, she curled one arm around his shoulders and cradled him to her. "Don't you ever scare me like that again," she whispered. "Do you hear me, Benjamin?"

He snuggled deeper into her embrace, snoring. She kissed the top of his head.

She held him well into the wee hours, as frightened by the surge of affection she felt for this man as for his brush with death. She'd wanted to remain aloof, but that part of her plan was a spectacular failure. Leaving him would cause a huge void in her life, a gaping hole in her heart, but at least she would know that he still walked this earth. And she'd had a hand in that.

It wasn't much. But it would have to do.

She dried her eyes with a corner of the sheet, and tight-ened her hold on Sinclair.

A scratch on the door woke Quincy. She scrambled out of bed just before Matilda entered the chamber, bearing a breakfast tray.

"I thought you must be hungry by now, sir," she said softly, setting the tray on the table. "I also brung you more lemonade and honey. Cook says as how you asked for lots of it yesterday."

"Thank you, Matilda." Quincy tried to rub the grit from her eyes. They burned as though she'd been out in a fierce windstorm. While the maid knelt at the hearth to build up the fire, Quincy checked on Sinclair. His breathing seemed easier, and his forehead felt cool to her touch. She let out a sigh of relief and said a quick prayer of thanks.

Removing the cover from the plate on the breakfast tray, she took a deep breath of the enticing aromas. Her stomach growled.

"Sir, is Lord Sinclair going to die?"

Quincy glanced at Matilda, who now stood only a few

feet away, her hands clasped before her. "No. He may feel like death warmed over when he awakens, but he will soon make a full recovery."

Matilda's face brightened. "I'm glad, that I am." With a last look at the sleeping earl, Matilda bobbed a curtsy and headed for the door.

Quincy halted her with a question. "Where is Jill this morning?"

"She's fitting Lady Sinclair for a new gown, sir. I think it's the one she plans to wear to the wedding."

"Wedding?"

"Lord Sinclair's. We was worried the gown might be for a funeral," she glanced at her feet, "but now we're sure it's for his wedding. Will you be needing anything else, sir?"

"No, thank you. You may go." Quincy barely heard the door close. Her heart hammered in her ears. Who could Lady Sinclair think her son was marrying? Surely she would know before his mother if Sinclair had decided on a bride.

She suddenly felt icy cold, ready to shatter into a thousand tiny shards. No, Lady Sinclair must be mistaken. Or premature. Yes, that was it. Premature. Sinclair could not have chosen a bride so soon.

The only sounds Quincy heard were the ticking clock and crackle of the fire. She stared down at Sinclair. His chest hardly lifted with each breath. He *was* still breathing, wasn't he? She rested her hand over his heart.

"My angel," Sinclair murmured. His mouth curved in a sleepy smile, and his fingers curled around her own in a firm grip.

"My lord?" she whispered.

He didn't respond. She looked at their entwined fingers, his strong hand holding hers. Her heart contracted painfully. This would never do. She was supposed to leave him, not fall deeper in love with him.

Love. Tears pressed at her eyes again, a distressing development in itself at how frequently they appeared these days. She stared down at this man she loved, this sweaty, phlegmy, unshaven . . . beautiful, generous, caring man. The man she had to leave.

She pressed a quick kiss to the back of Sinclair's hand and set it down on the blanket beside him. His smile faded, but he did not awaken.

She wondered if Thompson had collected his shilling from Grimshaw yet. Matilda had behaved as usual, so perhaps she had a few hours yet before word spread. Quincy returned to her now cold breakfast, to contemplate her cold future.

Sinclair opened his eyes slowly as the clock on the mantel struck twelve, and took stock of himself. His head and body ached abominably, and it felt as though an iron band constricted his chest. But, as Quincy had predicted, he had not died.

The soft noise he heard were her snores. Quincy dozed in the chair pulled near his bed. Sinclair frowned. Such devotion on the part of another female would not cause any comment, but Mr. Quincy might raise a few eyebrows if word got around. Sinclair was absurdly glad she'd stayed with him.

Faint sunlight filtering through the drawn curtains showed the remains of a meal on the table. Sinclair's stomach growled. He reached for the bell pull, but stopped.

Sometime during the night, there had been an altercation between himself, Thompson, and Quincy. Bloody hell, he hadn't said or done anything to give her away, had he?

Might it have all been just a dream? Such fantastical images flashed before his mind's eye, of soldiers and surgeons, flames and beasts, angels and devils. If he concentrated hard enough, he could disentangle the real from the imagined. If only he could keep his eyes open . . .

Chapter 18

"Mr. Quincy, sir?" Jill had come to collect the luncheon tray and halted at the door, tray balanced on her hip. At Quincy's raised eyebrows she continued. "There's a situation, I mean, something's happened and I don't know what to do about it." She cast a nervous glance at the sleeping earl.

Bracing herself for the worst, Quincy followed Jill out into the hall. "Tell me what has happened, and we'll proceed from there."

The maid lowered her voice. "I think Matilda has gone. She took the big basket like she was going to the greengrocer's, but Cook said Matilda hates going there because the old goat likes to pinch."

It took a moment to register that the problem had nothing to do with her or Sinclair. "Perhaps she had a change of heart?"

Jill shook her head. "I tore my stocking and went to get another—I share a room with Matilda—and all her clothes is gone. And it was Finlay's turn to serve tea, but Grimshaw couldn't find him."

"Perhaps Finlay just—I suppose his clothes are gone, too?" Jill nodded. Quincy shook her head in disbelief. An-

251

other match in the household! "Isn't this something you should tell Mrs. Hammond? Or Harper?"

"But I can't!" Jill set the tray on a table in order to twist the end of her apron. "Mrs. Hammond and Mr. Harper are having a discussion in her office, and he said they wasn't to be disturbed. I'd tell Lady Sinclair, but she's out making morning calls. And that ain't the worst of it!"

"No?"

"There's no one downstairs to answer the door but Celia, and she can barely close it."

"Surely Grimshaw can—"

Jill shook her head. "Grimshaw said Finlay was fickle, and some other things I just can't repeat, and he took Cook's sherry and locked hisself in the cellar! What should we do, sir?"

Quincy fell into the hall chair beside Sinclair's door and dropped her head into her hands, hiding her laughter. Oh, this was just too much.

"Sir?"

Quincy held up one finger. "A moment, please." She took deep breaths until she felt she could look at the maid with a straight face. Then she stood again, and with a few quick instructions put Jack on duty downstairs, arranged for Daisy to serve tea when Lady Sinclair returned, and asked Jill to bring up a tray for Sinclair. Harper, she decided, could deal with the drunken, disillusioned Grimshaw later. At least Thompson couldn't collect on their wager yet.

Rearranging the staff was undoubtedly overstepping her bounds, but what else could she do if the housekeeper and butler were having a "discussion" in the housekeeper's office? And if the staff continued to leave at the present rate, they would have to hire trained replacements. Lady Sinclair supported Quincy's rescue attempts now, but probably would not continue to do so at the expense of a smoothly functioning household. Another problem, but one Quincy couldn't deal with just now.

Sinclair woke an hour later, long enough to eat a small bowl of chicken soup. He seemed distracted and made no effort to speak. Quincy attributed his silence to nothing more than an attempt to conserve his strength and prevent additional coughing fits, and was not surprised when he soon dozed off again.

She stared at his relaxed face, darkened by three days of beard. Next time he awoke, she would have Jack or Thompson shave him and possibly help him with a bath, too. That had always seemed to make Papa feel better.

Thinking of his disarray, she gave a thought to her own. She'd been wearing the same clothes for a day and a half, and her last soak in a tub, at Brentwood, was a fond but distant memory. Not to mention the need to find her spare spectacles, to replace the pair Thompson had stepped on last night. Or was that this morning? She'd ruined more pairs of spectacles in the short time she'd been working for Sinclair than in the previous five years combined.

While she debated whether or not she had time to go home before he awoke again, Lady Sinclair scratched on the door and let herself in.

"How is he doing?" she whispered, standing near her son. She stretched out a hand to touch his forehead and brush aside a few strands of hair.

"Much better, my lady. His fever broke this morning. He should be back to his usual self in a few days."

Lady Sinclair sighed. "You have no idea how relieved I am. I know I should not worry so—he is a grown man, but—"

"I understand." Quincy briefly touched Lady Sinclair's shoulder, then retreated, afraid she'd overstepped her bounds again.

"You do, don't you?" Lady Sinclair gave her quick jasmine-scented hug. "You have done wonders, child, but you must be careful not to exhaust yourself."

"As a matter of fact, I was just planning to go home and—"

"No need for that. Your sister packed a few of your things. One of the footmen was supposed to bring up your bag, but there seems to be a shortage of staff at the moment."

"Beg pardon, my lady," Harper said, opening the door. "I've put Mr. Quincy's things in the adjoining chamber, as you requested."

"Thank you, Harper."

Quincy thought the butler looked rather flushed—perhaps he was sickening, too? Then the import of Lady Sinclair's words sank in. "My sister?"

"We had a delightful visit, your grandmother, sister, and I. Lady Fitzwater is a bosom bow of mine, you know. I thought it best if we put your things in the nearest room." She cupped Quincy's cheek and smiled into her eyes, then led her to the chamber next door. "Besides, there does not seem to be enough staff to prepare a guest room just now. Luckily I had them prepare this one last week. It's quite odd. I was certain we had enough staff this morning. I shall have a chat with Mrs. Hammond, if she has recovered. She did not look at all herself when I saw her a few moments ago."

Lady Sinclair drifted down the hall toward the stairs, lost in thought. Quincy stared after her, then shook her head and shut the door behind her.

The room was equally as large as Sinclair's, and neatly decorated in dark green and white. Everything matched, from the pair of mahogany chairs near the window, to the green and white striped curtains, coverlet and bed hangings. With a start, Harper's words sank in. This was the adjoining suite to Sinclair's.

The countess's rooms.

Lady Sinclair had specifically requested Quincy's things be placed here. She had servants prepare it last week.

Sinclair had not been ill last week.

Quincy stared in the direction Lady Sinclair had departed.

Harper had set her portmanteau on the bed, unopened. Wisps of steam rose from the hip tub near the hearth, beckoning to her. No sense letting the hot water go to waste. She could think while she washed. Quincy locked the doors, then stripped off her clothes to enjoy a long soak in the tub. Sinking into the water, she decided there was no hidden meaning to Lady Sinclair's actions, after all. As she had said, there was simply no staff available to prepare a different room.

But the hot water was not as soothing as usual. What

could Lady Sinclair have possibly discussed with Grand-mère, Lady Fitzwater, and Melinda, and had a delightful time doing it?

Quincy stepped out of the tub before the water cooled, something she rarely did when given the luxury of a bath, and dressed in fresh clothes. Melinda had packed several changes of linen, including freshly starched cravats, but she had not included spare spectacles. Drat.

She looked with longing at the undoubtedly soft bed, wishing for nothing more than a few hours to stretch out and test its comfort. A crash from next door recalled her to her duties.

"Sinclair! What in heaven's name are you doing?" Quincy marched over to the earl, who was sprawled on the floor near the knocked-over bedside table.

"Damn leg gave way," he said, sitting up. His gravelly voice reached the upper register on the last syllable, reminding Quincy of the squire's adolescent son. "What the devil are you grinning at?"

"Glad to see you are feeling much more the thing," Quincy said, pulling him to his feet. She didn't think he'd appreciate her observation concerning his fluctuating voice, so she kept it to herself.

The earl continued his silent brooding after climbing back into bed. She dosed him with the honey-whiskey-lemonade, saw that he ate another bowl of soup, and retreated to the sitting room to work.

She returned only when Jill brought the tea tray at four. Sinclair refused when Quincy offered him a cup. He stared into the middle distance, slowly rubbing his right thigh with the heel of his hand. His expression was foreign, yet somehow familiar.

Papa. Quincy abruptly sat down. Papa had often worn that same expression when his weakening condition confined him to bed, when the simple act of dressing left him exhausted.

"Were you trying to get out of bed, or returning to it when your leg gave way?"

Sinclair's gaze snapped into focus on her. "Returning." His left eyebrow raised in a silent question.

She sipped her tea and bit into a biscuit before she spoke again. "Sometimes Papa would overexert himself. Once he helped push a cart that was stuck in the mud near our cottage, and had to spend the next two days in bed to recover his strength. He spent his last few months as an invalid. He could not take care of us as he had before." She took another sip. "But his infirmity did not change the way we felt about him."

Sinclair's hand stilled. He stared at her. After a long silence, he held his hand out for a cup of tea.

With the earl eating more and his fever broken, Quincy thought she might be able to go home to her own bed that night. She couldn't actually *sleep* in the countess's room— that had just been a place to freshen up. Besides, she very much wanted Melinda to tell her about their chat with Lady Sinclair.

Almost as if he sensed her intention to depart, Sinclair's sleep became restless. It was hard enough seeing him toss and turn, but when she heard him moan, it was more than she could bear. She took Sinclair's hand in her own. The earl quieted immediately. So long as she was near, his sleep seemed peaceful.

The household settled in for the night. Harper grumbled about having to stay on duty so late to open the door for Lady Sinclair when she returned. He had no choice, since Grimshaw's snoring could be heard from his resting place behind the locked cellar door, and no one had been able to rouse him or find the spare key.

Jill was occupied helping the new maid, Carrie, determine what duties she was still able to perform. Lady Sinclair had encountered Carrie earlier that evening, just after the maid was cast out of her former employer's home when it was discovered the recently betrothed heir had been rehearsing his wedding night with Carrie. Her baby was due in four months.

Thompson entered without knocking, carrying a quilt under one arm. "His lordship still won't let you leave?"

Quincy watched him build up the fire. "You haven't collected on your wager yet."

"There's no hurry." He draped the quilt over Quincy's lap, leaned in to whisper in her ear. "I admire a lass with bottom." Quincy froze. "Yours is especially fine." He touched the tip of her nose. "No bruise. That's good. His lordship would never forgive himself if he'd hurt you."

"Thompson—"

"If you need anything in the night, Mr. Quincy, I'll be out in the hall. The new upstairs maid has right fine ankles." With a rakish grin, he left.

Quincy realized her jaw was hanging open. She snapped it shut. Impending doom suddenly felt more . . . pending. She still had to leave, but perhaps the scandal could be avoided, after all.

She struggled in vain to find a comfortable sleeping position in the chair, then gave in and sat up with a sigh of disgust. Sinclair's sleep was disturbed if she left for the cot in the closet, so what might happen if she dragged the cot out into his room? She did not want to spend another night sitting up.

But she was so tired. She didn't have the strength to move the cot. She could ask Thompson to move it, or she could simply stretch out on the floor. No, her feet were already chilled from the draft down there.

She didn't dare risk sitting beside Sinclair like last night. Her luck just wouldn't hold; someone was bound to walk in and see. She stared longingly at his bed. It was quite large. In fact, he took up less than a third of it, as he lay on his side with his knees drawn up. The foot of the bed was not used at all. She could sit down there, lean against the bedpost, and stretch out her legs. Just for a few minutes.

Sinclair did not stir as she settled at the foot of his bed, the quilt over her lap. Ah, much better. She yawned and tried to rub the grit from her eyes. She would sit there just for a few minutes, to restore the circulation to her limbs. Just a few minutes . . .

* * *

Something was different. Not wrong, but different. Sinclair lay still, listening, letting his eyes adjust to the dim light cast by the dying fire. There it was again, a shift on the bed not created by himself. "Quincy?" he whispered. The chair beside his bed was vacant. He slid out from under the covers, stood up, and looked around the room.

There was a large lump on his bed. Peering closer, Sinclair recognized Quincy's inert form, sprawled across the end of the mattress. He gave a soft chuckle, which turned into coughing. When he could breathe again, he picked up the blanket off the floor and draped it over Quincy. If he had started to shiver after being out of bed such a brief time, surely she must be half frozen.

He watched her sleep for a moment. She had tirelessly stayed by his side for how many days now? When he was far from at his best. Making him drink that foul tea, bathing his brow, murmuring soothing nonsense when he was sick to death of coughing. Calming his mother's fears. What had he done to deserve such devotion from a woman as wonderful as Quincy?

As soon as he recovered from this blasted illness, he would have the banns read. They would be married within a month. He would be able to tuck her in properly every night—at his side. They would finish what they had begun in the shepherd's hut, spend a lifetime exploring each other, and hide from no one.

He pulled the blanket higher on Quincy, trailed his fingers across her cheek, kissed her forehead, then climbed back into bed.

Lady Sinclair returned from the card party just before midnight. She seemed not at all surprised it was the butler who opened the door for her instead of the usual footman. It had been a topsy-turvy day for the servants, indeed.

Despite her son's protestations, she still checked on him before seeking her chambers each night. His condition was improving steadily, as Quincy had assured her it would. This late, Sinclair would certainly be asleep and never know of what he termed his mother's coddling.

Thompson opened the door for her, then she stepped into the darkened chamber and shut the door against the light from the hall. "Benjamin?" she called softly. There was no answer.

Sinclair rolled onto his back and moaned. He pulled the covers closer to his chin and shifted his feet.

Lady Sinclair moved to cover him with the blanket bunched at the foot of the bed, but jumped back when an arm shot out from under it. Lady Sinclair covered her mouth with her hand to muffle her surprise. She watched as Quincy flung an arm out and trapped Sinclair's roving feet. Sinclair slid farther down in the bed, as though seeking warmth, until his feet brushed up against her midriff. Quincy wrapped one arm around his feet, over the blankets, and was still.

Even in the dim light from the fire, there was no way to mistake the smile that curved Sinclair's mouth.

Lady Sinclair tiptoed from the room, a satisfied expression upon her features.

Quincy awoke to the muted sound of voices outside in the hall. Morning sunlight leaked through the curtains. She yawned and stretched, reveling in the feel of the soft down mattress beneath her and the warm quilt covering her.

Down mattress? Something pushed against her ribs. She peered over the top of the quilt. It wasn't a dream— Sinclair's feet were pressed against her ribs, through the blankets. She gave them a fond pat, in danger of becoming a caress, then slid off the foot of the bed before someone came in and saw the unorthodox sleeping arrangement. Sinclair mumbled something, rolled over onto his side, and resumed his stentorian breathing.

He had slept through the entire night. That meant the crisis the previous night had indeed been the turning point in his illness, as she'd hoped. He would soon be well enough for her to leave. Her throat constricted, her eyes burned.

Jill scratched on the door and entered just as Quincy finished folding her blanket.

"Morning, Mr. Quincy," the maid said softly, setting the breakfast tray on the table. "Have a good night?"

"What?" Quincy stared at her with wide eyes.

"I—I just wondered if the earl had a good night—if he's getting better, that is."

"Oh. Yes. Yes, he's much improved." Quincy stepped over to the table and lifted the cover off the plate, inhaling deeply. So much improved, in fact, that last night was probably the last time she would ever sleep in the earl's bed.

She suddenly remembered waking up lying atop his chest in the hut. Thinking of what they had done, the pleasure they had given each other, her toes curled. How Sinclair had made her feel when he held her in his arms, cradled and protected. Cherished.

She straightened her cravat and pushed those thoughts to the farthest reaches of her mind. Someday, years from now, she would allow herself to pull out the memory and relive it. Now it was too fresh, too painful, knowing it would never be repeated.

Alone again, Quincy ate breakfast, then worked at her desk in the sitting room, with the door closed. She penned a few notes in Sinclair's hand, declining more invitations for the upcoming week. Tradesmen's bills she sorted and filed. She'd worry about the last wages owed Finlay and Matilda later. She found the name and address of Sinclair's solicitor, and copied it onto a piece of paper she tucked into her pocket.

Just before noon, she heard movement and voices in Sinclair's bedchamber. If she was going to leave him, she should start getting used to not being near him. After waiting a suitable interval, and the outer door had opened and closed again, she knocked and entered. "Good morning, Sinclair."

He was just settling back in bed. "Few more minutes, and it will be afternoon." He leaned against the stacked pillows, an odd little smile on his face as he tilted his head to one side and looked at her.

His gaze was unnerving. After having been naked in each other's arms a few days before, it wasn't fair that he could still make her blush. "Would you prefer to have Thompson or Jack shave you after your bath?"

He stroked the stubble darkening his cheeks and chin, that odd smile still playing about his mouth. "Are you trying to tell me in your own subtle way that I stink?"

"Of course not." She reached to push up her spectacles, then remembered she wasn't wearing them. "Merely that I thought a bath might make you feel more yourself. And unless you intend to grow a beard, I thought you must wish to remove the whiskers."

He sat up straighter. "I would rather shave myself, thank you. I have already requested a bath be brought up." He coughed, then squinted at her. "You've bruises under your eyes. Have you been here all night again?"

"Which is why I thought I'd take the rest of today off. My cat hardly recognizes me anymore." Sir Ambrose was the only warm male she'd be cuddling up with in the future. Might as well get started.

Sinclair's smile fell. He looked crestfallen, but she must be mistaken. Now that he wasn't delirious with fever, it shouldn't matter much to him whether she was present or not.

"Give my compliments to your grandmother and sister."

Before she could reply, Jack knocked and entered, carrying the hip bath. Jill and Carrie were right behind with buckets of steaming water.

Quincy gathered up her belongings from the adjoining suite. While she was packing the portmanteau, she heard Sinclair request Jack bring the top two folios from the stack on his desk downstairs. She covered her face with her hands. If he was asking for his folios again, he was truly on the road to recovery. Soon he wouldn't need her at all. She sniffed and finished packing.

Feeling the need for fresh air, she declined Elliott's offer for a ride home in the carriage and started walking.

Sinclair was a strong man. Within a fortnight, he would be back on his feet. Back to his exercise regimen, back to the social rounds.

Back to selecting a wife.

Quincy sighed and kicked a stone. Lady Sinclair was already preparing a gown for her son's wedding, so he must have made his selection. She decided the most likely candidate would be the shy redhead, Miss Prescott. Lucky girl. The next time Sinclair fell ill, his wife would attend him in the sickroom, not Quincy.

She should feel relief that it would be someone else's duty to spend the night in the uncomfortable chair beside his bed, deal with his surliness, demand that he drink willowbark tea.

His wife would be the one to mop his brow, help him change into a fresh nightshirt, curl up on the bed beside him. His wife would be the one to tease and banter with him, sleep in his arms, run her fingers though the tight curls on his muscular chest and abdomen, stroke him until he groaned in ecstasy. His wife would be the one to kiss him, touch him, taste him.

No! A wave of possessiveness slammed through Quincy. *She* wanted to be the one to do those things. Even when he was crotchety and coughing, she wanted to be near him. He was the man who rescued orphans and hired down-on-their-luck ex-soldiers, who saw the humorous side to a household in chaos, who put other people's needs above his own.

Having realized that her affection for Sinclair went far beyond fondness or friendship, there was only one thing to do. She took off her hat and banged her head against the nearest lamppost.

Also realizing she was drawing attention from passersby, she put her hat back on and resumed walking.

It was utterly selfish of her to feel this way, because Melinda's needs were far more pressing than her own. Quincy needed to concentrate on her goal of buying a cottage and getting Mel out of the city, not mooning over an unattainable earl.

But, oh, how she wished . . . She stopped and stared at a lamppost in stupefaction. How she wished Sinclair had selected herself as his wife.

How could she have been so foolish as to fall in love with Sinclair?

Chapter 19

Sinclair select her for his wife? Impossible. Would never, could never happen.

Even if, miracle of miracles, he returned her feelings, even if he lowered himself to consider the daughter of a mere baron, how could he overlook how unsuitable she'd made herself to be anyone's wife? She sighed again and started to cross the street.

"Watch where yer goin', you son of a—"

Quincy jumped back, just avoiding the wheels of a passing hackney, and landed on her rump in the mud.

"Here now, Quincy!" a familiar voice bellowed. Quincy looked up and saw Sam the butcher in his cart, close behind the hackney. Sam handed his reins to the young woman seated beside him and climbed down. He reached out one beefy paw and yanked Quincy to her feet. "Not injured, are you, lad?"

"Just my dignity," she replied, retrieving her hand. She brushed at the mud, but gave up on the futile task and picked up her portmanteau.

Sam clapped her on the shoulder, nearly knocking her off her feet. "Angie," he said to the woman in the cart, "this here's the smart lad I been telling you about. Mr. Quincy, this is Angie, apple of her Papa's eye." Angie blushed and nodded.

Quincy bowed. "Pleased to make your acquaintance, Miss . . ."

"Missus," Sam filled in. "Mrs. Mayhew. Going to give us a grandbabe by midsummer's eve." Sam's barrel chest, already of formidable size, expanded another inch or two.

Angie blushed again.

"My felicitations, Mrs. Mayhew. I will have to get used to thinking of you as a grandfather, Sam," Quincy said.

Sam beamed. "Tell you what, Quincy, why don't you join us for supper tonight? Make it a big celebration, what with Angie just coming home again. And bring your sister, Melinda. My oldest boy Patrick wouldn't mind seeing her again, if'n you know what I mean." He chuckled and nudged Quincy in the ribs, almost sending her into the street.

"Thank you for the kind offer, but I wouldn't want to intrude—"

"Nothing of the sort. Come tonight and Angie will tell you all about the riots at the tin mine up at Birmingham. You can't even read about them in the papers yet!" Sam leaned close and lowered his voice to a stage whisper. "That's why I made Angie come home, don't you know. No telling what them miners might do, and we wouldn't want them involving the foreman's family, eh?"

Riots at a mine? And not in the newspapers yet? "I'd be delighted to come, Sam, Mrs. Mayhew." She crossed her fingers behind her back. "But I'm afraid Melinda has a previous engagement."

Sam's smile faded, but only slightly. "We'll see you at six, then." He shook Quincy's hand again, climbed back into the cart, and slapped the reins.

Quincy hurried the rest of the way home, her mind racing even faster than her feet. Once before she had heard rumors of upcoming changes at a mine that she had invested in. When the dust cleared a month later, she had quadrupled her investment's value. If only she'd had a hundred pounds invested then, instead of ten! The profit from that transaction had paid their expenses for several months. If only Papa had listened . . .

But she had no energy to spare for such useless ruminations. As she entered her lodgings, she wanted to eat, then sleep, then get up and go to Sam's and eat again. And hang on every syllable Angie uttered.

"Mr. Quincy! You've come just in time," Lady Fitzwater called from down the hall.

Quincy set her bag inside their quarters and forced a smile. "Good afternoon, Lady Fitzwater. In time for what?"

"Luncheon, of course! Come, your sister and grandmother are already in the dining room with my other guests. We don't want to keep them waiting." Lady Fitzwater tucked her arm through Quincy's and half dragged her into the dining room. "Everyone, look who showed up in the nick of time," she announced.

Eight pairs of eyes turned toward Quincy. She swallowed hard, then pulled out the chair and seated Lady Fitzwater before taking the only vacant seat, next to Melinda, across from Lord Palmer. She nodded greetings to Lady Fitzwater's other renters, Miss Stanbury, Reverend Gladstone, and Lieutenant Wheeler.

"Lord Sinclair must be running you ragged," Palmer said.

"He's been a bit under the weather," Lady Fitzwater said before Quincy could reply. "But Lady Sinclair assured me this morning that he is doing much better. Isn't he, Mr. Quincy?"

"Yes, my lady, he is much improved." Quincy gratefully sat back as the footman placed dishes and silverware before her, then filled her plate.

"Sinclair never had much use for doctors," Sir Leland said. "Has he sent one packing yet?"

"I would wager he has his secretary tending to his needs, not some fusty old doctor," Lord Palmer interrupted. "Isn't that so, Mr. Quincy?"

Quincy dropped her fork. Palmer couldn't possibly mean what she thought he meant. Could he? Her palms felt damp, but she wouldn't give Palmer the satisfaction of seeing her dry them. If even his friends were speculating on Sinclair's relationship with his secretary, it was past time for her to leave.

"Our Jo is quite experienced when it comes to dealing with illness," Grandmère jumped in.

"I don't know what we would have done last winter without Jo," Melinda added. "Grandmère and I were both quite ill."

"Now, now," Lady Fitzwater came to Quincy's rescue. "You're making the boy blush. Eat up, everyone!"

Quincy managed to get through lunch without choking. Unable to decipher the looks exchanged between Leland and Palmer, she did her best to ignore them, as well as the long looks they each gave her. Again and again she reached to push up her spectacles, only to remember they weren't there.

At last the meal was over and she escaped to her room. She tried to dismiss Palmer's innuendo as merely a figment of her guilty conscience. She tossed and turned so much, Sir Ambrose jumped down from her pillow and stalked away, his tail twitching in annoyance. Eventually she fell into a fitful sleep, interrupted when Melinda shook her shoulder.

Supper at Sam's was all she hoped for. Angie described upcoming changes at the mine that involved laying off some workers, hiring others, and incorporating new equipment. The owners had hushed up things so well, London papers hadn't heard of the unrest yet.

Quincy barely kept from rubbing her hands together in glee. This was exactly what she needed. And this time, thanks to Sinclair's extravagant raise, she had more than fifty pounds to invest. There was always a risk inherent to any investment, but the payoff—money for their cottage and getting Mel out of London—was worth it.

She thanked her hosts by reading the younger children a story, and included Angie in the reading and penmanship lesson.

Early the next morning, she took a hackney into the City, to the office of Sinclair's solicitor. Reginald Chadburn, Esquire, did not keep her waiting long enough for her to experience more than a niggling doubt about the wisdom of what she was about to do. She barely had time to remove her hat and gloves before the clerk ushered her into his office.

A short, stout man in his fifties, Chadburn urged her to be seated. "How can I be of service to you today, Mr. Quincy?"

Quincy pushed her spare spectacles up on her nose and plunged in. "Lord Sinclair is not feeling well, and has charged me with a few tasks. I will need your help to carry them out." She quickly outlined her strategy for moving the earl's investments.

"Certainly. I'll draw up the necessary papers and personally bring them over this very afternoon."

"Bring them over?"

"For Lord Sinclair's signature, of course."

"Of course." She cleared her throat. "Just ask for me when you arrive, and I'll be happy to take the papers in to him. I'm afraid he's still contagious."

Chadburn's eyebrows shot up into his wig. "Contagious?"

"Nothing serious, I assure you, but we don't wish to take any chances."

"No, we do not. Better to err on the side of caution, I always say." Chadburn consulted his pocket watch, and they agreed to meet at the earl's town house at three that afternoon.

When she arrived a short while later, Sinclair was awake, wearing his emerald satin dressing gown, sitting up in the chair drawn close to the window. Morning sunshine bathed his features, making his chestnut hair gleam, putting color back in his cheeks. He scratched at a hint of whisker stubble on his chin as he flipped through one of his ever-present folios.

She wanted to gather him in her arms. Wanted to feel his arms around her, wanted him to whisper words of love in her ear. Wanted to burrow under the bedclothes with him, their naked bodies entwined.

She hoped his future wife, whomever she was, would appreciate moments such as this. Private, quiet moments, nothing and no one in the world but the two of them.

There was no use pining for what could never be, for her. She cleared her throat, all business again.

"Good to see you sitting up again, my lord," she said, handing him the morning newspaper. He seemed alert. Now would be a good time to tell him about her plans for his investments, and confess that she'd discovered the full extent of Johnson's thievery.

"Good to be sitting up." Sinclair opened the newspaper, scanned the front-page headlines, then handed it back and dropped his folio on the table. "World hasn't come to an end yet. It will all wait another day." He leaned his head back and closed his eyes, his hands folded in his lap.

Quincy pressed her lips together. News regarding his investments could wait, too. She made to rise, but stole a moment to gaze at him again. Just looking on him made her heart feel warm, her pulse speed up. His vulnerability made her wish for all sorts of impractical, impossible things. Things that she gave up the right to on the day she became Mr. Quincy.

Years from now, she would pull out the bittersweet memory of this time, and cherish it all over again.

She forced her attention to the paper. No mention of the doings at the mine yet. Tomorrow, most likely, the story would break. Then, with Mr. Chadburn's help, she would have to move fast.

Sinclair opened his eyes and caught her staring at him. She pushed her spectacles up on her nose. "Care for some tea, my lord?"

He nodded, his expression slightly troubled as he returned her regard.

She poured the tea. As he took the cup, his fingers brushed hers. Sinclair seemed in no hurry to break the contact. She looked up, both of them holding the cup, to meet his steady brown gaze upon her.

"I realize the past few days have been less than ideal," he began.

She was in no hurry to break the contact, either, and gave him an encouraging nod.

He shifted the cup to his left hand, holding her hand in

his right. "The coming days will be much better, I promise. Until then, I just, ah, that is . . . Thank you."

She squeezed his fingers. "You're welcome." When she would have pulled away, he tugged her closer, leaning forward, until he raised her hand and kissed the back of her fingers, his lips warm and smooth upon her skin.

Her heart stopped. They had done far more intimate things with each other just a few days ago, but this was different. This was a courtly gesture, common among the aristocracy, one he'd doubtless performed hundreds if not thousands of times.

But no one had ever done it to her. And while she was Mr. Quincy, no one else ever would.

While she struggled to bring air into her lungs and her thoughts tripped over themselves, unable to form a reply, he gave her a smile, stood, and went back to bed.

His brief cough made her stand. She handed him the glass of honey-lemonade. "I'll be in the next room if you need anything." He nodded, and she walked to her desk, still dazed.

Several times throughout the day she heard him move from his bed to the chair, and back again after a brief interval. She should tell him about the moves she was planning for his investment portfolio. Instead she kept thinking about his hand holding hers, his lips on her skin. And not just on her hand.

As the clock struck three, Thompson opened the sitting room door to tell her there was a visitor for her. Blast. Mr. Chadburn. And she had forgotten to tell Sinclair.

She greeted the solicitor in the drawing room where Harper had seated him, and went back upstairs with the papers before even thinking to offer him refreshment.

Sinclair was asleep when she knocked and entered his bedchamber. Judging by the volume of his snores, he would not awaken anytime soon. He needed the rest; she wouldn't wake him up. She chewed her bottom lip in thought, then shrugged. Nothing could be done about it.

She signed Sinclair's name to the papers and took them back to Mr. Chadburn, her conscience clear. After all, she was not cheating the earl. Everything she did was in his best interest, just as she had promised when he hired her. How fortunate that what was in his best interest benefited her as well.

As he took the papers from her, Mr. Chadburn handed her a new folio. "Here's the monthly report on the Three Soldiers Inn. Has his lordship made a decision on the prospectus I sent over last week?"

"Prospectus?"

"For the inns in Lancashire, and one in Manchester. If he still plans to buy one or more of them, we need to complete the transaction soon."

"Ah, no, I don't believe he's made his decision yet."

Chadburn stood, putting on his hat. "Let me know the moment he does, will you? Rumor is there's another buyer sniffing around, and the price may go up."

"Yes. I'll do that."

The moment she was alone, Quincy tore open the folio. Income, expenditures, planned improvements, everything one needed to know about the operation of the Three Soldiers Inn. The same inn she and Sinclair had stopped at on their way to Brentwood. As she had suspected, Sinclair was the anonymous benefactor, the one with more pounds than sense.

She hugged the folio to her chest. She wanted to throw her arms around him. She settled for a deep sigh of contentment, and went back upstairs to work.

The earl also happened to be asleep during the next three visits from Mr. Chadburn. It could only be a coincidence that Quincy scheduled those appointments for just after luncheon, when Sinclair was most likely to nap.

"How does he do it?" Mr. Chadburn asked her one afternoon several days later. He had just delivered the news that their latest series of moves had netted a profit of ten thousand pounds for Sinclair, and five hundred for Quincy. She barely kept from dancing a jig of joy in front of the solicitor. "How did he know just when to buy and when to sell? We've been two days ahead of the newspaper, and all other investors, all week. Has he a Gypsy with a crystal ball?"

Quincy returned the solicitor's smile. "Let us just say Lord Sinclair listens very carefully to everyone he meets."

Chadburn nodded as though Quincy had just imparted great wisdom, and left with her new instructions, whistling a jolly tune. Likely he had made the same investments.

This profit meant she now had enough to buy the cottage she and Mel and Grandmère had wanted for so long. Just a little longer, a few more transactions, and she would have enough funds to comfortably furnish and stock it in plenty of time to get Mel out of the city before winter arrived. Her sister's life would be saved.

The door to Sinclair's room was open when she returned to her desk, and he was sitting up. Still bubbling with joy, she grabbed several folios from her desk and sat across from him.

"This came for you." She handed him the monthly report. "You great looby."

The swift change of expression on his face, from confusion to understanding to bashful, almost made her laugh aloud.

"They're doing quite well, but I agree, they still need Chadburn's monthly visits. Soon you'll be able to cut those back to quarterly, as the men are quick learners." Before he could say anything, she handed him the other folios. "Manchester is the best choice of these three. Better cash flow, better location, more forgiving while new innkeepers learn their trade."

"You think you know all my secrets now?" Sinclair leaned toward her, his voice low and husky.

Quincy licked dry lips. "You talk in your sleep." She watched with satisfaction as he considered what he might have revealed. She had no intention of telling him all he'd said was her name. Over and over. And over. "I told you when you hired me that my actions would be in your best interests. You should know that while you've been ill, I—"

The hall door burst open and Lady Sinclair entered in a swirl of burgundy skirts. "Benjamin, dear, tell me you're feeling much more the thing."

While Sinclair assured his mother she should indeed go

out that evening with Lady Fitzwater and Leland as her escorts, Quincy scurried back to her desk. Her intent to tell Sinclair of his change in fortune was thwarted when he fell asleep immediately after his mother left, and he did not awaken before Quincy went home for the day. Tomorrow she'd tell him.

The next morning, Harper greeted Quincy at the door and informed her his lordship was dining in the breakfast room with his mother. "Leaning heavily on his walking stick, and had to rest on the landing when he came on to coughing," Harper said, "but 'tis good to see him do justice to Cook's meals again."

Quincy murmured agreement and hurried upstairs. She could put it off no longer. It was time to tell Sinclair of her efforts to repair his finances. And if he was well enough to take his meals downstairs, he no longer needed her care. There was no longer a need to subject him to the risk of scandal by her remaining in his employ. Thompson still had not collected on his wager, but there was no telling how long keeping her secret would amuse him.

Alone in Sinclair's sitting room, she sagged against the wall, blinking back a sudden tear. She should be happy. The goal she had worked so hard for, for so long, was now within her grasp. Her investments were now worth more money than she'd ever possessed, and the profit for Sinclair was even greater. She could move her sister to the country, where Mel would be safe and healthy.

But it meant leaving Sinclair.

No! She couldn't. Not yet. But Thompson knew her secret, as did a footman at Brentwood. So would others, if she stayed too long. She would not subject Sinclair and his mother to more scandal than they'd already been through. It was time for her to leave.

She railed at fate a minute more, then wiped the tears from her eyes and moved on. She would concentrate on one step at a time, and avoid thinking about the empty years, alone and without Sinclair, yawning before her. She enlisted Thompson's help in moving her account books and other accoutrements from Sinclair's sitting room back down to the library.

"I'm about to give notice, so you can collect from Grimshaw soon."

"You're leaving?" Thompson dropped the books on her desk. "I'll miss you, m'dear." Quincy looked up in surprise as he patted her shoulder.

His hand was still on her shoulder when Sinclair walked in.

"That will be all, Thompson," he said, scowling.

"Yes, my lord." The footman bowed to Sinclair and backed from the room.

"May I say you are looking much improved, my lord?" Quincy said, pushing up her spectacles. This was the first time she'd seen him fully dressed since the day they'd ridden back from Brentwood. He was still pale, and his clothes hung a little loose, but he looked worlds better than he had that terrible night when she thought he was dying.

"You may." He gave her a grin as he dropped into his chair and unfolded the newspaper he'd carried tucked under his arm, and began to read.

Quincy mentally rehearsed what to say. Sinclair might be upset at first when she told him what she'd done with his investments while he was ill, but that was sure to pass when she told him of the profit. She had completed the task of investigating Johnson's thievery, the reason he'd kept her on. And after she confessed that at least two servants knew her secret, he would agree that it was best if she left his employ immediately. She cleared her throat.

"Bloody hell!" Sinclair shouted.

Quincy shut her mouth without saying a word.

Sinclair dropped his feet to the floor and leaned across his desk, his eyes fixed on the paper before him. "Quincy, you aren't going to believe this. Here, read it for yourself." He handed her a folded section of the newspaper, his finger stabbing an article.

It was a tiny notice, almost buried among the advertisements, concerning a ship headed for Boston that had gone down in a storm in the Atlantic. All hands were believed lost.

"My lord?"

"That's the ship Johnson and Florence sailed on. I watched them board just before she lifted anchor."

Quincy looked from the paper, her gaze locked with Sinclair's as they registered the loss. The thieving secretary was truly beyond their reach.

She swallowed, still determined to confess before she lost her nerve. "Sinclair, I need to tell you about something I did while you were ill—"

"My lord?" Harper tapped and opened the door. "There's a, ahem, person to see you. I've put her in the drawing room."

Sinclair took the card from the silver tray Harper handed him. He let loose a string of expletives and tossed the card on the fire. "I suppose seeing her is less trouble than trying to avoid her," Sinclair said at last. He reached for his walking stick. "If I don't return in five minutes, come rescue me," he tossed to Quincy over his shoulder as he left.

She and Harper exchanged puzzled glances, then the butler closed the door behind him. Quincy tried to turn her attention to the morning's mail, but accomplished little as she kept glancing at the clock.

Chapter 20

❦❦**M**y dear Lord Sinclair," Serena, Duchess of Warwick, gushed as Sinclair entered the drawing room, a sinking feeling in his stomach.

She stood and stretched out her hands for him to kiss. "I vow, I cannot tell you how concerned I have been. First you disappear from polite company, then you decline the invitation to my little soiree. I had to assure myself nothing unfortunate had happened to you."

"Didn't you just?" Sinclair murmured as he kissed the air a good six inches above her gloved knuckles. The invitation must be what Quincy had tried to tell him about.

Serena's perfume clogged Sinclair's lungs. He tried to step back, searching for breathable air, but Serena tugged him down on the sofa beside her. "Actually, I have been feeling under the weather," he said. Perhaps if she thought what he had was catching, he would soon be rid of her.

"So it was not just me you were ignoring? But of course. I feel so much better now."

Sinclair coughed, a heavy, wet sound. Serena looked alarmed, so he repeated the exercise.

"Sinclair, are you all right? Shall I summon someone?"

He continued to cough. Serena held her scented handker-

chief to her mouth and scooted away from him on the sofa.
Ah, clean air at last. But she remained in the room, so he
continued coughing. He had to look away; her expression
of distaste and near panic almost made him laugh.

"My lord, I—" Quincy broke off as she stood in the doorway, gaping at Serena. Sinclair glanced at the clock; she
was right on time. Quincy shook herself and hurried forward, and grasped Sinclair's arm as she helped him to his
feet. "I warned you about overtaxing yourself, my lord.
Forgive us, your grace. Lord Sinclair is not yet himself."

Sinclair leaned heavily on Quincy's shoulder as he
limped from the room, still coughing. He was about to give
up the fatiguing ploy when they reached the staircase, but
he glimpsed Palmer and Leland handing their hats to
Harper at the front door. If he stopped and visited with
them, he'd have to endure more of Serena's company.

He gave them a jaunty wave and bent his concentration
on climbing the stairs with his stiff leg, still leaning on
Quincy.

Quincy glanced over his shoulder at the visitors. "I will
take care of everything, my lord," she said quietly.

"Never had any doubt," Sinclair replied between gasps.
Quincy always took care of everything. She'd become the
one constant in his chaotic household.

Perhaps this pretend fatigue was not much of an act after
all. His chest ached from coughing. He should have thought
of a different ploy.

Quincy helped him into his bedchamber and summoned
Thompson to attend him, then scurried away. Sinclair
heaved a sigh of disgust and sat on the bed, rubbing his
thigh. In addition to the usual ache, it was also stiff. Too
much time in bed and not enough walking had undone
much of his work. He'd been sleeping entirely too much
lately, but at the moment he wanted nothing more than another nap. He leaned back and closed his eyes.

In that gray area between sleep and awake, he relived the
moments of Quincy caring for him, holding him, doing her
damnedest to make sure he lived through the night.

He'd been ten when his six-year-old brother had become

ill. He'd been at his side when he coughed and wheezed, there when the wheezing turned to a tortured struggle to breathe. Still there when he went silent, never to laugh or play again.

He'd relived that panic as fluid filled his own lungs, certain he would soon join him in the hereafter. But Quincy, his angel of mercy, had been at his side, ordering him to breathe, to cough, to clear his lungs. As a good soldier, he'd followed her orders, and been rewarded with her embrace. She'd stayed at his side all night, ready with whatever he needed, even if it was just her comforting presence.

When he'd kissed her hand, the temptation to tug her closer until she sat on his lap was almost overwhelming. He wanted to embrace her as she had held him, to massage her stiff muscles, to smooth the creases of concern from her face. He wanted to kiss her sweet lips, but not at the risk of sharing his illness, and had settled for kissing her fingers. The dazed look on her face had been priceless. He should have realized no one had ever done that to her before. What other things had she missed out on that he could rectify? He would make a list and check them off, one at a time, after they were married.

The next morning Sinclair paced his bedchamber. Much to his disappointment, he'd slept so long the previous afternoon, Quincy had already departed for home before he awoke. He'd wanted to quiz her about her reaction to the duchess. Her look of venom at seeing Serena, however brief, was unmistakable. Quincy couldn't be jealous, could she?

It was also high time he left the house. He hadn't ventured farther than the garden in over a week. Time to go for a long walk, and see his solicitor. Quincy had been right about the property in Manchester. He would tell Chadburn to make an opening offer on the inn.

But first he'd join his mother for breakfast. He nicked himself shaving, and made a mental note to get on with finding a new valet. He cursed as he tossed the second ruined cravat on the floor. He would *not* call for Thompson or Harper. He could get dressed by himself. It might take until noon, but he would damn well tie his own neckcloth.

His mother knocked and poked her head in the door while he was mangling the fourth cravat. "Coming downstairs, dear?"

"As soon as I finish this." He yanked the wrinkled linen from his neck.

"Why don't you just have Quincy tie your cravat again?" She smiled. "I shall see you downstairs."

Reaching for a fifth cravat, Sinclair froze. "Again?" How did Mama know . . . ?

He finally got a knot tied to his satisfaction—seven was always a lucky number—limped downstairs, ate breakfast with his mother, who beamed at him, and called for Harper to bring him his hat, gloves, and walking stick.

Sinclair was about to walk out when he thought he heard voices from his library. Another visitor? He opened the door. The voice belonged to Quincy, who was alone, pacing before the window with the morning's mail in her hands, thinking aloud.

"Good morning," Sinclair called.

Quincy jumped and threw the mail in the air. "G-good morning, Sinclair." She pushed her spectacles up, then bent down to retrieve the mail.

"Nice rescue yesterday," he said, leaning against the doorframe. He watched Quincy reach for letters with shaking hands. Heavens, she was skittish this morning.

"M-my pleasure, my lord. Are you feeling better?"

"Without Serena's perfume polluting the air? So much so, I'm off to visit my solicitor."

"Solicitor? But . . ."

"What is it?" He watched Quincy's shoulders slump as she stood up, the mangled mail in her hands.

"I've been trying to tell you, that while you were ill . . ."

"Yes?" He stepped farther into the room, a sudden sense of foreboding heavy in his gut.

Her words tumbled out in a rush. "I bought and sold mining shares in your name. A lot of shares."

He raised his eyebrows when she paused for breath. The sense of foreboding hadn't eased.

"Chadburn has all the details if you want to review them,

but you made a tidy profit, enough to replace all the money Johnson stole. With interest."

Profit? Interest?

He wanted to whoop with joy, to catch her up and swing her off her feet, even if his damn leg would probably give way and they'd end in a heap on the floor. But something in her expression gave him pause.

How did Quincy know about trading mining shares? More importantly, *this* is what had her quaking with trepidation? She should be pleased with her accomplishment, not looking like she was on her way to her own execution.

The imp of mischief made him at least tease her. "You forged my signature to do the buying and selling?"

She stiffened. "Of course."

He grinned. "Living up to your promise? Everything you do is in my best interest?"

The smile she gave him contained more sadness than joy. She nodded. "There's more, but . . . it will keep until you return."

Sinclair waited a moment in case she changed her mind, then left, that feeling of foreboding returning, stronger than ever.

The clerk ushered Sinclair into Chadburn's office right away.

"Lord Sinclair!" Chadburn fairly shouted, standing up to greet the earl. "How good to see you up and about. I did not expect to meet with you until this afternoon. Let me see if my assistant has drawn up the papers yet."

Sinclair held his hand up. "What papers?"

Chadburn's bushy eyebrows snapped together. "Authorizing the sale of your tin mine shares, of course. Aren't those the instructions you gave your secretary to pass on to me?"

"Ah." Sinclair sat down, relieved he had not forgotten something. "I have not been myself lately, and do not, er, clearly recall giving instructions for you. However, Quincy assured me that things have gone well."

Chadburn gave a short bark of laughter. "If these decisions have been made under the influence of your illness, you may not wish for the return of good health, my lord." He chuckled.

"Care to elaborate?"

"Thanks to your incredibly fortunate timing and action, you have added over thirty thousand pounds to your coffers in the last se'ennight. You may not recall doing so, but I have the papers with your signature right here."

Chadburn showed him the documents, complete with his forged signature, which outlined the series of buying and selling actions Chadburn had undertaken, per the earl's instructions as given by Quincy. "I admit I thought the moves odd at first, but after the first profit, I started investing a little of my own, as your secretary had done. Thanks to your knowledge and daring, we've each earned a tidy sum, too."

Sinclair let the news sink in, resting his chin on his fist. As Quincy had said, all the money Johnson had stolen was replaced, and more. True to her promise when Sinclair hired her, her activities with her illicit skill had indeed been in his best interest. But how had she known about the changes at the mining companies near Birmingham?

Then the thought hit him—Chadburn said Quincy had invested, too. He sat up straight. Had she earned enough to buy her cottage? If so, she could even now be planning to leave him, to move her sister to the country. Is that what she had been trying to tell him?

The offer on the property in Manchester could wait. He had to get back to Quincy. He made excuses to Chadburn and hurried out to the street, headed home, shivering with a sudden chill. She could leave his employ at any time.

Leave him.

He couldn't allow that.

He cursed his limp, slowing him down even more than usual after so many days abed. He had gone only a few steps when Elliott drove around the corner and pulled the team up beside him. With all the changes in the household staff, it was good to know at least Elliott had not been affected. "Impeccable timing, as always."

"Yes sir, Cap'n."

Sinclair climbed into the coach. "Home, Elliott, and spring 'em." He braced himself against the squabs as the coach set off as quickly as traffic would allow. There was nothing to distract him now, as his thoughts tumbled over each other.

Quincy had bathed his fevered brow, shared the warmth of her body when he was half frozen, and put him to bed when he was foxed. She had seen him at his worst, and not run screaming into the night. She had rescued his household from chaos, extracted his mother from her mourning, and restored his lost funds. Josephine Quincy had become indispensable to his well-being.

She had taken over his heart just as assuredly as she had his account books.

Beneath her starched cravat and masculine coat lay a very warm and real woman. Intelligent, witty, a delightful companion, someone he could look forward to meeting at the breakfast table every morning for the next fifty or sixty years. And as for the nights before . . . He wanted to untie that cravat, slide her coat from her shoulders, and caress her lemon-scented skin. Kiss her senseless. And then he'd get serious about making love to her. That morning in the hut, delightful as it had been, was only a taste, a mere hint at the pleasures that awaited them.

But he was a man of honor, and there was only one way to have the Honorable Miss Josephine Quincy. One sure way to prevent her from leaving him.

He had assumed that she knew he intended for them to marry, didn't need to actually say the words aloud. Knowing the hand that fate had dealt her so far, he now realized Quincy would make no such assumption. He smacked his forehead.

In fact, after living as Mr. Quincy the last few years, she might even resist his proposal, in a misguided sense of not wanting to blemish his family name or some such nonsense. It should be easy enough to dissuade her, though, once he started kissing her.

All his problems faded in memory, solved. Now he just had to figure a way to explain to Mama that he was going to marry his secretary. And get the secretary to agree . . .

* * *

Quincy paced the library, methodically shredding a handkerchief. Sinclair would return from his solicitor's any moment now.

She should have told him, should have given notice before he left, gotten it over with. She shouldn't have told Thompson to collect on his blasted wager. Now she feared word about her true identity would spread among the staff before she could warn Sinclair.

What a coil. She tossed the fragments of her handkerchief onto the fire.

Perhaps she could draw on Thompson's sympathy for Melinda's plight, convince him to hold off a while longer. Even though a footman knew, perhaps Sinclair would let her stay on long enough to reach her goal, to provide for her sister. She just needed a little more money, to furnish the cottage. And she didn't want to leave his employ. Didn't want to leave *him*. Not yet. Soon she would have to, but not yet.

But even if Sinclair did not make her leave, how much longer would Thompson keep quiet? How much longer would she put Sinclair at risk for scandal? Now that Sinclair's strength was returning, he didn't need her.

How should she tell him? "By the way, my lord, two of your footmen know my little secret"? That would never do. How about, "Sinclair, I—"

"Yes?"

Quincy whirled around toward the door, hand over her pounding heart. Sinclair leaned against the doorjamb, an odd expression on his face.

"Um." She couldn't squeeze any intelligible sounds from her throat. She took a deep breath to try again, but he closed the door and walked toward her. Was that a smile on his face? Another step closer. He reminded her of Sir Ambrose, stalking his dinner. Two steps closer. Is this how the mouse felt? "I need to—"

"To what?" he said softly. Another step.

Quincy stepped back and pushed her spectacles up. "To tell you—"

"Yes?" His odd smile broadened.

For every step he took forward, she took one back. Why couldn't she seem to catch her breath? Surely he could hear her heart pounding.

"Tell you about—" She bumped into the bookcase at her back. Trapped in the corner. Now what? Why did he keep coming closer? She caught a whiff of the spicy masculine scent unique to Sinclair.

"Tell me later," he whispered. With languid movements he reached up and lifted off her spectacles. "Do you know you have the most adorable habit of pushing these up when you're nervous?" He tucked them in his pocket. "Why do I make you nervous?"

She blinked. "Wha—what are you doing?"

It was definitely a smile. "Just this." He cupped her face in his hands, then caressed her bottom lip with the pad of his thumb. With a last look into her eyes, so close she could see the tiny flecks of gold in his, he leaned closer still and pressed his lips to hers in a tender kiss.

Heaven. His mouth was soft and warm, gently insistent, as he tasted and explored. Ever so much better than she had imagined, even better than she remembered. She raised her hands to his shoulders, to pull him closer, to press her body to his. Sinclair moaned in pleasure. Or had she made that sound?

"Something I've wanted to do for days now." He left her mouth, to kiss a trail down the side of her neck, making a delicious shudder shimmy all the way down to her curling toes. She quivered when he flicked his tongue behind her ear.

"Oh, me too."

The room began to spin. Sinclair caught her and tilted her face up to his, his strong arms supporting her back. Good thing, because her knees had turned to jelly.

She gave up her perusal of his lush mouth and raised her gaze to his eyes. The unfamiliar emotion revealed there was desire, confirmed by his body pressed against hers. Something she'd never thought to see from Sinclair again, certainly an emotion she'd never thought would be directed at her. She had barely registered it when he kissed her again, his large clever hands caressing her back, massaging his way from her neck to her hips, his touch decadent and sure.

He wrapped his arms around her, enveloping her in his secure embrace. She rested her face against his chest, absurdly pleased by his rapid pulse beneath her cheek. She wiggled her hands beneath his waistcoat to stroke his corded muscles, wishing she could get under his shirt, too.

"Chadburn told me what you did with the mining shares."

She felt his voice as much as heard it, a rich rumble in his chest that transmitted itself all the way down to her toes.

"Told me about your investments, too."

He had to bring that up? They could discuss it later. Just let her seize one more moment of joy, hold on to it a moment longer. This would have to sustain her for a lifetime. She squeezed him tighter.

He leaned back to slide his hand along her shoulder to her neck, and caressed her cheek with his thumb. She became lost in the way he looked at her, with affection and yearning. Never in her most foolish dreams had she imagined she would receive such a look from any man, let alone from someone she loved so much. Well, maybe in her *wildest* dreams . . .

After several long moments, Sinclair gathered her snugly in his embrace, resting his chin on top of her head. "The past few weeks have been tortuous. Can't tell you the number of times I worried that I had said or done something to give you away, to give *us* away." He chuckled again but abruptly leaned back in the embrace. "No one else knows, do they?"

Quincy took a deep breath, felt the floor beneath her feet once again. "Only two people. One is Thompson. He—"

"Thompson!" Sinclair dropped his arms. "I thought I was dreaming when I saw him hold you. How did he find out?"

Hmm. "Let us just say it was unintentional." Her face grew hot under Sinclair's narrow-eyed scrutiny. Well, he insisted. "You called me your angel, and held my hand to your heart. While Thompson was in the room."

"*I . . . ?*" He had the grace to look sheepish.

"If it's any comfort, he'd suspected something was amiss ever since he carried me out of the warehouse that first week I was here." She thought it best not to mention his wager with Grimshaw just yet.

Sinclair turned serious. "You could have been killed that day." His fingers cupping her head, he drew her closer, brushed his lips across hers, then trailed kisses along her jaw and nibbled on her earlobe. The tingling in her stomach grew and flared out to encompass her entire body. "You must allow me to reassure myself that you are whole and healthy." His feral smile returned. He tugged on her hands, drawing her forward as he walked backward until he sat on the sofa, and pulled her down onto his lap.

"Your leg!" She tried to get up, but he wrapped his arms around her.

"Never felt better." He nuzzled her neck, his hands stroking her shoulders, sliding inside her coat, delving under her waistcoat. He fingered her cravat. "I can hardly wait to see you in a gown. After we're married, you can—"

Quincy jerked back. "Married?"

Sinclair cradled her face in his hands. "It's the only cure for what ails us. I predict our recuperation will take, oh, at least thirty or forty years." He traced her lips with a fingertip. "Besides, we have to marry. You have hopelessly compromised me."

His smiling, handsome upturned face was her undoing. She knew several reasons—logical reasons—why they could not, should not marry, but they all fled her mind. Just as she had so often longed to do, she kissed him full on the mouth.

"Good afternoon."

They turned startled gazes on Lady Sinclair, who stood in the doorway, her expression unreadable. Oh, bloody hell. Quincy struggled to get up, but Sinclair tightened his hold. She remained on his lap, her face flooding with heat, her heart beating double-time.

"Good afternoon, Mama," he said. Quincy felt his racing pulse belie his calm voice.

Lady Sinclair closed the library door behind her. Her face and voice betrayed no emotion. "What have you to say for yourself, Benjamin?"

Quincy's face grew even hotter, sitting on Sinclair's lap in full view of his mother, especially since she could feel the reason he needed her to stay there. A true lady would faint right about now, wouldn't she? She certainly felt light-headed. That was the first step, right?

"You may wish us happy, Mama. We are to be married."

"But—" Sinclair silenced Quincy with a squeeze.

"All I can say is, it is about time." Lady Sinclair broke into a broad smile.

Quincy was too stunned to speak.

Sinclair looked from his mother to Quincy and back, slack-jawed.

"You chose an interesting method to seal your betrothal, Benjamin. A quick kiss would have sufficed." She settled into the wing chair. "Have you set a date yet, Josephine?"

"You knew?" Sinclair nearly choked on the words. He cast an accusing glance at Quincy.

She shook her head, unable to form a sentence. Lady Sinclair had known? "How?"

"You have your grandmother's features, my dear."

Quincy thought back to her first interview with Lady Sinclair, the way she had studied Quincy's face. A phrase came back to haunt her: *"You seem like someone who is comfortable with secrets."*

"Yes, my dear, almost from the beginning." Lady Sinclair's eyes sparkled with good humor. "Your grandparents cut quite a dash in society when I made my come-out. Such a romantic pair! All of us green girls wished to have a handsome man rescue us and fall prostrate at our feet with love, like Randolph did with Dominique." Lady Sinclair gave a dramatic sigh. "And while Benjamin is not quite prostrate, I recognize a love match when I see one." She shifted her gaze to her son. "I was beginning to worry, Benjamin. I never would have believed you could be so obtuse."

It was Quincy's turn to squeeze Sinclair into keeping silent.

Lady Sinclair sat up, her voice becoming very matter-of-fact. "We'll need to find you a dressmaker, Jo. One who can keep a still tongue." She snapped her fingers. "Of course! Jill is utterly wasted on cleaning and polishing. We'll set her and your sister to sewing your wardrobe, at least the beginning of one. I am certain Melinda will not mind. I don't imagine you have any gowns at all, do you?"

The room spun around her again. Events were proceeding entirely too quickly. She hadn't even agreed to Sinclair's proposal yet, though technically he hadn't asked, he'd just assumed. As heartfelt declarations of love went, his hadn't exactly been the stuff of which a girl dreamed. Not that she had harbored any such romantic fantasies. "No, my lady. I haven't worn a dress since I was fourteen." The last of her gowns had been made over to fit Melinda long ago. She hadn't so much as a chemise to her name.

"And I'll wager you've grown a bit since then." Her eyes sparkled. "Say good-bye to your secretary, Benjamin, and give her back her spectacles. We have a hundred and one things to do, and the sooner we get started, the better." She walked to the door, opened it, and asked Harper to send for Jill and the coach.

Sinclair dutifully retrieved Quincy's spectacles from his pocket, perched them on her nose, and had just enough time to kiss her again before Lady Sinclair turned around.

"Come along, Jo." She held her hand out. "I vow I have not had this much fun in ages."

Chapter 21

Once they were in the coach on the way to Lady Fitzwater's home, Lady Sinclair related the bare essentials of the situation to Jill.

The maid's wide-eyed glance darted between Lady Sinclair and Quincy, until Quincy felt like she'd grown a second head. She supposed she should get used to the staring.

Lady Sinclair led the way to the Quincy family quarters, Jill and Quincy obediently following. Grandmère and Melinda did not seem at all surprised when Lady Sinclair began issuing orders in her gentle voice, and no one but Quincy was startled when Lady Fitzwater made an appearance, personally bringing them a length of muslin.

"I declare this is the most excitement I have had in years," their landlady said, dropping the fabric on the table.

Quincy cast an accusing glance at her grandmother. "You told?"

"Of course she did not," Lady Fitzwater interjected. "And you did nothing to give yourself away, either, dear girl."

"Then how?"

"You have your grandmother's—"

"Features," Quincy finished.

289

"Especially the eyes," Lady Sinclair said. "They change color from gray to green depending on your mood and what you're wearing. Just like your grandmother. She was quite the matchmaker."

Quincy glanced at her grandmother, who blushed and stared at her sewing.

The other women had Quincy turn this way and that as she stood on a stool in the center of the room, clad only in one of Melinda's shifts. Designed for Melinda's more curvaceous figure, the garment hung loose on Quincy and ended several inches too short. Under their assessing gaze, she crossed her arms over her chest and stared with longing at her familiar trousers and shirt, draped over the back of a chair. Her spectacles had been consigned to a dark cupboard, along with Papa's boots and other items she would no longer need as Miss Quincy.

She felt like a marionette, with well-meaning tyrants controlling the strings.

The five women plotted and planned, measured and draped Quincy's figure. Strips of lace were held up to her cheek, lengths of silk and muslin hung over her shoulders, all in an attempt to find the most flattering colors, the best styles for her figure. They discussed how to dress her short hair. Bonnets, reticules and shawls were brought out, on loan until she had a chance to purchase her own.

Outnumbered and outflanked, Quincy decided to surrender with grace.

It was a heady experience, being the center of attention, to have everyone seeing to her needs instead of the other way around. Whether she wanted them to or not.

For so many years, she had pushed away thoughts of having delicate things for herself, content with buying the occasional gewgaw for her sister or grandmother. Now she ran her hand over burgundy velvet, an azure silk fichu, a beaded reticule. Wool trousers were eminently practical, but there was something to be said for sarcenet.

"Are you sad?" Mel whispered as she draped a length of seafoam green cotton around Quincy. A frown creased her brow.

Mummified by the fabric, Quincy could only shake her head. "That was a sigh of contentment," she whispered back.

"Good, because Grandmère's been looking forward to this day for more than five years."

So have I. Quincy swallowed a lump in her throat. With a farewell glance at her trousers as they were buried under discarded fabrics, she jumped into the current discussion, arguing volubly against the pink chiffon in favor of the periwinkle blue sarcenet.

The debate soon veered to which modiste to visit first. Quincy wondered what Sinclair was doing while she became Miss Quincy. What would he think when he saw her dressed in a gown for the first time? Would she measure up to his expectations? Would he think of her the same way as when she wore men's attire, have the same feelings for her?

"Is tomorrow too soon for an at-home, do you think?" Lady Fitzwater asked the room at large.

"Yes!" Quincy said.

"No!" Melinda, Grandmère, and Lady Sinclair said in unison. "We can have at least one afternoon gown finished by then, can't we, Jill?" Melinda added.

"Yes, my lady."

"But—"

"Hush, *ma chère,*" Grandmère said to Quincy. "You'll ruin the fitting."

Sinclair entered the front hall of Leland's house, his stomach fluttering with anticipation. He had not seen Quincy—his dearly beloved Josephine—since yesterday afternoon. Mama had invited him this morning to Lady Fitzwater's at-home, and promised a surprise. He had learned long ago to be wary of Mama's "surprises."

He tapped his foot as the footman slowly opened the drawing room door and announced him. His gaze swept the room. Melinda and a friend, an auburn-haired beauty in light green, chatted with Leland and Lord Palmer near the fireplace. Lady Fitzwater and Mama were in earnest conversation with Mrs. Quincy—no, he must think of her as Lady Bradwell.

He gave proper greetings to his mother and her co-conspirators, while stealing glances at the door. Surely Jo should arrive soon?

"Why don't you go join the other youngsters?" Lady Sinclair suggested, her eyes sparkling. Lady Fitzwater beamed at him, and Lady Bradwell smiled into her teacup.

He nodded and walked away. Undoubtedly he was spoiling their plotting.

"Pull up a chair," Leland called as Sinclair neared the small group.

"Dash it Sinclair, you've ruined our afternoon," Palmer said with a smile. "We were so enjoying having the ladies to ourselves."

Melinda and her companion blushed.

"May I say you look quite charming this afternoon, Miss Melinda?" He raised her hand and kissed the air just above her knuckles. She looked grown up with her long brown hair twisted into an elegant knot instead of the plaits he was used to seeing her wearing.

She glanced at Leland and her blush deepened. "Thank you, my lord." Melinda's companion plucked at the folds of her skirt, until Melinda elbowed her. "May I introduce you to my sister, Miss Josephine Quincy? She has been visiting friends in Chelmsford and only just returned to us."

Sinclair's heart stopped. He stared at the auburn-haired beauty. This was his Jo? Leland jabbed his toe into Sinclair's calf, reminding him of the audience. "Charmed, Miss Quincy," he managed to get out. He kissed her proffered hand before he dropped onto the chair.

This willowy apparition of feminine beauty was his Quincy? Wavy auburn hair framed her face and just brushed her creamy shoulders. She plucked at the folds of her skirt again and removed a gray hair that likely belonged to her cat, then reached two gloved fingers to push up spectacles that weren't there, no longer hiding her eyes. They were green, and wide with apprehension.

Leland reached over and pushed Sinclair's mouth shut. "Take care, old chap," he said, laughing. "You're drooling."

"I believe you have an admirer, Miss Quincy," Palmer said.

"You are too kind, Lord Palmer." She stared at her folded hands in her lap.

Sinclair shook his head to clear it. "Not at all. I have heard many favorable things about you. From my secretary."

"Oh, you mean our cousin, Joseph," Melinda said, staring directly into Sinclair's eyes.

"Fancy that," Palmer said, brushing invisible lint from his sleeve. "Cousins so similar in appearance. And named so similarly, too."

The foursome darted glances at Palmer, then everyone but Leland averted their gaze.

"What do you—" Leland broke off as the footman announced three more callers, a mama and her two marriageable daughters. They headed for Sinclair's group by the fireplace after cursory greetings to Lady Fitzwater.

More new arrivals were announced, including the other three boarders in the household, followed by a maid with a heavily laden tea tray. In the ensuing hubbub, Leland asked Melinda to take a turn about the room with him. With much blushing on her part and nervous adjusting of his eye patch on Leland's part, they began to stroll the perimeter of the room.

"What an excellent notion," Sinclair said, standing up. "Miss Quincy, would you do me the honor of accompanying me on a stroll?" He held his hand out to her, then tucked her hand in his elbow as she stood beside him, and they stepped in unison.

Fortunately he knew the layout of the room by heart, because he could not tear his gaze from her. He still could not reconcile this feminine vision to the one who'd kept him company the previous few weeks—the no-nonsense secretary who'd summarily dealt with merchants accustomed to cheating an earl, rearranged his chaotic staff when no one else had the presence of mind to do so, and ordered him to bed when he became ill. The same vixen who had joined him in bed on more than one occasion.

"You're quite a managing female," he said softly.

Quincy finally met his gaze. "Was that an insult or a compliment, my lord?"

They stopped near the doors leading to the garden. Without the heels on her leather shoes, the top of Quincy's head only reached to Sinclair's cravat. She tilted her head back to look at him, her green eyes flashing.

The urge to kiss her was so strong, Sinclair tugged her out the door, down the steps, and into the garden. "Benjamin, not 'my lord.' I want to hear my name on your lips." He brushed a lock of her hair from her face. "Say something so I'll know it really is you."

She leaned against him. "Would you like me to remove my gloves so you can see the ink stains on my fingers, Benjamin?"

He chuckled, and dropped his gaze from her face, traveling slowly past the strand of pearls encircling her neck, lingering on the light green fabric that clung to her breasts, finally to her hand clutching a reticule at her waist. She had not the generous curves of her younger sister, but was perfectly proportioned for his Quincy. "How is it no one else saw you for what you are?" He cupped her cheek in his bare hand, savoring the feel of her soft skin.

She closed her eyes, leaning in to his touch. "I learned long ago that people generally see what they expect to see, and nothing more." She glanced at the terrace doors, and the growing crowd in the drawing room.

Sinclair followed her gaze. "Right, no need to draw an audience. We can be private later. Shall we continue our walk?" He tucked her hand in the crook of his arm, keeping his free hand over hers, and started down the path. "I've missed you, you know."

Quincy gave an un-ladylike snort. "It's been less than twenty-four hours since your mother took me away."

"The longest hours of my life."

"After your experiences in war, and your injury? And illness? I find that hard to believe."

Sinclair stopped. "Believe me."

He watched the pulse fluttering at her throat as she stared at him. For a long moment neither of them drew breath. Then she smiled and started walking again.

"How do you like your new costume?" he said as they passed a patch of tulips basking in the sunshine.

She looked up at him with a broad grin, the same bold and irreverent look he'd come to adore. "It's rather drafty, actually." She clutched the lace beside her shoulder, trying to cover more of her chest with it. "When I first saw my reflection, I thought there was a bit too much . . . me . . . on display. Grandmère said she'd been saving these pearls, had almost given up hope of me wearing them, but I think they only draw attention to the problem. Your mother and Lady Fitzwater assure me the neckline is quite proper, though I can't help feeling a bit exposed."

He chuckled. "I can imagine, after so many years of wearing shirts and cravats and coats."

"And waistcoats."

"And waistcoats." They stopped beneath an elm, its leaves still just tiny buds reaching for the sun. Sinclair studied her again, wishing he could trace with his finger the lace edging on her bodice, dip down inside . . . Voices floated from the steps as other couples followed their lead to stroll in the garden. "You have no idea how much I want to kiss you," he whispered.

The suggestive look on her face said she wanted to kiss him just as badly. "I think the Trio would frown on that. They've been schooling me on ladylike behavior, and I'm fairly certain kissing in public is something in which a lady does not indulge."

Sinclair raised her hand to his lips. "I would never sully your reputation. I can restrain myself, let me see . . . three weeks. Yes, three weeks and four days. We can have the banns read starting this Sunday, then hold the ceremony at St. George's. Or would you prefer a more intimate setting, at Brentwood Hall, perhaps?"

Her eyes sparkled with tenuous joy. "You're sure you still—"

"Hallo there," Lord Palmer said from behind them. "Sinclair, Miss . . . Quincy. Getting better acquainted, I see."

Sinclair grimaced in mock anger, then faced his friend. "Do join us, Palmer," he said. "Miss Quincy was just telling me about Chelmsford. I must visit it some day."

"How quaint." Palmer turned toward Quincy, a glint in his eye Sinclair had not seen since before Waterloo. "When do you expect your cousin Joseph to return, Miss . . . Quincy?"

"I really could not say, Lord Palmer."

Sinclair's gaze darted between Quincy and Palmer, a sense of dread invading his stomach.

"Pity," Palmer said. "He was quite intriguing, wouldn't you say, Sinclair?"

"You seem awfully interested in him," Quincy interjected.

Palmer lowered his voice. "You should know I am always interested in matters that concern my friends, Miss Quincy."

Sinclair draped his arm across Quincy's shoulders and drew her close. "There is nothing to be concerned about, Palmer. Mr. Quincy is gone. He stayed only as long as he was needed."

"I see." Palmer looked unconvinced.

"Do you?" Sinclair lightly caressed Quincy's upper arm, a gesture calculated to be reassuring and possessive.

Palmer looked as though he wanted to say more, but held back as another couple strolled past. "I hope you know what you're doing, Sinclair. Good day, Miss Quincy." He executed a stiff bow and walked back into the house.

Sinclair followed his friend's progress, then turned back to Quincy. Her head was bowed, hands covering her face. His stomach clenched. "Quincy, darling, what is it?"

"I knew it was too good to be true." She looked up, her eyes bright with unshed tears, and slowly shook her head.

His throat tightened at the raw pain in her voice. "You're not making sense." He'd never had much luck understanding females, but he thought he'd understood Quincy.

Her chin came up. She blinked back the tears. "What do you think you were doing?" She pointed at the terrace door, where Palmer had just stepped indoors. "You as much as told him that we— Ooh!" She swatted at his outstretched hand and stalked down the path.

Sinclair fell into stride beside her. "I let him know Mr. Quincy was none of his concern."

"By letting him think that we—"

"But we soon *will* be, my dearest Josephine. In three weeks, four days." Quincy stopped in mid-stride. "And since when have you concerned yourself with what others think?" he added.

Quincy spun to face him. Startled by her sudden movement, he stepped backward, and stumbled on an uneven section of the path. A flash of concern replaced her anguish. "Where is your walking stick?"

"I have no need for it." He longed to wrap his arms around her. Conscious of their surroundings, he instead traced her pearls, warm and smooth, like her skin, with one fingertip. "There is nothing to fear from Palmer. As my friend, he will keep his speculations to himself."

She shook her head again. "It *does* matter to me what other people think—about you, your mother, your friends." Despite her feminine finery, he had never seen her look so wretched. "Don't you see? You'll be dragged through the gossip columns within a week. We can't marry."

Her words hit harder than if she'd planted him a facer. "We . . . what?" Before Sinclair could hear her explanation, Lady Fitzwater stepped out onto the terrace.

"Yoo-hoo, Miss Quincy!" she trilled. "Please come in. There are several gentlemen begging to meet you! Sinclair, you naughty boy, you can't keep her to yourself, you know!"

"We're not finished, Quincy."

"It's bad form to keep our hostess waiting, my lord." Quincy made her way to the terrace. Lady Fitzwater shook her head and gave him an unmistakable *"tsk, tsk."*

Sinclair watched the door close behind them, then sat on the nearest bench, his shoulders slumped, oblivious to the chattering couples walking in the garden. What did Quincy mean, they couldn't marry? Whyever not?

What was the terrible thing people would gossip about if they married? That she had leg-shackled herself to a cripple? It was one thing to kiss him, but another to shackle herself to a cripple. Like Serena. He'd had a moment of panic there, thinking she was repulsed by his scarred leg. But then good sense had returned. Quincy was nothing like Serena—her demand for his walking stick stemmed from concern, not repugnance. The same concern for fellow beings that was as much a part of Quincy as her wry sense of humor and wavy auburn hair.

While Quincy cared for everyone else, she didn't give a fig for what people thought of her.

He sat up. People would look down on *him* for marrying her. That's what she thought?

Nigel. Her ex-fiancé had taught her a valuable lesson, she'd said. Thanks to that cowardly bastard, she still believed she was unsuitable to be anyone's wife.

Sinclair pounded his fist on his knee. He was a damn earl, by God. He could marry whomever he wanted, and he wanted Quincy.

But how to convince the stubborn girl?

Ah, that must be at the heart of the issue. She had only been a girl, Miss Quincy, for less than one day. She did not yet see herself the way he did, as an attractive young woman.

Time. That was it. All he had to do was give her more time as Miss Quincy, let her interact with her peers in her new role.

Mama's upcoming soiree would be the perfect opportunity. The invitations had gone out weeks ago, but he knew several men whose nephews and younger brothers could be added at the last moment—young bucks who would fall over each other to win the favor of a new Incomparable like Miss Quincy. Their fawning adoration would be just the ticket to boost her confidence. Allay all her fears. In less than a month she would be his wife, just as he planned.

Sinclair strolled back indoors, whistling.

* * *

Quincy endured yet more introductions to faceless people by Lady Fitzwater, pasting a smile on her face as she rejoined her sister. She went through the social niceties by rote, her mind reviewing the recent events.

She had been caught up in the whirl of her transformation to Miss Quincy, with all the requisite feminine accoutrements, though she still felt like an imposter. She had been living a masquerade for so many years, she did not *feel* like Miss Quincy, even wearing a dress.

But the Trio's delight in making the change had been infectious. Her concern about expenses had been allayed by Lady Sinclair, who insisted on paying for much of her new wardrobe and accessories, explaining it was money that Quincy deserved anyway from her investments on Sinclair's behalf. She thought Lady Sinclair's logic was fuzzy, but went along, not wanting to be a spoilsport.

She had even begun to believe that perhaps she got the fairy-tale ending after all—the dashing hero, well, the limping hero, wanted to take her away from all her worries and live with her happily ever after. Her sister would be saved, and Quincy would marry the man of her dreams.

Until Palmer had brought her crashing back to reality.

If even Sinclair's best friend disapproved of their alliance, what would others think?

Sinclair's entire household knew Mr. Quincy, and servants' gossip spread faster than fire in a powder keg. He and his mother would be the laughingstock of the ton once word got out he'd hired a female secretary. The new scandal would dredge up talk of the old one. He'd be shunned, given the cut direct. Lady Sinclair would become a recluse again. Sinclair would grow to resent it, resent her for causing it. They had already endured enough scandal. She wouldn't be the cause of another.

Sinclair was a reasonable man. As soon as they could steal a moment of privacy, she would explain her reasoning to him, make sure he understood. He would agree it was for the best that they break off their friendship.

Quincy steeled herself as Sinclair came back indoors.

She entered the conversational foray, looking for an opportunity to speak with him alone. Like lancing a boil, 'twas best done quickly.

But no boil had ever hurt this much.

Chapter 22

Sinclair paced in his library, watching the clock's hands drag their way toward nine. It had been three days since Lady Fitzwater's at-home. Three agonizing, tortuous days since he'd last seen Quincy. The managing trio of his mother, Lady Fitzwater, and Lady Bradwell had conspired to keep them apart.

Jack, his one-legged footman, had kept Sinclair apprised of Quincy's activities. While Jill had been sewing on Quincy's gowns, Quincy had been suffering through shopping trips for feminine fripperies, and deportment lessons taught by the Trio.

He did not envy her, having to learn all over again to curtsy rather than bow, and all manner of ladylike behaviors. Undoing five years' worth of habits could not be an easy task.

Quincy's masculine mannerisms had served her well in the past, but they had almost been her undoing at Fitzwater's three days ago. Two bucks had been affronted when she'd jumped into their discussion of the corn laws, and one young lady was insulted by Quincy's disregard for her millinery confection. Quincy was far more appreciative of a sturdy wool coat than a flimsy bonnet that would droop in the lightest drizzle.

Would that change, he wondered? Would her outward transition extend to changes on a deeper level? He tried to picture a simpering Quincy, but couldn't. No, the person who'd badgered him into keeping her employed was too strong to be affected by mere clothing. She was still his Quincy. Though he could no longer admire her legs and derrière, outlined in her trousers, the low necklines currently in vogue offered some compensation. Perhaps she'd wear trousers when they were alone. That idea held interesting possibilities.

After they were married, they'd set the ton on its collective ear with the way he planned to carry on, spending time in each other's company. A *great* amount of time in each other's company. No separate bedchambers for the earl and his countess. After the brief taste he'd had in the shepherd's hut, he wanted to wake up with Quincy in his arms every morning, fall asleep with her every night.

The clock struck nine, promptly followed by the sound of the knocker, heralding the arrival of the first guests to his mother's soiree. Ten more minutes and he could join the group gathered in the drawing room. Join Quincy. His Jo.

And join the men he'd added to his mother's invitation list. Far outnumbering the husband hunters Mama had initially invited, they were eminently eligible bachelors, the best Town had to offer. Not only would Quincy be fawned over by the young bucks, she could meet other gentlemen, other potential suitors, and interact with them as Miss Quincy. With their reaction, she'd soon realize they would envy him, not look down on him, for having her as his bride. She'd come to her senses, they'd have the banns read, and be wed in three weeks. Just as he planned.

He mentally rehearsed all he wanted to say to her, to be sincere but not overeager. To bite his tongue when she conversed with other gentlemen. To not let anything slip regarding their previous relationship. As far as the ton knew, they had just met a few days ago, and not for the world would he damage her reputation. Society had forced her to play a role to survive, and he'd be damned if she'd be punished for it.

He wiped the eager grin from his face, replacing it with a polite smile, and entered the drawing room.

Leland had accompanied his mother and the Quincys, and sat close to Melinda on the sofa, their heads bowed in deep conversation. Other groups clustered about the room, while his footmen passed trays of champagne and hors d'oeuvres. The new maids had taken one look at the gentry and frozen. Fortunately he could count on Thompson and Grimshaw to carry out their duties without incident, especially since, for Thompson at least, it meant the chance to peer down a few bodices.

"Sinclair, dear boy, how good of you to join us," Lady Fitzwater called, just audible above the hubbub from the newly arrived crowd.

Sinclair kissed his mother's cheek, then the air above Lady Fitzwater's knuckles. He scanned the room while greeting the ladies, trying not to be obvious about it.

"She's over there," Lady Fitzwater said in a stage whisper, nodding toward the far side of the room. She winked at him as he excused himself to join Quincy's group.

Quincy was surrounded. In a poor tactic, most likely to avoid attention, she'd sat in the corner farthest from the door. But how could she have thought to escape attention, dressed in a delectable light blue gown trimmed with sapphire ribbons, matching slippers, and her grandmother's pearls caressing her throat? She had caught the attention of several young bucks who now clustered around her like the fawning subjects of a queen. Young ladies, not to be deprived of male company, had inserted themselves into the crowd of bodies. Quincy was trapped.

Sinclair edged his way into the cluster, absently chatting with the empty-headed debutantes who should have stayed in the school room until they had absorbed knowledge of something, anything, beyond husband-hunting. He was generous and democratic in giving attention. He greeted the brazen Lady Louisa and quiet Miss Mary briefly enough that they could read no intent in his remarks, and exchanged pleasantries with shy Miss Prescott just long enough to have her look him in the eye instead of his neckcloth.

Just as he was beginning to doubt he would ever reach Quincy's chair, his mother came to the rescue. She seated herself at the pianoforte, adjusted her wedgewood blue skirts, and began to play for a young couple. The duet became a trio, then half a dozen more joined in. The group around Quincy broke up, to join the gathering around the pianoforte or greet newcomers. A silver-haired gentleman sat beside Mama on the bench, turning pages for her. Sinclair recognized him from the theater.

Quincy met Sinclair halfway across the crowded room. "She seems to be enjoying herself," she said with a nod toward the couple seated at the pianoforte.

Grimshaw passed by, circulating a tray with glasses of champagne. Sinclair snagged two glasses and offered one to Quincy. "I'm beginning to wonder if this evening was planned for me or for her," Sinclair said. "I don't even know his name."

"Coddington, a widowed marquess with fifty thousand a year."

Sinclair raised one eyebrow, then lowered it. "Ah, yes. You know everything that goes on in this household."

Quincy shook her head. "I overheard a couple of tabbies less than five minutes ago. Lady Stanhope is quite jealous."

"I stand corrected." Sinclair noticed two cubs hovering close by, silently pleading with Sinclair to introduce them. He *should* introduce them to Quincy. After all, the purpose of the evening was for her to interact. He held his arm out. "Care to take a turn about the room with me, Miss Quincy?" She took his proffered arm and they stepped away from the cubs. "Have you been introduced to many of the other guests?" he inquired. *Have you seen how they think you're fine as six-pence?* "I believe they represent the best of those on the Marriage Mart. Both genders."

Before she could reply, there was a great crash and a shrill scream as Thompson bumped into Lady Stanhope, and his tray of champagne glasses slid down her generous backside to the floor. The room fell silent except for Lady Stanhope's gasping. Oblivious to the mess he'd made, Thompson gawked at Quincy.

Sinclair pinned him with a stare. "Is something wrong, Thompson?"

"It's . . . But she's . . . er, no, my lord. So sorry. Terribly clumsy of me." He bent to pick up the shards of glass, stealing sideways glances at Quincy even as Grimshaw arrived with rags and a dustbin.

Several ladies rushed forward to whisk Lady Stanhope to a private room, and the hum of conversation resumed. Sinclair started walking again, Quincy at his side, right where she belonged. It took a moment to realize she was leading him toward the French doors and the relative privacy of the balcony beyond. He missed their hours alone in the library, too. He quickened the pace.

Outside, rain earlier in the day had washed the city, leaving behind the crisp, clean air a spring night. The mellow tone of a lark was a counterpoint to the hum of conversation and music from the drawing room. Sinclair leaned closer to Quincy in the velvet darkness, inhaling her fresh scent, a hint of lemon. She stood before him, her hands resting on the stone railing, much of her shoulders and upper back left bare by her dress. Her shawl hung low, almost slipping from her elbows.

Shielding her from the doorway with his own body, Sinclair gave in to temptation and reached with one finger to follow the lace edging on the top of her bodice, tracing a path from one shoulder, down and across her spine, up to her other shoulder. She stayed perfectly still for his touch, like a cat having its chin scratched. He could almost swear she purred.

"I've never seen Thompson falter before a woman before," Sinclair leaned in to whisper in her ear. "You felled him with your beauty." As long as he was so close, he dropped a kiss beneath her earlobe, and another on the back of her neck, brushing her hair aside to land it in the spot that he knew from personal experience made her quiver with desire.

This time her quivering turned to outright laughter. "What fustian. He was just startled, that's all." She turned in his arms, her smile fading as she gazed at him.

He'd do anything to get her smile back. "You've met the other guests? Been treated well? Put your fears to rest? The women will be jealous, and the men will envy me for capturing your hand." He raised the aforementioned hand for a kiss.

The cut of her gown revealed the rounded tops of her breasts, and he licked his lips as he watched them rise and fall as she took a deep breath. "No, Sinclair, we can't—"

Someone else stepped out on the balcony, someone whose cloying perfume overwhelmed all other scents. Sinclair bit back a groan. Serena, Duchess of Warwick.

"Josephine, you sly minx," the duchess said, slapping Quincy on the wrist with her fan. "Trust you to find the most eligible *parti* in a gathering full of them." She slid her arm possessively around Sinclair's elbow and batted her kohl-rimmed lashes at him. "I hope you are fully recovered from your illness, my lord? You look quite virile once more."

Sinclair glanced from the duchess to Quincy and back again. He'd never had the chance to quiz her about her reaction to the duchess that day in the drawing room. "I was not aware you two were acquainted."

"Serena and I grew up in the same village," Quincy said, rubbing her wrist. Her tone was calm, but her jaw was clenched.

"Yes, and we always seemed to end up sharing everything," Serena said. She brought her other hand up, imprisoning Sinclair's arm. "How is your new secretary working out, my lord? A fascinating fellow, I hear."

Sinclair resisted the urge to squeeze her lovely neck until her face turned blue. "He's gone. No longer in my employ."

Serena opened her eyes wide. "Gone? But I'm sure he hasn't gone very far." She leaned closer, all but rubbing her body against his. "I'm sure he could come back. Why don't we meet tomorrow to discuss it, hmm? Just you and I." She ran her tongue along her upper lip, then her full bottom lip.

Sinclair's stomach lurched.

"Are you sure your husband won't miss your company?" Quincy batted her eyelashes at the duchess, her expression innocent.

Another couple stepped onto the balcony. As everyone shuffled to make room, Quincy tugged on Sinclair's free arm. "Excuse us, your grace," she said, "but Lady Sinclair is signaling for us. We'll have to continue our discussion later."

Sinclair disengaged Serena's fingers from his arm and followed Quincy back into the drawing room. Once inside, Quincy let go and ducked under Grimshaw and his passing tray of champagne glasses. By the time Sinclair did a *pas de deux* to keep from colliding with the footman, Quincy had disappeared in the crowd.

Sinclair searched every group, every cluster of people, but Quincy was nowhere to be found. Admitting defeat, he headed for the pianoforte. Luckily the song had just ended. "Mama," he hissed, sitting beside her on the bench, "how could you invite that . . . that . . . duchess into our home?"

Lady Sinclair closed the lid over the keys. "I thought you had invited her. Is something wrong? I saw Jo leave and she did not look happy. Whatever did you say to her?"

"I say, old chum," the silver-haired gentleman said, leaning around Lady Sinclair. "Is something amiss?"

"Coddy, dear, my son is just being obtuse. Again." She pinned Sinclair with a grim stare. "Whatever it is, fix it."

Sinclair groaned and stood up. "Fix it, indeed," he muttered as he ducked out the door and headed for the back stairs. For the love of Juno, how was he to fix this mess?

Quincy marched back to the Fitzwater's house alone, ignoring the stares from other pedestrians, her broad strides straining the seams in her new gown. How dare Serena? How dare she! Serena had always gotten what she wanted. She had never shared with Quincy, she simply took. And then batted her long lashes and got away with it.

Well, not this time. She wasn't getting Sinclair.

Fate had conspired to keep Quincy from having Sinclair, but that didn't mean her childhood nemesis could have him, either. Quincy thought back to the petty tyrant Serena had been as a young girl, thought of the pain she'd inflicted on Sinclair when she'd cruelly spurned his offer, calling him a cripple. It was past time for the tart to receive her comeuppance. Quincy was just the person to dish it out.

By the time Quincy reached her rented rooms, she had devised a plan. She headed straight for Grandmère's chamber and pulled the trunks out from under the bed. Quincy riffled through them until she found the ribbon-bound bundle of paper. "Sorry, Grandmère," she said, untying the faded cords, "but I'm sure you'll understand." Quincy thumbed through the stack, past the missives from her grandfather, past the wedding and birth announcements, until she found the obituary. She paused for a moment, reading the long-memorized lines about her mother and still-born brother.

"I haven't forgotten my promise, laddie," she said with a faint smile, looking up. "As soon as I get to heaven, I fully intend to throttle you for leaving us in this predicament."

Quincy set back to work. Stacked beneath the obituary were the letters and notes of sympathy, including the one she sought.

"Bless your excruciatingly correct parents, Serena," Quincy whispered. She read the very proper message of sympathy from the Doughty family. At the bottom of the neatly penned note were the signatures of the earl and countess, and their daughter Serena.

By the light of a single candle, Quincy practiced the loops and swirls until she had it just right, hoping the adult Serena's handwriting had not changed much. White paper would never do, she decided. Riffling through Grandmère's things once more, Quincy found her stash. Lavender, yellow, pink. Grandmère had pink paper? Lavender would be best. And for the pièce de résistance, Quincy chose the most exotic-smelling of Grandmère's tiny bottles of scent.

My dearest Sinclair, Quincy wrote. *Why don't we meet tomorrow to continue our discussion? Just you and I. You know where and when.* Quincy signed Serena's name with a flourish, added a drop of perfume, and sealed it with drips from the melting candle.

Not bad. Besides, with any luck, Serena's husband had never seen her handwriting beyond signing the parish register after their wedding. The Duke of Warwick didn't seem the type to write *billets-doux*, and Serena's goal had been to inspire them, not pen them herself.

Now for the real problem—getting the note into the duke's hand. Could she risk dressing as Mr. Quincy and delivering it to his club herself? No, too many people knew that Cousin Joseph had left town. She needed a co-conspirator, someone unknown to the duke or Serena.

Sam the butcher, or his sons? Melinda would have to ask him, since Joseph was officially gone and Mel had taken over giving the lessons. No, they would all ask too many questions.

That left . . . Thompson. Quincy cringed. He had been a tad surprised upon seeing her tonight, but at least he hadn't said anything. Well, nothing coherent, anyway. And he apparently hadn't collected on his wager with Grimshaw. She wrote a note to Thompson and wrapped it around the duke's note, along with a couple of coins. She went out into the hall and found one of Fitzwater's footmen, the one who often winked at Mel, and gave him another coin in exchange for his promise to deliver the package into Thompson's hands.

Quite pleased with herself, and suddenly exhausted, Quincy shucked off her new gown and fripperies, pulled on a night rail, and was sound asleep before the other ladies came home.

She awoke the next morning with a pounding headache and second thoughts. The note put Sinclair in a bad light. Stupid, stupid, stupid, she should have addressed it to "my dearest lover" or similar drivel. What if the duke took umbrage with Sinclair? He might call him out, they'd fight a duel, they could both be hurt. Or worse. Both men were innocent in the affair. Well, the duke had shown poor judgment in marrying Serena in the first place, but still . . .

She had to get the note back from Thompson. Now.

And there was one more thing. The interlude on the balcony last night proved she was not immune to Sinclair's charm. He could easily seduce her into marriage, and everything she had tried to avoid would come crashing down around their ears anyway. Serena's threat had made it clear how easily Sinclair, and his mother and friends, could be hurt if she continued to associate with them. She wouldn't put them through it. Wouldn't put *him* through it. No one else should be punished for choices *she* had made.

With a sinking heart, she realized the only way to avoid it now was to leave. Never see Sinclair again. She clutched her stomach.

She had the profit from her investments. If she was frugal, made a shrewd bargain, she could still buy a cottage and furnish it. Move Mel and her grandmother to the countryside, away from Serena's venom.

"Good morning, Grandmère," Quincy called, entering the kitchen after she'd dressed.

"Where did you go so suddenly last night, miss? I'm not in the habit of making excuses for you. And why are my things strewn all over my room?" Grandmère sat at the table, holding out her teacup for Mel to refill. The lines etched on the elder woman's face seemed deeper than usual. Quincy winced.

"You missed seeing Serena last night," Mel said, bringing out another cup for Quincy. "Did you know she married a duke?"

"No, and yes." She accepted the filled cup and faced her grandmother. "I did not miss Serena last night, and she did not miss me. Nor did she miss Mr. Quincy a fortnight ago when she paid a call on Sinclair."

"Oh, dear."

Mel fell into her chair. "She recognized you? Oh my."

"Yes. Oh my." Quincy related the essentials of their meeting last night, and Serena's request of Sinclair. Her audience made suitable noises of disgust and dismay.

When Quincy finished, Grandmère spoke quietly. "Are you going to let her affect your decision in regards to Sinclair's offer?"

Quincy bit her lip. "How early can we pay a call to thank our hostess?"

Grandmère frowned.

"You still haven't explained the mess you made in Grandmère's room," Melinda said.

Grandmère's eyes suddenly widened. "My colored paper. Tell me you didn't."

"I did. I merely repeated Serena's words, and added a few of my own."

It was Mel's turn to frown. "What are you talking about?"

"Jo's been practicing her creative penmanship again."

"On colored paper?" Mel squealed in delight. "You sent a note to the Duke of Warwick?"

"But now I realize it may not have been the wisest course of action, and I need to go to Sinclair's to get it back."

"I cannot believe Lord Sinclair agreed to participate in such a scheme!"

"Of course not. He knows nothing about it, and I'd like to keep it that way. May we go now?"

"You can't go anywhere looking like that, Jo," Mel said, standing up and looking at Quincy's back. "You've done up your buttons all crooked."

Quincy rolled her eyes in disgust. "Well, the back is a foolish place to put them!"

Grandmère and Mel shared a chuckle at Quincy's expense, then resisted all her attempts to hurry them. Two hours passed before they left to pay a call on Lady Sinclair, and even then, Grandmère warned, it was still too early to be quite proper.

"Lady Sinclair will join you shortly," Harper said, ushering them into the salon. His butler's mask was firmly in place, though Quincy caught him casting surreptitious glances at her.

She winked at him. He stumbled on the edge of the carpet on his way out.

The three had barely seated themselves when Lady Sinclair bustled in and rang for a tea tray. "It's my son, isn't it?" she said grimly, coming to sit beside Quincy. "What did the beast say or do to you? Tell me, and we'll make it right." She took Quincy's hands into her own, patting them.

"No, my lady, you don't understand," Quincy began.

"It's the Duchess of Warwick who is being beastly," Mel piped up.

Quincy shot her a quelling look. Lady Sinclair turned to Mel in surprise.

"Warwick, you say?" Lady Sinclair frowned. "I don't usually repeat servants' gossip, but"—the Quincy women leaned closer as Lady Sinclair lowered her voice—"the duchess' maid was dismissed by the duke himself last night. Their graces had a shocking row; woke up the entire household. Then they became completely silent, and—" Lady Sinclair looked to make sure she had everyone's attention—"no one has seen the duchess since."

Melinda and Grandmère gasped. Quincy felt the blood drain from her face. What fateful acts had she set in motion?

Lady Sinclair took a sip of tea. "The duke told her grace's maid that they had no more need of her services, and sent her on her way with a purse full of coins."

Quincy felt sick. Melinda and Grandmère spoke at once.

"What do you suppose—"

"You don't think he really—"

"Stop!" Quincy shouted. She rested her shaking hands on her lap. "I don't wish to hear any more of the Warwicks' affairs, if you please."

"Of course not. Forgive me for bringing it up." Lady Sinclair patted Quincy's hand. "Now, my dear, what did my son—"

"Good morning, ladies."

They turned in unison at the male voice, to see Lord Palmer entering the room.

"Hope you don't mind the intrusion, Lady Sinclair. Just popped in to see your son, but he ain't in the library."

"Not at all, Lord Palmer. Do join us." Lady Sinclair rang for a fresh pot of tea. "I'm afraid it may be a while before he returns. He went out for one of his long walks this morning."

Palmer had sat down, but rose again. "That being the case, I'll catch up to him at our club, and leave you lovely ladies to your coze." He tipped his hat and left.

Quincy groaned. She had to get out of here. It would be hours before she could speak to Sinclair. Hours during which her relatives, and Lady Sinclair, would try to talk her out of her decision to reject Sinclair. And what on earth could the duke have done to Serena? She had only wanted Serena given a set-down. She wanted the hussy out of the way, not six feet under. If the duke had taken drastic action because of her note, Quincy would never forgive herself. He didn't deserve to hang.

"Now then, where were we? Ah, yes, my son." Lady Sinclair patted Quincy's knee.

"If you'll excuse me, I, um . . ." Quincy stood and edged toward the door. "I just remembered that we left a kettle on the hearth. No, don't worry," she put her hand out to her grandmother and sister, who hadn't moved, "I'll take care of it."

Caught up in her thoughts, she didn't even notice which servant opened the front door for her and wished her a good day. She jumped when Palmer spoke to her on the sidewalk.

"I understand felicitations are in order, Miss Quincy."

Quincy stared at him, openmouthed.

"I know it has not been formally announced yet, but Sinclair has asked me to stand up with him as his best man."

"H-he has?"

Palmer nodded. His coach pulled up then, and he gestured for his coachman to follow as he fell into step with Quincy. "I am gratified to see the changes wrought in him since making your acquaintance, Miss Quincy. He is once again the jolly fellow I remember from our school days. And the changes in his mother are even more remarkable."

"Thank you."

"But I must confess I am concerned. I fear his past relationship with a certain secretary could mar his chances for long-term happiness, should anyone learn the true nature of that relationship."

Quincy held her hands to her aching stomach. "I don't know what to say, my lord," she said, wishing her voice wouldn't shake, "other than to assure you that Lord Sinclair's future is of as much concern to me as it is to you. I would never pursue my happiness at the expense of another's."

"Just as I thought," Palmer said, raising her hand to kiss the air above her knuckles. "I admire the courage of your convictions. Good day, Miss Quincy."

"Good day, Lord Palmer." Quincy watched him climb into his carriage, then walked home in a daze, her thoughts going in a dozen different directions.

Was Serena really dead? If she and the threat that she presented were gone, was there anything to prevent Quincy from marrying Sinclair?

Thompson and Wilford could probably be persuaded to keep quiet, since neither had said anything so far, at least nothing that she knew about. Or would there be someone else who would reveal Quincy's secret and shatter Sinclair's happiness?

Maybe next week, next month, next year. Maybe never. Could she take that chance?

Chapter 23

"You're just in time, miss," said Lady Fitzwater's footman as he let Quincy into the house. "They've just gone in to luncheon."

"But I'm not expected."

"Anybody who's about the house is expected, miss."

Quincy followed him to the dining room, where Lady Fitzwater, two other women, and Miss Stanbury, one of Lady Fitzwater's boarders, were being served.

"Miss Quincy!" Lady Fitzwater called. "How good of you to join us. May I introduce Miss Pippen and Miss Jesperson, dear friends of Miss Stanbury?"

Before Quincy finished the how-do-you-dos, the footmen had set her place and brought her soup. The meal passed quickly in congenial conversation, and Quincy allowed herself to be distracted from her earlier introspection. She was caught up as their discussion moved from dealing with coal porters and other merchants to the benefits and possible dangers as more gas lines were laid in London. Miss Jesperson had recently invested a portion of her pension in a gas works, and shared the results of her research.

Not once did the subject of fashion come up, except for Miss Pippen whispering to Miss Stanbury that her shawl's fringe had fallen into her soup. And they included Quincy in their little group as a matter of course.

With a start, Quincy realized she had not been involved in an all-female conversation such as this since she was fourteen. Instead of boys and deportment, they discussed how to run households and stretch budgets.

Shortly after they retired to the drawing room, Lady Fitzwater's two other boarders, Lieutenant Wheeler and Reverend Gladstone, joined them. After the requisite introductions, the animated discussion resumed. This was no proper social call; no one left after twenty minutes. Just a small group of friends enjoying each other's company.

Quincy had almost forgotten the simple pleasure of intelligent conversation with people not related to her. She reveled in the moment, refusing to worry about her past or her uncertain future. She did not worry about doing or saying something too feminine for her male counterpart. She was even growing accustomed to wearing a dress and corset-slip instead of breeches and a coat.

This was what she wanted for her future. These ladies dealt with merchants and solicitors, and remained ladies. So would she. No more subterfuge. Mr. Quincy was banished forevermore.

As if sensing her thoughts, Lady Fitzwater caught her eye and gave her an approving nod. Quincy smiled back.

"I say," Lieutenant Wheeler said, "has anyone heard what happened with the Duke and Duchess of Warwick?"

Quincy's heart stopped, than started again at double-time. Everyone else in the room looked at the lieutenant with mild interest.

Wheeler answered his own question. "He packed her off to Northumberland, exiled for the Season. Apparently His Grace found a note she'd written to a paramour."

"How uncouth," exclaimed Miss Pippen. "She hasn't even produced an heir yet!"

The other ladies expressed shock and dismay, and applauded the duke's action.

Reverend Gladstone shook his head slowly. "A virtuous woman is a crown to her husband, but she that maketh ashamed is as rottenness in his bones," he intoned, quoting from Proverbs.

Quincy squeezed her eyes shut in pain. *She that maketh ashamed . . .*

Soon the conversation drifted to more general topics, and Quincy excused herself.

Grandmère and Melinda had returned to their quarters just before Quincy arrived, and were hanging up their shawls.

"Did you get to the kettle before it burned?" Melinda said.

"What kettle?" Quincy said absently, gathering paper, ink, and a pen. She sat down at the table and began to write.

"Jo, are you sure . . ."

Quincy looked up, determined not to be swayed by her grandmother's arguments regarding Sinclair's offer.

Grandmère waved her hand in dismissal. "Stubborn child."

The first note was to Sinclair, letting him know she would call upon him tomorrow morning. Since she had never formally accepted his proposal—for that matter, he hadn't formally proposed—she didn't need to break anything off, but she would tell him farewell in person. She bent the tip of the quill as she signed her name and had to sharpen it before continuing.

The second note was to Mr. Hatchett, a solicitor recommended by Sam the butcher. "He don't mind working for us common folks," Sam had said.

Feeling that she'd already imposed too much on Lady Fitzwater's servants, Quincy put on her shawl and set out to see the crossing sweeper two streets over. After paying the boy a few coins to deliver her notes, she headed for Mr. Chadburn's office, to have him liquidate her investments. It was time to set things irrevocably in motion.

After passing a restless night and refusing breakfast, Quincy paced in her room. At last it was time to leave. Much to her surprise, Grandmère and Melinda quietly fell into step beside her as they left the house. Grandmère leaned on her cane in her right hand. With her left, she gave Quincy's hand a squeeze.

"Lady Sinclair is in the drawing room," Harper informed them a few minutes later. "I am sure my lady will be pleased to see you." While he led the group upstairs, Quincy slipped away to the library.

She stood with her hands over her fluttering stomach. "Like swallowing a live toad before breakfast," she muttered, "nothing worse can happen all day." She opened the library door.

Sinclair stood near the wall, searching the book titles on the shelves. She stole a moment to study his profile. Strong jaw, well-formed figure, big enough to inspire confidence without being intimidating. Breathtakingly handsome. He wanted her to be his wife. He wanted to be her husband. She wanted to run into his arms and never leave. Quincy sighed. Why on earth shouldn't she marry him?

She that maketh ashamed . . .

"Good morning, my lord," she said, stepping into the room.

"Good morning, Jo." Sinclair's voice was soft and rich, meant for her ears alone. His gaze took in every inch of her before coming to rest on her face.

Her pulse raced. Staring back at Sinclair, she could not form a coherent sentence if her life depended on it.

"My compliments on a well-executed plan," Sinclair said, walking toward her, his limp pronounced. "I had not even devised a strategy yet, and I discovered yesterday that you'd already carried yours out. However did you get the note to the duke so quickly?"

Before Quincy could answer, Sinclair closed the remaining distance between them, wrapped his arms around her waist, and claimed her lips in a mind-numbing kiss.

Instinctively she brought her arms up around his neck, running her fingers through his silky hair, breathing in his delightful spice-and-liniment scent. She lingered in his embrace, savoring every sensation. The roughness of his chin, the softness of his lips, how his warm breath tickled her ear.

She could taste as well as smell the cinnamon toast he'd had for breakfast.

In his arms she felt safe and cherished, and the stirrings of something unfamiliar but wonderful. Happiness.

At last Sinclair let go, his breathing ragged. "Three more weeks, my love," he whispered, tucking back a tendril of her hair.

That broke the spell. With trembling fingers, Quincy straightened her gown. She also reached up and adjusted Sinclair's cravat and smoothed the lapels of his coat. "That's what I came to talk to you about. I keep telling you that we can't . . . But you . . . Oh, blast." She sat down, her limbs no longer able to support her weight.

Sinclair joined her on the sofa. He took her hands in his, massaging her palms with his thumbs.

She couldn't do this. She had to do this, had to leave. She took a fortifying breath and stared into his warm brown eyes. "Your limp is worse."

Sinclair seemed as surprised by her remark as she was. "I stumbled in the dark last night. 'Tis nothing. You were trying to tell me something?" He let go to rest one hand on her knee, his fingers gently massaging.

Quincy followed his lead, resting her hand on his thigh, just above his knee. She ran her fingers in lazy circles, caressing the strong muscles, then stopped when she realized she was perilously close to throwing him back against the sofa and kissing him until he begged for mercy.

Mercy. There was precious little of that in Society. Needing space between her and Sinclair to get through this, she stood, twisting the strings of her reticule. "Serena may be gone, but the problem she presented is not."

"What makes you think that?" Sinclair tried to pull her back down beside him, but Quincy stepped farther away, putting a chair between them. She gripped the chair's back, studying her white knuckles.

"I was Mr. Quincy for a long time. There is a veritable army of people who knew him, many of whom know or suspect he was a sham. When I became him five years ago,

I did so knowing that eventually I would be exposed. Ostracized. I resigned myself to the outcome because the benefits of what I could accomplish far outweighed the consequences. It was the only way I saw to fulfill my duty to my family. And only three of us could be hurt.

"But now . . . a lot more people could be hurt because of what I've done. People I care for deeply." She forced herself to meet his unwavering gaze, his expression unreadable. She let go of the chair to rub her numb fingers.

"I don't think—"

Quincy held her hand up, unwilling to risk him changing her mind. A muscle ticked beside his jaw. "You have worked so hard to be rid of the stares, to quiet the rumors. I know how much it bothered you, though you try not to let on. Hardly anyone speaks of the old scandal anymore. At last they're letting your father and old Lord Twitchell rest in their graves. Not only has your mother come out of grieving, she even has a suitor."

"My mother—"

His attempts at interrupting her were getting louder, even as her resolve weakened. "If I stay, when my past is exposed, everyone around me will be tarred with the same brush. There isn't a war for you to join this time, even if your leg was strong. I can't let the Sinclair family name be used for scandal fodder again. I won't be the cause of more pain for you. And you'd only grow to resent me. Be ashamed of me." She licked dry lips. "You can see why it's best for everyone if I leave."

Sinclair stood up, towering over her. "How dare you?"

Quincy took an involuntary step back.

Color flooded his cheeks, even as she felt the blood drain from her own. "How dare you presume to make such a decision for me? I'm the damn Earl of Sinclair, and I will marry whomever I choose." He raised his arm, his finger stabbing the air before her. "I chose *you*. How can you think I'm incapable of deciding what's best for me, for my family?"

"It's what I do," she whispered. "You said so yourself." She held her fists at her sides, her voice getting stronger. "I've always made these decisions for the people around me, always had to be the one with a clear head. In time you'll see I'm right. This is for the best." She spun on her heel, determined to get to the door before her tears fell.

She heard footsteps, then a crash and grunt of pain behind her. Sinclair was sprawled on the floor, the tipped-over chair beside him, his face a mask of agony. He sat up, hands clutching his right thigh. "I can't chase after you, Quincy."

She squeezed until her nails bit into her palm. "I don't want you to." She yanked the bell pull on her way out.

In the hall, she closed her eyes and tried to regroup. She briefly debated going in search of her grandmother and sister. No, they'd ask questions she wasn't ready to answer. She should go home and pack, get her money from Chadburn, go buy her cottage.

Grimshaw passed her, answering the summons. She was five steps from the door when Thompson crossed the hall. He started toward her, but stopped and stared for a suspended moment. Then he clicked his heels and dropped into a deep bow.

Quincy nodded an acknowledgment and hurried out into the street before he could see her tears.

Once back in her room, Quincy flung herself down on her bed and let the tears flow. When Sir Ambrose nudged her with his wet nose, she rolled onto her side and wrapped her arm around his soft, furry body, holding him close against her chest.

She hated this weakness. It was unproductive. Messy. But from past experience she knew that giving in now was the only way she could hold the tears in check during the day until she was alone in her bed at night. She rummaged through the pile of clothes on the floor, searching for a handkerchief. She found a pair of white gloves instead. Borrowed from Sinclair the night he took her to the theater, never returned. They still carried his scent, a strangely pleasant combination of liniment, bay rum, and Sinclair. She clutched the gloves in her fist, crying even harder.

She'd felt torn apart after her father's death, but at least she had years of happy memories to sustain her. It was the same after her mother's death—the intense grief gradually eased until she could think of the joyful times with her lost loved ones, instead of just the painful loss.

But she didn't have happy years with Sinclair. She'd had only moments of joy, few and brief, snatched here and there. Could they sustain her?

They must. They were all she'd get.

Gradually her sobs gave way to hiccups, and Sir Ambrose began to purr. At last she sat up. Her throat ached with spent emotion. She blew her nose, then held a damp cloth over her red-rimmed eyes. It was nearly time for her appointments. Yesterday she had instructed Mr. Chadburn to liquidate her investments. Now to see what real estate Mr. Hatchett had found for her. She smoothed and folded Sinclair's gloves, tucked one inside her reticule, and went about her business.

Grandmère and Melinda were putting away their mending when Quincy returned home late that afternoon. "We thought you would join us in Lady Sinclair's salon," Grandmère chided.

"I . . . had other business to attend to."

"One of Sinclair's footmen asked me to give you these," Melinda said, handing her two coins. "Said you dropped them."

Quincy turned them over on her palm. Perhaps Thompson was a bit of a gentleman after all. She looked up in time to watch Melinda tying her bonnet ribbons under her chin. "Where are you going?"

Mel blushed. "Leland asked me to walk in the park with him. You don't mind, do you?"

Quincy waved her off. "Enjoy yourself. Don't worry about me. I·have to pack, anyway. Our new solicitor, Mr. Hatchett, has already found several cottages for me to look at. I'm leaving early in the morning."

Melinda gave her a quick hug, then was out the door in a flurry of skirts and ribbons. Quincy watched the door close, then propped her elbows on the table.

"You are certain this is what you want to do, miss?"

Quincy massaged her temples. "This is what must be done."

Grandmère slowly nodded, looking every one of her sixty-three years.

Sinclair sat on the floor after Quincy left, his anger with her overriding the pain in his leg, the humiliation of his fall. How could she dismiss him, dismiss their feelings? What gave her the right to make the decision for them both?

He suffered through the embarrassment of Grimshaw calling for assistance to raise him from the floor. Still weak from his recent illness and accompanying inactivity, his leg had been taxed last night when he tripped over a bundle of laundry. His sudden movement just now, going after Quincy, had been too much.

Thompson skidded into the room, halting beside Grimshaw. Without a word spoken aloud, the two footmen picked Sinclair up and made the awkward, agonizing trip up to Sinclair's bedchamber. His useless leg refused to support any of his weight. Without any of the obsequious fussing he used to get from Broderick, Thompson helped Sinclair change into a dressing gown and retrieved the bottle of liniment from the bedside table.

"I'll do it myself," Sinclair said, snatching the bottle.

"Yes, my lord. Do you require anything else?"

"No. Get out." Sinclair flung his arm over his eyes. "Thompson?"

The footman paused at the open door.

"Thank you."

"It's been a trying day, my lord." He left, shutting the door softly.

Sinclair wallowed in his misery a few moments longer, then sat up and began to massage liniment into his leg. The task kept his hands busy, leaving his mind free to race.

How could Quincy think he would ever be ashamed of her? He was damn proud of the way she had pulled her family through rough times. Proud of her ingenious strategy.

Eventually I would be exposed . . . What did that signify? And if it ever happened, it would be a nine-days' wonder at most, until the next bit of gossip came along. Being

accused of killing his father's rival was a scandal; having a
female secretary was a flea bite in comparison.

Even if your leg was strong . . . Sinclair stared at the spot
on his thigh where Quincy had run her fingers. She had
jerked her hand back when she realized she was touching
his scarred leg. He ran his own fingers over the rough tissue.

The scar had repulsed her.

He sat up ramrod straight. She had it backwards. She
wasn't concerned that he would become ashamed of her,
but that she would become ashamed of him. *Your leg is
weak . . .* She would grow to resent being leg-shackled to a
cripple. He would cause her pain.

He corked the liniment and put it away, retrieved the
half-empty bottle of whiskey in its place, and poured a
glass. He swallowed the contents in two gulps. Coughed.

Yes, it was best for everyone if Quincy left now, before
his emotions became involved. Before she became deeply
involved in his life. Before he needed her.

He grabbed the bottle to refill the glass but stopped,
hauled back his arm, and hurled the empty glass against the
stone fireplace. The glass shattered into a thousand satisfying pieces, showering the room with shards.

He switched the bottle to his right hand, prepared to
throw it, too. He stared at the golden fluid sloshing around
inside. Quincy had done them both a favor. Better to back
out now, while they could both walk away with their hearts
and pride intact.

Walk away. He snorted.

He raised the bottle in a silent toast to his former almost-
fiancée, and drank.

He stayed in his bedchamber for three days.

On the fourth morning, Sinclair limped downstairs only
because Thompson, the incompetent fool, couldn't find the
last case of brandy. Harper was of no help either, continu-
ally closeted in meetings with Mrs. Hammond. Sinclair had
unearthed the case in the wine cellar, instructed Thompson
to bring the rest abovestairs, and was heading back to his
room with a fresh bottle when his mother accosted him in
the hall.

"Benjamin," came the command, "you will please join me in the dining room."

"No need to shout, Mama," he whispered, holding his head.

"I was not aware beards were in vogue," she said as soon as they were seated.

Sinclair ran his fingers over his stubble-covered chin and shrugged. "Ain't had time to shave."

Lady Sinclair withheld comment while the footman set a luncheon plate before her. "We'll need another place setting, Grimshaw," she said. "My son will be joining me after all."

Grimshaw scratched his head. "I'll see what can be done, my lady."

Lady Sinclair stared at the footman's retreating back. "Most odd goings-on lately. I don't know what to make of it."

"Most odd," Sinclair murmured, wondering if his mother would notice should he slip off the seal and drink straight from the bottle, seeing as how there were no clean glasses on the sideboard.

"Now then, about Miss Quincy."

Sinclair nearly dropped the bottle. "What about her?"

"I have not seen any of the Quincys in several days. I thought I instructed you to fix things."

Sinclair squinted, almost uniting the twin images of his mother. "Did fix 'em. She cried off. Said she didn't want to be leg-shackled to a cripple."

Lady Sinclair pursed her lips. "I find it hard to believe Jo would say that. I— Yes, what is it, Daisy?"

The maid stood in the doorway, blushing furiously. "So sorry, my lady, but we can't, that is, there ain't—"

"Spit it out, child."

"Beg pardon, my lady, but there ain't no dishes for another place setting. I could dump out the sugar bowl if you like."

Lady Sinclair's brows rose. "What happened to the dishes?"

"Nothing! That is, they're just dirty, like. All of 'em. There's a big stack from the party last week, plus what we've used since. Alice, the scullery maid, left to go out walking with one of the grooms three days ago, and she ain't come back."

"And no one has washed dishes since?"

"Everyone says it ain't their job."

Sinclair dropped his forehead to the table.

"Do we think Alice has come to any harm?" Lady Sinclair said, ignoring her son. "Did the groom return safely?"

"Ned says Bart, that's the groom, he talked about going to work for his cousin what runs a coaching inn. We think that's where they went."

Lady Sinclair sighed. "Find Celia, and the two of you start washing. I shall hire another scullery maid right away."

"Yes, my lady." Daisy bobbed a curtsy and fled the room.

With a loud clatter, Lady Sinclair set her dishes in front of Sinclair. "Eat." She sniffed delicately and wrinkled her nose. "I don't care if you have to chew parsley and spend all afternoon in the tub, but I want you fresh and presentable when you escort me to the Danforth's ball tonight."

"Yes, Mama."

"And Benjamin?"

"Yes, Mama?"

"I never thought I would say this to you, but," she sighed, "you are an idiot."

"Yes, Mama."

Sinclair ate. When no one answered the bell pull, he went down to the kitchen to exchange his brandy bottle for a pot of coffee. One glance at the teetering piles of dishes made him dizzy. He requested hot water for a bath and headed back upstairs.

He had plenty of time to think while he waited for the water, sitting in the chair Quincy had so often occupied while she nursed him. Many parts of her farewell speech had replayed incessantly in his mind over the last three days, but now he heard different phrases. *People I care for very deeply* . . .

Did Quincy really care? He thought of how many sleepless nights she had spent watching over him. Cradling him in her arms. Protecting his mother, lessening her worries about his illness.

A knock on the door was followed by a parade of servants with his tub and buckets of hot water. No one spoke or met his gaze, though Sinclair thought he heard Thompson mumble something about it being "high time" on his way out.

Once he'd scrubbed himself raw and shaved, Sinclair sat back in the now-tepid water and stared at his thigh. He'd grown accustomed to the scar, he realized. The sight of it no longer nauseated him.

Five years ago he'd fled London, shaking with grief and impotent rage. Nothing he did or said convinced the scandalmongers he hadn't murdered old Lord Twitchell. Leaving meant he couldn't cause any further humiliation to his grieving mother, and it deprived the scandalmongers of more fodder by the simple expedient of depriving them of his presence.

Brentwood hadn't been far enough away. Hell, all the way across the English Channel was barely far enough. He'd thrown himself full-tilt into his new life in the army. Couldn't prove it by his chaotic household of late, but he'd taken an unorganized group of soldiers and turned them into a cohesive cavalry unit. He liked to think his leadership had saved a few lives on the battlefield. And, all right, he'd admit it, he'd hoped news of any acts of heroism he'd be able to perform would get back to London, and buff some of the tarnish from his family name.

But after surviving his first few battles, he'd lost interest in what Society thought of him. What mattered was serving his country, and saving the men of his unit. His disfigured leg was merely a souvenir of doing his duty.

Duty. To country, to family. A word Quincy knew well. She had skipped adolescence to take up adult responsibilities, in the name of duty.

Won't be the cause of more pain for you . . . With a sudden calm, Sinclair realized she had left him, rejected him, in the name of duty. An act of selflessness. *Not* because he limped.

More people could be hurt . . . His mother, most certainly, even Lady Fitzwater and Leland, would be hurt by a scandal. Quincy didn't know them well enough to gauge their reaction to being the object of a scandal, and so had decided to spare everyone the possibility.

To protect them, she had left. He should accept her sacrifice, and get on with his life. As she had said, it was for the best.

Besides, he'd already humiliated himself once by running after her. He wouldn't make the same mistake twice.

Chapter 24

❧

S inclair stared into the hall mirror and made a final adjustment to his cravat. Before lowering his hands, he discreetly exhaled in front of his palm. Satisfied, he took his last sprig of parsley and tucked it into the vase of tulips on the console table.

"You look much improved, Benjamin," Lady Sinclair said, descending the staircase in an elegant green gown.

"I pity Lord Coddington, missing such a vision as you are this evening, Mama." Sinclair kissed his mother's knuckles and helped her into the waiting carriage. "I hope you two have not had a falling out?" He leaned his walking stick against his knee.

"Of course not." Lady Sinclair settled her skirts as Elliott set the carriage in motion. "He is expecting to always escort me everywhere, and I cannot in good conscience let him take that for granted. I will, however, save two waltzes for him."

Sinclair leaned his head against the window and closed his eyes. At least someone in the household was happy.

Once through the receiving line, Sinclair saw to it his mother was settled with a group of friends, then fetched her a glass of punch before heading off to the card room. He passed Lady Louisa and Miss Prescott, who both tried to catch his eye, but he pretended not to notice.

Perhaps by the Little Season he could once more contemplate the idea of finding a wife. He would not shirk his duty to marry and carry on the line, but surely it could be put off a few months. He snagged a glass of champagne from a passing footman, hoping it would ease the sudden pain in his throat. It was difficult to swallow around the large lump lodged in his gullet.

"Good evening, Lord Sinclair," greeted a redheaded young man as Sinclair stepped through the card room doorway.

"Evening, Alfred." Palmer's nephew barely had time to nod before Leland joined them.

"Well, if it isn't the Matchmaking Earl himself," Leland said, grinning broadly. "Made any more matches lately?"

Sinclair wanted to be angry or even annoyed, but couldn't muster the energy. Unwittingly, he'd made successful matches for everyone in his household, it seemed, but himself. He tried to shake off his melancholy. "Pleasure to see you too, old chum. And yes, as a matter of fact, I understand my former scullery maid and one of the grooms are quite happy together now."

Leland let out a bark of laughter, slapped him on the back, and began explaining the joke to Alfred. Sinclair wandered away to find a game to join.

He gave up on the card room after an hour. No sense in losing all the money Quincy had won back for him.

Quincy.

Sinclair felt a sudden need for fresh air. He pushed through the sea of bodies. Where was that damn balcony door?

At last he found it. Just as he stepped over the threshold, he realized there was already a couple shrouded in the shadows, lovers undoubtedly escaping the crush for a stolen moment of privacy. He froze when he recognized Palmer and his wife.

They were not kissing, or even talking. They were simply leaning against each other, forehead to forehead, with Lady

Palmer's arms wrapped around her husband's waist. Palmer slowly stroked his wife's back.

The scene felt more intimate than if he'd walked in on them making love. He quickly withdrew, and casually blocked the doorway when another couple headed his way. The man scowled, but Sinclair didn't budge until they had passed by.

Clutching one hand to his stomach, Sinclair made his way back to the ballroom and circled the dance floor until he found his mother.

"Sit down, dear," she said, tugging him down beside her. "Whatever is the matter? You look positively ghastly."

"I think the crab cakes disagreed with me. You don't mind if we go home early, do you?"

"Evening, old chap," Coddington said, emerging from the crowd. He handed a cup of punch to Lady Sinclair before taking the seat on her other side.

"I am certain Coddy would see me home if you need to leave." Lady Sinclair turned to her cicisbeo. "I'm afraid my son isn't feeling well."

"Eh, what's this?"

Sinclair felt his cheeks grow warm. "It is of no concern, truly," he said. Belatedly he realized he was still clutching his stomach with one hand.

"The crab cakes, eh? Meant to warn you about those. Lord Danforth tends to buy his fish a day late." Coddington went on to describe several stomach remedies, and their results, in excruciating detail.

"Oh look, dear," Lady Sinclair said at last, interrupting Coddington's monologue. "Isn't that your friend Lord Palmer? He looks so happy. She must have told him."

"Told him what?" Sinclair watched Palmer and his wife glide past in the waltz. Oblivious to several stares, Palmer held his wife with his left hand, his empty right sleeve tucked in his pocket, as they moved gracefully across the floor. The look on his face could only be described as rapturous, matching Lady Palmer's expression. In a room filled with ennui, their joy stood out like a beacon.

"Their timing is perfect. They should be able to enjoy the

rest of the Season before heading to the country for her confinement," Lady Sinclair added with a smile of her own. She turned to face her son and stared at him expectantly.

Sinclair felt her gaze, but remained focused on the Palmers, reliving a memory from France.

In the aftermath of a battle, he'd found Palmer in a field hospital, his right arm a bloody stump just below the shoulder. Palmer refused medicine and food, repeatedly telling everyone within earshot he was better off dead. At last Lady Palmer arrived. She threw herself across his chest, weeping copious tears, for precisely three minutes. Then she ordered him a meal, a bath, and a shave, barking commands like a general. And like a general's, her orders were promptly obeyed, even by Palmer.

Palmer had recuperated quickly, if the muffled noises from his tent at night were any indication. With his wife at his side, he calmly faced a future that would be far different from the life he had planned.

With his beloved wife at his side, Palmer could face anything.

Sinclair wanted Quincy at his side.

Duty be damned. Scandal be damned.

He wanted Quincy beside him, beneath him, on top of him. He wanted her in his library, in his carriage, in his bedchamber.

He wanted Quincy. In his life.

The music ended. Sinclair stared back at his mother.

"Well?" she said. She reached for his hand, which he was again clutching to his stomach. "The stomach remedy you need . . ."

Sinclair stared down at his whitened knuckles and unclenched his fist. His tight expression relaxed into a smile. "I know just what I need. Good night, Mama." He kissed her on the cheek, then left so abruptly his chair teetered before settling.

"I knew I had not raised an idiot."

"What's that, my dear?"

"I said I believe you requested this dance, Coddy. Shall we?"

* * *

The street was clogged with carriages. At just past midnight, it seemed everyone in Town was traveling at once.

Sinclair stood on the Danforth's front steps and pulled up the collar of his coat to keep out the cold rain. He calculated how long it would take Elliott to reach the front of the line, then navigate the crowded thoroughfares. Damn. Sparing a glance for the cloudy sky, Sinclair crossed the street, dodging between carriages and ignoring a coachman's curses, moving as fast as he could with his cane.

After four blocks his leg throbbed. After eight blocks, he was limping badly through the downpour. By the twelfth block, he grabbed on to walls and lampposts and railings for support. Anything to remain upright and moving forward. His eyes stung and his legs felt on fire, but he didn't stop until he reached Leland's house.

He let himself in through the kitchen door, startling a scullery maid on her pallet before the fire. When she took a deep breath to scream, he tossed her a coin and kept going out to the hall.

The sound of his squelching shoes echoed off the walls, as did his labored breathing. His coat dripped with every step. He vaguely thought about leaving a generous vail for the maids.

At last he reached the Quincys' door. He took several deep breaths and ran a hand though his soaked hair, pushing it out of his eyes, before he softly knocked. A minute passed. Just as he reached to knock again, the door creaked open a few inches and Melinda's sleepy face appeared.

"Yes?" A moment later her eyes flew open in recognition and she let out a startled "Oh!" Sinclair heard a soft murmur, and Melinda spoke over her shoulder. "It's Jo's earl!" she whispered.

The door swung wide open and Lady Bradwell pushed Melinda aside, gesturing for Sinclair to come in. "What is it, my lord?" Lady Bradwell said as she tied the sash on her dressing gown. "Is your mother all right?"

"Yes, she's fine, thank you." Sinclair stepped into the doorway, looking past the two ladies to the door of

Quincy's room. "I'm terribly sorry about the lateness of the hour, but I must speak to Quincy right away."

The ladies exchanged a glance. The hairs on the back of Sinclair's neck rose.

"I'm afraid that's not possible, my lord," Lady Bradwell said.

Sinclair adjusted his wilting cravat. "I know it's late and this is highly improper, but—"

"But she isn't here!" Melinda interrupted.

"Not . . . at this hour?" His voice rose. "Where is she?" The ladies exchanged another glance, making Sinclair swear under his breath. "Where is she?" he demanded.

"She left three days ago with her new solicitor to look at cottages," Lady Bradwell said.

All the breath left Sinclair's body at once. "Three days?"

"You know how fast Jo proceeds once she has a plan," Melinda said proudly.

Sinclair leaned against the doorjamb and closed his eyes. He snapped them open when an idea occurred. "You must know where the properties are located. Did she leave you a list?"

Lady Bradwell shook her head. "I haven't been able to tell that girl what to do since the day her mother died. We don't even know when she'll be back. She was in a hurry to be gone."

Sinclair's leg gave out and he slid to the floor. If only he had come to his senses three days ago. Or not let the love of his life leave his library in the first place.

"Oh!" Lady Bradwell rested her hand on his shoulder. "I just remembered the name of the solicitor."

Hope flared in his chest. "Yes?"

"His name is . . . it's . . . Mel, help me. The solicitor that the butcher recommended."

"Hatfield? Hallett?"

Sinclair groaned and struggled to his feet.

"Hatchett!" the ladies cried in unison.

"Thank Juno," Sinclair muttered. "Thank you, Lady Bradwell," he added, louder. "I shall pay a call on him in the morning."

"Godspeed finding my granddaughter," she said as he left, "and good luck once you do!"

Sinclair had to open the door himself when he arrived home a short while later. Not a servant was in sight. His footsteps sounded unnaturally loud in the hall as he made his way toward the kitchen. Turning the corner, he almost bumped into the housekeeper, just exiting the butler's pantry. Mrs. Hammond's face was flushed, as was Harper's when he appeared a moment later.

Eyeing the pair, Sinclair stood still. Mrs. Hammond blushed even brighter. The awkward silence continued. Nobody moved.

"Are you two in love, or just cuddling in the corners?" Sinclair said at last.

Harper stepped forward, inserting himself between Sinclair and Mrs. Hammond, and raised his chin. "Yes."

Sinclair nodded. "I'm going to obtain a special license tomorrow. If I get one for you, too, will you make an honest woman of her?"

"I—I that is . . ." the butler stammered.

"Oh my. Oh my lord." Mrs. Hammond stared at the floor.

"We've discussed the possibility, neither of us is getting any younger, but—"

"My offer comes with one condition, however," Sinclair interrupted. "Take a week's honeymoon, and report back here in eight days. And make sure every blasted servant who works for me knows I have no objection to married employees. Is that clear? I don't care how many more matches are made, as long as they damn well stay here!"

"Yes, my lord!" Mrs. Hammond gushed.

"Thank you, my lord," Harper said. He took his intended's hand and squeezed it, then gave her a quick kiss on the cheek. "Does this mean Miss Quincy will soon be joining the household permanently, my lord?"

Sinclair couldn't hold back the grin that spread across his face. "I hope so, Harper. I certainly hope so."

Resuming his walk toward the kitchen in search of food, Sinclair heard the unmistakable sounds of kissing, and grinned again.

* * *

"What do you mean, you can't find them?" Sinclair dropped his feet to the floor and glared at Wooten across his desk. It had been three days since he'd hired the Bow Street Runner again, charged with the task of finding Quincy and/or her house-hunting solicitor, Hatchett.

Wooten switched his wool cap to his left hand to plow his right through his greasy hair. "I said I ain't found them *yet*. Just need more time. I'm only here because you told me to report today."

Sinclair groaned in frustration. "Go. Leave. Find Hatchett, or Miss Quincy, and don't come back until you do. Just send me written reports on your progress."

"Aye." Wooten bowed and left the room.

Thompson knocked on the library door a moment later. "Beg pardon, my lord."

"What now, Thompson?" Sinclair made an effort to keep from shouting. With the butler, housekeeper and Quincy all gone at once, the household was in shambles. This morning his coffee had been served in the sugar dish, and sugar served in a salt cellar. Heaven only knew where the salt now resided.

Even Lady Sinclair had given up on creating order from the chaos. Yesterday she had decamped for Lady Fitzwater's home with two trunks and the parting words, "Fix it." And the highly recommended Bow Street Runner hadn't found so much as Hatchett's office.

"Couldn't help overhearing that you're looking for a solicitor named Hatchett."

Sinclair stopped pacing. "You know of him?"

"That runner's looking in the wrong places. Hatchett works for common folks. His office is above a dressmaker's shop. You have to go through the fitting rooms in back to get to it."

"What a lovely view he must have," Sinclair said dryly.

"Oh yes. Hatchett likes the ladies, that he does." Thompson started to grin but stopped and cleared his throat. "I could go down there if you like, my lord, and see what can be seen."

Sinclair shook his head. "Even better, Thompson, you're going to take me there."

Within an hour Elliott stopped the coach a few doors away from the dress shop. Thompson jumped down from the driver's bench and led Sinclair through a maze of fitting and storerooms to the office in question.

Hatchett wasn't there.

His assistant was.

After much blustering and bellowing on his part, and a generous bribe on Sinclair's part, Angus Leach was persuaded to produce a sheet of paper listing several properties for sale.

Pocketing the coins, Mr. Leach pronounced his conscience appeased by "such an obviously upstanding peer of the realm," and his tongue loosened. "Such a pretty young thing, Miss Q. And so eager! I would have dropped everything to accompany her on a trip to the country, too," the solicitor's assistant said with a broad wink.

Sinclair barely restrained himself from strangling the blackguard.

Thompson, however, had less self-control, and planted Leach a facer. "Mind how you speak about your betters," Thompson growled, gripping him by the collar.

Leach nodded vigorously. Thompson let go and Leach slumped back in his chair, blood trickling from one nostril.

Sinclair stared at his footman, who glared back as though daring the earl to reprimand him. Thompson's heated defense of Quincy stirred a hazy memory, of Thompson with his arm around Quincy.

Time to ruminate on it later. Now he had a list of properties Quincy had gone to look at. She'd already been gone for six days, accompanied by a man known to "like the ladies."

"Let's go, Thompson," Sinclair said, spinning on his heel and heading for the door. "We have work to do, and Mr. Leach needs to freshen up."

As they threaded their way through the noisy crowds on the sidewalk, Sinclair glanced back at Thompson, trying to bring the hazy memory into focus. The big footman stepped sideways to avoid an costermonger, and bumped into a flower girl. Thompson grabbed the girl by the shoulders to steady her. To her obvious delight, he did not release her right away, but playfully grinned at her and kept one arm around her shoulders.

Sinclair froze. Noise from the street faded as the memory became clear. He remembered Thompson holding Quincy. Stroking her hair, touching her face. In his employer's bed-chamber, with Sinclair practically on death's doorstep only a few feet away. It might have been innocent, just offering her comfort when she was all done in caring for Sinclair.

"My lord?"

Sinclair shook himself out of his reverie. "Thompson," he said, casually resting one hand on the footman's shoul-der, "you know I plan to marry Miss Quincy, don't you?"

Thompson was still grinning. "Of course, my lord. Entire household is counting on it. What's left of the household, that is."

"Then you may consider yourself warned." Sinclair kept his expression mild, but there was steel beneath his calm tone. "If you ever lay a hand on my wife again, I'll have your guts for garters."

Thompson gulped. "Y-yes, my lord."

Chapter 25

Sinclair settled in at his desk with the list of cottages and a map. Choosing the property most likely to appeal to Quincy should be a simple exercise in logic.

Bluebell Cottage was moderately priced and located only a half day's ride from his own country estate. With a start, Sinclair realized it was the very cottage he and Quincy had seen on their ride to Brentwood so long ago. He crossed it off the list. Quincy was too pragmatic to want to live near a constant reminder of something, or *someone*, she'd given up.

Castallack Cottage was just outside Birmingham. For her sister's health, Quincy wanted a cottage in the country, not another city with noxious fogs. He crossed that one off.

Broxham was at the back of beyond, in Kent. The tracks that passed for roads there were barely passable even in good weather. He crossed that one off, too.

Waverly Cottage, in Danbury, was the least expensive on the list and had a large garden. Danbury was also where the Quincys had lived until coming to London. He crossed it off.

That left only a timbered cottage outside of Cheltenham. Close to a moderately sized town for employment and shopping, with no apparent drawbacks. Sinclair pictured the wooded vales and rushing streams of the Cotswolds, and knew the area would appeal to Quincy.

By dawn the next morning, Sinclair was astride his bay mare, heading for Cheltenham, the special license tucked in his pocket. He imagined the look of surprise and delight on Quincy's face, and his chest swelled.

As the morning mists cleared, so did Sinclair's head. Quincy had decided that duty demand she reject him, in order to protect him and those around him. He would have to convince her otherwise. Knowing her stubborn nature, he would have to be very persuasive indeed.

Two kisses should do it. Perhaps three.

He was still smiling when he rode into Cheltenham late that afternoon and quickly located Plough Cottage. It was dark. Ivy crept up the walls and obscured the windows. He trampled fading tulips in an overgrown flower bed as he peered through a ground-floor window. No footprints disturbed the dust-covered floors.

Scowling, he mounted his horse and rode back to the coaching inn.

"Ain't no one lived there in ages, ducks," said the serving maid, when Sinclair asked about the place. She plunked down a tankard of ale and a platter of stew. "Not since old Archibald Plough hanged himself in the rafters. Thinking of buying it?"

"No," Sinclair said, sniffing the stew suspiciously. He pushed the platter away and took a swig of ale. "I thought a friend was interested in it, though."

Sinclair retreated to his room, his stomach growling, and took out the list of properties to study again. This was simply a setback, a mere miscalculation. He knew Quincy well enough to figure out which property she'd want.

Danbury. He'd been too hasty in crossing it off the list. Lady Bradwell and Melinda had regretted the necessity of leaving the village. He had no doubt Quincy could easily fool the villagers into accepting her as herself instead of her cousin Joseph.

Sinclair set off again before dawn, his spirits light.

By midnight, his confidence plummeted.

Waverly Cottage was brightly lit, a welcoming candle in the window. But the candle was for the seafaring son of the tradesman who had purchased the property earlier that week.

Sinclair took a room at the nearest inn and collapsed on the bed. His head ached, his leg throbbed, and his stomach growled. He took out the list and studied it again.

"Quincy, my love," he murmured, "where have you hidden yourself?"

Hidden. Yes, of course! Where better to escape notice then the back of beyond?

He ate a hearty meal, which eased his stomach, but even after half a bottle of brandy, his leg still throbbed. The damp sea air did not help matters. The pain was of little consequence, however, for tomorrow he would see Quincy.

It took two days to locate Broxham Cottage. The going was rougher than he anticipated, and the Kentish folk seemed to take pride in their impassable roads. His mare threw a shoe the second day, and Sinclair was forced to walk the last mile, slogging through ankle-deep mud. Filthy and bone-weary, he was not surprised when the innkeeper asked for payment in advance.

In better spirits after a hot bath and hearty meal, he took out his list once more.

Only two properties left. Perhaps he didn't know Quincy as well as he thought. He couldn't believe she would buy in Birmingham. The detriment to her sister's health would be as bad or worse than living in London.

That left only Bluebell, on the way to his country estate.

Why would Quincy want to buy near Brentwood? Living near his estate would be a continual reminder of what she had given up. Quincy was far too practical and pragmatic to indulge in sentimentality. *Josephine,* however . . .

With a hitch to his breathing, Sinclair remembered what she looked like as Josephine, properly gowned and coifed. She appeared as beautiful and fragile and feminine as any other debutante. Outer trappings couldn't disguise her independence and fierce determination, but perhaps deep down she was as sentimental and emotional as any other woman.

Early the next morning, the blacksmith had barely hammered home the last nail when Sinclair mounted his mare and set off for Bluebell Cottage. He felt certain he would find Quincy by the end of the day, but he'd been certain, and wrong, before.

Perhaps Quincy hadn't bought any cottage. Perhaps she'd dismissed them all and gone back to London with Hatchett to find others to look at. Perhaps she was with Hatchett this very minute, fighting off his advances.

Sinclair spurred his horse to a gallop.

He wanted to continue straight to the cottage, but his horse was exhausted. Sinclair reined in at the coaching inn late that afternoon and ordered a meal and a private room. He quizzed the serving maid when she arrived with his food.

"Mr. Hatchett stayed a week," she said. "Left in a hurry, he did, even though he'd paid for another week in advance. We haven't had that much entertainment in ages." She chuckled.

"Entertainment?" Sinclair forced his hand to uncurl from a fist.

The maid pulled out a chair and sat down, then leaned across the table and lowered her voice. "We knew the lady with him wasn't his Missus, though he kept trying to act like she was. But she wouldn't have none of it, no sirree! Insisted on rooms at opposite ends of the hall, she did. One morning she comes down to breakfast, pleasant as can be. But when he comes down, his left eye is swelled right shut! He calls for his carriage, and she says, 'Good-bye, Mr. Hatchett. 'Twas a pleasure doing business with you!' He stomped out the door—oh, the things he said!—and we ain't seen him since."

Sinclair barely heard the last part over the pounding in his ears. He tried to contain the excitement in his voice. "Do you know where the lady went?"

"Oh, she ain't gone nowhere," the maid said, standing up. "She's still here. Well, not right now, she ain't. She goes out every morning and comes back for a late supper in her room." She suddenly frowned. "This is a respectable inn. We don't want nothing havey-cavey going on with our customers."

Sinclair smiled and handed her several coins, which she tucked into her apron pocket. "I can assure you my intentions are honorable. Do you by chance know the shortest way to Bluebell Cottage from here?"

She did, and Sinclair gave her another generous tip before rushing out the door, his meal untouched.

The maid's directions sent Sinclair climbing over a stile, limping through a horse-dotted pasture, over another stile to a footbridge across a stream, and into a dense copse of oak trees. Low-hanging limbs tore at his clothes and hair, but Sinclair pressed on. Just when he began to think the maid had sent him halfway to Wales, the trees gave way to a garden at the back of a white cottage, surrounded by flower beds. Bluebell Cottage.

As he caught his breath, Sinclair stood at the edge of the trees, studying the anthill-like activity on the property.

Workmen scurried back and forth, carrying boards and bundles of thatch. Gardeners scythed the lawn and pruned rosebushes. A painter clung to a ladder on one outside wall, and hammering and sawing echoed through the open door and windows.

Suddenly there was a snap from the roof, and someone yelled "Look out, Miss Quincy!" as a bundle of thatch rolled down the roof and fell over the edge.

Sinclair watched in horror as the bundle struck the painter on the ladder.

Quincy barely heard the roofer's warning before something hit the back of her legs, and her feet skidded forward on the rung. She grabbed at the rail to keep from falling but only managed to slow her descent. The paintbrush and bucket landed with a wet smack on the ground below. She found herself hanging upside down, her shins painfully wedged between two rungs. Blinded by her skirts, stars danced before her eyes.

"Cor blimey, you killed 'er!" someone shouted.

Quincy shoved the skirts from her face. The world tilted

at a crazy angle, but nothing seemed damaged. At least not permanently. "Davey, I thought you said you were done with the roof," she said.

"I'm ever so sorry, Miss Quincy," Davey said, peering over the edge of the roof. "The string on the last bundle broke. Are you all right?"

"I am fine, Davey." She looked straight out and saw several of the workers staring in shock or coming toward her. "It's all right," she called to them. "You can go back to work now." Davey withdrew from the edge, though a few of the workers still gawked at her. She gave an unladylike grunt as she reached up to free her feet, wondering how she was going to extricate herself without causing injury or providing further entertainment for her workmen.

"Lucky thing you are fond of trousers," came a familiar but unexpected voice close by.

Quincy dropped back, still upside down but now eye to eye with the newcomer. "Sinclair!" She couldn't help the silly grin that nearly split her face. It had only been two weeks since she'd last seen him, but her memory was no match to this living, breathing vision before her.

Wait—why was he here? Something must be wrong. "Grandm—"

"And your sister are both fine. Everyone is fine."

She relaxed a fraction, and pushed her shifting skirts aside.

"I had been concerned about your welfare, off on your own this past fortnight, but I see you have matters well in hand." Sinclair's eyes twinkled, even when viewed upside down.

"Miss Quincy, I'll get you down, I'll—" Davey came running around the corner but skidded to a halt as he caught sight of Sinclair.

"If you don't mind, *I'll* get her down," Sinclair said, reaching for Quincy. "Hang on to me, love." Lifting and supporting her with one arm, he pulled her free of the ladder. But instead of setting her on her feet, Sinclair held her close to his chest, one arm under her legs, the other behind her shoulders, and gazed into her eyes.

Her insides melted. His heart beat next to hers, his breath ruffled her hair, strong hands held her secure. She could stay here forever.

Quincy realized the workmen were staring. Hang the workmen. Sinclair had called her his love! She had bid him farewell, yet here he was, just in time to release her from an uncomfortable predicament. He shifted his grip, his thumb stroking her shoulder. Her heart beat even faster.

Someone coughed. Oh, very well. Trying to be respectable was often a pain in the arse. "You should, ah, put me down now," she said.

"I should?" His smile was warm and beguiling, his voice low and soft, a verbal caress. A shiver danced down her spine. "Very well, madam, if you think it best."

He set her down, not letting go until she was steady on her feet. With shaking hands, she smoothed her skirts over her trousers. Melinda's old gown was almost ready for the dustbin. Paint blotches covered many of the grass stains, and numerous small tears made the dress immodest without the trousers and shirt beneath.

"Miss Quincy?" Davey had not moved away. Other workmen began to gather, staring at Sinclair suspiciously.

"Everything is all right," Quincy assured her foreman, glancing from the workers to the man at her side. For the first time she noticed his mud-splattered clothes and muck-covered boots, and his hair looked like he'd combed it with a rake. Beautiful. She couldn't stop grinning. "The Earl of Sinclair is my, ah . . . former employer."

"Betrothed," Sinclair quickly added.

She stared at him. No, she couldn't have heard him right. They'd agreed it wouldn't work between them. Besides, she'd already bought the cottage and begun repairs. It was almost ready for her family to move in.

"Employer?" Davey took a step closer, standing several inches taller than Sinclair. The other workers stepped closer also, still holding their tools—scythe, hammer, thatch hook.

"She was my secretary," he told the men, though his gaze never left Quincy. "And a damn good one, too. But it was a secret. When I asked her to be my wife, she felt it her duty to protect me from scandal in the event anyone discovered her secret. So she left me."

Quincy swallowed the lump in her throat. "To protect your mother, too," she whispered.

Sinclair shook his head. "Mama doesn't require your protection. She prefers your presence. And I don't need your protection, either." He puffed out his chest and looked down his nose at her. "You think the Earl of Sinclair and the Dowager Countess cannot face down scurrilous gossip?"

Quincy started to smile, then remembered how the scene had ended. "But you agreed with me! When I said—"

"I did not agree, not in the slightest. You took unfair advantage of my condition and left before we had finished our discussion."

He took both her hands in his, gazing intently at her with his warm brown eyes until she thought she would melt. "I've recently learned a valuable lesson from my friend Palmer. Some still cannot bear the sight of him, as if his missing arm was contagious. But he suffers the slings and arrows with good grace, secure in his love for his wife, and her love for him."

"But even Palmer said—"

"He'll come around when he sees how happy we are together." Still holding her hands, he got down on one knee.

Tears blurred Quincy's vision. She barely heard him over the thunderous pounding in her ears.

"I have been utterly heartbroken since the moment you left. I think your duty now should be to alleviate my misery. I'll buy you all the cottages you want, if only you'll live in one of them with me."

Though her thoughts were in tumult, she knew she could not give in. "But this one . . ." She gestured at the cottage behind her.

"Would make a lovely wedding gift for your sister. I think she and Leland would be quite happy here."

Mel and Leland? She nodded. A good match.

His voice broke when he spoke again, and she now realized the twinkle in his eye was an unshed tear. "I can face anything if the woman I love is at my side. You make me whole, Quincy. I need you, because I love you. Will you marry me?"

His upturned face was almost her undoing. Logic and duty be damned, she wanted to say yes, she wanted Sinclair. Wanted him as she had never wanted anyone or anything before. Wanted him with every fiber in her being.

But even more than all that, she wanted him to be happy. And he never could be, not in the long-term, not with a scandalous wife.

Her throat choked with unshed tears, Quincy pulled him to his feet. He did not let go, even as he towered over her, twining their fingers, caressing her cheek with one hand.

"Jo?"

She closed her eyes, leaning into his caress, for one brief moment. "Nothing has changed," she whispered. It took several attempts at swallowing the lump clogging her throat before she could speak again. She cursed the hitch in her voice. "You feel this way now, but once my secret is revealed, once you and your mother are the object of scandal again . . . I can't put you through that. Either of you. I won't."

His shoulders slumped. One hand dropped to his side, though he still held her fingers. He pinched the bridge of his nose. Suddenly he gripped her shoulders with both hands.

"All right. We'll forget this conversation happened. But you still need to come back to London. I, er, wasn't entirely truthful, earlier." His gaze dropped to their boots as they stood toe to toe, close but not quite touching.

Her heart pounded anew. "What . . . Who—"

"My mother." He chin almost on his chest, he looked at her through his sinfully long lashes.

"Is she—"

"She was making such great progress, with a suitor, with hiring and training orphans, but I fear . . ." His gaze slid away again.

"What? What has happened, Benjamin?" The intimate appellation slipped out. He didn't seem to notice.

"I fear she has taken on more than she can handle in her fragile state."

Of their own volition, her hands wrapped around his arms, stroking the firm muscles beneath his dusty coat.

"She has expanded her efforts, *your* efforts, of rescuing the orphans and vagrant soldiers, by founding a charity. She is planning a ball to kick it off. She is very determined, but I fear it is too much for her. If the event is not successful, if the charity is not well-received, it may set her back. I don't want her to regress, to become a recluse again."

"I understand your concern, but I don't see how I—"

"You could help Mama, make certain of the ball's success."

"But I've never planned so much as a card party, let alone a ball. She needs—"

"She needs *you*. She *likes* you. She'd accept your help where she would refuse it from anyone else. And you are the most managing female I know. You could have planned Wellington's assault at Vittoria. A ball will be a snap for you."

Quincy's cheeks heated at his praise.

"Are you going to make me beg you to help my mother?"

It meant returning to London in Sinclair's company, spending time in his home again. Being near him, yet not being able to have him. Exquisite torture. Agonizing joy. She closed her eyes and swayed on her feet, landing against Sinclair's chest. His arm went around her, a haven of security. "I could," she said into his cravat.

"Could help Mama?"

"Could make you beg."

He tipped her chin up with one finger. "Please?"

She fell into his warm brown eyes, twin pools of melted chocolate. Lost. How could she deny this wonderful man such a simple request? "Yes."

Sinclair let out a whoop, and before she had dealt with the shock of that, he wrapped both arms around her and swung her off her feet, spinning in a circle, her skirt fluttering in the breeze.

He set her down and kissed her on the forehead. Instead of releasing her, he kept his arm around her shoulder as she faced the workmen who had stayed close by, unabashedly eavesdropping.

Quincy cleared her throat and clapped her hands. "All right, back to work! We're running out of daylight!" In a softer tone, she called Davey to her side. "I have to return to London for some unfinished business. I'm relying on you to see that everything is finished as planned, and on budget."

"Yes ma'am, Miss Quincy, you can rely on me." He tugged his forelock, started to leave, but turned back. "She's an odd duck, but a right 'un," he confided to Sinclair before walking away.

"Couldn't agree more," Sinclair said.

Quincy frowned, trying to decide whether she should take umbrage or not. She'd just realized his calling her a "managing female" was a compliment, and now she was an "odd duck."

"It's too late to head back to town tonight," Sinclair said, giving her shoulder a squeeze. "How about giving me the grand tour?"

She proceeded to show off her property, enjoying the weight of his arm across her shoulder. His walking stick was nowhere in sight, but he didn't need it with her at his side. She wrapped her arm around his waist, happy to assist him over the uneven ground. The added closeness of walking as though joined at the hip, pressed to each other's sides from ribcage to thigh, was purely coincidental. Pure bliss.

Back in London, Sinclair accompanied Quincy to the door of her family's quarters within Leland's house, and left her only after obtaining her promise she'd call on his mother in the morning.

Then he went in search of his mother, to convince her to move back home so she'd actually be there when Quincy came to call.

He found Lady Fitzwater and his mother having tea in the front parlor. "Mama, would you care to stroll in the garden with me?" he said as soon as the niceties had been observed.

She raised her brows, but agreed, and soon they were outside in the relative privacy of the garden. He tried to hide how heavily he was leaning on his walking stick but she noticed anyway, and sat on the bench nearest the door.

She patted the seat beside her. "Out with it, Benjamin. What have you done now?"

Sinclair flipped his coattails aside and sat. Live toad, first thing in the morning. He cleared his throat, clasped his mother's hand, and looked her in the eyes. "Have you considered founding a charity for orphans? You could hold a ball for it."

Quincy's knock on Sinclair's door the next morning was answered by Thompson. "Is Harper ill?" She handed her bonnet and shawl to the footman.

"No, Miss Quincy, he's um, on holiday. Yes, on holiday."

The butler must not have gone on holiday in some time. She followed Thompson upstairs to Lady Sinclair's salon. He announced her at the doorway, then left with a deep bow.

Lady Sinclair greeted her with a hug. "I'm so glad you agreed to come back and help me with my little project," she gushed, leading Quincy to her escritoire. Lady Sinclair pulled papers out of the top drawer. "Here's what I have planned so far. I'm afraid the house is still at sixes and sevens, so we'll need to hire outside staff for much of the work. What do you think?"

Quincy studied the notes. Heavens, so little had been worked out, one might think they had started planning the ball only yesterday. Good thing Sinclair had enlisted her support. "I think it will be a smashing success."

Lady Sinclair beamed at her, then drew more paper from the desk drawers, along with pens and ink, and they started making lists of things to do, people to see. Caterers, musicians, florists, additional staff, and the all-important guest list of those likely to support the charity.

They worked through the day, stopping for meals, and started again the next morning. Lady Sinclair was pleasant to work with, an amiable companion, but Quincy longed for somewhere, and *someone*, else. She had felt far more at home in Sinclair's library, with its mismatched oversized furniture, than with the delicate pieces in his mother's salon. And as for working with Sinclair . . .

But at no time did she hear his voice, hear his distinctive tread in the hall outside. She had no valid excuse to go down to the library and see him. With a sigh, she returned to penning the invitations.

"We shall deliver these in person," Lady Sinclair announced after lunch.

"We?"

"Of course. But first we'll see what progress Jill has made on your wardrobe, then we'll go out to Bond Street and get any necessities you are still lacking. Tomorrow we can begin our morning calls and deliver the invitations. We'll have ever so much fun!"

"We," it turned out, meant Lady Sinclair, Lady Fitzwater, Grandmère, and Mel. Quincy felt like driftwood caught up in the tidal wave of the Trio and her sister. They draped and pinned her for more dresses, dragged her from shop to shop, and Mel continued her barrage of questions about their cottage and its renovations.

Quincy allowed them to help her choose feminine accessories while shopping, but steered them toward the more practical, economical choices. She never lost sight of the fact that she would soon be moving to the cottage. Sturdy was more important than pretty.

At what must have been the tenth shop they visited that afternoon, Lady Sinclair perched another bonnet on Quincy's head while the Trio debated its merits. It was the same bonnet she had seen in the window, next to the tobacco shop, the day she'd had lunch with Sinclair and his friends at their club.

Not too fussy, not too plain, Quincy loved it. Then she saw the price on the dangling tag. She removed the bonnet and set it back on the shelf. "We've already bought so many things. I really don't need this."

As Lady Fitzwater and Grandmère began to protest,

Lady Sinclair gave her a nudge. "My treat, dear. Tell me again how much money you made for us with Benjamin's mining shares?"

Quincy grabbed the bonnet. "You're right. You can afford it."

"Did I miss something, Margaret?" Lady Fitzwater said, interrupting their shared laugh.

"Never mind, Fitzy," Lady Sinclair said. She gestured for her footman waiting outside to come collect their purchases, and they were off to the glovers next door.

After the fittings and shopping excursion came the dreaded morning calls. Now that Grandmère's ankle had healed to the point she was able to get about with a cane, she and Fitzy had joined Lady Sinclair's cause, and all insisted Quincy and Mel be included in the social rounds. Quincy wasn't sure if the added numbers would provide a distraction from any social gaffe she might make, or increase the pressure on her, thereby increasing the chances of making a gaffe in the first place.

"I've been meaning to compliment you on your manners, Miss Quincy," Lady Fitzwater began as the Sinclair coach pulled away from Lady Bigglesworth's town house.

Wedged between her sister and grandmother, Quincy fidgeted with her gloves. "Oh?"

"You've done quite well. You haven't tried to cross your legs even once in the last two days, and your stride is most ladylike."

"Most of the time," Melinda added.

"I believe," Lady Sinclair interrupted before the sisters could argue, "that her manners are always appropriate to her situation. Whatever her situation may be."

"Hear, hear," Grandmère added.

"Thank you, my lady."

The coach pulled up at another grand house. Quincy descended the coach steps with caution, sure she would slip up now that Lady Fitzwater had complimented her. The five ladies were shown into the drawing room and announced. Nearly a dozen other people were already gathered, and Lady Sinclair made the necessary introductions.

Quincy remembered to curtsy and murmur something appropriate, and their hostess, Lady Danforth, poured tea and passed a plate of cakes. Quincy had never met most of the people before, but she knew of them, thanks to studying *Debrett's* prior to choosing Sinclair. The tedious conversation was briefly interrupted by the arrival of Lord Danforth, who took a seat beside his wife.

The strain of remembering everything she should or should not say or do threatened to segue into boredom. Where was the forward Miss Ogilvie and her hussy of a companion when one needed a diversion?

The butler announced the next group of callers, which included the Duchess of Warwick.

Melinda choked on her tea. Quincy glanced at Grandmère, who shrugged.

Serena sailed into the room with two other ladies and a cloud of perfume. More introductions, tea and cakes, and polite nothings murmured all around.

"I am surprised to see you in Town, Miss Quincy," Serena said. "I did not think you had the blunt for a Season."

Two could play this game. "I'm surprised to see you in Town also, your grace. I heard you were on a repairing lease in Northumberland."

Serena flushed. Quincy bit back a grin. Score one.

"I went home briefly on account of . . . an old friend, but everything is fine now. I fully intend to enjoy the rest of the Season while my husband takes the waters in Bath." Serena leaned forward, her expression concerned. "Are you certain you wish to stay for the Season? It can be dangerous as well as expensive—many girls accidentally ruin themselves."

Melinda gasped at the veiled threat.

Quincy refused to react with anything but icy disdain. "Quite certain. Thank you for your concern." She stood up, more than ready to leave. Melinda and Lady Fitzwater stood also, as did Serena, while Lady Sinclair helped Grandmère up. In the shuffle as Serena stepped away, the tip of Grandmère's cane scooted out and Serena tripped. She fell, landing in Lord Danforth's lap.

Amidst the nervous laughter and shocked titterings, they

took their leave. Once in the coach, Melinda burst into laughter. "Did you see her face?"

"Did you see *his*? Poor man." Quincy gave in and joined her sister.

"Thank you for the use of your cane, Dominique."

"My pleasure, Margaret."

"I missed something again, didn't I?"

Chapter 26

Separation would be the death of him. Since bringing Quincy back to London, Sinclair had been allowed to see her only during morning calls, for twenty minutes at a time, and never alone. The Trio made certain of that. Wait for the ball, they said. He should live so long.

He saw Quincy every night, though. His dreams were vivid, intense, and had him sloshing the ewer of cold water over his head in the morning. Only a few days to go.

And then what? She'd already rejected his proposal twice. *Nothing has changed*, she'd said. So what the hell was he to do? He needed to think.

Sinclair went for a long walks. Purportedly to strengthen his leg, but mostly because he couldn't bear to be in his library without Quincy. He was going mad. She was everywhere, yet not there at all. He couldn't even visit with her in the salon while she helped his mother—one of Mama's conditions for abetting his subterfuge. It was easier just to leave the house entirely.

His leg was improving, though still weaker than before his illness. He pictured Quincy massaging liniment on his thigh, and then moving her hands elsewhere . . .

". . . Is back in town?"

Sinclair snapped his attention back to the present, and realized Palmer had fallen into step with him on the sidewalk just outside Brooks's. "Beg pardon?"

"I said, did you know that Serena is back in town?"

Sinclair froze. "Thought the duke killed her."

"*Hoped* he'd killed her, you mean." Palmer grew serious. "You know she'll cause trouble."

Sinclair nodded, and cursed the day he'd met Serena. He followed Palmer inside the club. Neither spoke until after the waiter brought their drinks.

"My estimation of Miss Quincy's character rose considerably after she had the good sense to reject your suit, but are you certain she is worth pursuing?"

Sinclair pictured Quincy when he'd seen her at the cottage, trapped upside-down on the ladder, splattered with paint, dirt smudges on her face. He grinned. "A bothersome wench, to be sure, but"—he held his hand to his heart—"I can't imagine living without her."

Palmer nodded, chuckling. "It's hopeless, then." He raised his glass for a toast. "To the lovely Josephine, and may you have many happy years together."

They drank. "Now, what do we do about Serena? A frontal assault is out of the question."

Palmer refilled their glasses. "Can't just throttle her, either. Warwick might take exception."

Sinclair sat up straight. The solution he'd been seeking was simplicity itself. Make something change. "We'll attack from the flank."

"Eh?"

"We'll need your wife's help, as well as my mother and Lady Fitzwater." Sinclair explained his idea, and they spent the next hour planning their strategy.

That night, Sinclair dreamt he was waltzing with Quincy at the charity ball. She was soft and warm in his arms, light on her feet, her faint but intoxicating scent of lemon wafting about them. His angel, the love of his life, her smile so sweet and meant just for him that his heart swelled until it felt too large to fit within his chest.

Everyone important in his life was present—his mother,

her grandmother, sister, their friends. All were watching them dance together, graceful, in perfect harmony.

Until his leg gave way.

Quincy slipped from his grasp as he collapsed in an ungainly heap at her feet. Everyone laughed. Pointed at him. Laughing, taunting, jeering. They called him cripple. His leg was on fire, the pain making his eyes water, nausea washing over him. But worse than that—Quincy kept waltzing, with another partner who appeared from nowhere. The faceless man danced away with her in his arms. She didn't even look back.

Sinclair sat bolt upright in bed, panting, sweat trickling down his face. He ran a hand through his hair. "Just a dream," he muttered. "Just a dream." He slid out of bed to splash his face with water. Back under the sheets, his pulse gradually slowed but the images from the dream refused to fade. The clock struck two. He lay there the rest of the night, wide awake, his leg throbbing, the dream playing in his mind over and over.

"I can't believe we're going to a ball, Jo!" Melinda fidgeted while Quincy did up the buttons on her dress for the charity ball—their first ball ever.

"Me too." No fairy godmother required; it had been her own doing. Hers, and Sinclair's, and his mother's. Emotionally exhausted by vacillating between the elation of getting to dance with Sinclair tonight, and the agony of knowing that tomorrow she would return to her cottage, never to see him again, she had settled for trying to enjoy each moment as it came.

Mel's buttons done up, Quincy spun around so her sister could do hers in return. Since it was also likely their last ball, she was determined that Mel should enjoy the evening to the fullest.

She straightened her gown and peered in the mirror. Melinda and Jill had made another beautiful creation for her, this one in light green silk with emerald ribbons. It brought out the green in her eyes, the red highlights in her auburn hair. It made the best of her figure, such as it was.

Her foolish, feminine side hoped Sinclair liked it. The dress, too. Perfect for dancing, it had full skirts that swirled around her ankles, revealing a peek at her silk stockings—one of the few luxurious purchases she'd allowed herself.

In less than an hour she'd get to dance with Sinclair. She'd dreamt about it countless times, and at last it was about to happen for real. They would be in public, with hundreds of other attendees, but she didn't care. Sinclair. Holding her in his arms again.

It would be torture, having only this night, this one chance to dance with him. She had agreed to come back to help Lady Sinclair, and now that obligation was almost fulfilled. Tomorrow she would begin preparations for moving to the cottage.

But tonight . . .

"If you can drag yourself away from your reflection for a moment, would you help me with my hair, please?"

"Of course, Mel." Quincy put aside her ruminations and returned to practical matters. Once Mel was satisfied with her own chignon, she turned to Quincy's hair.

Quincy was about to embark on her first major public appearance as a female with a secret past that wasn't so secret. She checked that Sinclair's white glove, her good luck charm, was tucked in her reticule. Tonight she'd need all the luck she could get.

Soon they were both ready, and with Grandmère, met Sir Leland and Lady Fitzwater in the hall, and the five set off in the Fitzwater carriage. To distract herself from worrying about making a fool of herself at the ball, Quincy decided to play matchmaker. She made certain that Mel was squeezed between herself and Sir Leland for the ride, with Leland on the far left so that Mel was not on his blind side. Quincy took up more than her share of the bench, making Mel sit even closer to Leland.

"No need to be nervous, my dear," Lady Fitzwater said, patting Quincy's knee. "Your beau has everything well in hand."

"My what? And what is well in hand?"

Melinda rested her hand on Quincy's lap, where Quincy

had unconsciously been shredding a handkerchief. Quincy tucked the shreds into her reticule.

"About the duchess, of course."

Quincy's stomach flipped again. "What about the duchess?"

"Sinclair didn't tell you? Naughty boy." Lady Fitzwater clucked her tongue.

"Fitzy, I'll handle this." Grandmère leaned forward. "While you had your final fittings today, we—that is, Lady Sinclair, Lady Palmer, Fitzy and I—spread a little gossip on our morning calls."

"Gossip?"

"Not gossip, really," Lady Fitzwater said. "Just the tale of how you and Sinclair met."

"How we met?" Not caring that she sounded like a parrot, Quincy fell back against the cushions, feeling faint.

"It's all part of his plan to thwart Serena," Melinda said.

The coach pulled up just then, preventing Quincy from extracting any further details. She exited the coach first and waited on the sidewalk for the others to join her. Music floated on the night air, as the musicians inside the town house tuned their instruments.

Without consulting her, Sinclair had put a plan in motion to thwart Serena, which involved spreading word of how she and Sinclair had actually met. Compared to this, the first time she'd appeared in public wearing breeches and chopped-off hair had been a snap. And just as life-altering.

Thompson and Grimshaw stepped outside and assisted Grandmère indoors and up the stairs. Much as Quincy wanted to turn back and go home, she hurried after them.

In the hall, Jack and a new one-armed footman were taking wraps from arriving guests. Harper spotted her amidst the mass of bodies, and abandoned his post by the ballroom door.

"Miss Quincy, may I say what a pleasure it is to see you again." He bowed deeply.

Quincy saw a flash of gold. "Harper, you old dog!" Ignoring everyone else in the foyer, she wrapped the butler in a hug, and ended it by grabbing his left hand and staring at the gold ring. "This was the reason for your holiday? And where is Mrs. Hamm—, er, Mrs. Harper?"

"Right behind you, dearie."

Quincy spun around. The housekeeper looked years younger and her eyes twinkled. Quincy wrapped her in a hug, too. "Congratulations."

"Thank you. So much has changed, and so quickly! When Harper and I returned from our honeymoon, we found we have two new maids, and a scullery maid, all orphans, and—"

"Don't forget the new footmen, Mrs. H."

"Right you are, Mr. H. Two new footmen, foot*boys*, actually, and . . ."

As the housekeeper prattled on, Quincy felt suffused with warmth. She'd missed these friends dreadfully.

While she chatted, Grimshaw and Thompson helped Grandmère up the staircase to where Lady Sinclair formed the receiving line with Lord Coddington at her side. Lady Sinclair was resplendent in a yellow silk gown, her face lit up with a bright smile.

But where was Sinclair? Quincy's stomach did another flip. She hurried up the stairs, trailing Melinda, who clung to Leland's arm. Grandmère and Lady Fitzwater had already moved on to the ballroom.

"Ready for your debut, Jo?" Lady Sinclair pressed Quincy's icy fingers between her warm hands.

The butterflies were back, in full force. She stood straighter. "Yes."

"Everything will be fine, I promise you." Lady Sinclair kissed her on the cheek. "Now, if I could just locate my son . . ."

The musicians finished tuning and began playing. Everyone but their little group drifted into the ballroom. With the hall almost empty, Quincy saw Sinclair approach from the far end. He looked magnificent in black evening clothes, an emerald stickpin winking in the candlelight from the folds of his cravat. The butterflies in her stomach evaporated. It was ridiculous, how good she felt just seeing him again. Soon she'd be in his arms.

But he was taking an awfully long time to arrive. The rose fog cleared, and she realized his movements were slow, his gait deliberate and painstaking. She went to meet him.

"You came down the back stairs, didn't you?" she said as he raised her hand to his lips.

"I've missed you, too," Sinclair said, lowering her hand but not releasing it.

"You only do that when you're hurting, so no one will see." She leaned around him, looking for telltale signs of dust on the seat of his trousers.

"It's nothing." Sinclair pulled her back. "I am fine."

"You are not fine, you're limping. Badly." She touched his right thigh. "What happened?"

Sinclair pulled both her hands into one of his and cupped her cheek in his palm. "I'm gratified by your interest in my person, but it's nothing, really."

At her growl of exasperation, he relented. "I may have overdone my physical training in the last day or so. And had a minor accident involving a wet bar of soap. But I am fine." He gave her a soft kiss on the cheek and lowered his voice. "Nothing will keep me from dancing with you tonight, my sweet, and holding you in my arms."

"But your leg, you need to rest—"

"I will, tomorrow." A devilish glint came into his eyes. "Consider that if you'd but marry me, I'd get a great deal of bed rest. Well, perhaps not rest, but we'd certainly spend plenty of time in bed."

Shocked at his words, Quincy felt the blush to the tips of her toes, and a shudder of excitement. She blushed even hotter.

He gave her a knowing smile, the wretch. "Go join your grandmother before she sends out a search party, and I shall play the good host before Mama shoots me." He kissed her hand once more and pushed her toward the ballroom.

Harper announced the group stepping through the doorway before her, then whispered an apology that he had already announced her when the rest of her party had entered, not realizing that she had, ahem, lollygagged with his lordship.

Thompson was waiting for her just inside. "If you'll come with me, Miss Quincy," he said, "I'll show you to Lady Bradwell."

She trailed Thompson through the crowd. The room was rapidly filling with people, most of whom she recognized from morning calls though she'd forgotten their names.

"Such a romantic tale," she overheard one matron saying to another. Thompson stopped, mostly hidden by a potted palm, and held one finger to his lips. Quincy peered between the palm fronds, and recognized the speaker as Lady Barbour, one of Lady Sinclair's friends.

"Most romantic," Lady Barbour continued. "I wasn't the least surprised, you know. Her grandparents met through unconventional means, too. It's in the blood."

"Oh, yes, blood will tell," her companion replied, "I remember Randolph Quincy well." She gave a dramatic sigh, and both ladies giggled.

Matrons giggling over her grandfather? The two ladies moved on, and after a moment, so did Thompson and Quincy. He stopped at the next palm, however, in time for Quincy to eavesdrop on Lady Danforth and a friend.

". . . And so Sinclair went along with her charade. He couldn't in good conscience let her family suffer."

"But wearing trousers!"

"Oh, pish. I've thought of wearing them myself a time or two. They look to be quite comfortable for gardening or riding."

"Hmm. Perhaps some day we'll all wear trousers." The two ladies accepted glasses of champagne from Grimshaw, and stepped away to greet newcomers.

Quincy craned her neck to look up at Thompson. "Sinclair is really telling everyone how we met?"

Thompson started walking again. "You'll still need to watch out for some of them high sticklers, like Lady Bigglesworth. They'd rather see a body starve than break some bloomin' rule."

"Of course. Trying to make it a charming, heartwarming story only solves part of the problem. There is still—"

"Her Grace, the Duchess of Warwick," Harper announced.

"Speak o' the devil," Thompson muttered.

Serena glided into the ballroom accompanied by a handsome colonel in full regalia. Her hand resting on the arm of her cicisbeo, Serena scanned the room until she spotted Quincy.

Their gaze locked. Quincy stared back at the duchess from across the crowded room, all ambient sounds drowned out by the sudden pounding in her ears.

"Oi there," Thompson said with a grunt, trying to uncurl Quincy's fingers from his arm. "You're cutting off me circulation."

Quincy ignored him. Serena hadn't moved.

Lady Bigglesworth sailed toward Serena, and they made a great show of kissing the air beside each other's cheek. Before Lady Bigglesworth could lead her and the colonel to Lord Bigglesworth, Serena turned back to Quincy and mouthed the words "I warned you." She then bent her head close to Lady Bigglesworth's ear, deep in conversation.

"That's it, stand tall, Miss Quincy," Thompson said, patting Quincy's hand.

She nodded and did as he suggested, and they continued walking. The butterflies in her stomach were fluttering in a frenzy, and Grandmère's welcoming smile did nothing to ease them. From across the floor, she caught Lady Bigglesworth's eye. The grand dame looked like she'd just sucked on a lemon, and abruptly turned away.

The cut direct did not feel like the slap in the face she'd expected. Probably because Serena was involved. "Did you see that?" Quincy asked Melinda.

"See what?"

Since Mel hadn't taken her eyes off Sir Leland, Quincy grumbled, "Never mind," and tried not to fidget. The insult had been aimed at her, thankfully, not at Sinclair or his mother.

The musicians finished their piece. Silence fell across the

room as everyone directed their attention to the balcony, where Lady Sinclair stood.

"I'd like to thank you all for coming tonight," Lady Sinclair began. "Your generous donations will help feed and clothe and train unfortunate souls so that they may improve their lot in life. With your help, they can become productive members of the populace, no longer indigent. They can become workers rather than beggars."

She paused, waiting for the burst of applause to quiet down. "I could not have done this without the aid of the Honorable Miss Josephine Quincy. Though we may have met under unusual circumstances," there was a small titter of laughter, "Miss Quincy has had a profound impact on my life. That is why the charity shall henceforth be known as the Jo Quincy Foundation for the Homeless." She gestured, and all eyes turned to Quincy.

Registering the polite applause, Quincy swallowed a lump in her throat. Lady Sinclair had never mentioned the name for the charity before. This was beyond anything she'd expected.

Then it hit her. Her secret had been publicly revealed, and the world had not come to an end. She scanned the faces turned toward her, people still clapping hands, applauding her and Lady Sinclair. No one seemed scandalized by her outré life as Mr. Quincy. Well, no one but Lady Bigglesworth, and since Quincy had never before met anyone so eager to be outraged, she hardly counted. The people she respected, those whose opinion mattered to her, did not look at her any differently.

Lady Sinclair blew Quincy a kiss, then turned to the orchestra leader. "Maestro, if you please." The musicians struck up a waltz.

Couples moved on to the dance floor, including Lord Coddington escorting Lady Sinclair. Their progress was impeded by the many people wishing to talk to her. So much for the ostracism Quincy had feared.

She had been wrong. Was it possible for her to have the happy ending, after all?

Suddenly Sinclair stood before Quincy. He bowed and

reached for her hand. She curtsied, and Sinclair led her to the dance floor, the space crowded with other couples.

"Not nervous, are you?" He gave her a reassuring squeeze while still maintaining the proper distance between them.

"Not when I'm with you." The truth of the statement surprised her. She had barely learned the steps of the waltz two days ago, at Lady Sinclair's insistence, and had only danced with her sister. With over a hundred other people in the room, the cream of the ton, the potential for disaster boggled the mind.

Yet Quincy couldn't spare a thought for anyone or anything else. She was too busy enjoying the experience of being held in Sinclair's arms, staring into his warm brown eyes. His hand in the small of her back, guiding her, the heat of his touch tangible even through his gloves. Gliding without effort, nothing but them and the music. Heaven.

They circled the room once, twice, other couples calling out greetings as they passed.

All too soon the music ended, and Sinclair escorted her back to her grandmother. Her heart beat faster as he remained at her side. Tall, handsome, and if his chest puffed out any farther, in danger of popping buttons.

She wanted to talk to him, alone, but there was no chance. She was swarmed by curious well-wishers. Everyone wanted more details of Mr. Quincy and "his" employment with the earl, but were too polite to ask blunt questions. She redirected their attention to the Foundation. Melinda was no help, as she and Sir Leland headed to the dance floor, eyes only for each other.

Men kissed her hand, and several people—of both genders—actually winked at her. Lord and Lady Palmer stopped by—he was one of those who winked—before going off to dance. Sinclair stood at her side, his arm often going around her shoulders. She took comfort in his contact, though she felt herself blushing when he rubbed his thumb across her shoulder or stroked the bare skin below her sleeve.

Not everyone was charmed by the story of their meeting,

however. The Bigglesworths were noticeably absent among the greeters, as was Serena. But enough people congratulated her on the Foundation that Quincy almost ceased worrying.

Since propriety dictated that she and Sinclair dance together only once more, and she was trying to be exceedingly proper, Quincy allowed her dance card to be filled in for every dance, save the last waltz. Being sought after in this fashion was a heady sensation, indeed. Men whom she'd previously conducted business with as Mr. Quincy now wanted to partner her in the quadrille and Scottish reel. And there were an embarrassing number of waltzes scheduled—something Lady Sinclair had planned without her knowledge—all of which were claimed.

Sinclair smiled indulgently as Quincy was led off on the arm of yet another curious admirer.

"Now there's a sight I thought I'd never live to see," Lady Bradwell said, drawing his attention.

"How's that, madam?"

"My Jo, the belle of the ball."

Lady Sinclair appeared with Lord Coddington, and now linked her arm through Sinclair's. "She is, isn't she?"

"Never expected anything less," Lady Fitzwater joined in.

Sinclair nodded, his chest swelling even farther. He never expected anything less of Quincy, either.

Since his mother and Lady Fitzwater remained standing, Sinclair was forced to stand also. Once he lost sight of Quincy amidst the dancers, he glanced at the refreshment room, wishing he could indulge in something stronger than punch. His leg had ached nonstop since his spill in the ditch weeks ago, and it hadn't improved with riding cross country to search for Quincy. This afternoon his new valet, a boy, really, had dropped the wet soap just in time for Sinclair to step on it. He'd ended up in a heap on the floor, the pain in his leg beating a tattoo in his brain.

For Quincy's sake, he'd forgone even one glass of brandy. The pain wasn't so bad that he'd had to scoot downstairs on his backside, as she thought, but without her to lean on he had gone up that way several times in the last few days.

The truly frustrating part was not the discomfort itself, but the weakness. He had worked so hard to strengthen the muscles, but it seemed to have all been undone by the stress of the last few weeks. Waltzing with Quincy had been wonderful, but if he couldn't sit and rest, there was no way he'd be able to dance again later. As his mother and Lady Fitzwater showed no signs of sitting any time soon, he'd be lucky if he didn't embarrass himself before the evening ended. Perhaps a subtle hint was in order.

"Ladies, if you'd like to sit and rest, I'd be happy to fetch you each a glass of punch."

"Darling boy," Lady Fitzwater said, promptly settling in a chair beside Lady Bradwell.

His mother couldn't hide a quick glance at his leg, but she too sat down. "Thank you, Benjamin, but don't you wish to stay with us? Thompson should be by in a moment with another tray."

"With all these women to gawk at, no telling how long he'll be," Sinclair said, already stepping away from the Trio.

He saw a clear path to the refreshment room, only thirty feet away. If he didn't have to dodge sideways, if he could walk straight forward, his limp was slight. What a time to need his walking stick.

Twenty feet to go. A couple crossed in front of him, but they moved fast enough that he barely brushed the lady's skirt without breaking stride.

Ten feet to go. Sweat broke out on his brow and made his shirt cling to his back. Just get the punch, make it back, and then he could rest for an hour or more, with no one the wiser. Except for his mother. And Quincy. And . . . Oh, hell, everyone knew. Once he sat down, it would take more strength to get up again than he possessed at the moment.

Five feet.

His vision dimmed.

Sinclair realized Serena had simply blocked the light as she suddenly stepped in front of him.

He was trying to behave like a gentleman tonight, so he resisted the urge to toss her out on her ear. "Good evening, your grace," he said with the slightest of bows.

"I suppose you expect a donation to the charity from me." Anger flashed in Serena's eyes, and a hint of something else. Not remorse, though. But not capitulation, either.

"From you?" Sweat rolled down the small of his back, but he stood ramrod straight. He glanced at the jovial crowd swirling around them, and gave a sad shake of his head. "Even Bonaparte knew when to surrender."

Serena's bosom heaved with her sudden intake of breath, and sparks flashed from her eyes. She stepped aside and spun on her heel, presenting her back to him.

Instead of feeling insulted at the cut, Sinclair appreciated that she'd cleared the path, and continued to the refreshment room.

He downed one glass, again wishing the punch was made of stronger stuff. He refilled his glass and scooped up three others, two in either hand, and headed back to the Trio.

Thirty feet, and he could rest for an hour.

He didn't even make it halfway.

Like a tide, the crowd swelled and surged around him. Just as they began to separate, Serena appeared at the edge of his vision, looking very pleased. Her posture seemed odd, and too late, he realized why.

She'd stuck her dainty foot out in front of him.

In agonizing detail, he watched himself fall. He tried to catch himself. Stepped awkwardly on his bad leg. Right knee buckled. Left foot slipped. Right knee slammed into the parquet floor. Forgetting the glasses in his hands, he reached out to keep his chin from slamming into the floor. Punch splattered, glass shards flew, ladies gasped.

The musicians kept playing.

Stars exploded behind his eyelids as Sinclair squeezed his eyes shut against the waves of pain and nausea. He rolled onto his side and struggled to draw air into his lungs.

Palmer knelt beside him, his large hand on Sinclair's shoulder. "Ben?"

The music stopped. Murmurings were more audible now. "Disgraceful, getting drunk at his own ball," someone muttered. "No, no, his leg gave out," someone else whispered back.

Sinclair risked opening his eyes, to reassure Palmer that he wasn't dead, though speech was still beyond his capability at the moment. His breath came in gasps, his leg a lump of molten lead. Every nerve ending screamed.

The crowd moved back as Thompson and Grimshaw closed in with rags, broom, and dustbin, and quickly removed all evidence of Sinclair's fall, save for Sinclair himself still sprawled on the floor.

Just like his nightmare.

He dimly registered Palmer trying to pull him to his feet, but rose no farther than sitting up. His leg refused to obey the simplest command. Stabs of pain accompanied each beat of his heart.

The crowd moved back, allowing him a glimpse of Quincy miles away, deep in conversation with the colonel who'd accompanied Serena. Serena stood a few feet off, smiling with triumphant satisfaction.

His worst nightmare come to life. Unable to stand or even speak, he watched helplessly as Quincy walked toward the French doors with the colonel, her back to Sinclair.

Would that the ground open up and swallow him. He closed his eyes against a fresh onslaught of pain that had nothing to do with his leg.

Quincy tried again to disengage her hand from the colonel's arm, tired of his inane conversation. The newness of being the belle of the ball had worn off, and she wanted nothing more than to be back with Sinclair, counting the moments until they could dance together again. But the colonel seemed determined to drag her out the double doors.

A commotion behind them caught her attention. She turned to investigate, and her heart froze. Sinclair sat on the floor, swaying, his head hanging down. Palmer stood behind him, looking pained and helpless.

Wrenching free of the colonel, Quincy dashed across the dance floor to Sinclair and dropped to her knees beside him. She plucked Palmer's handkerchief from his pocket and wrapped it around Sinclair's bleeding hand.

At last Sinclair looked up at her, and her heart almost broke. She wanted to wrap her arms around him, to comfort him, but knew he wouldn't appreciate the gesture just now.

"I'm sorry," he whispered. "You shouldn't—"

She shocked him into silence with a quick kiss on his mouth, and patted his leg. "Anything broken?"

He shook his head.

She turned both his palms over and eased his gloves off. "I don't think you'll need stitches. The bleeding's already stopped. Sometimes you can be so clumsy."

Several people in the crowd gasped, but her comment had the desired effect on Sinclair. He sat up straighter, one corner of his mouth curved in a faint smile.

Heedless of her gown, Quincy rearranged herself until she was sitting cross-legged beside Sinclair, her full skirts in a puddle around her, still holding both of his hands in hers. "Your mother is a great hostess. Her ball will be talked about for weeks to come."

Palmer dropped to the floor on the other side of Sinclair. "Her guests will be dining out on this story for the rest of the season," he added as Lady Palmer joined them on the floor.

"Just this Season?" Melinda said, sitting next to Quincy. Sparing a glance for his best breeches, Leland shrugged and sat down, too.

"Let's not be greedy," Lady Sinclair said, as she and Fitzy sat down. "Another nine-days' wonder will come along soon."

"Perhaps we're starting a new trend," said Lady Danforth as her husband helped her down to the floor.

Surrounded by family and friends, Sinclair looked around in astonishment, watching the guests drop down with varying degrees of grace to sit on the floor, including, after a lengthy pause, Lord and Lady Bigglesworth. Even the colonel sat down cross-legged. All of the guests sat on the floor.

All except Serena, who was left standing, alone.

"If you can't join us, we'll join you," Quincy said.

Sinclair's breathing was almost back to normal. He cleared his throat and pitched his voice just loud enough for Quincy to hear him over the chattering crowd. "I don't think I'm going to be able to keep my promise and give you the last waltz."

Quincy leaned in close, her lips nearly brushing his ear, a tantalizing whiff of bay rum and essential Sinclair teasing her senses. "It doesn't matter," she whispered. "I love *you*, not your dancing ability."

She wiggled closer to Sinclair, her voice at a normal pitch. "I think we can safely assume that everyone now knows I worked for you as Mr. Quincy."

His brows raised. "You think?"

She pressed on, ignoring his sarcasm. "They seem to enjoy being in on it, rather than scandalized by it." She glanced at the Bigglesworths. "Most of them, anyway." She made sure Sinclair was looking her in the eye before she spoke again. "Listen carefully, because I don't say this often. I was a fool."

He didn't contradict her.

"I should have trusted that you and your mother could handle whatever repercussions there might be." She twined their fingers together. "Sinclair, will you marry me?"

The crowd fell silent.

For one heart-stopping second, Sinclair did nothing. Then he kissed her. He cradled her face in his powerful hands, his kiss demanding and accepting, tender and tantalizing, leaving her trembling when he whispered "Yes" against her lips.

The crowd cheered.

"That's my Jo," Grandmère said with a sniff. Lady Fitzwater handed her a handkerchief. "Never does anything by half."

"About bloody time the Matchmaking Earl made a match for himself," Leland announced.

Sinclair wrapped his arms around Quincy as the on-lookers laughed. He should be ecstatic. After all, Quincy had just agreed to be his wife, or rather, asked him to be her husband. But one thing still bothered him. He tilted back in their embrace to see her face. "My leg is weak," he said.

She looked puzzled. "And? So?"

As far as she was concerned, it didn't signify.

With blinding clarity, Sinclair realized it really didn't matter. It didn't matter if he never walked without a limp. For all that, it didn't matter if he never walked again.

Not when he had the woman he loved at his side. His throat clogged with emotion, he raised her hand to his lips.

"Besides," Quincy said, leaning in close again, her eyes sparkling with mischief, "If we can't waltz, I know you'll make up for it later. Right after our wedding."

Sinclair threw back his head and laughed. Heedless of the crowd, he pulled Quincy into his embrace. He had everything he wanted, right here in his arms.

Roses are red, violets are blue,
but these books are much more fun than flowers!
Coming to you in February from Avon Romance . . .

Something About Emmaline by Elizabeth Boyle

An Avon Romantic Treasure

Alexander Denford, Baron Sedgwick is a gentleman much envied for his indulgent and oft-absent wife, Emmaline—who is in fact a mere figment meant to keep the *ton* mamas at bay. But one day Alexander starts receiving bills from London for ball gowns in his imaginary bride's name, and he realizes a real Emmaline is about to present herself, whether he likes it or not!

Hidden Secrets by Cait London

An Avon Contemporary Romance

A missing boy, an unsolved murder, the feeling of impending danger. Marlo cannot figure out how they are connected—until she finds and develops an old roll of film that unlocks the past. But as she gets closer to the truth of the missing boy, she must choose between two men for protection. And if she makes one wrong move, it will be her last . . .

In the Night by Kathryn Smith

An Avon Romance

A life of crime is not what Wynthrope Ryland wanted for himself, but he will do what he must—if only to protect his dearest brother, North. Moira Tyndale, a stately viscountess, is to be the victim of this ill-timed theft, but she is also the one woman who can tempt him . . . or perhaps, somehow, set his wrongs to rights.

Stealing Sophie by Sarah Gabriel

An Avon Romance

Connor MacPherson, a Highland laird turned outlaw, must find a bride—or steal one. Intending to snatch infamously wanton Kate MacCarran, he mistakenly abducts her sister, Sophie—recently returned from a French convent. Quickly wedded, passionately bedded, Sophie cannot escape, and cannot be rescued—but perhaps this is not such a bad thing after all!

REL 0105

Avon Romances—
the best in exceptional authors and unforgettable novels!

THE SWEETEST SIN   by Mary Reed McCall
0-06-009812-0/ $5.99 US/ $7.99 Can

IN YOUR ARMS AGAIN   by Kathryn Smith
0-06-052742-0/ $5.99 US/ $7.99 Can

KISSING THE BRIDE   by Sara Bennett
0-06-05843-3/ $5.99 US/ $7.99 Can

ONE WICKED NIGHT   by Sari Robins
0-06-057534-4/ $5.99 US/ $7.99 Can

TAMING TESSA   by Brenda Hiatt
0-06-072378-5/ $5.99 US/ $7.99 Can

THE RETURN OF THE EARL   by Edith Layton
0-06-056709-0/ $5.99 US/ $7.99 Can

THE BEAUTY AND THE SPY   by Gayle Callen
0-06-054395-7/ $5.99 US/ $7.99 Can

MASQUERADING THE MARQUESS   by Anne Mallory
0-06-058787-3/ $5.99 US/ $7.99 Can

CHEROKEE WARRIORS: THE CAPTIVE   by Genell Dellin
0-06-059332-6/ $5.99 US/ $7.99 Can

DARK WARRIOR   by Donna Fletcher
0-06-053879-1/ $5.99 US/ $7.99 Can

MUST HAVE BEEN THE MOONLIGHT   by Melody Thomas
0-06-056448-2/ $5.99 US/ $7.99 Can

HER SCANDALOUS AFFAIR   by Candice Hern
0-06-056516-0/ $5.99 US/ $7.99 Can

Available wherever books are sold
or please call 1-800-331-3761 to order.   ROM 0904

Avon Romantic Treasures

*Unforgettable, enthralling love stories,
sparkling with passion and adventure
from Romance's bestselling authors*

GUILTY PLEASURES *by Laura Lee Guhrke*
0-06-054174-1/$5.99 US/$7.99 Can

ENGLAND'S PERFECT HERO *by Suzanne Enoch*
0-06-05431-2/$5.99 US/$7.99 Can

IT TAKES A HERO *by Elizabeth Boyle*
0-06-054930-0/$5.99 US/$7.99 Can

A DARK CHAMPION *by Kinley MacGregor*
0-06-056541-1/$5.99 US/$7.99 Can

AN INVITATION TO SEDUCTION *by Lorraine Heath*
0-06-052946-6/$5.99 US/$7.99 Can

SO IN LOVE *by Karen Ranney*
0-380-82108-7/$5.99 US/$7.99 Can

A WANTED MAN *by Susan Kay Law*
0-06-052519-3/$5.99 US/$7.99 Can

A SCANDAL TO REMEMBER *by Linda Needham*
0-06-051412-6/$5.99 US/$7.99 Can

HIS EVERY KISS *by Laura Lee Guhrke*
0-06-054175-X/$5.99 US/$7.99 Can

DUKE OF SIN *by Adele Ashworth*
0-06-052840-0/$5.99 US/$7.99 Can

Available wherever books are sold
or please call 1-800-331-3761 to order.

RT 0804

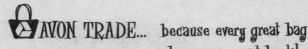

AVON TRADE... because every great bag
deserves a great book!

Paperback $12.95
($17.95 Can.)
ISBN 0-06-058958-2

Paperback $12.95
($17.95 Can.)
ISBN 0-06-058441-6

Paperback $12.95
($17.95 Can.)
ISBN 0-06-059568-X

Paperback $12.95
ISBN 0-06-059563-9

Paperback $12.95
($17.95 Can.)
ISBN 0-06-008546-0

Paperback $12.95
ISBN 0-06-059580-9

Don't miss the next book by your favorite author.
Sign up for AuthorTracker by visiting *www.AuthorTracker.com*.

Available wherever books are sold, or call 1-800-331-3761 to order.

ATP 0105